LORDS OF MISR

The Scots always required strong kings, and
the early Stewarts failed to provide them. Into
the consequent power-vacuum there was no lack
of strong men to pour, Douglases pre-eminently.
When the chief of these, the second Earl
thereof, was slain at the Battle of Otterburn
– of Chevy Chase as the English named
it – and foul play was alleged, amongst the
suspects the name of Stewart stood out. Not the
old King Robert II, Bruce's grandson, feeble
weary and half-blind, but his tribe of tearaway
sons, legitimate and otherwise. Young Jamie
Douglas, himself bastard of the powerful Lord
of Dalkeith and esquire to the dead Earl, on
Otterburn field vowed himself to avenge his
master – despite the fact that by the very nature
of things he was taking on the most eminent
and unscrupulous men in the kingdom,
Robert Stewart, Earl of Fife and Menteith
(later Duke of Albany) and Alexander Stewart,
Earl of Buchan, the notorious Wolf of Badenoch.

**Also by the same author,
and available in Coronet Books:**

The Robert the Bruce Trilogy
Bk 1: The Steps to the Empty Throne
Bk 2: The Path of the Hero King
Bk 3: The Price of the King's Peace

Montrose: The Young Montrose
MacGregor's Gathering
The Clansman
Gold for Prince Charlie
The Wisest Fool
The Wallace
Chain of Destiny

Lords of Misrule

**The First of a Trilogy of Novels on
The Rise of The House of Stewart**

Nigel Tranter

CORONET BOOKS
Hodder and Stoughton

Copyright © 1976 by Nigel Tranter

First published in Great Britain 1976
by Hodder and Stoughton Limited

Coronet edition 1978

_____

*Apart from actual historical personages and events,
the characters and situations in this book are
entirely imaginary and bear no relation to any real
person or actual happening*

This book is sold subject to the condition that
it shall not, by way of trade or otherwise, be
lent, re-sold, hired out or otherwise circulated
without the publisher's prior consent in any
form of binding or cover other than that in
which this is published and without a similar
condition including this condition being
imposed on the subsequent purchaser.

Printed and bound in Great Britain for
Hodder and Stoughton Paperbacks, a
division of Hodder and Stoughton Ltd.,
Mill Road, Dunton Green, Sevenoaks,
Kent (Editorial Office: 47 Bedford
Square, London, WC1 3DP) by
Richard Clay (The Chaucer Press), Ltd.,
Bungay, Suffolk

ISBN 0 340 22303 0

PRINCIPAL CHARACTERS

In Order of Appearance

LADY EGIDIA STEWART, LADY DALKEITH: Sister of the King; wife of the Lord of Dalkeith.

JAMIE DOUGLAS: Illegitimate eldest son of Sir James, Lord of Dalkeith. Esquire to the 2nd Earl of Douglas.

SIR JAMES DOUGLAS, LORD OF DALKEITH: Statesman and wealthiest noble of the kingdom. Chief of the second line of Douglas.

SIR JAMES LINDSAY, LORD OF CRAWFORD AND LUFFNESS: Lord High Justiciar, chief of the name of Lindsay, and son of Lady Dalkeith by an earlier marriage.

JAMES, 2ND EARL OF DOUGLAS: Most powerful noble in Scotland, Chief Warden of the Marches and Justiciar of the South-West.

ROBERT II, KING OF SCOTS: Grandson of the hero-king, Robert Bruce.

JOHN STEWART, EARL OF CARRICK, HIGH STEWARD OF SCOTLAND: Eldest surviving son of the King and heir to the throne — later Robert III.

ROBERT STEWART, EARL OF FIFE AND MENTEITH: Second surviving son of the King; later Governor of the realm and Duke of Albany.

DAVID STEWART, EARL OF STRATHEARN: Fourth surviving son of the King.

WALTER STEWART, LORD OF BRECHIN: Youngest legitimate son of the King.

GEORGE COSPATRICK, EARL OF DUNBAR AND MARCH: Great noble. Justiciar of Lothian.

LADY GELIS STEWART: Youngest of the King's legitimate daughters.

MARY STEWART: One of the King's illegitimate daughters. Maid-in-Waiting to the Lady Gelis.

SIR ARCHIBALD DOUGLAS (The Grim), LORD OF GALLOWAY: Great noble; later 3rd Earl of Douglas.

JOHN DUNBAR, EARL OF MORAY: Great noble. Wed to another daughter of the King. Brother of Earl of Dunbar and March.

MASTER JOHN PEEBLES, BISHOP OF DUNKELD: Chancellor of the realm.

SIR WILLIAM DOUGLAS OF NITHSDALE: Illegitimate son of the Lord of Galloway. Warrior and hero.

SIR HARRY PERCY (HOTSPUR): Great English noble and champion. Heir to the Earl of Northumberland.

JOHN BICKERTON: Son of Keeper of Luffness Castle. Armour-bearer to the Earl of Douglas.

GEORGE DOUGLAS, EARL OF ANGUS: Young noble. Founder of the Red Douglas line.

LADY MARGARET STEWART, COUNTESS OF ANGUS: Widow of late Earl of Mar; Countess of Angus in her own right. Mother of the boy Earl of Angus.

LADY ISABEL STEWART, COUNTESS OF DOUGLAS: Daughter of the King. Wife of 2nd Earl of Douglas.

LORD DAVID STEWART: Eldest son of the Earl of Carrick; later himself Earl of Carrick and Duke of Rothesay.

LADY ANNABELLA DRUMMOND, COUNTESS OF CARRICK: Wife of King's eldest surviving son. Later Queen.

ALEXANDER STEWART, EARL OF BUCHAN: Known as the Wolf of Badenoch. Third surviving son of the King. Lieutenant and Justiciar of the North.

DONALD, LORD OF THE ISLES: Great Highland potentate. Son of eldest of the King's daughters.

MASTER THOMAS STEWART, ARCHDEACON OF ST. ANDREWS: Illegitimate son of the King.

LORD MURDOCH STEWART: Eldest son of the Earl of Fife.

SIR ANDREW STEWART: One of the five foremost illegitimate sons of the Earl of Buchan, Wolf of Badenoch.

SIR ALEXANDER STEWART: Eldest of above. Later Earl of Mar and victor of Harlaw.

SIR WALTER STEWART: Still another of above.

MARIOTA DE ATHYN (or MACKAY): Mother of above, mistress of Buchan.

LACHLAN MACKINTOSH, 9TH CHIEF: *Mac an Toishich*, Captain of Clan Chattan.

FARQUHAR MACGILLIVRAY: *Mhic Gillebráth Mor*, 5th Chief.

MASTER WILLIAM TRAIL, BISHOP OF ST. ANDREWS: Primate.

DOUGLAS GENEALOGY

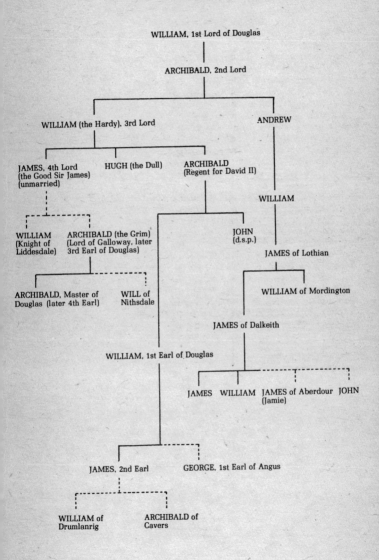

STEWART GENEALOGY

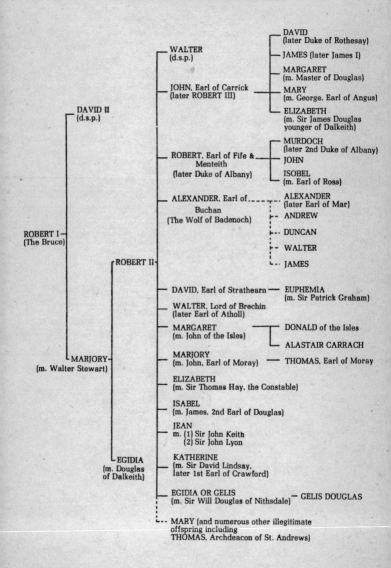

ROBERT I — (The Bruce)

DAVID II (d.s.p.)

MARJORY (m. Walter Stewart)

ROBERT II

WALTER (d.s.p.)

JOHN, Earl of Carrick (later ROBERT III)
- DAVID (later Duke of Rothesay)
- JAMES (later James I)
- MARGARET (m. Master of Douglas)
- MARY (m. George, Earl of Angus)
- ELIZABETH (m. Sir James Douglas younger of Dalkeith)

ROBERT, Earl of Fife & Menteith (later Duke of Albany)
- MURDOCH (later 2nd Duke of Albany)
- JOHN
- ISOBEL (m. Earl of Ross)

ALEXANDER, Earl of Buchan (The Wolf of Badenoch)
- ALEXANDER (later Earl of Mar)
- ANDREW
- DUNCAN
- WALTER
- JAMES

DAVID, Earl of Strathearn — EUPHEMIA (m. Sir Patrick Graham)

WALTER, Lord of Brechin (later Earl of Atholl)

MARGARET (m. John of the Isles)
- DONALD of the Isles
- ALASTAIR CARRACH

MARJORY (m. John, Earl of Moray) — THOMAS, Earl of Moray

ELIZABETH (m. Sir Thomas Hay, the Constable)

ISABEL (m. James, 2nd Earl of Douglas)

JEAN m. (1) Sir John Keith (2) Sir John Lyon

KATHERINE (m. Sir David Lindsay, later 1st Earl of Crawford)

EGIDIA OR GELIS (m. Sir Will Douglas of Nithsdale) — GELIS DOUGLAS

EGIDIA (m. Douglas of Dalkeith)

MARY (and numerous other illegitimate offspring including THOMAS, Archdeacon of St. Andrews)

I

I

THE GREAT HALL of Stirling Castle made a fair representation of Bedlam, and had done for some time. It was fuller than usual, of course, with so much of the country's nobility assembled; and the meal and entertainments, hastily arranged but on a lavish scale, had gone on longer than usual also. The more fastidiously-minded of the women had retired discreetly considerably earlier, and that included three of the King's daughters and the Countess of Carrick, wife to the heir of the throne. Those who chose to remain tended to have anything but a restraining influence, their skirls and screams contributing to the general uproar in significant degree, with effect on wine-taken men. And such as had disarranged clothing were by no means all serving-wenches, entertainers and the like; some, in young Jamie Douglas's opinion at least, were certainly old enough and distinguished enough to know better. His own step-mother, for instance — if that was the right description for his father's second wife, when even the first was not Jamie's mother — the Lady Egidia Stewart, was behaving unsuitably, and with the French ambassador, her gown torn open almost to the navel. Her husband, the Lord of Dalkeith, like her brother the King, was asleep, head fallen forward on bent arms amidst a pool of wine at the Douglas end of the dais-table; but her sons by two of her previous marriages were present and very much awake; and Jamie considered that they must find the spectacle embarrassing — although the eldest of them, Sir James Lindsay 12th Lord of Crawford and Luffness, Lord High Justiciar of Scotland, admittedly did not demonstrate anything of the sort, as he knelt on one of the tables further down the hall, amongst toppled flagons and empty platters, boxing with a brown Muscovy bear of the dancing variety, its keeper weeping and declaring that there would be injury done, while most of the wolfhounds in the room bayed and slavered their excitement. Jamie Douglas was no prig, and appreciated his fun as much as most young men; but he felt that the present occasion and company was not the most suitable for it, that things were getting out of hand, and the important business of the evening was still to be concluded.

He himself was heedfully sober. He was rather inclined that way, anyhow, but had been specifically warned by his master, the Earl of Douglas, to hold himself prepared to act scribe, if necessary, in case none of the trustworthy churchmen were in a state to wield a quill. He was sitting near the head of the esquires' and pages' table, at one side of the great smoke-filled apartment, where he was really quite close to his lord at the left of the dais-table — the King's left, that is, the male Stewarts being all on the right, naturally. Normally the table-plan was T-shaped, the dais-table on its slightly-raised platform crosswise at the head of the hall, the main board stretching down the room slightly to one side, leaving ample space for the servitors, the entertainers and spectacles, with the esquires down the far wall. Tonight, on account of the large numbers present, an extra lengthwise board had been inserted, parallel; so there were in fact three tables reaching down the room, complicating precedency arrangements, cramping the service and the entertainment and adding to the present uproar.

Jamie dutifully kept his eye on the Earl of Douglas. He had been only six months promoted esquire to his hero and chief, after serving for four years as page; and he recognised well the great honour the Earl had done him — and perhaps to some extent, his father — in making the appointment. For many young lords in their own right would have been glad to be principal esquire to the puissant head of the most powerful house in Scotland; and for an illegitimate son, even of the wealthy Lord of Dalkeith, aged only eighteen, to be selected, had been unexpected and the cause of some heartburning. Although Jamie would not have admitted as much, he rather suspected that the Countess Isabel of Douglas had had something to do with it. The beautiful daughter of the King, she had always shown him especial kindness, as a page, and had on occasion called him handsome. He did not know whether his typically dark, almost swarthy and somewhat sombre Douglas features were handsome or not, nor greatly cared; but he was glad that he was well-built, tall and wide-shouldered, since so much in life depended on that. He was taller than the Earl, indeed.

James, 2nd Earl of Douglas, clearly was sober also tonight; and likewise and evidently less than approving of the way the evening was shaping. A dark, stocky, thick-set man in his early thirties, with strangely still though rugged features, he sat glowering, shoulders hunched, staring distastefully down on the pandemonium of the hall. But every now and again, he would glance along the dais-table itself, to his right, past sundry notables and his snoring monarch, to where John, Earl of Carrick sat immediately on the King's right, quietly reading in a curling parchment, amidst all the hubbub, an odd sight; and beyond him to the next seat where his brother, Robert, Earl of Fife and Menteith sat back, stiff face raised towards the smoke-dim hammer-beam ceiling, eyes closed — although no one would ever suggest that that man would be asleep. Two more of the King's sons, David, Earl of Strathearn and Walter, Lord of Brechin, the youngest, sat still further along, the first staring moodily, the second sprawling hopelessly drunk; but neither of these concerned the Douglas. It was their elder brothers, John of Carrick, heir to the throne, and Robert of Fife, the real power behind that throne, who were the objects of his assessment and speculation, of his less than patient waiting. And it was not often that the chief of the Douglases had to exercise patience in public.

The two princes, on whom the entire success or otherwise of the evening hinged, could not have been less alike, in appearance as in character, although sons of the same mother — which was by no means always the way with the royal offspring — and only some two years apart in age. John, although but fifty-one years, looked an old man already, gentle, sad and studious in aspect, delicately featured with great expressive eyes, hair and beard already grey, diffident and awkward of manner. He was the second son of Robert the Second, the first of the Stewart kings — the eldest, Walter, had died young — and although he had qualities of intellect and great compassion, these were scarcely those most demanded for the next King of Scots; and it would be safe to say that he represented the major disappointment of the kingdom, to himself most of all. Some of the poor folk loved him after a fashion, for he was kindly towards them, when princes were expected to be otherwise, humble-minded, generous. He had been kicked in the knee by a horse, long ago — it had to be a Douglas horse that did it — and the bone had set badly, so that John Stewart limped through life thereafter, where the Scots expected their leaders to stride manfully.

Robert Stewart, as it happened, was scarcely popular either; nor did he stride with much élan, to be sure. He was not pitied — he was feared. A tall, slender, stern-faced man, good-looking in a spare, long-featured way, he had a tight mouth, watchful almost colourless eyes and a severe manner — an unlikely Stewart in fact. Always well if soberly dressed, where his brother John was untidy and careless to a degree in his clothing, he had for years now taken more and more of the rule of the kingdom into his own long-fingered hands, as the aged, half-blind and failing father Robert the Bruce's grandson, sank towards senility. Although that certainly did not mean that Scotland was well or adequately governed, in the year 1388, nor had been for a decade. If men did not love Robert of Fife, they tended to feel that putting up with him was probably the lesser of evils — they had little choice, anyway — for the next brother was Alexander, Earl of Buchan no less, the terrible and notorious Wolf of Badenoch so-called, not present this night for, praise God, he was apt to confine his outrageous activities to the northern half of the kingdom, where he reigned as Justiciar and Lieutenant of the North; the thought of *him* governing the realm was enough to come between a man and his sleep. And the other two surviving princes, David and the second Walter, were by way of being nonentities.

So the Earl of Douglas watched and waited, with smouldering impatience. That his glance seldom lingered on the slumped and open-mouthed person of King Bleary himself, held its own significance.

Jamie felt for his beloved and admired master, who was patently bored to an extremity. The Countess Isabel, his wife, had left the hall an hour since. The Papal Legate, who sat on his right, spoke Italian, Latin, French and Spanish, but neither Scots nor English; and the Earl of Douglas's scholarship in such matters had been neglected. On his left he had long exhausted the conversational resources of George, Earl of Dunbar and March, a somewhat morose man although a good enough soldier. The entertainment itself was fair enough of its kind, a gipsy troupe now dancing with wild abandon to screaming fiddles, the women half-naked and becoming more so; but there was a time and place for all things, and it had been a long and active day, of tournament and pageantry and chivalric sports, in all of which the Earl had taken his major part, indeed largely organised by himself as an excuse to gather together this large assembly of great and lesser nobles and chieftains without the monarch or his heir suspecting what was afoot. But there was important work to be done this night yet, and the hour was already late. Worse, too many of the lords and knights on whom so much depended, were already either drunk or so drink-taken that they would be increasingly difficult to handle and bring to a state of usefulness. The thing was nearing the impossible.

It was all, as so often, John of Carrick's fault. The man had a genius for upsetting things and people — all with the best will in the world, which made it the more irritating. Tonight he was a danger to the plans of better men — or at least more active and venturesome men. Every endeavour had been made to contrive his absence from the table, but he had confounded all by turning up, late, to sit beside his father, a right which scarcely could be denied to the heir to the throne. Since his arrival, the project had been either to get him to leave early, through offence, disgust or boredom; or else to make him sufficiently inebriated for his presence not to matter. It had not worked. John could drink deeply too, on occasion, like all the Stewarts — but not tonight. And although clearly he was not enjoying the proceedings, he stayed on in his seat, having brought in his wretched parchment with him, the study of which seemed to console him. As far as Douglas could see, it was poetry or something such. Yet the business of the evening could not be proceeded with whilst Carrick was present, or conscious, for fear of his interference, his disapproval, his influence on the King. It was galling in the extreme. Young Jamie recognised all this, since he was in some measure involved himself — but he could not help being a little sorry for the unfortunate prince nevertheless.

At length, the Earl of Douglas could stand it no longer. Pushing his wine-goblet away, he raised his head, caught Jamie's eye and beckoned. The young man rose, and made his way round behind the dais-table to his master's side, stooping between him and Dunbar. The Earl gestured him round to the other side, where the Papal Legate's ignorance of the language would afford better privacy.

"This is damnable, beyond all," he jerked, low-voiced. "We must get him out, somehow, or nothing will be done this night. I swear Robert could have got him away, if he would — but Robert is none so keen on this project himself, a plague on him! I can think of one thing only, Jamie — the Lady Gelis. We must use her."

The esquire's swarthy features flushed. Like many of the younger men there, he was helplessly, hopelessly in love with Egidia Stewart, youngest legitimate daughter of the King, usually called Gelis to distinguish her from her aunt, the Lady Dalkeith. Almost all the Stewart women were handsome but Gelis was a raving beauty, a darkly lively, sparkling creature of just twenty years, all gaiety, verve and challenge, in person as in personality. She now sat at the far right end of the dais-table with the usual bevy of lordlings around her, two of Jamie's legitimate brothers amongst them, a noisy colourful group. Jamie had, in fact, been disappointed in her that she had not long since left the hall with her elder sisters and other discreet ladies — for in his mature opinion that room was now no place for fair and virtuous young women. But, of course, it had been *her* day. As the only unmarried princess, she had been Queen of the Tourney. She was clearly loth to end the day's excitements.

"Get her out of here," the Earl James went on. "You are friendly with her, I hear. She should have been gone long since. Then have her send for the Earl of Carrick, her brother. He dotes on her, all know. Some upset, outside. A tulzie — some young fools. She is troubled — sends for her brother to escort her to her chamber. He would not come back, I think."

The younger man all but wailed. He would gladly have laid down his life for Scotland's greatest soldier and chief of the name of Douglas, his master. But this command was beyond him. "My lord — how can I?" he protested. "She will not leave because *I* ask her to. She smiles on me, on occasion — but that is all. I have no power with her. All these around her are more important than I am. How shall they take it if I come urging the princess to leave them . . .?"

"Damnation — then get your precious brothers to take her out, boy."

"Why should she go? But if *you* asked her? Or better, my lord — if you asked my lord of Carrick to take her, himself. Say that the company grows unruly, too ill-mannered, that she would be better away. He would take it from you . . ."

Douglas frowned. "There would have to be more noise, horse-play, around her before I could do that. But — you go, Jamie, and stir up some buffoonery. Seem the worse for wine, if you like. Raise a turmoil. Then I can approach Carrick. Off with you."

Unhappily Jamie Douglas did as he was commanded. It was appallingly unfair. The very last thing he wanted was to raise an uproar, make an object of himself in the eyes of Gelis Stewart. Damn the Earl of Carrick!

At the end of the table it was as though a separate little party was in progress, heedless of what prevailed in the rest of the great apartment. Seven or eight young men, sons of the highest in the land, eddied around the princess, sitting on her bench, on the table-top itself, even on the floor at her feet, laughing, chattering. One, the Master of Dunbar, heir of the Earl thereof, was singing a madrigal to her, plucking soulfully at the strings of a lute as ac-companiment.

Perplexed, Jamie eyed them all. He insinuated himself to the side of his half-brother and namesake, James Douglas Younger of Dalkeith, nearly two years his junior but born in wedlock and so heir to their father. They were good enough friends. The Dalkeith family, like most other noble houses there represented, made little difference between the legitimate and illegitimate, save in the all-important matters of heritable property and titles.

"James," he muttered in the other's ear. "You are to make a to-do. A noise, something of a riot. Fight. It is the Earl's orders. No — hear me. He wants the Lady Gelis to be in the midst of a turmoil. So that my lord of Carrick can take her out. No questions, of a mercy! Do something. Pick a quarrel with Willie — as though you were drunk. Go on."

His brother peered at him. "Are *you* drunk, Jamie? Taken leave of your wits?"

"No. It is the Earl James's orders, I tell you." He grabbed his other brother, William, a year younger still. "Willie — come, pick a fight with James," he urged, in a sort of commanding whisper. "Or with me. All of us. We have to make a noise . . ."

His normally far-from equable and pacific kin gaped at him and at each other. Some of the other lordlings were following their gaze, likewise. All knew Jamie as the mighty Earl of Douglas's principal esquire, and so with his own importance. But they would take ill out of any interference with their evening's pleasure.

"What is it, Jamie?" That was Gelis Stewart herself, kindly enough. "Your brows are even blacker than usual — which is a wonder! Is anything wrong?"

He cleared his throat. "No. That is — no. It is these, my brothers. They, they should be gone. The hour is late. Willie is but fifteen." He reached out to grasp the youngster's shoulder — and whether out of brotherly regard for the command to seem to quarrel, or from a more natural resentment at this high-handed intrusion, the youth twisted violently away. Jamie, however, hung on, and the other brother took the opportunity to join in, an arm round Jamie's shoulder, in turn. The trio, lurching together in a reeling huddle, cannoned against the table — and Jamie judiciously swiped a wine-flagon and a goblet with his free arm, so that both crashed to the floor, spilling blood-red contents. Angrily now, some of the lordlings sprang up, and George Dunbar ceased his serenading.

Turmoil, of a sort, was achieved.

Normally, to be sure, such goings-on in the presence of the monarch would not have been permitted for a moment, and royal servitors would have hurried forward to hustle the offenders out. But this was not a normal occasion, the monarch was fast asleep and had been for an hour at least, as had many another, and the rest of the hall resounded to such noise and uproarious mirth that what went on up here was scarcely noticeable. But it was sufficiently noticeable for the Earl of Douglas, who rose and went to tap the heir to the throne and High Steward of Scotland on his hunched shoulder, to speak and point.

Catching sight of this out of the corner of his eye, Jamie heaved a sigh of relief, and almost relaxed his pushing and pulling at his youngest brother. But the turmoil must not stop too soon, of course, so he continued with some token struggling. Alexander Lindsay, son of Sir David of Glenesk and another princess, the Lady Katherine Stewart, came to separate them, in laughing remonstrance — and was turned upon for his pains. As one or two others came to Lindsay's aid, the scuffle took on a new dimension. Gelis Stewart was scolding them all, only half in laughter.

Jamie had a momentary glimpse of the cold eye of Robert, Earl of Fife and Menteith, considering them remotely from up the table. Then, thankfully, he realised that the Earls of Douglas and Carrick were beside the princess, stooping to speak with her.

Disentangling himself from the other young men took a little while, none sure what it was all about but now roused and the wine in them making its presence felt. Then Jamie, receiving a buffet on the head from his master of all people, staggered aside, to glower distinctly querulously at the entire scene. He saw his brothers scowling at him similarly, the Earl of Douglas stalking back to his seat, and the Earl of Carrick limpingly escorting the Lady Gelis from the hall — although she looked back in some bewilderment as she went.

He found another young woman looking speculatively at him, likewise, and from much closer at hand.

"That was a strange business, Jamie Douglas — and not like you," she said. "What does it mean, I wonder?"

He frowned at her; Mary Stewart, half-sister and lady-in-waiting to the princess, a comely, cheerful and friendly creature, popular with all and particularly well-endowed as to figure, one of the many royal bastards about the Court. Jamie and she, as a rule, got on very well together. "It means that this hall is no place for princesses—or for other decent young women!" he jerked. "Ought you not to be following your mistress?"

"I see," she said, slowly. "I see something — but not all. I shall enquire more, hereafter. Your doublet is torn. If you bring it to me in the morning, I might stitch it for you — and learn the rest, perhaps? A good night, Jamie." And dipping a less than respectful curtsey, she turned and hurried after the prince and princess.

Some little time and explanation was required to achieve detachment from his brothers and the other sprigs of nobility. By the time this was accomplished, his lord was beckoning to him again.

"You did well, Jamie," the Earl said briefly, as though it was all normal duties for an esquire. "Now to serious business." He looked along the table. "His Grace seems sufficiently asleep still. We can

19

make a move. You have the list of the men we want, lad? Have them to come to the Chapel-Royal. Not all at once — one at a time. Such as are not too drunk. But no others, mind. And tell Lyon to bring on his more women dancers — the gipsies. They will keep the rest ogling, for they are to throw off most of their clothing! You have it all?"

"Yes, my lord. Shall I inform the Earl Robert of Fife?"

"No. He would not take that kindly, I think! I will do it. Off with you, now, Jamie."

The Earl of Douglas rose again, and moved along to the Earl of Fife's position, to stoop and say a word or two. That self-contained individual altered neither attitude nor expression, but he did incline his stiff head somewhat. Douglas moved further, to David, Earl of Strathearn, and again spoke quietly. That handsome but rather weak-featured prince looked a deal more interested and would have started up, but the other pressed down on his shoulder and indicated to wait for the elder brother, Fife, to make a move. He glanced at the sprawling Walter Stewart of Brechin, snoring drunk, and shrugging, went back to where the Lord of Dalkeith, second man of the Douglas clan, slept head on arms, and shook him into wakefulness.

"James — waken, man," he urged. "Have you your wits? Aye, well — at last we can move. Not you, not you. The King sleeps on. You and my lord Bishop here, the Chancellor, to stay and see that all is in order here. If any could call this uproar order! The drinking and entertainment are to continue. See that we are not disturbed, in the chapel — that is important. If His Grace wakens, assure him that all is well and we will be back. Not to leave the hall. With wine he will fall asleep again — he always does. You have it?"

Yawning, his older kinsman managed both to nod and shake his head at the same time. "Aye — but I do not know that I like this, James," he said. "It smells of deception, of trickery, bad faith towards His Grace. Our oaths as Privy Councillors . . ."

"Like it or no, it is the only way, man. You know that. God knows I would prefer to have it otherwise — but it is this, or nothing. And I have worked sufficiently hard to bring it thus far. Are we to be tied for ever by a degrading, weakly-signed truce and an old done man's palsy? Ha — there Robert rises now. He has been hard enough to move, I tell you — no warrior that! I will

20

after him. See you to matters here. We will be back anon. Where is Archie of Galloway? Ah, here he comes . . ."

In company with the tall stooping eagle of a man who was Sir Archibald Douglas, Lord of Galloway, third in the Douglas hierarchy, by-named The Grim, the Earl of Douglas slipped out of the hall by the dais entrance, in the wake of the Stewart princes.

*   *   *

In the Chapel-Royal of Stirling Castle, distinctly chilly in bare stone, the illustrious company gathered. Carefully selected, these were the most powerful nobles and most puissant and experienced warriors on the land — with two or three militant churchmen amongst them including the mitred Abbots of Melrose and Dryburgh. Jamie Douglas had found only two or three too far gone in drink to be able to attend, although some were scarcely at their brightest owing to the long wait. Significantly the French ambassador was present, the only non-Scot. The Earl Robert of Fife sat in the chapel's throne, as of right, and looked down on them all coldly, with a sort of steely patience. He did not suffer fools gladly, however high-born.

"Your attention, my lords," he said at length, the very slight impediment emphasising the clipped manner of speech rather than the reverse. "You have been brought here, I hope, to good purpose. A considerable endeavour is intended. On the realm's business. As commander of His Grace's forces, I am concerned. The Earl of Douglas will explain. Proceed, my lord." The Earl Robert was no great talker.

The Douglas was not either, really — although he had his own forceful eloquence on occasion, and a sort of dogged sincerity which could be very effective. "My lords," he said, "and Monsieur le Comte. As you well know, this realm is still smarting from the invasion of King Richard of England of three years back, when he burned much of our land, the abbeys of our good friends here, Melrose and Dryburgh, also the towns of Berwick, Coldstream, Roxburgh, Haddington and part of Edinburgh. And my lord of Dunbar and March's castles of Dunbar and Ercildoune — and attempted mine of Tantallon." A brief hint of a smile flickered on his dark, strong features.

A rumble of agreement, almost a snarl, rose from the company.

"There are stirrings again, over the English March. It could be that Richard Plantagenet, to draw attention from his misrule, thinks to do what his thrice-damned forebear Edward sought to do, and could not — to make Scotland but an English province. The great Bruce and our forefathers stopped that. We may have a similar task. It may not be so, but it behoves us to recognise the danger." He held up his hand. "Wait. We did not strike back at Richard three years ago, as we should have done, and as our French allies desired. For we were weak, lacked armies and armour. His Grace was occupied with other matters, and re-signed a truce, a truce the English had just broken . . ."

"His Grace was feart!" Archie the Grim barked, an outspoken man. "His Grace turns the other cheek. We all know that — and pay the price. Get on with it, James — to the meat of it. Enough of old history!" As Warden of the West March of the Border, the Lord of Galloway was much affected by the constant English threat and the inefficacy of the one-sided truce.

"Quiet, Archie," his chief said, but conversationally. "We never doubted that King Richard must be taught his lesson, my friends — but there has been lack of opportunity. With King Robert otherwise minded." He glanced over at the King's sons briefly, but neither made any comment. "Until now. We have tidings which favour us at last. Richard is beset with troubles. Many of his lords have risen against him, led by his own uncle, Gloucester and nephew Bolingbroke — Warwick, Arundel and the rest. The Lords Appellant, as they are called. They say that John of Gaunt, Richard's other uncle, of Lancaster, is also behind them. You all know of this. They have seized London. This, in the South. Now, in the North too, is trouble. I have sure word that open feud has broken out between the Percy and the Neville. It has been simmering from long, cousins as they are — and now they take opposite sides in this matter. You know what that means — the two greatest houses in the English North at war with each other. Wardens of their East and Middle Marches. The West March will be drawn in — nothing surer. The Border lies open to us, my lords, if we but force it."

There was a stir of excitement now. The Earl of Douglas was Chief Warden of the Marches, on the Scottish side, as well as head of the most powerful Border clan. If he believed that the English Borderline was open to them, none would doubt it.

"What is proposed, my friends, is that we muster a large force. Swiftly and secretly. And strike into England whilst they are thus at odds with each other. As we should have done long since."

Men eyed each other with varied expressions — although undoubtedly the majority feeling was gleefully favourable.

"And the truce, my lords?" the Abbot of Melrose asked. "The signed truce with England."

"To lowest hell with the truce!" somebody cried, and many there shouted agreement.

"No doubt, sirs. But the King's royal signature is upon it," the prelate insisted. "And the Great Seal of this realm. Moreover, the original truce is endorsed and sealed by His Most Christian Majesty of France. Such great raid as is suggested would break it. Break the King's royal word. Can any here think to do that?"

All eyes turned on Robert, Earl of Fife. That careful man examined his finger-nails and made no comment.

The Douglas cleared his throat. "The full truce expired in the spring of this year," he reminded. "Since when, as you may know, there has been renewal only by letter. Not by any meeting or full treaty. The Great Seal not appended. His Grace's signature to the letter, yes. But ... what His Grace has signed, His Grace can unsign!"

There were many exclamations at that, both appreciative and questioning. The other abbot, of Dryburgh, spoke up. "His Grace is a man of peace, my lord. Hating war. He will not revoke that letter, I think."

Douglas looked at the Earl Robert — but still got no help from that quarter. David of Strathearn spoke up, however. "My father will sign," he asserted. "Sign *something*, Master Clerk, never fear!"

Douglas, frowning, spoke quickly. "Here is why we have to go about this matter with some care. Why the tourney was held today, to bring you together. Why it required to be done thus. Why you are all here, in the King's castle and presence. Yet His Grace not to know the reason. Nor my lord of Carrick. If the Earl John was to hear of this, he would inform his father — nothing surer. Since he is of a like mind. We, who are differently minded, must needs use this device — distasteful as it may be. If we are

23

agreed, my lords, the Earl Robert here will present a paper hereafter to his royal sire, for signature. He, h'm, assures that it will be
signed. For His Grace ever signs what the Earl Robert puts before
him. The writing will be small and difficult. His Grace's eyesight is
not good. What is needed must be done. For this realm's weal and
safety. A copy will be given to the envoy of His Majesty of France,
to send to Paris." He looked over at the French ambassador. "You
understand, Monsieur?"

The Frenchman nodded. "*Parfaitment, mon ami.* It is well
thought of. My royal master, I swear, will be well content. He no
more loves Richard Plantagenet than do you!"

Douglas sought not to let his relief show. Much depended on
the French envoy. "Good, Monsieur le Comte. And ... the arms
and armour?"

"*Certainement.* The arms and armour you must use, yes.
Would that I might come with you, my friends, to use it. At last.
Mais non — that would be indiscreet, I fear."

Not only the Douglas sighed thankfully. All around major satisfaction was expressed. Three years earlier, the King of France had
sent to Scotland the magnificent gift of 1,400 complete sets of the
finest armour, with arms to match, along with 40,000 gold livres in
money — partly to keep the Scots in alliance but more to be used
as a threat against the English, to help ensure that King Richard
kept the tripartite truce by not invading France. But though the
gold was distributed — Douglas himself had got 7,500 livres, as
Warden of the Marches — the arms had remained unused. For
King Charles VI had prudently sent the precious goods in the
strict care and control of a strong party of French knights, ostensibly to instruct in their usage, but in fact to ensure that they were
used only for purposes directly favourable to himself. The pro-
jected invasion had never taken place, and the arms went unused
and undistributed — although much coveted throughout Scotland. Their French guardians had been constantly and carefully
renewed, and so far no appeals had been sufficient to weaken their
grip. The getting of these armaments into good Scots hands without offending the King of France and endangering the Auld Alliance, had been a major preoccupation for these three years.

"The plan is this," Douglas went on. "Some of us have
discussed it, at Aberdeen, a week past. And put it to my lord of
Fife, who I rejoice to say is in agreement — for I need not say that

it could not be attempted lacking that agreement. We will cross the Border, as soon as may be possible, in two arrays, one on the Middle March, one on the West. To further divide the English strength and confuse them as to which is the main assault. We shall require powerful forces, for this is no mere raiding, but war. Many men — knights, mounted men-at-arms, foot. You, my lords, have the men. We judge that 50,000 would be an apt number. And they must be mustered swiftly and secretly — secret from Stirling as well as from Newcastle and Carlisle! That will be difficult — but it is necessary. Royal orders to halt, to disperse, would be . . . embarrassing!"

Men considered the implications of that, thoughtfully — although some snorted their contempt for any such orders from any source. Coldly the Earl Robert intervened.

"We must not receive such orders. Or I, as commander of the forces of the Crown, cannot proceed. Mind it."

"Secrecy and haste, then, are vital, my friends. We will muster where we may be well hidden. On the southern skirts of my Forest of Ettrick — where none but shepherds and herdsmen will see, and these my people. Muster at Jedworth. The forces will thereafter divide, one to go south directly, by Tynedale. That will be the lesser force. The other will ride down Liddesdale and Eskdale, to the Sark and Carlisle."

"Who leads?" That was Sir James Lindsay, the Justiciar, the same who had been table-fighting with the bear. Men held their breaths for the answer.

"My lord Earl of Fife and Menteith is commander over all. Under him, my Lord of Galloway leads the West array. I lead the East, with my lord Earl of Dunbar and March deputy."

There was fairly obvious relief at this announcement, although the Earl David of Strathearn stirred restlessly.

"Now as to men." Douglas stared round him at them all, at his most bull-like. "Numbers, my friends. Start with you, Lindsay. How many? Within the week?"

"A thousand," that cheerful young man said promptly.

"Not sufficient. From your lordships of Crawford, Luffness, Byres and Barnwell. Double it, man!"

"It is the time, James. Only a week! But . . . very well. I will try for two thousand."

"Good. Archie?"

25

"As many. Give me two more days, James and I will make it *three* thousand. From Galloway."

"The extra two thousand must follow. I know that you have many men away in Ireland with your son Will. But we cannot wait. Every day increases the risk of discovery. Dunbar, how many?"

"I will not be beat by Archie Douglas! Four thousand from my two earldoms. But only for the East array. I will not have them under any other command." And he glared at Robert Stewart.

"Let Douglas watch out, then!" David of Strathearn gave back. "He is welcome to you, and them. I would not risk such cattle — or you, Dunbar — in any command of mine! Lest you desert to the English. As is your family's habit!"

There was uproar in the Chapel-Royal.

Between them, Douglas and Fife in time gained approximate quiet.

"Of a mercy, restrain yourselves," the former requested. "Or we are lost before we start. Jamie — are you noting these numbers? On your paper? Moray — you?"

"My lands are all in the North, James. I could not get men down in time. But from my small Merse baronies I can find you a hundred or two. Say four hundred at most. All horsed." The Earl of Moray was Dunbar's younger brother and married to another of the princesses, Marjorie.

"Your Merse mosstroopers are worth three spearmen and more. Now — my lord of Dalkeith knows of this ploy, and promises one thousand. Myself, I will bring six thousand. And I will vouch for another thousand from my young kinsman of Angus. How many is that, Jamie?"

"Ten thousand Douglases, my lord. And, wait — six thousand and four hundred others."

"A start. Hay — my lord Constable? What of you . . .?"

"How many Stewarts?" the Earl of Dunbar demanded, interrupting, and staring at Strathearn and Fife.

There was a murmur of support from not a few present. The Stewarts in fact, fairly new come to a position of major power through the Bruce connection, were much less rich in manpower than many of the other great nobles. And the one who could have raised most, holding their only inherited earldom — as distinct from their earldoms gained by judicious marriage — was John of

26

Carrick, Lord High Steward, not present. He, and the Wolf of Badenoch, in the far North.

"I will bring fifteen hundred," David of Strathearn said, scowling. Most men doubted if in fact he could raise half that.

"And I five hundred." That was Sir John Stewart, Sheriff of Bute, a bastard of the King and a stout fighter.

"Enough!" The Earl Robert raised a hand. "The Stewarts will be sufficiently represented. Leave it so. Douglas — proceed."

And so the count went on, the great magnates now gleefully vying with each other to embarrass the unpopular Stewarts by the numbers of men promised. Eventually Jamie could excitedly announce a total of 45,000.

A day was fixed for the muster, at Jedburgh, eight days hence.

The Earl Robert rose from the throne, to indicate that the meeting was over. He led the way back across the courtyard to the Great Hall.

All appeared to be as it had been there, save perhaps that there was even more noise and cantrips. King Robert still slept soundly — he had a great capacity for sleep — and his youngest son Walter was now on the floor. The Lord of Dalkeith was only just awake, blinking owlishly; and Bishop Peebles of Dunkeld, Chancellor of the realm, was playing cards at the dais-table with his chaplain. Somebody had up-ended two tables, trestles, at the foot of the hall, and using these as barricades, battle was being done by a number of the young nobles, including Jamie's brothers, with tankards, platters, belts, even ladies' shoes, as weapons. The Lord Lyon, as official master-of-ceremonies, had given up all attempt to control the situation, and had retired, with his heralds, to a corner of the room where they played dice, unable to leave until the monarch chose to make his departure.

Distastefully eyeing the scene, the Earl of Fife drew a paper from his doublet, and turning to look for Jamie Douglas, pointed peremptorily at the inkhorn and quill which hung from the esquire's belt. Given these, the Earl moved to his sleeping father's side, and unceremoniously shook the royal shoulder.

The King of Scots came approximately awake, blinking rheumy, red-veined eyes, the reason for his by-name of King Bleary. He had once had quite noble features. "What . . . what's

27

to do? What's to do, eh? It's you, Robbie? Och, I must have dozed over. Aye, dozed. Robbie — I'm needing my bed . . ."

"To be sure, Sire. I will have you escorted to your chamber forthwith. But first, here is a paper to be signed. A small matter to do with the Marches, for James Douglas. A crossing of the Border, which requires your royal signature, he says."

"Och, it's gey late for papers, Robbie. The morn will do fine, will it not? Forby, the Douglas seldom begs *my* leave to cross yon Border! He's aye at it. He's Warden, is he not?" The voice was quavering, thick.

"No doubt, Sire. But Percy and Neville are on the rampage and better that Douglas has your authority to deal with them. I might even have to assist him myself. To, h'm, keep the peace. His Grace of England, I fear, cannot keep his lords in order."

"Percy and Neville? Och, the ill limmers. Trouble-makers . . ."

"Exactly, Sire. Sign you here, then, and it's done with."

Mumbling, the old man took the quill in a shaking hand and made some sort of crooked signature where directed.

The Earl Robert straightened up, with the paper. "Very good, Your Grace. And now, to bed." He looked around. "Lyon — His Grace retires."

Thankfully the chief herald signed to his trumpeters, and thereafter a loud if distinctly ragged fanfare blared out. All in the hall capable of doing so stopped whatever they were doing, and stood, if only approximately, whilst the King of Scots, on the Earl Robert's arm, hobbled from the chamber.

The Lord of Dalkeith stretched and yawned. "Thank God that is over," he said. "Did it go as you wished, James?"

"As well as could be expected, yes. We shall require more men yet — but I will find them, never fear." The Earl of Douglas shrugged. "It has been a tiring evening."

"I wonder that you ever got Robert Stewart to play this game of yours, James. It is not like him. That man is no adventurer! You will be advised to watch him well. He may be your good-brother, but I know him better than you do. Ah, well — I'm for my bed. If I can find that wife of mine. Jamie — go seek the Lady Egidia. Or . . . no, perhaps better not, better not . . ."

II

THE GREEN HOLLOW of the haugh of the upper Jed Water,
at the Kirkton of Southdean, was a stirring sight in the
August evening; indeed it stirred like the inside of some vast
anthill. Hidden amongst the foothills under the great Cheviot
ridge of Carter Fell, it lay some ten miles south of Jedburgh and
within four miles of the actual Borderline at the pass of Carter
Bar. The Scots leaders had chosen it as the mustering-place, in
preference to Jedburgh itself, for secrecy's sake. Jedburgh was on
the main Middle March road south, into Redesdale in Northumberland, and there was considerable coming and going along
the road when there was no state of war between the two countries. Travellers, packmen, wandering friars and the like would
not fail quickly to carry word southwards of any large concentration of armed men at Jedburgh, the nearest Scots town to
the Border in this Middle March; and the English would be
warned. Southdean, however, was off the main Carter Bar route,
where the Jed Water made a major bend westwards amongst the
jumble of green braes and hollows, and could be approached
inconspicuously from more than one direction. It had the further
advantage of offering a hidden west-by-south route, for the division of the army which was going to invade England via Liddesdale, Sark and Carlisle.

Army was indeed a true description of the concourse assembled
in the skirts of Cheviot that August evening. Here was no raiding
band or skirmishing force, but a vast concentration of well-armed
and equipped manpower, and of suitably varied categories. There
were widely differing estimates as to numbers; but the total was
almost certainly nearer to fifty than forty thousand, and still growing. There were probably forty thousand foot alone, spearmen,
halberdiers and the like. Of lords' mounted men-at-arms, or lances
as they were usually termed, there were five or six thousand; and
as well as these, a couple of thousand Border mosstroopers, also
mounted — indeed who could never be parted from their horses,

so that it was said, their wives and womenfolk came very much second in importance. There were also some five hundred archers, an arm in which Scotland was always weak, and so representing a major achievement, many of them supplied by Holy Church, and most of these mounted. And, of course, there was the chivalric and knightly host itself, the lords and nobles, the lairds and gentry, with their esquires, standard- and armour-bearers, pages, chaplains and bodyguards, adding up to another five hundred at least. For a private, volunteer and notably unofficial venture, Lowland Scotland had done the Douglas proud — for it was that Earl's idea, of course, from the start.

Jamie Douglas at least swelled with pride at the sight of it all. As chief esquire to the great Earl himself, he was very much concerned, naturally; and moreover he had a personal stake in the business now, for in token of affection and esteem, and especially to mark the occasion, his father had made over to him, illegitimate though he was, the small estate of Aberdour in Fife. He had not yet actually got a charter of the lands, admittedly, only the Lord of Dalkeith's verbal declaration; but that was enough, for his father was a man of his word. And on the strength of it, he had hired three horsed men of his own for this venture. He was a laird now, even if only in a small way, with a 'fighting tail', and a stake in this gallant affair.

Not that Jamie had much time for prideful musings. His master kept him more than busy, and there was a constant stream of tasks to be done — for though in theory Robert, Earl of Fife and Menteith, was commander-in-chief, all the organising fell to the Douglas. Most there accepted this as right and proper anyway, for he was well and away the foremost warrior of Scotland as well as its most powerful subject — and of course chief Warden of the Marches into the bargain. At a lift of the Douglas's finger, more than half of that host would have made a right-about-turn, marched to attack Berwick-on-Tweed, turned for home — or on the Stewarts, to rend them. All knew it, including the Stewarts.

Jamie had come out of the parish kirk of Southdean, or Sooden as the Border folk call it, where a more or less continuous council-of-war had been in progress for the last two hours. The Earl of Douglas wanted Pate Home of Hutton for advice on a scouting party for upper Redesdale. Pate was a freebooter and horse-thief of considerable notoriety, and had appeared before the Wardens on many a charge; but none knew the wild empty hills flanking Rede and Coquet and Aln, over the English March, as did he. He would be found in the Earl of Dunbar and March's assembly, presumably ...

The lively scene of the huge armed camp spread over the grassy braes and hollows, all colour and movement, was exhilarating for a young man. His attention, however, became concentrated on a particular corner of the whole, near the riverside, where there seemed to be some especial commotion, shouting, quarrelling. It was in the sector occupied by the Mersemen, the East March Borderers, always a contentious lot and followers — if that was the word — in the main of Dunbar and March. It was where Pate Home was to be looked for, anyway, so Jamie Douglas made his way thither.

As might well have been anticipated, the trouble proved to be about a horse, these being Borderers. And no ordinary horse. A magnificent black Barbary stallion, with one white fetlock, was the centre of controversy, amidst a throng of vociferous competitors, with three individuals all apparently claiming if not actual possession, at least some hold on the animal — and to emphasise their claim each gripping some part of its harness. Will's Wat of Foulsyke asserted that he had seen it first, and therefore he had prior claim. Dand Elliot in the Haremyres held that he had reached the brute first. And Mark Turnbull of Ruletownhead, the only one of lairdly status, declared that he it was who had given authority to bring the animal back into camp; therefore its disposal was also a matter for him. The crowd took voluble sides.

Jamie was certainly not anxious to get mixed up in a Marchmen's dispute about horseflesh, being a reasonably prudent young man; but he was intrigued, and much admired the stallion. Innocently he asked to whom it belonged, thus saddled and bridled.

He was all but submerged in a flood of scorn and invective, and was but little the wiser as a result, save for the realisation that there seemed to be an underlying assumption that it was an *English* horse, and therefore fair game. Pricking up his ears, he approached the burly Mark Turnbull, tugging his elbow.

"I am my lord Earl of Douglas's esquire, sir. Where came that horse, friend?" he enquired, civilly.

The other, who undoubtedly otherwise would have shaken him

off, possibly with a blow, paused at the Douglas name. "Ha, cockerel — what's that to you? Or to Douglas?" he demanded. "Will the Douglas buy him off me?"

"That remains to be seen. I but asked where it came from?"

"Och — from a bit den, off the waterside, a half-mile up." Ruletownhead pointed southwards. "Back some ways. Hidden in a clump o' saughs."

"*I* found it," Will's Wat insisted. "It's mine, by God!"

"I set hands on it first. That's Border law . . ."

"Why should it be any of yours?" Jamie enquired. "A fine beast, saddled and bridled, and hitched in bushes. *Somebody* owns it . . ."

All stared at him, pityingly.

"That's an *Englishman's* horse, bairn!" Turnbull explained, with what might pass for patience. "Any Englishman's beast is forfeit, this side o' the March."

"But — how do you know it belongs to an Englishman?"

"Do you reckon we wouldna ken a kenspeckle brute the likes o' this? If it belonged *this* side o' the March, man?"

"But there are thousands of horses in this valley, now, from all over Scotland. Horses you do not know."

"Sakes, boy — how long since you left your mother's breast? This stallion has been ridden long and fast, *today*. Hidden the south side o' this camp. Look at its houghs and hooves. Yellow clay. There's no yellow clay within a score o' miles, this side o' the March. But there is in Redesdale, no more'n eight mile south. In England. Rochester, Otterburn, Elsdon. And why hide the crittur there, if it was a Scots horse? It was hidden — nothing surer."

"Then . . . this is serious! Important. It is not just the prize of a good horse. But what it was doing there. And where is its master . . .?"

"How can we tell that, laddie? There are thousands o' men here. Strangers. He could be any o' them . . ."

"I'm thinking I might know that beast," a new voice spoke up, from the rear. "I'll wager I've seen it running with the mares in Twizel's parks. It's a beast I'd no' be like to forget. Will Clavering of Twizel's stallion."

"Twizel! Clavering!" Jamie turned to the speaker, a thin, hatchet-faced man of early middle years, sardonic as to feature. It was Patrick Home of Hutton himself. "Ha — it's you, Hutton.

32

Are you sure? The Claverings are well-connected, are they not? Powerful folk? This could mean much. Danger."

"Powerful?" Home shrugged. "I'd no' so name them! But Will o' Twizel is kin to Clavering o' Tillmouth, chief o' the name. Likewise Shellacres and Grindon."

"In other words, an important Northumbrian squire. Here amongst us. And we about to invade Northumberland! A spy. What else? We must take him. Quickly. Hutton—you would know him? By sight?"

"Guidsakes, lad — what's one damned Englishman amongst 50,000 of us?" the Turnbull scoffed. "We've got his horse—which is what matters!"

"Hutton — could you find this man? Clavering?"

"In this concourse? Amongst thousands! I have seen him but twice, close, man . . ."

"Then we must do it differently. Take his horse back to where you found it, Ruletownhead. And then set men, hidden, to watch it. The owner will go back for it, presently . . ."

There was immediate protest. They could watch the den without the horse, to be sure.

"No! If he hid the brute thus warily, he will make wary return. He might well perceive it gone. Take fright. Make his escape. Never fear — you shall have the horse. But get the Englishman first." Young James drew himself up, and raised a hand high. He was not a Douglas for nothing. "I speak in the name of the Douglas. Will you have me go bring my lord Earl to you? And your own Lord of Dunbar? Aye — then see to it, and swiftly, my friends. And you, Hutton—my lord seeks word with you, forthwith. In the Kirk. Come, now . . ."

The little church was packed to overflowing, and with the cream of Scotland's nobility — yet the smell, of a warm summer evening, was as of lesser men, of sweat and leather and horse and unwashed humanity. Men in chain-mail, half-armour and protective clothing tended to smell. The Earl Robert sat in the parish priest's stall, and all others had to dispose themselves as best they could. The Lord Maxwell, Deputy Warden of the West March, was holding forth on the division of forces and objectives, when Jamie brought Pate Home to Earl Douglas's side.

"My lord," he whispered, "here is Hutton. But there is something more. Something amiss. I fear there is a spy in the camp."

33

The Earl, seated uncomfortably on a saddle on the earthen floor, sat up. "Eh?" A spy? What mean you . . .?"

Hastily Jamie muttered the essence of the matter, while the Lord Maxwell scowled in his direction.

"Clavering of Twizel, eh? I have heard of him. You sure of this, Pate?" Douglas made no attempt to lower his voice.

"I canna be sure, my lord. But it is a notable stallion, with the one white fetlock. I ken no other like it. And it comes from the English side, I'd swear."

"Aye. Then this must be seen to. Jamie — I need you here, by me, for the writing." The Earl turned to scan the serried ranks of Douglas lords and lairds behind him — and that church might almost have been a Douglas court. "Will — see you to this. Jamie will tell you. And swiftly. Then come you back, Jamie." He faced the front again. "A matter of some urgency, my lord Robert," he mentioned. "Proceed, Maxwell."

Jamie took Sir William Douglas, Lord of Mordington, outside, and informed him of the situation. He was his own uncle, younger brother of the Lord of Dalkeith, a cheerful extrovert. He would cope adequately.

Back in the church, the vital discussion on the division of forces, and who was to go with whom, continued. It had been agreed that the main thrust would be made in the west, for both the Percys' and the Nevilles' home areas were in the east, in Northumberland and Durham, and an invasion on the west side of the Pennines would probably gain greater impetus and get further. The Eastern assault would be more in the nature of a diversion, a distraction to draw off the opposition, hard-hitting and fast-moving but with limited objectives. The question hinged on personnel and personalities.

Archie the Grim, of Galloway, a veteran fighter, was to command the west force, under the Earl Robert his friend, who was no warrior; but a preponderance of the lords wished to accompany the Earl of Douglas, whose dashing reputation as a soldier promised the greater honour, chivalric credit and general excitement. It was this vexed issue which was holding up the planning — to the Earl Robert's distinct offence. The popularity of Douglas as against Stewart, was all too obvious.

As it happened, soon after Jamie's return, there was a diversion which to some extent redressed the balance. A commotion at the church-door heralded the appearance of a small group of new-comers, mud-spattered, travel-stained, clad for war, and led by a slender, long-featured rapier of a man, only in his twenties but with a careless air of leadership. Sufficiently swarthy to be recognised as a Douglas, he was of the sort to grip and hold the attention.

There was a major stir at this development, even the Earl of Douglas rising to greet the newcomer; and the grizzled Archibald of Galloway pushing forward, to grip the young leader by both shoulders. He was indeed Archie the Grim's son, though not his heir, illegitimate but the light of his sire's fierce eye nevertheless — Sir William Douglas of Nithsdale, the most gallant blade in the land, and next to his chief probably the most successful soldier into the bargain, young as he was, and already in line for the title of the Flower of Chivalry. Moreover, it was whispered, he might well be the light in another eye also — the Lady Gelis Stewart's.

"So you are back, lad!" his father cried. "Well come — and in time for a new and fair venture. How did it go, Will?"

"Well, my lord — passing well." For such a long dark face, the young man had a most winsome smile. "We landed at Cairnryan yesterday, rode to Threave — and spurred on here hotfoot when we heard of this venture." He bowed to the Earl of Douglas. "Yours to command, my lord."

"Aye, Will. I rejoice to see you. Safe. And Ireland? Did you prosper?"

"To be sure. We made our mark. Those treacherous kerns will not forget Douglas for a while. Nor will their English masters. We fought two battles, slew their leaders, burned their pirates'-nest of Carlingford, and sank the English fleet based there. And coming back, by Man, we taught that isle that the Scots were its true masters, not the English. There will be no more pirates preying on our Galloway coasts for long, I swear!"

"Good! Good, I say, Will — bless you! The Irish needed that lesson. Man likewise. Here is an excellent token and portent for our present attempt. Not only Galloway and Douglas, but all Scotland is in your debt ..."

The Earl was interrupted by a hammering noise from the chancel of the church. The Lord Robert Stewart was banging his dirk hilt on the arm of the priest's stall.

35

"My lords," he said thinly, tonelessly, into the hush he achieved. "May I remind you that this is a council, and under my authority, as Great Chamberlain of Scotland. Not some Douglas tryst and caleerie. We will proceed with the business. You were saying, my lord of Crawford . . .?"

"Earl of Fife," the Douglas declared, level-voiced but tellingly. "On Douglas territory and in *my* presence, Douglas business is all men's business! Perhaps in the territories of one or other of your ladies, in Menteith or in Fife, it might be different! But not here."

There was a quivering silence at this blunt reminder of basic realities. More than half the men in that building were either named Douglas or linked with Douglas in marriage, interest or vassalage.

The Lord Walter Stewart of Brechin, youngest of the King's legitimate sons, burst out with hot words. But his brother, the Earl David of Strathearn, gripped his arm.

"*I* welcome Sir William of Nithsdale, and rejoice at his success," he said clearly. "His Grace, our royal father, will be grateful, I have no doubt."

Archie the Grim was not usually renowed as a peacemaker, but he essayed the role now, in his strange friendship with the Earl Robert. "I crave the forbearance of all," he exclaimed, his harsh voice creaking in unaccustomed placation. "My son's arrival. and his good tidings, much bemused me. My lord of Craw-ford — proceed."

Young Lindsay of Crawford, whose mother was a Stewart but now wed to a Douglas, coughed and looked at the Earl Robert — who stared directly ahead of him, expressionless, utterly self-contained, but none doubting his wrath. "Very well," he said, doubtfully. "But, to be sure, here is a new situation, is it not? A new force landed in Galloway, from Ireland. In the west. Will my lord of Nithsdale fight with the west array? Or the east?"

"My son, I think, will ride with his father," Sir Archie said.

"To be sure, my lords — that I will."

There was a new stir in the kirk. If the dashing young Will of Nithsdale with his victorious force, was going to be on the west front, then some of the sprigs of nobility present were prepared to reconsider. Some shifting of positions became evident. Jamie Douglas knew a pang of something like resentment, in that his romantic distant kinsman should seem to be able to steal some of the popularity of the Earl James, his chief. And there was the matter of the Lady Gelis's rumoured favours . . .

At anyrate, the problem of the division of the forces seemed to have become much eased and the council-of-war was able to proceed to tactics. David of Strathearn was advocating a by-passing of Carlisle and a drive down on Lancaster, when there was another interruption. Douglas of Mordington came back with a prisoner.

The stocky, red-faced, youngish man, looking distinctly apprehensive, was indeed Clavering of Twizel. They had caught him returning in round-about fashion for his horse. Mordington presented him urgently before his chief, ignoring the Earl Robert.

"I am Douglas," that man informed the captive grimly. "Chief Warden of the Marches. I require to know your business in this camp on my territories, Englishman?"

"I . . . I had reason to travel to Jedworth, my lord," the other declared, glance darting around the hostile faces. "I saw . . . many men. I came to discover what it might be. So, so great a gathering."

"Why were you riding four miles off the Jedworth road, sir?"

"I thought to ride by, by Fulton, my lord. I could win to Fulton this way . . ."

"Why Fulton?"

"I might buy cattle there. As at Jedworth. On occasion I deal in cattle, my lord Earl."

"You were looking for cattle? Scots cattle? To buy?"

"Yes, lord. To buy."

"Search him, Will. Discover how much siller he has on him."

A rough search of Clavering's person produced only three nobles, a half-noble and some groats.

"You were buying no cattle this journey, sirrah," the Earl declared. "You lie."

"No, lord — no! I was but spying out the prospects. For buying. If the prospects were good, I would come again. With the money. With drovers . . ."

"Aye — spying out the prospects! *That* I will believe, Englishman! But not for buying. For stealing! You ride alone. Secretly.

You hide your horse in a brake. Come spying through this camp . . ."

"No, my lord — no! On my soul I swear it! I am an honest man I have broad acres. No need to steal cattle . . ."

"How many Borderers have? Yet cattle-stealing is as life to them. As Warden, I am left in no doubts as to that! On both sides of the March. I say that you were spying the prospects for a raid. Choosing a route, a secret route. To drive back beasts stolen from Fulton and other lands, through these quiet hills and into Redesdale. You planned a prey . . ."

"In the name of the Blessed Mary and all saints — no! I am no reiver . . ."

"Fulton is a vassal of mine, my lord James," Kerr of Altonburn put in. "He is in the camp. Have him in, and see if he knows this man."

"I do not *know* him," Clavering asserted hurriedly. "I was told that he bred good cattle."

"Aye — so you went to spy them out. By back ways. Instead of riding honestly up to his door, from Jedworth. I say you are a liar, and a poor one, Twizel! Enough of this. You were intent on stealing Scots cattle. And you know the penalty for cattle-reiving, in my warden's court. Hanging, sir! You will hang."

With a wail, Clavering sank down on his knees. "My lord Earl — mercy, I pray you! Mercy! Of your lordship's clemency. I did not come to steal. On my immortal soul, I swear it! Hear me. That is not why I am here. I can explain . . ."

"It was not cattle, then? You lied in this also?"

"No, lord — not cattle. I came . . . I came . . . otherwise. To discover what was to do. So many men a-move on the Border. My lord Harry Percy sent me. He was concerned — all were. At Berwick. He feared a raid, a great raid."

"Ha! Here is a horse of a different colour! But equally lies, I'll be bound!"

"Truth, lord — truth. The Percy had had word. In Berwick. He is Governor of Berwick. Word of mustering men. He sent me to discover the truth. Others also. I followed a company of men, riding down Teviotdale. To here. At a distance . . ."

"So! You were spying, indeed? You confess it. Not for cattle, but for men! On Scots soil. Spying on me, Douglas! And you think to escape hanging by confessing it?"

38

"It . . . it is warfare, lord. Not reiving. I am captured, yes. A prisoner. You cannot hang a prisoner-of-war. A ransom. My kin will pay a ransom."

"Tush! Think you Douglas is interested in ransoming such as you? You are a spy, sir — no prisoner in fair fight. And should hang. Unless . . .?"

"Unless, lord?" The other in his eagerness grabbed the Earl's arm.

Distastefully he was shaken off. "Unless you can offer us some information that is of value to us. Information that is sufficiently valuable to exchange for your valuable life, Twizel! How think you?"

The other bit his lip unhappily.

"Yes or no, man?"

"I know little, sir . . ."

"You come from Berwick. Twizel is near to Berwick. If Hotspur Percy is concerned, does he muster men?"

"Yes, lord. At Berwick. And at Alnwick."

"How many?"

"Not many. As yet. He does not know your numbers. Or . . . or intent. There is the truce . . ."

"You claim a truce? And yet would be treated as a prisoner-of-war! You must make up your mind, Clavering."

"Yes, lord. No, lord. I . . ." Helplessly the man shook his head.

"Percy musters in Berwick and Alnwick? But not in great numbers as yet. What else? What of Neville?"

"There is trouble with the Lord Neville of Raby, sir. Percy and he are at odds, although cousins. There is word of Neville raiding in the south. But I know not . . ."

"Where in the south?"

"They say in Weardale and Allendale and Stanhope. But I have no sure word. The dale country . . ."

"And Clifford? And the Bishop of Durham? On whose sides are these?"

"Both support Hotspur. The Prince Bishop is already in arms on the Percy's behalf. In those south dales. And my lord of Clifford making thither from Cumberland."

"Then why does Hotspur sit in Berwick town, his southlands raided, and leave Neville to be repelled by his friends? It sounds not like Hotspur!"

39

"King Richard's orders, my lord. The Percy is Governor of Berwick and Warden of the East March. And there have been whispers of trouble in Scotland. His brother, Sir Ralph Percy leads in the south. For the old Lord of Northumberland . . ."

"I say that is not like Harry Hotspur! There is more to it than any King's order, I swear, to keep him. Tell me, sirrah — if you value your neck."

Clavering swallowed. "I think . . . I do not know, lord — but I think that the Lord Harry intends to make a sally into Scotland. From Berwick. Should a raid develop into England. To, to draw the Scots back. I do not *know*, you understand, my lord. I but heard that it was so . . ."

"That sounds more like the Percy! So — we have it, now? You have, I think, earned your neck, Englishman — from us. But earned a hanging, I'd say, from Hotspur! Take him away. But hold him secure. He may aid us further, yet."

The unhappy informant was escorted out.

"What now, then, James?" the Earl David asked. "Do we change plans?"

"Not on the west, I think. Here in the east, we must consider anew."

The Earl Robert made one of his few interventions. Although little of a warrior, he was shrewd of mind. "If Clifford leads a Cumberland array to aid Ralph Percy in the south-east, he will cross by the Irthing, by Gilsland and Haltwhistle and the South Tyne. The hills between grow ever higher and wider to the south. Cumberland, Westmorland, Furness and Lancaster should lie unprotected. Our main thrust should go far and fast. But there is danger. Ralph Percy, Clifford and the Bishop, when they gain word of our Scots thrust, could make their peace with Neville, and march westwards through the hills of Teesdale and Lunedale, across the spine of England, to cut us off. From Scotland. If Neville joined forces with them, we could be caught."

"My own thinking, entirely," Douglas nodded. "They must be diverted, therefore. Into believing the main thrust to be in the east. That will be my task. A swift-moving mounted force, stopping for nothing, until it menaces Ralph Percy's flank in the southern dale country. Then burning and harrying, and a slow retiral. Drawing them after us. Leaving them with little time to spare for you, in the west. *You* to strike fear deep into England."

40

"It will serve . . ."

"And what of our Scots East March?" Archibald of Galloway demanded. "If Hotspur invades from Berwick, meantime?"

"We must allow for that, yes. Detach a force to hold him. Will Douglas — Mordington is on his way. In the Merse. Take you, say, two thousand or so of Mersemen. They will know and defend their own country best. Keep the English back from the Merse and Lothian. They will not be in large force."

"Not to come with you, my lord? Into England? On this venture . . . !" That was almost agonised.

"Someone must defend the Merse, Will. Your lands are there. You know it all. But, see you — it may not be for long. You may be able to join us. For when Hotspur hears that it is *Douglas* wasting his homelands of Keeldar, Coquet, Alnwick and the rest, threatening his town of Newcastle — as hear he will, I shall make sure — I wager he will ride south in haste, King Richard's orders or none. And either forget the venture into Scotland, or else send but a token force under some lesser man. *I* would, in his boots."

None there found fault with that reasoning.

So it was agreed. The Douglas, with fastest movement requisite, did not want to be encumbered with foot, or large numbers. His force would consist of lords and knights and esquires, with their men-at-arms, plus a contingent of Border mosstroopers and a share of the mounted archers, 3,000 would serve. Another 2,000, a mixed force, would follow along behind him, more slowly, to consolidate, protect his rear, burn and harry, and help confuse Hotspur. Mordington would take his 2,000 and head north-eastwards however reluctantly. And the main body, over 40,000 still, would march south-westwards, over the Note o' the Gate pass into Liddesdale and so down to Esk, to cross into England east of Carlisle, and thereafter southwards for Lancaster.

III

JAMIE DOUGLAS RODE cheerfully down Redesdale, a little
uncomfortable in his new shirt of French chain-mail, but
heart singing within him. Without actually thinking the
matter through, it seemed to him that this was what he had been
born to do, that all his life hitherto had been just a preparation,
leading up to this fine sunny morning's adventure. He, James
Douglas of Aberdour, was off to war, well-mounted, armed,
equipped and 'tailed'; indeed he was now riding on the soil of the
Auld Enemy, and in the most gallant of company. The green
Cheviots rose steeply on either hand, the sparkling Rede sang and
chuckled on their right, the larks shouted their praise above them,
and they clattered down the winding, twisting drove-road, part of
it of Roman construction, they said, at a fast trot, 3,000 strong and
under the proud banner of Douglas. For a young man, it was the
best of worlds.

There were many other banners flying this morning, and no
lack of Douglas colours amongst them; but the main great
undifferenced standard of the house today was not borne by
Jamie, nor yet by Bickerton the armour-bearer, but by the Earl's
fourteen-year-old illegitimate son, Archibald Douglas of Cavers.
The other members of the Earl's personal retinue were present
also—John Bickerton, son of the Keeper of Luffness Castle for Sir
James Lindsay, but still Douglas's armour-bearer; Master Richard
Lundie, chaplain; and Simon Glendinning and Robert Hart,
junior esquires or senior pages. To them, riding immediately
behind the Earl and his supporting lords, were attached a group of
Douglas lordlings — James and William, Jamie's legitimate
brothers, and Johnnie, otherwise; William of Drumlanrig, only
thirteen, the Earl's other illegitimate son — unfortunately he had
no lawful offspring as yet; young Douglas of Mains; Douglas of
Bonjedward and others. There was some regret that the hero, Sir
William of Nithsdale, had gone with the west force — but not on
Jamie's part, who had room in his heart for but one hero at a time.

They made a stirring, lively company in their youthful high spirits, brave armour — most of it worn in earnest for the first time — and colourful heraldic surcoats worn over the steel. Behind them the winding column stretched far out of sight, for even 3,000 horsemen on a narrow road, three-abreast and in close file, will cover well over two miles; and there were the sumpter horses behind that.

The first sizeable English village, Otterburn, fifteen miles from the Borderline at Carter Bar, came in sight of the head of the column, under the grassy braes and outcrops of Fawdon Hill, a cluster of grey, low-browed and reed-thatched cottages, with a sturdy peel-tower on a mound behind. There were some quite fair cattle and sheep grazing on the slopes around, and some useful horseflesh in the in-fields. But though these aroused a succession of acquisitive growls, especially from the mosstroopers, the Douglas had given sternest orders that there was to be no harrying and reiving at this stage, however tempting, indeed no pausing at all. They would have their sport later, he promised.

But Douglas himself was interested in the Otterburn area, as they rode by — as he was in every strategic site. He pointed out to his companions, the Earls of Dunbar and Moray, the Lord of Crawford, Sir William Keith, the Marischal and others, how the place was made for defence, the flooded low ground of the Rede meadows proof against cavalry attack, the river itself unfordable here, the slopes behind steep, with scrub woodland for cover, and retreat-lines into the hills. The Earl was an experienced campaigner, but he also had a natural-born eye for tactical country.

After Otterburn, the valley of the Rede much opened out to high, rolling moorland and wide vistas, with the Cheviots drawing back, the river itself swinging away southwards to join the Tyne at Bellingham. Pate Home of Hutton, in charge of the forward scouting party, was waiting for them at the Elsdon Burn. He reported that the country lay unroused, apparently unsuspecting, the folk at their harvesting. Whatever rumours Hotspur had heard at Berwick, he did not seem to have sent warning south.

All that day the Scots rode southwards, unopposed — and for once not leaving a blazing desolation behind them. By Rothley and the Scots Gap they came to the great Hadrian's Wall of the Romans, and crossing Tyne by a quiet secondary ford near Wylam, were able to camp sufficiently secretly in the extensive

43

Chopwell Woods, just over the County Palatine border, Durham city itself only some fifteen miles to the south-east, a lively demonstration of the Douglas capacity for swift and prolonged advance.

But the two days that followed were a disappointment, at least to Jamie Douglas and many another non-veteran campaigner. Nothing would shake the esquire's pride and faith in the Earl of Douglas; but it seemed to him that his hero was on this occasion scarcely living up to his reputation. For nothing very gallant or exciting transpired. Scouting parties were sent out into the dale country ahead and towards Durham itself, and these in due course sent back information that Sir Ralph Percy, Hotspur's brother, was in intermittent action against Neville's forces in the Blanchland area of the Derwent valley, aided by the Prince-Bishop of Durham and a considerable contingent. This meant that Durham city would be largely unmanned. The Douglas was not intent on any confrontation — the English forces combined seemed to add up to almost 10,000 against his 3,000. His objective was to distract, divide further if possible and draw the enemy eastwards away from any possible crossing of the Pennines into Westmorland and Lancashire where they might menace the main Scottish thrust. This sort of programme offered little of glory and chivalric élan, such as Jamie and other untried warriors had looked for in the great adventure. It did not seem like the famous Earl of Douglas, somehow, to allow himself to be used merely as a species of decoy, he with the greatest military reputation in Scotland, whilst the western army achieved all the action. After all, it had all been Douglas's idea, in the first place.

What did transpire was less than dramatic. The Scots force was split. The Earls of Dunbar and Moray, with about 1,000 men, went to harry the flanks of Percy's force, up Derwent — not to risk any battle but to worry and mystify the English, and thereafter to retire north-eastwards burning the land as they went. Douglas himself, with the bulk of his force, made a hasty descent, by night, on Durham city, to threaten it — they could not expect to capture it even if they had wanted to, secure behind its strong walls. It was hoped that this would sufficiently alarm the warlike Bishop to bring him back in haste to the rescue, and so not only weaken Sir Ralph Percy but have the effect of bringing Hotspur himself hurrying south to protect Newcastle and the populous coastal plain.

Jamie found the night dash to Durham exhilarating enough. But once there, circling round and round the silent walled city yelling threats, soon palled, with nothing more effective possible lacking siege machinery. Just before dawn they drew away northwards again, the Earl apparently satisfied, but now grimly giving the order to burn, burn.

The setting alight to the surrounding countryside thereafter, with villages, mills, farms and cot-houses going up in flames, over a wide swathe of North Durham, might be strategically sound and even in keeping with the accepted standards of Border warfare; but it seemed scarcely in the chivalric tradition and unsuitable work for a knightly host. Jamie, and others who felt like him, could hardly put this point of view directly to the Earl; but something of disappointment and reaction did become evident in that savage, smoke-filled early morning. Jamie was in fact seeking to comfort his young and vomiting brother, amongst screaming horses and bellowing cattle, weeping women and cursing men, priests and friars on their knees praying, all in the ruddy glare of burning Finchale Priory monastic buildings — not the church thereof, for all churches were being spared, by order — when the Earl James rode by, armour gleaming red.

Reining up, he looked down on them. "You mislike it?" he asked them, harshly. "Your tender stomachs turned, eh? Then remember this night laddies. And remember that we are but babes at it, compared with the Plantagenet — all the Plantagenets. Seek that it will not happen in Scotland again, as it has done times without number — why we are here. Remember Kelso. Roxburgh, Haddington, Teviotdale, Tweeddale, Melrose. Now — have done with your puking and play the man. Remember your name — Douglas! Jamie — come with me."

At last the Scots began to gather again, company by company, on the high heath of Chester Moor seven miles north of Durham. Although the new day was bright ahead of them, behind was almost as dark as night still, under the pall of smoke lit by a red and evil flickering. Few were depressed, unhappy, sickened, it seemed — indeed excitement and elation ran high, destruction clearly engendering its own fierce exultation.

They rode back to Chopwell Woods. The other party was late in arriving; but Dunbar and Moray were also well content with their night's work. Percy had been lured out, and was warily probing behind them, but only slowly, not risking any major confrontation before he could discover the Scots' full numbers and intentions. They had carried out token burnings over a fairly extensive area around Slayley, Dipton and Hedley.

Weary as they all were, Douglas was not prepared to allow them rest. He was anxious to have the Tyne between them and Ralph Percy before they halted — for to be caught on the wrong side of that major river, by a superior force, could be fatal. They headed north, as they had come.

Just before noon they rested at last, in the Horsley Woods, only nine miles up-river from Newcastle. And there, stiff and jaded, as the invaders snatched what rest they could, the news was brought that Harry Percy himself had arrived at Newcastle, having evidently ridden through the night. He appeared to have brought no large force with him.

At this word of Hotspur's near presence, a noticeable change came over the Earl James. He was as a man re-invigorated, personally challenged. For long there had been especial antagonism between the great houses of Douglas and Percy, that of rivalry rather than feud. Their interests tended to clash at points innumerable, their positions almost complementary, the two most powerful families of the Border area. Douglas was Chief Warden on the Scots side, and it was probably the similar appointment of Harry Percy, in place of Neville, on the English side, which had sparked off the present fighting. As well as this, there was the more personal aspect. Hotspur, as his nickname implied, was renowned far and wide as a high-spirited, potent and gallant figure of that age of chivalry, probably the most famous champion in England, headstrong, arrogant, courageous and a law unto himself. Douglas, Scotland's most famed warrior, was born to cross swords with him. Undoubtedly, with Hotspur's arrival on the scene, a new dimension developed. Jamie was not alone in suspecting that this situation lay largely behind the entire present Douglas involvement.

Nothing would do but that the Scots must ride for Newcastle at once. Hotspur must be challenged — and before his brother came up with reinforcements. There would not be any large garrison in the town — Ralph Percy would have taken all he could. If Harry Percy had ridden south, fast, with only a comparatively small company, it could represent a notable opportunity. Newcastle's town walls were not nearly so strong as Durham's, despite the more powerful castle. They might be able to lower the Percy's pride somewhat — and not before time.

Infected by their leader's enthusiasm, they rode out of Horsley Wood, by Houghton to the Roman Wall, and along it eastwards by Heddon, Throckley and Walbottle, until from the Nuns Moor Newcastle came in sight. On a ridge of the rolling common of the Town Moor, hidden by thorn scrub, broom and whins, they halted, to gaze down.

Newcastle, although sunk in the valley of the Tyne, at the first point inland from the estuary at which it might be bridged, was not nearly so tightly enclosed by banks and braes as was Durham. In consequence, the town had spread itself more widely over the valley-floor, sprawled indeed, to the detriment of its defensive capabilities. Protected on the south by the river, its walls tended to ramble and be extended in the other directions, the newer extensions less high and thick than the old, with obvious weak spots. The main gate, leading to the bridge and dominated by the tall castle, looked potent enough, however.

From their viewpoint the newcomers could see two gates, and both were open — as might be expected, in early afternoon. But undoubtedly they could be closed before any rush of Scots could reach them, however swift. There was a wide fosse before the walls themselves, moreover, which would narrow any attack to the recognised crossing-places. No surprise headlong assault was going to get them into the town.

But Douglas had a notion. He had been to Newcastle many times and knew the lay-out of the town. Since these two northern gates were open, it was likely that others were also. It ought to be possible to make their way down fairly close to one of the lesser western ports unobserved, via a wooded ravine of a sizeable burn they had crossed, which dropped from the common land of The Leazes, an extension of the Town Moor south-westwards, near enough perhaps to rush the West Gate before it could be closed. No large numbers would be required, or suitable, for this. It might not prove possible, but would be worth the attempt.

The Earl himself would lead this sally. He selected 300 men only. The rest would remain in their present position until the gate-rushing attempt was launched; then they would show themselves, and ride straight down upon the main northern gate, to

47

cause maximum alarm and distract attention from the western assault, hopefully preventing aid being sent there.

Jamie went with his master, better pleased with this sort of warfare. The 300 rode back on their tracks, into the main open forested lands between Arthur's Hill and Scotswood, until they picked up the Lort Burn they had noted. They were surprised to see no herders or cattle on the Town Moor and The Leazes; no doubt the night's burnings had alarmed the owners and all had been withdrawn to safer grazing. The dean or ravine of the burn wound and twisted, making awkward going, with the men having to dismount and lead their horses; but inevitably it led approximately in the right direction, towards Tyne.

When they reached the level ground and their cover began to thin out, Douglas himself, with Sir James Lindsay, Jamie close behind, crept forward and up a low bank, to reconnoitre. They found that they were on the edge of open waste haughland, which gave the impression of being flooded in winter, with the town walls rising no more than a quarter-mile away. Unfortunately there was no gate opposite. The only one visible on this side, presumably the West Gate, was some distance further to the south-west.

The Earl cursed. "Too far," he jerked. "Near half-a-mile. Unless they were asleep, they could have the gates closed before we could reach them. Even at the gallop."

"We could win further along this burnside, without being seen," Lindsay pointed out. "The bank will give us cover some way yet, so long as we are not mounted. We would get that much nearer yon gate."

"Not near enough." Douglas pointed. "You can see how far we could go, unobserved. It would still leave 600 yards of open ground to cover. And there is the fosse to cross. It will not serve."

"My lord," Jamie put in, diffidently eager. "They would not close the heavy gates, surely, for three or four men, seeming to be unarmed travellers. If these could ride openly, then seek to stop the gates being closed. It might give time for the rest to win across."

"Dangerous work for the three or four, laddie! They could be overwhelmed and cut down. And keeping the gates open might not be easy."

"They would have surprise to aid them. And the gates could be blocked in some fashion. *I* would go."

"How would you block the gates?" Lindsay demanded. "You cannot carry anything sufficiently heavy . . ."

It was the Earl who answered him. "Those beasts!" he exclaimed, pointing. There was quite a number of cattle grazing in the haughland, no doubt brought down from the Town Moor and commons for safety. "Use them. Drive a dozen before you. Then hamstring them, in the gate-mouth. They will not easily move hamstrung cattle in a short time. And the brutes will give you some cover, forby. That is it, Jamie — you have it! They will not be able to close the gates till the beasts are dragged clear. And we will ride the moment we see you within the gates. But . . . it may cost you dear, boy. You will not be able to wear armour."

"When they see you all coming at the gallop, my lord, they will not concern themselves with such as us."

So it was decided. Jamie, his half-brother William and two mosstroopers used to handling cattle doffed all armour, shirts-of-mail and helmets, and with only their dirks at their sides, mounted and rode openly out from their cover towards the grazing cattle, while the rest of the party continued on down the burnside, behind the lessening bank, leading their horses.

Jamie and his companions felt exceedingly naked as they trotted unhurriedly towards the gate, slantwise across the haughs. They had no difficulty rounding up sufficient cattle-beasts; indeed they picked up almost too many of the animals which, looking askance at the horses, moved off in front of them fully a score strong. There was a great temptation to rush it, now, to cover the ground as quickly as possible before those gates were closed in their faces and the arrows started to fly. But Jamie resisted the urge, and held back his colleagues. Haste would only arouse suspicions.

A new problem began to materialise, which successfully distracted their minds from their personal fears. This was the tendency of the cattle to run on too far and too fast, ahead, and so enter the gateway before they could be stopped. Fortunately the fosse came to the rescue, the deep and wide ditch dug well out from the wall-foot. It was fairly dry at this season, but much rubbish from the town had been cast into it, making the bottom all but impassable, and the trotting cattle, clearly not liking the look of it, turned at right angles along the lip. The horsemen, cutting across, were able to catch up without hastening unduly.

Before the West Gate, of course, the fosse was bridged by a road. They reached this still with no challenge from whoever kept the gate. Three men were seen to be standing in the entry watching them, but displaying no signs of alarm. The cattle were still in front, and need not appear to be being driven deliberately. With a flash of inspiration, Jamie raised his hand in part salute, and then pointed at the beasts, and shouted,

"Stupid brutes! A plague on them! Turn them back, see you — turn them." He hoped that his voice would not reveal him as a Scot. The Northumbrian tongue was not so dissimilar.

Possibly the three men would have sought to turn back the cattle anyway, since they presumably would not be welcome in the streets. Anyhow, they answered the appeal, waving their arms, shouting, and trying to prevent the beasts' entry. The creatures, confused, had horses behind them however, and pressed on through the gatehouse pend. Chaos ensued.

It could hardly have worked out better for Jamie's purpose, a score of hulking beasts jammed in the entrance pend, men disputing their passage, yelling horsemen behind. Reaching for their dirks, the Scots leapt down.

What followed was not for delicate stomachs. Stooping, four of them slashed with their knives at the great tendons at the back of the hocks of the cattle-beasts' hind-legs, to hamstring them and bring them down, the mosstroopers at least expert at the grim task. Bellowing with pain and fright the wounded animals collapsed by the rear, unable to move. In only a few moments that gateway was a heaving, roaring mass of disabled livestock such as would take much time and labour to clear — and the town-gates, could not be shut until it was.

There was, indeed, no attempt to shut them. Bent low, and busy amidst the distracted animals, the four Scots did not hear or see the eruption of their fellow-countrymen, from the cover of the burnside 600 yards away, until they were in full charge, well out into the haugh. But the three at the inner end of the gateway did, since they were facing that way — and a terrifying sight it must have been. They turned and bolted; and their flight was joined by two more from the gatehouse above, racing away up a narrow street of thatched houses. The West Gate was left in the charge of the four Scots and the frantic cattle-beasts — such as could still move going pounding after them into the town.

The Earl's contingent came thundering up in great style — and found nothing more dramatic to do meantime than to put out of their misery and clear away about a dozen suffering bullocks. A cheaper entry into a walled city would have been hard to imagine. Congratulations were showered on Jamie and his companions.

The Douglas wasted no time on such inessentials. With Lindsay, Bickerton and others he drove his horse somehow over the struggling mass of bullocks and pressed on beyond the gateway. They found that they were still not within the city itself, but in a sort of adjunct to it, and enclave, with a number of houses, hutments, byres, stables and what looked like a tannery and brewery. Beyond this area rose another and higher wall, with a second and stronger gatehouse.

Pulling up, the Earl frowned. It was clear that this was the original city wall and West Gate, and that, with the place growing, new wall had been added, in this section, further out. Edward I had first walled-in Newcastle almost a century before, and his grandson Edward III had extended it in places. This was one of the extensions.

There was obvious alarm, panic indeed, ahead, with folk streaming from houses and buildings and hurrying off up the central street. The Scots leaders spurred forward. If they could reach the second gate while it was still open to admit these people, they could perhaps hold it open. Douglas yelled for men to follow him.

Jamie left off putting cattle out of their misery, gladly, mounted and rode on. He could hear distant shouting, cheering and clash from northwards. Evidently the main body had moved down upon the northern or New Gate, as arranged.

He came up with the Earl to find him taking cover behind the gable of a house which jutted into the access street, which was the principal road out, to Carlisle.

"Archers!" he was warned, briefly.

Peering round, he saw an open space, used as a bleaching green apparently, with behind it the tall double towers of a gatehouse in the high walling. In the open, two horses lay transfixed with arrows, Lindsay's and Bickerton's, the second the unfortunate

51

armour-bearer had lost thus — although the armoured men themselves were safe. Bowmen could be seen standing between the crenellations of the tower-tops. The last of the townsfolk were pushing in through a small postern door at the side of the great gateway between the towers. This wider entry was not closed by the usual massive gates, but by a piled-up barricade composed of carts, ploughs, barrels, joists, furnishings and the like — and was being added to feverishly as they watched. Presumably the gates themselves could no longer shut — or they might have been detached and used for the new gateway.

The Earl was swiftly weighing up the tactical situation. "All to dismount," he told Jamie. "Bowmen forward. The best armoured to me."

It took some time to organise the attempt, the few archers they had brought along to seek to keep down the heads of the enemy bowmen on the towers, those Scots who had protective coats-of-mail, mainly gentry these, to form up under Douglas himself, to rush the barrier on foot.

That sally was not a success. For one thing, men weighted down with steel, whether plate- or chain-mail, or both, were inevitably slow-moving and anything but agile. Instead of being able to rush the barricade they only blundered towards it. They might be fairly proof against arrows, but not against the thrusts of long pikes which, though they did not pierce the armour, could knock the men down. And clambering on and over upturned carts, ploughs and barrels was far from ideal footwork for such burdened men, used to fighting on horseback. They could not bring their swords to bear, and the few lances they had brought were no match for the twelve-feet-long pikes. The defenders had almost every advantage. With townsfolk throwing missiles of all sorts, and more pikes being rushed up, Douglas regretfully ordered a retiral. The forty or so who had made the attempt had to support or drag back with them fully a quarter of their number, mainly with damaged limbs caused by falling or being knocked over on the unstable barricade. Jamie aided his half-brother Will, groaning with pain; and young Archie Douglas of Cavers, standard-bearer, was also amongst the casualties. This was no more knightly combat than was hamstringing cattle-beasts.

The Earl now was in a quandary. If they had had the armoured war-horses and destriers which were the normal mounts for chivalry, it would have been comparatively easy; but on such slow and heavy creatures they would never have been able to reach here in the first place, covering scores of miles a day. Their light mounts were unprotected against archery. The English were always strong in bowmen, with their long yew-bows and cloth-yard shafts which Scotland could not match. Any attempt to rush this barricade clearly would have to be done by *unarmoured* foot, protected by some sort of portable shield or covering — like the sows for sheltering teams working a battering-ram, in siege-machinery. But that would take time to make. Bringing in large numbers of men from the main body would solve nothing here, for the entrance gateway between those drum-towers was narrow, and only a limited number of attackers could fight therein, at a time. Not having come prepared for siege warfare, they were held meantime.

On the other hand, they had gained a useful salient into the city, here, with houses and buildings for cover, and a safe approach to the outer walls at least. They would endeavour to hold on to this enclave. It was the best place that they were likely to obtain from which to threaten the town. Douglas ordered his men to convert the houses and buildings into strong-points, and the archers to prepare many fire-arrows for an attack on the thatched roofs beyond the inner walls. He also sent for the two Earls and other leaders to come round from the demonstration before the main northern or New Gate, for a conference. And he sent out many more small groups to scout around in all directions but especially south-westwards. They must on no account be caught in the rear by *Ralph* Percy.

What would Hotspur do now, they all wondered? He was certainly not the man to lie low meekly and do nothing.

IV

WHETHER OR NOT Sir Harry Percy was weary, and resting after his hurried dash southwards of sixty miles from Berwick, he gave remarkably little sign of his presence in Newcastle that day — so that, indeed, the Scots began to wonder whether their scouts had been misinformed and he was not there at all. His reputation was such that it was expected that he would react vigorously and at once to their attacks; but nothing of the sort developed that afternoon or evening. There were no counter-demonstrations, no counter-attacks, no intimations that any other than the normal garrison and Town Guard were in control of the city. A stout defence was mounted, admitted — but that would have been looked for, anyway.

The Earl of Douglas was in two minds as to what to do. He was, after all, in a highly dangerous situation, deep in enemy country which he himself had aroused to fury, with a comparatively small force of 3,000 and at least four English hosts in the vicinity—Ralph Percy's, the Bishop of Durham's, Hotspur's own northern column based on the Northumberland's seat at Alnwick, and the Neville's. Not counting what numbers faced them here in Newcastle itself. Prudence suggested that he should withdraw to a secure defensive position somewhere to the north, with good lines of retreat; but of course, it was not prudence which had brought the Scots here in the first place. On the other hand, they had no siege engines or equipment, and therefore little hope now of entering a walled and defended city. It had been Douglas's hope that pride, vainglory and chivalric *élan* would have been strong enough to force Hotspur into some sort of retaliation and challenge, especially against a Douglas presence. None materialised.

It was decided that they should wait until the next day — but ready for immediate retiral, with one-third of their numbers keeping open an escape-route northwards. Meantime they would fortify their enclave within the walls, keep up intermittent demonstrations, sallies and aggressive gestures all around the perimeter, and seek to construct a timber-and-hide shield for an assault on the barriers, with long poles for pushing obstructions out of the way, and scaling-ladders of some kind.

As evening wore on, news from the scouts was that Ralph Percy, with some 4,000 men, largely foot, was now directly south of Newcastle in the Washington vicinity, examining that devastated area but still heading northwards heedfully, possibly awaiting instructions from his elder brother. The Bishop was hastening back to Durham. There were also messengers from Gordon and the Scots rearguard division, announcing that they were now in the Rothbury district and in skirmishing contact with a Percy force of some 2,000 based on Alnwick. Considerably relieved that no immedate threat appeared to be posed by these various enemy units, Douglas set his sentries, and settled to a much-needed night's rest.

Daylight revealed no change in the situation. But over the breakfast fires braising good English beef, a middle-aged knight, fully armoured but without helmet, rode out from the postern at the West Gate, under a white flag, proclaiming himself to the sentries to be none less than Sir Matthew Redman, Captain of the Castle of Berwick, and requesting to be conducted to the Earl of Douglas.

The Earl, sitting in the morning sunlight in the brewery yard, savoury chop in hand, rose courteously to greet his visitor. He suggested that the Englishman dismounted and took breakfast with them.

"I cannot greatly recommend the ale, Sir Matthew — but the beef would be excellent, if only it had had a little longer to hang."

"I thank you, my lord Earl — but I have already eaten," Redman said, remaining in his saddle. "I regret that our English beer is not to your taste. But no doubt we will be able to offer you better hospitality later, when you are the guest of the Lord Harry Percy. He sends me to you to give you welcome to his father's Northumbrian domains. He wishes with all his heart that he had had longer notice of your coming, so that Percy might have greeted Douglas more fittingly."

"That is kind, sir. But perhaps it is not too late for such personal greetings? Assuming that Hotspur is sound in wind and limb? I have feared for his good health since yesterday, when on arrival we saw naught of him!"

"Sir Harry was at his meal when you arrived, my lord — and does not like to be disturbed. Thereafter he slept a little, having been in the saddle the previous night. He trusts you will forgive him?"

"Gladly. I but anticipate our meeting the more. When am I to have the honour, sir? Assuming that Sir Harry is sufficiently rested and able?"

"Any time you choose, my lord. He will be waiting at this West Gate, to receive you, in person. There is some small blockage, impedimenta, chattels lying there, which the townsfolk have left — you know what these burghers are — but that will not stop you? Or if you would prefer to go to the New Gate, to the north, he will meet you there, with pleasure. Unfortunately that gate has jammed shut. The timbers swollen, perhaps. But it may be that if you were to push, whilst we pulled, Sir Harry thinks a meeting might be effected. Or anywhere else you care to choose, my lord, around the walls?"

"I see. Hotspur is not so hot, this fine August morning, that he would venture *outside* his walls to meet me, in more knightly style than in dragging rubbish and pushing ill-made gates, Sir Matthew?"

"Alas, the Percy is desolated. But he must needs remain on hand within, to greet another visitor, his father-in-God the Prince-Bishop of Durham, who is also expected at any moment. Less distinguished than the Earl of Douglas, of course, but a man of venerable years. Also, his own brother Sir Ralph Percy is coming. Obligations, you will understand."

"I understand you, yes. But you can inform Sir Harry that the Bishop has changed his mind, and found pressing business in Durham. And Sir Ralph is making but slow progress northwards, having difficulty with heath-fires and the like. This warm weather. You would observe the smokes? So Sir Harry would have time enough, I think."

For the first time, the other looked a little put out. "You . . . you may have been misinformed, my lord," he said. "But I will tell the Percy what you say."

"Do that, Sir Matthew. But I would not have him to disturb his arrangements one whit. For a man so clearly set in his ways, feeling his years perhaps, that would be troublesome. Tell Hotspur — if I may still name him that? Tell him that I will meet him at this West

56

Gate just as soon as I have comfortably finished my breakfasting. And gladly. Perhaps we may be able to clear away your . . . impedimenta. I give you good morning, sir."

Jamie Douglas had had much ado to restrain his mirth during this exchange. It shed a new light on his beloved but normally rather dour and unforthcoming hero. He had never before heard him speaking like this, so much master in an affray of words, as distinct from deeds. The Englishman went off less pridefully than he had come.

The Earl was less dilatory than he had sounded, when Redman was gone. Tossing aside his meat, he quickly gave his orders, all indecision gone.

The renewed assault on the West Gate was launched within an hour of Hotspur's challenge, although the shields and sows were scarcely complete. There were two of these, each about twenty feet long, of a size to negotiate the entrance gateway. Consisting of planking torn from buildings and coated with raw hides from the slain cattle, to help baffle arrows, they were really no more than simple, angled shelters with slits left at eye-level, and cross-bars for holding up and carrying, behind and beneath which men could advance in comparative safety upon the barriers. Once the obstructions were reached these could be canted upwards somewhat, while some of the men inside worked, still under cover, to clear the obstacles away, reinforced by others bearing long poles and beams, with which to push. Behind would creep the main assault.

Since there could be no secrecy about this attempt, the Earl made the most of it, with trumpets blowing and hundreds of throats shouting the continuous chant of "A Douglas! A Douglas!" Bowmen were stationed at strategic points, to shoot blazing arrows over the walls, in the hope of setting fire to thatch within; and the main mass of the Scots, who could not be employed on this restricted front, were set to galloping to and fro around the perimeter walling, yelling challenge and threat, as at Durham, to alarm and preoccupy the citizenry.

Douglas and his officers did not demean themselves by creeping under the mobile canopies, but stood in a knot under his great banner just out of bowshot, watching, ready to move in whenever opportunity offered. To Jamie, in his shirt-of-mail again, it was frustrating just to stand by idly, whilst others adventured all; but with such limited space as the gateway provided, there was little else that they could do.

The canopies proved very effective, and though arrows stuck quivering in the planking and stones and spears and other missiles were showered down on them from the wall-walk and gatehouse parapets, they continued to move inexorably onward, one behind the other, the bearers secure beneath. Perceiving the uselessness of assailing these, quite quickly the English diverted their assault on to the crouching ranks which followed after. More or less unprotected, these suffered heavily. It was as well that it was only from above that they were vulnerable, the canopies in front also protecting them from low-level attack, or the attempt would have proved costly indeed.

The first canopy reached the start of the barrier, amidst screams and yells and trumpetings, with smoke beginning to billow up from within. Here it moved slightly at an angle to one side, to allow the other to come up alongside so that they formed a sort of wide spearhead. The front curtains were tipped up somewhat now, necessarily because of the obstructions — which themselves, however, tended to form a protection against arrows. Leaving only a third of their number inside to support the things, the others stooped to tug and pull and heave at the miscellaneous obstacles. The polemen, sometimes three to a beam, moved forward to push the more massive objects.

Unfortunately the besieged, in the interim, had greatly added to the pile of impedimenta — were still adding to it. Indeed, faster than the awkwardly-stooping attackers could clear the barrier at one side, it was enlarged at the other. The following men were unable to help or make any real impact on the situation, for so soon as they appeared from behind the canopies, or mounted the barricade, they were the targets for accurate and close-range archery. The armoured knights again pressed ponderously forward, but once more they were halted by their sheer inability to climb effectively over upturned carts, wheels, ladders, barrels and the like, sheathed in heavy and hampering steel. Arrows did them little harm, but the occasional shaft found its mark in crevice, joint or visor. The long pikes, however, were still a menace, and thrown spears and stones helped to topple unsteady armoured feet.

After a grim half-hour of this, with only the fire-arrows appearing to have been very effective, the Earl himself shaken from sundry falls, he recognised that nothing was to be gained as against quite considerable losses, and reluctantly gave the order to retire. To the jeers and cat-calls of the defenders, the Scots began the awkward and dangerous process of disengagement. It was simpler to advance behind those canopies than to retreat, especially with casualties to drag back.

It was Hotspur's turn, now. New trumpets rang out from within the walls and, against a pall of dirty black-brown smoke, a magnificently armoured figure in black plate mail, gold inlaid, over chain, and a great helm plumed with the blue and gold Percy colours, appeared on the gatehouse parapet, flanked by a scintillating group of knights. They all looked a deal more fresh and polished, less travel-worn and smoke-blackened, than their Scots counterparts.

"I am Percy," a strong voice called, casually authoritative though with a distinct burr, as his trumpeter left off. "I regret that Douglas has been unable to join me for the hospitality I promised. Some lack of endeavour, is it not? We must try harder, I say. Strive more manfully to overcome all obstacles! Do you not agree, my lord?"

Douglas drew a deep breath. "I had never thought to see Harry Percy, once named Hotspur, hiding behind old carts and ale-casks!" he gave back. "If these are your favoured defences, sir, my folk will make a song about them, I swear! A song which will resound for generations to come. Can you not hear it? 'Harry Hotspur and the Farmyard Midden!' Or perhaps 'The Percy at the Garbage Gate!' A ballade — a notable ballade!"

"The singing will be otherwise, I think. Scarcely by the Scots! And speaking of such things, is not the Douglas motto *Jamais Arriere*? Never Behind? Yet I vow I saw you, my lord, creeping far behind your front men in their pigeon-cotes or coney-hutches! We must seek a new motto for Douglas. *Toujours Arriere*, perhaps? Always Behind? That would serve. Or, say . . ."

He broke off as an arrow clanged against his breastplate, setting him staggering back a pace, though quickly he recovered his stance, unharmed.

"No!" Douglas cried hotly, to his archers. "Not the Percy. He is mine! The others if you wish. Not the Percy."

Taking him at his word, the Scots archers, furious at the Percy mockery, let fly their shafts at the knightly throng on the parapet-

59

walk. Promptly English arrows came winging back, and the exchange of civilities broke up in a hurry in mutual disagreement.

Douglas did not allow the previous set-back to discourage him. If the barricade was impossible for them, and the shut gates likewise, without siege engines, only the walls themselves were left. He had ordered the manufacture of some sort of scaling ladders. Since normal, lengthy step-ladders with wooden rungs could not be fabricated in haste they had to make do with rope-ladders. These were contrived out of twisted straw and bracken, with wooden cross-pieces inserted at convenient intervals — awkward admittedly but just possible for the task. Great numbers were required, each about twenty-five feet long and with a crosswise pole of about six feet at the top end, which could be thrown up over the wall-head, with the intention of catching in the crenellations, and holding. It would not be easy to make them so catch, and the defenders could of course cast them down or chop the ropes through. So large numbers were needed; and the men manning the walls would have to be kept busy and distracted, on a wide front. To assist in this, orders were given to collect large quantities of straw, hay, dead bracken, whins and anything else burnable, from the surrounding haughs, commons and woodlands, this material to be piled up in heaps to the south and west, from which direction the wind blew, to provide a comprehensive blanket of smoke, under the cover of which the attempt could be made.

While this was being organised, a scout came to report that Sir Ralph Percy had arrived just south of the city. And even as Douglas considered this news, another messenger from Pate Home appeared, to announce that the Percy and his force were in fact crossing the bridge over Tyne into Newcastle itself, making no move to ride round and attack the Scots from the rear, as might have been feared. Presumably he was still uncertain as to their numbers; or he may have been merely obeying his elder brother's orders. This, at least, was a major relief. Ralph Percy would not greatly add to their problems by merely reinforcing Hotspur inside the walls. Still, it would be wise to commence the wall assault before the newcomers had time to be deployed.

So the fires were lit, and the billowing clouds of smoke rolled over on the breeze to envelop all the western and northern portions of the town in their choking pall, to add to that of the burning thatches within. Under the cover, the ladder-throwers advanced against a very considerable stretch of the walling, coughing and spluttering, eyes streaming.

It was difficult and frustrating work. The walls averaged about twenty feet in height, and throwing the ropes up and over in itself was an awkward procedure, with all the protruding rungs and poles. Most casts fell back, and of those which went over, nine out of ten did not catch in the crenellations, and they too slithered back whenever pressure was put on them. Where they did take hold, there was usually a defender nearby to hurl them back, or chop through the ropes. The smoke helped — but it also hampered the attackers. They were unable to call the attention of many of their fellows to a ladder which was holding. Some Scots clambered up on to the wall-head, only to find themselves alone and unsupported.

Jamie Douglas, running up and down the perimeter and weeping copiously, with the task of keeping his master informed of progress, was not long in coming to the conclusion that this assault, too, was going to fail. Even those ladders which had gained a lodgement did not remain long in position, with teams of Englishmen running, crouching, along the parapet-walk, to clear them, with any Scots who had climbed them. The Scots archers did manage to pick off a number of these — but the smoke hindered them equally with the enemy, and some of their own fellow-countrymen fell to their arrows in the murky confusion. And when Ralph Percy's additional manpower began to stream up to reinforce the walls, the balance became quickly less favourable. The fuel situation, too, began to deteriorate, with the stocks of smoke-making material running out, and the sinking fires ever tending to produce more heat than smoke — on an August noontide which had become sufficiently hot anyway. The perspiring, sore-eyed, coughing attackers flagged, visibly.

Once again, the Earl of Douglas had to admit defeat, and call off the attempt.

The Scots morale was not helped when, as they were drawing off, the Percy himself, now accompanied by his brother, appeared once more above the West Gate, this time under a white flag.

"Warm work on a hot day, my friends," he called. "Clearly you are wearied. Sir Matthew tells me, Douglas, that you do not enjoy our simple English beer? So here is a pipe of prime Burgundy wine to cool your gullets. With Percy's much sympathy!"

Down from the parapet was lowered on a rope a huge ninety-two gallon wine cask, infinitely carefully, inch by inch, amidst much English cheering.

Douglas, ignoring the growling of his own people, with a great effort wiped the black frown from his features. He bowed, and as a further gesture removed his plumed helmet and handed it to Bickerton.

"I thank you," he shouted back. "I shall be glad to taste of your so famed hospitality. Which we have hitherto found hard to come at!" He paused. "But see you, Percy, we have, I swear, both had sufficient of this jousting at a distance, which appears to be deciding us nothing. Let us come to a decent decision, as between Douglas and Percy, I say. I have burned your lands — as you have burned mine, in the past. Let us settle this issue between us and our houses as honest knights should. Let us cross lances, you and I, in single combat, here before all. A joust, sir. You are namely at the business, I am told. Show us *how* namely, I pray!"

There was an obvious stir, up there on the gatehouse parapet. And not only there. All around him, Douglas's lieutenants and supporters looked astonished, doubtful or openly hostile to the notion. Most began to declare it foolish at the best, dangerous anyway, possibly disastrous. But the Earl shook his head. They had sustained four rebuffs, he pointed out. He had the spirits of his men to consider — of vital importance, deep in enemy territory. The men were no longer at their best. It was clear to all that they were not going to win into this city, by force nor yet by guile. But just to steal away, in defeat, must wound their spirits further, as indeed their fair name. This way, a retiral could be effected decently. If he won, they could go proudly. If he lost, it would be in fair fight and before the greatest champion in England — no reflection on the Scots.

The Percy seemingly was having a like difficulty in deciding the pros and cons of this unexpected proposition. Before it might be rejected, Douglas sought to clinch the matter by changing it from proposal to dare. He had a trumpet-blast blown.

"I, James Douglas, do hereby challenge Henry Percy in single combat!" he cried. "Mounted or afoot. With lance, sword, battle-axe or mace — the choice Percy's. To be fought until one or other yields or is carried off the field."

There was only a brief pause before Hotspur shouted back. "I accept. So be it. Let it be lance *and* sword. Mounted, to be sure. Prepare to fall, Douglas!"

"It is a match. There is space here, before the gate. I will meet you here, so soon as you are prepared. With no carts or casks to protect you, Percy!"

The total change which came over the entire scene and situation was almost laughable. From an atmosphere of war, anger and bloodshed, suddenly it tended almost to holiday, sportive excitement. With no longer the dread of vicious arrows picking them off, the Scots set about clearing a wide space before the old West Gate, laughing, even shouting wagers to Englishmen who began to work to clear a passage through the barricade. Equally cheerful sounds came from within. The fear of possible sudden death and terrible hurt, abruptly lifted, can produce almost hectic reaction.

Jamie Douglas did not know whether to rejoice or otherwise. He had faith in the ability and expertise of his renowned lord; but Hotspur's martial and chivalric fame was as notable — and he was bound to be fresher as well as being somewhat younger. Possibly better mounted too, for though the Earl had a superb Arab stallion, the sort of animal which was ideal for long and fast cross-country riding, it was on the light side for the tiltyard. Percy probably would not have a destrier available at Newcastle, admittedly; but he would certainly have a choice of heavier beasts. He had chosen the mounted duel, and no doubt knew what he was about. If the Douglas was to fail, and before all . . .

The contest was bound to differ from the normal tournament standard in more respects than the horses involved. The Earl was armoured mainly in chain-mail, with only cuirass of plate back and front, gauntlets and knee-pieces of steel, and no massive jousting helm — and it was likely that Percy would be in the same black plate armour he had been wearing. There might be jousting armour kept in the castle here, but it would be surprising if it fitted Hotspur, who was over six feet tall. Likewise, Douglas had no blunt jousting lance; and it seemed unlikely that, for pride's sake, Percy would insist on them using such, as against the sharp and shorter war lances. In other words, this was going to be a much more dangerous affair than in a normal tourney — just as so much more hung on the result.

The Earl was ready first — indeed little preparation was necessary, although John Bickerton fussed about tightening buckles and straps holding the cuirass-guards in place and testing every item of the stallion's trappings and harness, his lord pooh-poohing impatiently. Jamie attached a long Douglas pennon to the Earl's lance, aided his hero to mount and then handed him up his comparatively small shield, blue and white, with the Douglas heart.

To a lively fanfare, Sir Harry Percy rode out through the gap in the barrier, followed by a throng of knights and esquires, a gallant figure on a splendid bay and leading a matching beast. He did wear the same rich armour as before, with considerably more plate than the Douglas, and being taller anyway, made the more imposing figure. Visor up, he raised a gauntleted hand.

"Ha, Douglas!" he called. "I have brought you a better nag than your grey. It will be weary, perhaps. I would not have you further disadvantaged than you are already!"

"I thank you — but I am well content, sir," the other retorted. "Give your second horse to your brother, Sir Ralph. Then, when I have unseated you, he can seek to redeem the honour of your house!"

Percy laughed aloud. "Crow while you may, Scot! Your time is short." And he reined round, to ride off to the south end of the open space — so that Douglas, not he, would have the sun in his eyes.

"My lord — you should have drawn lots for that position!" Jamie protested. "He has taken the advantage, as of right."

"Let him be, lad — perchance he will need it! Give me my lance . . ."

"See you, Lord James," Bickerton put in, at the other side, low-voiced. "Take you this small mace. It could be useful. Should lance and sword fail."

"No, no. Lance and sword Percy said — so let it be. I need no mace."

"But, sir — he has already taken an advantage. This of the sun," the armour-bearer pressed. "Who knows what other trick he may spring? He has the fresher horse and the longer reach. And more plate-armour. Take the mace — if only as precaution." And he held up a short-handled, heavy spiked club, designed for piercing even steel plate.

"No, I said. Fool — put it away! Would you have all see it? See

64

Douglas doubting the outcome? Taking a weapon disallowed?"
And with a back-handed swipe of his steel gauntlet, the Earl swept
the proffered mace aside. Unfortunately it struck Bickerton slightly
on brow and cheek, one of its spikes drawing blood. Douglas trotted off to the opposite, northern, corner from Percy, Jamie running after, whilst the armour-bearer flung up hand to head, and
cursed savagely.

The two principals sat their mounts some 200 yards apart, the
furthest the open space would allow. The Earl of Dunbar and
March and Sir Ralph Percy paced out into the centre, bowed
stiffly to each other, agreed on a signal, decided that second lances
would be available should one snap, and that either side had the
right to carry off their champion unopposed should he fall. Then,
back at his own party, Sir Ralph gave the sign, and a long high
blast on a horn proclaimed that the fight was on.

Nothing loth, the protagonists shut down their visors, couched
their lances and dug in their spurs, driving their spirited mounts
forward, all dash and colour. A hundred yards was not a very
adequate distance in which to attain maximum speed, but these
were swift riding horses, not heavy destriers, and both were in fact
into the full gallop before they met. The sun was strong in
Douglas's eyes, it being early afternoon, and he was only too well
aware of the handicap. But by keeping his glance lowered and
peering through his thick, dark eyebrows, he to some extent
countered the effect. He was counting almost every hoof-beat of
his stallion — and at the same time warning himself not to under-
estimate his opponent.

Only a few yards apart, the Earl savagely jerked his horse's
head to the right. At that speed, the animal all but fell over its own
fore-feet, its rider keeping his saddle only by a remarkable mixture
of balance and agility. For moments the grey was directly across
the front of the bay, with Douglas's lance rendered useless. If the
Percy had been prepared for that extraordinary manoeuvre, the
other would have been at his mercy in those brief instants. But they
were both right-handed men, with their lances couched each at
that side, so it went without saying that they should ride to clash at
the same side. Percy did make a wild thrust, but it was uncoordinated and askew. Douglas took the lance-tip on his shield, off
which it slid harmlessly. But he himself could make no effective
riposte. He plunged on, past.

But already he was urgently, violently, reining back and round, his beast's forelegs now pawing the air. In only a few yards he had managed to turn completely, on the creature's hind-legs, mainly, and thereafter was spurring back whence he had just come, behind the Percy.

That man, possibly because of the restricting effect of his helmet, both as to vision and hearing — and also because the normal procedure after such an inconclusive pass would be for each to ride most of the way back to the perimeter positions before wheeling for another charge — was a little while in realising that his opponent was in fact hard at his heels. But when it did dawn on him, he reacted in no uncertain fashion — for it must look very much as though he was running away, with his rival chasing him, an intolerable situation for England's champion. Indeed, many onlookers, the Scots at least, had begun to howl with mirth. So Hotspur sought to rein round, almost as abruptly as his foe had done half-a-minute before. He achieved the difficult feat almost as effectively as Douglas had done — for both were superb horsemen, necessarily — and so again faced his enemy. But now their respective positions were vastly different. Percy, suddenly, had the sun in his eyes, and moreover was all but at a standstill; whereas Douglas was in full charge. Not only that, the Scot was prepared for the situation, had visualised and contrived it, and the Percy was not. Barely a dozen yards apart, it was too late for the Englishman either to take adequate avoiding action or to gather any speed. He aimed his lance at the other's breast and furiously hacked at his bay's sides with his sharp spurs.

But there could be no comparison between the impact of a lance with a full gallop behind it, and one with little more than trotting speed. The two protagonists met with a resounding crash, and both took the opposing lance-points on their shields. Percy's set back the Douglas in his saddle quite noticeably — more from his own momentum than anything else; but the Scot's weapon smashed Hotspur and his shield clean off his bay's back. The man fell backwards with a mighty clatter, his lance flying wide — and fell, not on peat-dust or soft turf, but on cobblestones, inside a great weight of steel plating. Sparks actually flew up at the impact. Sir Harry Percy lay still, in gleaming, colourful ruin.

The Earl, recovering his seat, glanced round, perceived the

situation, and rode on to his own corner, amidst the wild cheering of the Scots.

Jamie Douglas, all but beside himself with excitement, almost worship, was bubbling breathless enconiums as his lord trotted up. But, turning his mount again, the older man raised his visor and sat still.

"Wait you," he panted. "He may rise. It may not be finished."

But the Percy lay motionless — and clearly his supporters considered that enough was enough for, superintended by Sir Ralph, a large number of the English ran out from their side into the central space, to pick up and half-carry, half-drag the presumably stunned Hotspur back to the entrance gateway. The yells of the watching Scots became fiercer, more jubilant.

Douglas, narrow-eyed, moistened his lips. "It will serve, I think. Scarce my finest hour — but it will serve for our present needs." He raised a mail-clad arm to point. "See, Jamie—they have overlooked something, in their haste. Come with me."

Lance raised high now, its Douglas pennon fluttering, he trotted out again into the middle, Jamie running, all but skipping, behind. The English, with their inert burden, looked at them askance, but the Earl waved them on, genially.

"I pray that Sir Harry be not sore hurt," he called. "Air, and a mouthful of that excellent Burgundy, will revive him, I vow!" Pulling round somewhat, he leant over, to murmur to Jamie. "Hotspur's lance and guidon lad. Lying there still. Get it. Bring it to me. Quickly, before they perceive it."

The young man ran for the forgotten lance. The English began replacing the gateway barrier, presumably fearing a rush at it.

So, carrying both flagged spears, the Earl of Douglas rode back to his own people, barely five minutes after leaving them, to hilarious enthusiasm. He waved down all the plaudits, however.

"That was not a knightly victory," he declared. "That was but a strategem, an artifice of sorts. But necessary, since it was needful that I won. Presently, we can retire with honour, I think. Meantime, a beaker of that Burgundy, in sweet Mary's name!"

"There is a messenger here, James, from Home," the Earl of Moray said. "The Bishop of Durham is on the move again. Northwards."

"Ah! How far? And in what strength?"

"He left Durham an hour before noon, my lord. With a strong force. Horsed, in advance, perhaps 1,400 with 5,000 foot behind," the scout informed. "When last seen, the horse was at Rainton. They will have moved many miles further north, by this."

"Aye." Douglas dismounted. "This means that we must ride the sooner. But . . . decently." He turned to Dunbar and Moray. "My friends — have all our force assemble in groups and troops outside the walls. Save those who are here, within this part. These to show naught of readiness to move, meantime. You have it? Not to *look* as though we prepare to retire until I have spoken with the Percy again. We have a little time yet, I think."

After a due interval, the Earl had his trumpeter sound a summons, and then paced forward on foot, nearer to the West Gate again, Jamie at his side. He raised his hand.

"Englishmen," he called, "I seek word of the Percy. He suffered a misfortune. Too early an end to our joust. How fares he? Is he recovered? No serious hurt?"

After a few moments of silence, Sir Ralph answered, from a window of the gatehouse. "He is well enough, Douglas — after that scurvy trick! Stunned by his fall, that is all. It was no honest fight."

"It was a poor bout, yes. Too swift an end. But honest enough. I fear that the sun got in your brother's eyes. But if you are not satisfied, sir, perhaps you would care to come run a course with me, yourself? To retrieve this!" And in his other hand he held up, and let unroll, the long fish-tailed pennon with the Percy arms. "How say you?" And he flapped the thing casually.

There was a pause at the other side. Then another voice spoke up, not quite so strong and arrogant as before, but clearly Hotspur's.

"I will fight you again, Douglas — anywhere, at any time. Never fear. These fools dragged me off the field. We could have finished the bout."

"Ha, Sir Harry — I rejoice to hear you sound so well recovered. What happened to you was but a mischance, yes. I, too, am ready to meet you at any time. When, I hope, you will give me better sport!"

"Damn you, Douglas . . . !"

"Any time," the Earl repeated, holding up the pennon again.

68

"But . . . not today, I think? I would not have you riding another course, when shaken from your fall. It would be but a dull contest. Next time, we must not disappoint. Meantime, no doubt you will come for this guidon of yours? I am called back to Scotland, unfortunately. I cannot wait here while you recover your strength. But I will go but slowly. Wait for you between here and the Border. Till after tomorrow's night. Thereafter I shall carry your guidon to Scotland and plant it upon my castle's wall. Where you may come for it, if you care!"

"That you shall never do!" came back hotly, from the gate-house. "This I swear!"

"Very well, Percy — as you will. The remedy is in your own hands. Come take your guidon before I leave Northumberland. You will find it before my tent. I will wait for you until two nights from now — no more. Perhaps we shall see some sport, yet." And flicking the pennon mockingly, Douglas turned and strolled back to his own party. "Prepare to move," he called, but unhurriedly and quite openly.

"Do we give up, my lord — *now*?" Jamie asked, unhappily. "Flee, because of this Bishop's coming?"

"Can you count, boy? *I* count over 10,000 against us, when the Bishop comes up — perhaps more, since we know not how many Harry Percy has in this city. And Neville may be moving against us. We have heard no word of Neville. We flee, then — as far as the Town Moor, yonder!"

"The Town Moor . . .?"

"Aye. There is room there, for action. I will not be trapped down here, pressed against these city walls. When you go to war, lad, learn to use your head! It will help keep it on your shoulders! See, now — take this Percy guidon, and guard it well. Where is Bickerton? To rid me of this cuirass . . ."

"I will aid you, my lord," young Archie of Cavers volunteered. "John Bickerton has gone."

"Gone? How, gone? Gone where?"

"He mounted horse and rode away. Sore angered that you had struck him, my lord," Richard Lundie, the chaplain, explained.

"The fool! I did not strike him. Not of a purpose. I but thrust away that mace. What was he at, giving me the mace before all? The English must have seen it. Giving the Douglas a mace, when Percy had declared for only lance and sword, putting my honour

69

at risk! The man has lost his wits. And now he betakes himself off? Lindsay — what's amiss with the fellow? He is your man. I made him my armour-bearer on your commendation."

"I know not, my lord. He is a good fighter, and namely with horse, hawk and hound. His father keeps my castle of Luffness in Lothian, and sought my good offices with you. I am sorry that he has behaved so. If I had known of this temper . . ."

"Think no more of it, Sir James. I also am sorry — that the mace struck him. I shall tell him so, anon. When he has recovered from his spleen."

"The *Douglas* will never make apology to that, that underling!" Jamie protested. "He is a surly oaf. I have never liked him."

"If Douglas has behaved ill, he will make apology to any soever!" the Earl reproved. "It is the knightly code — and do not forget it. Any of you."

"Only a Douglas should be armour-bearer to Douglas," Will Douglas of Drumlanrig, the Earl's elder illegitimate son put in — who had coveted that position for himself, although only fifteen.

"Bairns — enough!" the Earl cried. "We have more important business than to haver here, about thin-skinned youths! When you find Bickerton, send him to me. Now — prepare to retire. In good order. Up to the Town Moor . . ."

So, in orderly fashion, with a fair amount of trumpet-blowing and marshalling, the Scots turned their backs on Newcastle town and marched up the quite steep braes and banks to the northwards, to the high common lands. Here, where they could not be approached unawares, there was room for manoeuvre and a choice of retreat routes, Douglas pitched camp. He had cooking-fires lit all along the lip above the city, so that there could be no doubts about their presence there; and before his own tent he set up Hotspur's lance with the Percy pennon. Sentries were posted all around, and scouting parties were out in force.

Just after sunset a messenger arrived from Pate Home to say that the Bishop of Durham had halted for the night at Birtley, just over 4 miles south of Newcastle. A close watch was being maintained on him.

John Bickerton was still not to be found, amongst the leadership, when the camp settled for the night.

V

PONTELAND LAY AT a crossing of the Pont River eight miles north-west of Newcastle, a bridge-hamlet with a small castle, really only a peel-tower, in a good position to levy tolls on the bridge-users. The Scots came to it in mid-forenoon and in no hurry. Douglas, in fact, was disappointed. Hotspur had not ventured out to seek retrieve his guidon, although the Scots had waited as long as they dared, with the Bishop reported on the move again and probing west-about — and moreover, word at last of Sir Ralph Neville with a large force heading north-eastwards from Derwentside. The object of the Scots exercise had been fully accomplished, therefore, and the main thrust, in Cumberland and Lancaster under the Earl of Fife and Archibald the Grim, was safe from any cross-country assault, to cut it off from Scotland. But the Earl of Douglas had hoped for better results in his personal exchange with Harry Percy. So he was dragging his feet somewhat, on his way home.

It was, of course, a risky game to play, for if the Percys joined up with the Bishop they would form an army many times the size of his own, and in their own country. But he based his calculations and hopes on Hotspur's famous pride and arrogance. The man must be smarting indeed, and was known to resent his Prince-Bishop's territorial pretensions anyway. Believing himself to have been bested by something of a trick, in single combat, he should be eager to prove that he was the better man in the field, especially in his own Northumberland territory amongst his father's vassals — without calling upon any churchman to aid him. Douglas would have wagered on him following them up, without waiting for the Bishop. His people most certainly would be keeping him well informed as to the Scots' progress and numbers. Yet rearward scouts reported no move out of Newcastle.

Ponteland was an excuse to delay for a little, at least. The owner of the little castle had the unlikely name, for a Northumbrian, of Sir Aymer d'Atholl. He was not exactly a renegade Scot, since he

71

had been born here and never lived in Scotland; but he was descended from the ancient Celtic Earls of Atholl, and his grandfather had taken the English side in the Wars of Independence, and in consequence had lost all his Scottish lands, and settled here. The Scots had not forgotten them, however, especially as the d'Atholls were not backward in the Border reiving activities.

So a halt was made, to assault and take Ponteland Tower.

John Bickerton had quietly taken his place in the Earl of Douglas's entourage that morning as they assembled to leave the Town Moor of Newcastle. He made no comment on his absence, nor indeed on the previous day's incident, curtly dismissing his colleagues' remarks and queries. The Earl had taken him aside, however, before they moved off, and had spoken with him for a minute or two — none knew to what effect. Now, Douglas sought him out, appointing him to go forward and demand the yielding of this castle. He went, stiff, expressionless.

So far as delay was concerned, Ponteland did not provide much excuse. Quite quickly Bickerton brought back Sir Aymer d'Atholl himself, a middle-aged, heavily-built, anxious man, with a cast in one eye, who had taken one look at the force arrayed against him and recognised the wisdom of a prompt surrender. The Earl made a gift of his person to Bickerton, to take back to Scotland for purposes of ransom — a gesture which drew not a little comment, some of it resentful. It even set Jamie wondering why his master must be so generous and forgiving. The general opinion was that there was more to this than met the eye.

Leaving Ponteland Tower's stables and subsidiary buildings alight, as a beacon for Percy — since the stone tower itself would not burn — they moved on north-westwards.

Two days earlier Douglas had sent couriers to halt their slower-moving rearward force, under Gordon of Huntly and Scott of Buccleuch, in the Wansbeck valley west of Morpeth. They would be more use there, keeping the Percys' Alnwick and Berwick groupings occupied and in check, and maintaining an open line of retreat for the main body, than they would have been had they come on to Newcastle. An extra 2,000 men, mainly foot, could not have opened that citadel; and they would have been only a hindrance to any swift withdrawal. Now they would join up.

They reached the Wansbeck in the Wallington area in the early afternoon—and had no difficulty in finding the second Scots force. Indeed it could be heard, if not seen, from miles off, with the continuous lowing and complaining of vast numbers of cattle. Gordon and Scott, if somewhat reproachful at the undramatic and pedestrian role allotted to them, had evidently decided to make the best of their opportunities otherwise, and had apparently collected the products of half the farms of Northumberland, such as would travel on the hoof, to compensate for lack of more martial excitements. And, it seemed, this huge concourse by the Wansbeck was not all; two other great herds had already been despatched northwards, under adequate guard.

Douglas found no fault with this. But he refused to halt for the night at this great camp, nevertheless. It was in no very good defensive position, for the Wansbeck was a comparatively shallow stream and could be forded easily at many points. This was no place to await the possible onset of Harry Hotspur. The Percy might come with many times their own numbers—and encumbered with all their booty, his new foot reinforcements would be of little service against a cavalry host. He must secure a very strong position, and adequate escape routes at his back. Otterburn, in the mouth of Redesdale, which they had noted on their way south that first morning, provided more or less what he required. It was another fourteen miles.

The Earl ordered the march to continue, and Gordon and Scott to bring on their people and the cattle at their best speed — but to be ready to disperse should the Percys' array overtake them. Pate Home and his rear scouts would give them warning.

It was dusk before the main force reached the long green Cheviot ridges, all pools of shadow, where the Rede issued from the narrows of its upland valley at Otterburn. But Douglas would allow no respite nor settling-in until he had made his defensive dispositions, pressing on a little way beyond the village. The river, and the wide low haughlands flanking it, wet and swampy, would protect his right; the steeps and escarpments of Fawdon and Greenchesters Hills would cover his left, provided they could deny the enemy the area in between the two heights, where the Otter burn itself came down from the north to join Rede. Admittedly the burn had carved for itself a fairly deep dean, or ravine, and this would make a useful frontal barrier. But there was a wide gap between the two hills to the north, and this would be the weakness of the position, and would have to be thoroughly plugged against

73

any outflanking move. Apart from this, the position was an excellent one, only marred by the fact that in the centre of it all on a steep knoll where a smaller burn joined the Otter, above the deep dean, rose the Tower of Otterburn. And unlike Ponteland, its owner did not acquiesce to the Scots demand for instant surrender. It was a much stronger place, to be sure, although no larger, a tall square parapeted tower of stone, with tiny windows and a door reachable only by a removable timber stair, at first floor level, all within a small, irregular, high-walled courtyard. Taking it would be no easy matter, without siege engines.

Satisfied that he had surveyed the terrain as well as was possible in the fading light, and recognised its advantages and its dangers, and aware that the tower could do him no harm, at least, the Earl allowed his host to make camp, partly on one side of the dean, partly on the other. He made use of the earthworks of an ancient fortified camp, on the higher ground west of the burn, as main base — evidently their Pictish ancestors, who had extended their sway further south than this, had also recognised the strategic usefulness of Otterburn.

During that moonlit night, although there was no word of the Percys, the continuous arrival of contingents of the vast cattle-herd, amidst much bellowing and stir, ensured that few of the Scots leaders, at least, achieved undisturbed sleep. The new arrivals and their noisy and complaining charges, were confined to the low haughland area flanking Rede.

In the morning Douglas held a council-of-war, for there was considerable difference of opinion manifesting itself amongst his principal colleagues and lieutenants. One school of thought, put forward by the Earl of Moray and the Lord Maxwell, mature and responsible men, considered that they had done sufficiently well in this expedition, and should return now safely to Scotland without further adventure or possible risk, their objectives accomplished. This waiting for Percy was perilous as well as unprofitable. Another proposal, put forward by some of the younger lords, was that they should now cross over to the west of the country, by the Tyne, Haltwhistle and the Gilsland Gap into Cumberland, to join up with the larger Scots army. This was supported by Sir James Lindsay of Crawford, Sir John Montgomerie of Eaglesham, Sir John St. Clair of Roslin and others. These, too, were doubtful of the business of waiting for Hotspur.

The Borderers, on the other hand, the Scotts, Homes, Kerrs, Gordons, Johnstones and the like, were in their element here, with the March not far at their backs, and most of Northumberland wide open to their depredations, were quite content for Douglas to wait, so long as they might make Otterburn their base and fan out left, right and centre but especially down into the richer coastal plain around Warkworth, Alnwick and Craster, in a glorious despoiling campaign such as generations of their mosstrooping forebears had dreamed of.

The Douglas heard them all out patiently. Jamie, in attendance, thought that perhaps he was even encouraging the discussion and prolonging the debate in the interests of his own preoccupation with Harry Hotspur, giving that hero more time to come up. As commander, the Earl had of course to balance the pros and cons of over-all strategy; but he also had to take into account the desires of the various component parts of his force. For this was no sort of disciplined military unit, save in that it voluntarily accepted himself as leader. Every man in it was in the fighting tail of some lord or laird, none belonging to any central authority. And none were being paid for attendance, save out of the pockets of the same lords and lairds. There was no such thing as a national army. Therefore a commander had to carry his supporting leaders with him at every step — or they could just depart and either return home or go campaigning on their own; often they did just that.

The Earl of Douglas therefore could not *command* all to his will, even though a fair proportion of those present were in fact Douglases. He had to gain his ends by more subtle means, if at all. He did so now by playing one view against another; and, being a man of action himself and recognising that words were less effective than deeds as a distraction, proposed that they meantime assailed Otterburn Tower, which was impudently holding out against them. None objected to this, at least — and delay was achieved.

The assault was not, and could not be, a very effective exercise. Large manpower was of no advantage. The position of the keep, surmounting a mound of solid rock, meant that there could be no mining or undercutting. The courtyard and outbuildings were fairly quickly taken and destroyed; but thereafter there was a stalemate. A battering-ram, contrived out of a tree-trunk, beat down the basement door and its iron yett; but this merely gave access to the vaulted ground-floor chamber, which had no communication with the upper parts of the building — and unlike a timber floor, the stone vaulting was quite fire-resistant and immensely thick. The only other door was at first-floor level, its removable timber staircase drawn up. The battering-ram could not get at this, even though attempts were made to erect a platform from which to assail it, while the arrows and missiles of the defenders on the parapet-walk high above made the attempt costly. The windows were all so high and tiny, that ordinary arrows could not find a mark, and fire-arrows were useless against a wholly stone building. Picking away at the lower courses of masonry, under cover of mobile shelters, was put in hand; but with walls eight feet in thickness, with iron-hard mortar, this was a slow process indeed. In fact, the little castle could only be starved out, through lack of water and food; but this might take days.

Nevertheless, as far as the Douglas was concerned, the attempt served its purpose. It used up time, constituted a challenge to hot-blooded men, and stilled demands for departure meantime. And it did not prevent quite a large proportion of the Border contingent from pursuing their favourite role of cattle-stealing, ranging near and far for beasts discreetly hidden away in remote valleys, deans and 'beef-tubs'.

In mid-afternoon Pate Home sent the anticipated news at last. The Percys were on their way, having left Newcastle during the forenoon, a host of perhaps 8,000. They had not so far linked up with the Bishop of Durham, who was advancing slowly northwards well to the west — seemingly keeping a wary episcopal eye on Sir Ralph Neville, who was also advancing on a more or less parallel line still further to the west. These two forces were still some thirty miles off; but the Percys only twenty or so when the message was despatched.

Now there was no talk of retiral or heading westwards. All was preparation. Messengers went out in all directions to warn the raiding bands. Douglas was content. He should have his confrontation.

Nevertheless, by dusk, the Percy had still not put in an appearance, and scouts reported him still five miles away on Ottercops Moor, although his forward pickets were probing much nearer. An hour later, Home himself rode into the Otterburn camp to announce that the enemy had in fact settled in camp below Hunterless Hill, at the west end of that moor.

Tomorrow, then, would see Douglas and Percy at grips, at last.

The Earl and his lieutenants made a final circuit and inspection of the position before turning in. He was still a little concerned about a flanking attack from the higher ground to the north. It was the one weakness of the site. He ordered a strong party under Scott of Buccleuch to occupy these heights on either side of the burn. And on the low ground north of the Rede itself he had all the cattle which had not yet been despatched northwards spread in a great belt half-a-mile wide, some thousands of beasts. Any surprise frontal attack would have to negotiate this living barrier. It seemed unlikely that Hotspur would make a night assault; but if he did, they ought to receive ample warning.

Reasonably satisfied, Douglas retired to his tent, as a pale half-moon rose over the ridges eastwards.

*　　　*　　　*

Jamie, in the esquires' tent behind his master's, was awakened by the horn-blowing from the low ground, an urgent ululant wailing. Only three or four seconds later the Earl's voice was shouting for his aides and leaders. Stumbling heavy-eyed out into the now quite bright moonlight, the young man found Douglas already standing before his tent. There was a confusion of noise from the riverside area now, the clash of steel, shouting and a great lowing of cattle.

"Dunbar, Moray, Lindsay, Maxwell to me — quickly, Jamie!" he jerked. "Archie—get Montgomerie, Gordon, Keith. Will—down to the haugh. Discover for me the position. Synton commands there—Scott of Synton. Richard—up to Buccleuch on the left. Discover if he finds any move there. Ha—Pate! Lacking your own presence this once, your scouts have slept, I think! Get forward and find me what's to do. Rob Hart—the horses. Simon — stay by me. Bickerton — my armour . . ."

Most of the leaders came hurrying, without being summoned. While Bickerton eased the Earl into his chain-mail shirt and buckled on the cuirass back and front, and other armour-bearers did the like for their own masters, Douglas rapped out his orders.

"You know your positions, my lords. All was arranged. From

77

the noise, Percy has elected to strike by the riverside — the marsh-land — first, hoping to turn our flank. That means he is on foot. Horses would be bogged down, there. No doubt he will try the left flank also. Maxwell — be ready to go to Scott's aid. You are on my left. Afoot, on those braes. Indeed, on this ground, most fighting will be on foot. You have the right, Dunbar. I move to the edge of this dean, meantime, to await information. I will seek to advance in the centre, if I may, towards the village. Is that clear?"

Not all of the awkward business of fitting on and buckling the armour was finished by any means, when Douglas pressed on to the lip of the ravine, where a better prospect of the area to the east was to be had. He was still helmetless, as were some others. Everywhere behind him men were assembling in their troops and companies.

Jamie found the waiting, the staring across the dark wooded trough of the dean, galling, nerve-racking, with the babel of sounds coming from a considerable distance ahead and to the right. Nothing was to be seen of any conflict, however bright the moonlight. But the Earl, fitting on his plumed helmet now, was not going to move further until he knew more, however eager his supporters. If Hotspur had chosen to attack under cover of dark-ness, unexpected for that man, then he was going to use that darkness and consequent confusion for his purposes. With a force apparently some three times as large as the Scots, he could be allowed no other advantages.

At last Will of Drumlanrig came running up from the low ground, all but speechless, partly with excitement. "Cattle . . . Englishmen . . . fighting . . ." he panted. "In the bog. In the river. Everywhere. Beasts crazed. Charging all ways. Blood . . . !"

"Quiet, boy!" his father snapped. "Take your time. Keep your wits. Speak plainly — or not at all."

'Y-yes, my lord. Yes," the fifteen-year-old said, swallowing.

"Answer my questions then, Will. Did you speak with any in command, down there?"

"Aye. With Scott of Synton and the Laird of Swinton. They said . . ."

"Wait. Are these alone? Do they have many men still down there with them?"

"Some, lord. I could not see many. The cattle . . ."

"But they have a front? *This* side of the cattle?"

"Yes."

78

"The English? *They* are amongst the cattle?"

"Aye — hundreds of them . . ."

"Tcha, boy — we are not concerned with hundreds but *thousands*! Now — what did Synton and Swinton say? Think, Will — did they say aught of the English strength?"

The boy chewed his lip. "Aye, sir. They said . . . Synton said that some were across the river. Mounted. He said to tell you that he believed . . . believed that they could hold them. Those in the haugh. With some more men. He wants more men . . ."

"Now we learn. He believes *he* can hold them, down there — with more men. Then, he cannot think that to be the main force. Of thousands. He could not hope to hold thousands. And the horse across Rede — a diversion, a flanking force, to ford higher and come down behind us. But we know there is no ford till Shittleheugh, three miles up. They cannot ride fast in this light in rough country. We have an hour before these can reach our backs. Did he say aught else, Will? Think."

"The cattle, yes. Swinton said that they had driven many of the beasts uphill. And were seeking to drive more. Up to the village, he said. To block Percy in the streets . . ."

"God's sake, boy — why could you not say that, at the first!" the Earl exclaimed. But he patted his son's heaving shoulders, nevertheless. "They believe Hotspur's main thrust is in the centre, through the village where lies the road. For his horse, to be sure. So Swinton would pack the street with cattle. It makes good sense, for Percy. This I would have done my own self, with another flanking force to the high ground northwards. Now we may hazard a move. My lords — you hear? I conceive Hotspur to advance on four fronts. One in the level haughs. One horsed across Rede, to scare us. One probably on high ground, to our left. And in the centre, moves his main force along the road, through the village where his horse may pass on good ground, thereafter to spread out like a doo's tail, to advance, mounted in the main, on this burn and dean. You have it?"

Cries of agreement supported his assessment.

"We can wait here for him, my lords. He must dismount to cross the dean. But that would give his flanking thrusts time. Time to work around us. Instead, we can go meet him. Seek to engage him before he can form a front in the fields and rigs this side of the village. If the cattle and the Mersemen have managed to hold him

79

up in the streets, his confusion could be our opportunity. If we are too late, we would retire promptly to his dean. How say you?"

There was a great shout for an advance.

"So be it," the Earl said grimly. "We give battle. But against three times our number. Do not forget it, because of this moon-light. If I fall, my lord of Moray commands in the centre, until my lord of Dunbar takes fullest command. If Moray falls, Lindsay of Crawford commands. Then Maxwell. Now — Gordon, take you another two hundred. Down to the haughs to aid Dunbar and Synton. Keith — mount you, and take one hundred horse west-wards, to halt this English cavalry which will seek to ford Rede at Shittleheugh. But be prepared to ride to our aid if we need it. Maxwell, on the left, be prepared to turn northwards, swing round without breaking the line, if Buccleuch requires aid. For the rest, leave all horses here. Get your people across this dean. Assemble them in a long front at the other side. No further advance until I order it. There will be no trumpeting before battle is joined. We hope for surprise. Off, now — and quickly . . ."

Assembling all on the eastern lip of the dean took longer than impatient tempers approved, in the darkness of the steep, tree-filled ravine; but at last all was approximately in order. The Scots centre consisted of about 1,600 dismounted men, armed with lances, swords, maces and bows, in four main com-panies — Maxwell on the left; Douglas himself, with Moray next; Lindsay and the Sinclair brothers on their right; and Mont-gomerie and Gordon still further to the right, to try keep touch with the Earl of Dunbar down on the low ground. The noise of battle ahead and to the right was still very confused; but clearly the cattlemen and their charges were holding up the enemy advance notably well — although this could not last for long.

Douglas raised the heavy iron mace he carried, high above his head — it would be of more use than a sword in what was to come, he declared — and amidst a low, muttering growl, infinitely men-acing, the long line began to move eastwards across the slantwise pasture-land, pacing steadily, unhurriedly.

It was Jamie Douglas's first real battle — as that of many another there. And far from what he, and others no doubt, had anticipated — on foot, in half-darkness, against an unseen enemy, with no brave cheering and slogan shouting, the business sounding more like the approach to a cattle-fair. Banners there were in plenty, but the colours were muted in the greenish moonlight. He carried a sword over his shoulder, the long two-handed war brand — he doubted if his wrists were up to wielding a mace effectively — and had a dirk at his side. He paced directly behind his lord, with Bickerton on his right and young Archie carrying the chiefly, undifferenced standard of Douglas on his left. Rob Hart strode beyond Archie, and Simon Glendinning beyond Bickerton, these last three's ages not adding up to more than forty-four between them. Richard Lundie the chaplain was not yet back from his errand to Scott of Buccleuch on the high ground. This at least was as visualised — the Earl's personal entourage in its due position. To the right of them Moray's gentlemen marched likewise. Behind, the men in their hundreds came on, clanking, rank upon rank. Jamie knew a distinct and awkward admixture of emotions — wild elation and sheer bowel-loosening fear struggling within him.

They seemed to go pacing across that hillside for a long time, opening ranks to pass clumps of whin-bushes or outcropping rocks, and closing again. It all felt highly unreal, somehow. They were nearing the village, but could distinguish nothing of what went on there, save for the noise. The light of the half-moon was peculiarly unsatisfactory in that it seemed to alter the relative sizes and shape of things, near and far, giving the impression of quite distinct prospects but obscuring detail and proportions. However, it would work that way for both sides. Quite a number of cattle-beasts were milling around before them, having escaped presumably from the constrictions of the village. From any way off it was hard to tell whether these were animals or groups of men.

A clash and shouting on their right, at no great distance, brought the line to a halt. Montgomerie's and Gordon's company had apparently come up with the enemy. The noise maintained and grew. Douglas waited, sending word up to Maxwell to pause likewise. They must learn what this signified. Hotspur might be seeking to avoid the village area by making a diversion closer to the river, with his main force. Or it might be no more than some extension or movement of the haughland fighting. The Earl sent runners to discover.

They came back sooner than might have been anticipated,

having met messengers from Sir John Montgomerie. He asked for immediate reinforcement. He believed that he was in fact facing the main strength of the English, who appeared to have left their horses behind also, and were advancing just above the edge of the haughs and water-meadows. Numbers he could only guess at, but it was a major thrust. He was forming a sort of schiltrom or defensive square, lances projecting like a hedgehog's spines — for they were clearly much outnumbered.

The Douglas was still hearing this report when Master Lundie came riding fast from the north, to announce that Buccleuch was under attack from a force which had come round the back of Fawdon Hill, seemingly in fairly large numbers, again afoot. Buccleuch was holding them meantime in the throat of the little pass of the Otter burn; but he required more men if he was to prevent them rounding his position by taking to the hillsides.

The Earl made up his mind with typical swiftness. He sent an order to Maxwell, on their left, to divide his force of some four hundred. To send half up to Buccleuch's aid; and to follow him, Douglas, with the other half. Then he commanded his own array to wheel round, almost at right-angles and right-handed. In line abreast again, but facing southwards now, towards the river, not eastwards to the village, the centre resumed its deliberate advance. Battle sounded straight ahead.

Their approach to the flank of the English host was aided by the presence of a scatter of thorn-trees and a larger than usual bank of whins, at an uneven stretch of the common land. In daylight this would have been of little service; but under the moon its shadows were as deep as though it had been quite a major wood. In consequence, the Scots perceived the line of their foes, indistinct but indubitable, considerably before they themselves were observed — the more so in that they were looking for the enemy in this position and the English were not. First with the bushes and thorns themselves as cover, and then with their dark shadow as backcloth, they were within two hundred yards of the Percy's flanks before the warning was given.

The Earl was ready, therefore, if his opponents were less so. "A Douglas! A Douglas!" the Scots cried, as they charged down the slight slope under a dozen banners.

Obviously there was a great mass of the enemy before them, parts of it engaged in an assault on Montgomerie's and Gordon's schiltrom but the major portion just marching westwards. Turning these two sections into a unified L-shaped front, to face the schiltrom and the north, was not the work of a moment, however alert and expert the leadership. The Scots were in amongst them before it could be achieved.

Jamie, running yelling behind his lord, forgot about fears and unease of stomach. The Earl went in, smiting hugely with his mace, and his esquire followed close. He tried to wield his great sword effectively, but found it awkward. It was altogether too long for such close work, too heavy for easy wielding. The Earl's shorter-handled mace was obviously infinitely more practical. After making two or three ineffective jabs at figures suddenly thrust up against him in the mêlée, and only avoiding an unexpected dirk-thrust by an inch or so, he recognised that practicalities were more important than sentiment and chivalric notions, and tossed his fine sword from him, a gift from his father on his eighteenth birthday. Instead, he snatched out his dirk, and felt the better man therefor.

Others were doing likewise around him. Lances and bows, as well as swords were being discarded as useless meantime. The dagger, the battle-axe, the club and the mace were the weapons for this in-fighting, on foot. The Scots perceived this rather more quickly than did their foes, undoubtedly. And they were aided by the element of surprise. Led by the Douglas and the other lords, Moray still helmetless, they drove on mightily, sending the front ranks of the English reeling back. Men went down before them in swathes, and soon the attackers were stumbling and tripping over the fallen bodies of their victims, their momentum slowing.

Jamie's duty, as esquire, was principally to protect his master in rear and flank. But that did not prevent him from some aggressive initiative of his own. A big round-faced fellow with a wide-open mouth and gapped teeth, presumably yelling, loomed up at his left, and stabbed viciously with a shortened sword, held part-way down the broad blade. Dodging aside, Jamie nevertheless felt the blow glance off his chain-mailed shoulder, leaving it numb, and knocking him back. But somebody close behind butted into him, cannoning him forward against the Englishman, not yet fully recovered from his swipe. Fending himself off with one hand, despite weakness of shoulder, Jamie drove down his dirk with the other, at the thick column of throat. The man went down in spouting blood. Pressure from behind toppled him full length over the fallen Northumbrian — thereby saving him from another English sword-thrust. Thereafter, prostrate, feet kicked, stamped on and tripped over him in all directions, a more horrible experience than any he had yet encountered. He felt little pain, but knew a great indignation, affront. It was some time before he could get to his feet, unsteadily, bruised and breathless, spitting grass from his mouth. His victim lay twitching beside him, but otherwise still. Stepping over the body, dirk held the more firmly, he pressed on, in suddenly trembling excitement, offence forgotten. He had slain his first foe. He was a full man now.

Detached from his group, Jamie recognised that his duty was to get back to his lord's side as quickly as he could. In the press, confusion and half-light he had some difficulty in discovering the Earl's whereabouts; but amongst the banners ahead, reeling and swaying and dipping crazily, he discerned one larger than the others, and thrust his way towards it. For safety's sake he chanted "A Douglas! A Douglas!" as he went, despite lack of breath. In the mêlée he could be attacked by friend almost as easily as by foe.

The Scots were doing less well now, however. The English had rallied, and some of their leaders fought their way back from the front assaulting the schiltrom to take command. Jamie realised, indeed, that the Douglas banner, along with others, was being forced back towards him. He found himself amongst a group of men momentarily at a loss, apparently detached, like himself, from their comrades and leaders, some wounded. He raised his voice urgently.

"I am a Douglas!" he shouted, waving an arm at them, with the dirk. "Come! Shout, all of you. Your loudest. Shout 'A Douglas!' Come on — to the Earl's banner. All shouting!"

There was probably no more than twenty of them all told. But tight-knit and yelling vehemently in unison, they no doubt sounded like reinforcements of many times that number. Especially as other Scots took up the cry in a renewal of vigour and enthusiasm. For a few minutes the tide of battle turned again.

The Earl of Douglas was swift to renew the slackened initiative. Uplifting his great voice, he bellowed "Percy! Percy! Hotspur! Here is Douglas! Percy — to me — and die!"

How far his challenge would reach in that uproar there was no knowing, powerful as were his lungs. But indubitably it had an effect on the ordinary English soldiery in the Earl's immediate vicinity, causing them to hesitate, glance around, even draw back a little, in the recognition that here was no business of theirs, a contest between the giants, a lordly feud not for wise but lesser men to interfere in. If it did not produce Sir Harry Percy, wherever he was, or his brother, at least it allowed Douglas to head a distinct forward movement again, his mace swinging and beating tirelessly.

The Lord Maxwell and his half-company came running from the north, to join the fray, shouting a new slogan, but welcome.

When Jamie at length won back to his due position, it was to find that his place immediately behind the Earl had been filled by John Bickerton. The others, Archie Douglas, Hart, Glendinning and Lundie were all still there, although Glendinning appeared to be wounded and Archie was drooping, tripping and stumbling, to the dire danger of the standard — no doubt its weight was beginning to tell on his fourteen-year-old wrists. Jamie, in fact, grabbed its pole as one more trip over a body all but brought it down.

"Take it, Jamie — take it!" the boy gasped. "I canna . . . hold it up. I'm no' . . . right." Vomit was in fact spilled all down the lad's front. Close range killing is not good for the stomachs of sensitive teenage boys.

So Jamie Douglas found himself acting standard-bearer, and requiring both hands to hold aloft the tall staff and banner. Which meant that there was no more dirking for him, meantime. Young Archie clung close to his side, panting, his own dirk drawn now, in white-knuckled fist.

Douglas, Moray and Lindsay had now swung round somewhat right-handed, seeking to cut their way through in the direction of Montgomerie's schiltrom — where, it was to be assumed, Hotspur himself would be fighting. Certainly several banners could be seen to be upraised thereabouts, although devices were impossible to distinguish in the poor light. As the leading Scots neared these, so the fighting grew ever tougher, with more and more armoured knights mixed amongst the ordinary men-at-arms and spearmen. Moreover, even the Douglas's arm was beginning to flag somewhat, with the weight of that deadly flailing mace. More than once the Earl staggered back from some blow he had failed to avoid, through growing weariness even though his mail protected him from actual wounding. Each time Bickerton, directly behind, caught him and held him up.

It was when a particularly heavy stroke from a knight with another mace sent the Earl reeling back, that it happened. Bickerton caught his master, as before — but this time his right hand rose high and fell again, in a swift gesture which had nothing to do with support for a tottering man. And Jamie had glimpsed the gleam of steel in the moonlight, in that right hand. The Earl's mail-clad body convulsed to a violent spasm, and uttering a loud groan, the bloody mace at last fell from suddenly nerveless fingers. Bickerton now had to hold up his collapsing lord bodily.

Jamie Douglas gazed, appalled.

With an enormous and evident effort, the Earl gained some sort of control of his buckling legs, and managed to stand approximately upright, swaying, mumbling. Bickerton let go of him, and he began to lurch sideways. Throwing the standard at Archie again, Jamie leapt to catch and seek to hold up the weighty person of his hero, babbling incoherencies. The others, Lundie, Hart, Glendinning, perceiving that the Douglas was sore hurt, gathered round him, while Moray, Lindsay and Maxwell moved forward, smiting, to form a protective front.

"My lord! My lord!" Jamie cried desperately. "The dastard! Oh, the foul dastard! My good lord . . ."

"My back!" the Earl muttered. "In . . . my back!"

Horrified, the young men crowded round their lord, young Archie dropping the standard altogether in his distress for his father. They gabbled their questions, and fears.

"Hold me . . . hold me up," Douglas got out, thickly. "Hold. Lead me . . . forward."

"My lord — no! My good lord," Jamie wailed. "Do not so. Rest, you . . ."

"No!" That was vehement, determined, however weak the voice. "I am . . . Douglas! A, a . . . dead man! But . . . old prophecy. In our line. A dead man . . . shall gain . . . a field!"

They were all supporting him now, but even so the Earl's knees gave way. Sagging forward, he was held. Head sinking, he saw his standard lying there before him.

Sir James Lindsay came, panting. "How fare you, Douglas?" he demanded.

"But . . . poorly," the Earl gasped. "I die. But . . . I die . . . like my forefathers . . . praise God! On the field . . . not in . . . my bed!"

"No, no. Not that. We shall save you yet, friend," Lindsay cried. And to the esquires. "Fools! Lay him down. Staunch his wound. Here is folly . . ."

"No!" Douglas was still master. "I say . . . no! Raise me up. Aye . . . and raise my banner . . . lying there. No foe . . . nor friend . . . to see . . . what case you see me in. Lest . . . lest . . ." His voice faded.

The Earl of Moray was there now, questioning.

"Raise me, I say." Almost miraculously there was an accession of strength in the quavering voice. "On, with me. My . . . command. I am Douglas. Shout it — my slogan! Conceal . . my death. Forward me . . . and my banner. Douglas . . . shall win the day . . . yet! My last command . . . to you all. Shout, I say . . ."

They shouted, then, in broken sobbing tones which, however, strengthened as they continued. "Douglas! A Douglas!" On and on they went, three young men staggering, panting, shouting, dragging the now inert figure of their master. And all around them, from other throats, the cry arose once more, "A Douglas! A Douglas!" with renewed vigour. But the Douglas himself spoke no more.

*   *   *

Although it seemed a long way that they carried their weighty burden over the uneven, corpse-littered ground, banner waving above them, it was of course not far before the esquires were up with the battling front line of the Scots fighters again. Here they must halt. Nor, in the nature of things, and in sheer self-preservation, could they continue to hold up the dead Earl, however loyal to his last command. The Douglas had said that dead he would yet win the battle; to this end they must *fight*, not just stand. So they lowered the mail-clad body to the ground. In doing so, Jamie discovered that the Earl's mace was still attached to his gauntleted wrist with its leather thong. Stooping, he detached it. This would be his, from now on — until he might use it to fullest effect, on John Bickerton, God willing!

If they could no longer bear up the Douglas's person, they could still shout his slogan, as commanded, whilst breath was in them. This they did, standing over the corpse, while above them Archie kept the great standard upright. The sight and sound of them seemed to put new heart into the entire Scots front. But it was no longer a forward-moving front, nevertheless. The fact was that they were now only some two hundred yards from Montgomerie's schiltrom, and in between was wedged the most knightly leadership of the English array, fighting on two fronts and standing fast, out of necessity. It was a matter of sheer ding-dong slogging, until one side or the other gave in.

At least, in these circumstances, it was not a chaotic mêlée and press of bodies, as before. There was room to wield a sword — or a mace. Jamie did so in a strange state of mixed pain, sorrow and utter determination, uncaring for any danger to himself, standing over the body of the man he had most loved and admired, stricken down by blackest treachery. As tirelessly as its fallen owner, he now swung the Douglas mace in that hacking, immobile battle, all but an automaton in his steely inward rage and outward calm. At his left Simon Glendinning had picked up a discarded English sword, and used it with dogged, dour ferocity, hurt already as he was. Rob Hart at the other side had never abandoned his, and made deadly play with it in persistent figure-of-eight pattern. Close at their backs, Chaplain Richard and young Archie of Cavers kept the standard aloft between them, each with a dirk in hand to protect the others' flanks and rear. They had now been joined by the Earl's other son, Will of Drumlanrig, with a battle-axe which he certainly had not had before. They made a tight, tense and dedicated group above their dead lord — and only Richard Lundie out of his teens.

Only esquires as they might be, they were dealing now with the cream of the North of England chivalry, dismounted admittedly but experienced as they were proud.

Rob Hart was the first to fall, struck down by a glancing battle-axe blow to the side of his helmet. Jamie felled the wielder immediately thereafter with his mace, but Rob lay still, over the Earl's legs. Will Douglas of Drumlanrig stepped into his place, straddling both, without pause. They still gasped "A Douglas! A Douglas!" breathlessly, sometimes only mouthing the words, Archie and the chaplain doing rather better at their backs.

Some timeless, incalculable time later, Jamie realised that Glendinning, on his left, was on his knees, swaying, sword still at last. Lundie, leaving the standard to the boy again, picked up that sword and took the other's stance at Jamie's side.

The greenish moon shone coldly down on Otterburn, and endless carnage. Will Douglas fell next, pitching against Jamie from a sideways blow. Now there was only the two of them, with Archie behind. It could not go on for much longer.

It did not. Jamie was dazedly, almost blindly, involuntarily swinging his mace at one more armoured figure in plumed helmet who loomed up before him when some corner of his consciousness perceived a difference. This man was waving a steel-gauntleted hand, not thrusting a sword or axe. Then he recognised the coat-armour of Montgomerie of Eaglesham, the three gold fleurs-de-lis on blue. Reeling drunkenly now, he stayed his blow.

"Hold!" Montgomerie was shouting hollowly. "Hold, you!" He raised his visor and spoke more plainly. "Hotspur has yielded! To me. Sir Ralph is down, wounded. Where is the Douglas? The day is ours. Ours, I say! Where is Douglas?"

Lindsay came lurching from the left, as Jamie shook his head wordlessly.

"There is Douglas — dead!" the Lord of Crawford panted. "So we win? Win the day — too late! It is as he said. A dead man shall win it!"

"Dear God — Douglas?"

All around them now the battle was disintegrating, slackening, as the word was shouted, screamed, laughed. Men were throwing down their arms, fleeing or yielding, as the news that Hotspur had surrendered swept the field. Cheers rose above the shrieks and groans of the dying and wounded.

Moray came up, bleeding from a cut brow, fair hair caked with blood. He was leading Sir John Lilburn, his last opponent, as prisoner. Everywhere the Scots were grasping at weary bewildered English knights as captives, the richer-clad the better, meet for ransom, even fighting each other for prize specimens. In only minutes that dreadful scene was changed from one of desperate battle and bravery to one of bickering, huckstering, riot and shameful greed, like some evil fair.

But not around the fallen Douglas, where the young esquires had piled up a quite distinct semi-circular barrier of enemy slain

in their protective efforts. Scarcely knowing what he did, Jamie
Douglas sank to his knees scrabbling to open his master's visor,
sobbing openly now. The dead eyes, open still, gleamed palely in
the moonlight.

Lindsay shook his head. "Here is the sorriest victory we shall
ever see!" he exclaimed. "The noblest of our race the price of
it."

"*Your* price, my lord—yours!" Jamie burst out, voice breaking. "Slain by your man. The dastard Bickerton! Keeper of your
castle . . ."

"What? What are you saying? Are you mad, sirrah? Your wits
unhinged . . .?"

"I saw him, I tell you. Saw him stab my lord. In the back. Saw
the dirk. Oh, my lord, my dear lord!"

"How can this be? His mail . . .?"

"Bickerton? Where is he?"

"I'll not believe it. Here's folly . . ."

"Turn him over," Moray commanded. "Let us see his back."

They rolled the Earl's corpse over — and in doing so had to
move Rob Hart's body. He groaned — so he was not dead, at
least. But none had eyes for him at that moment. All stared at the
Douglas's armour, at the back.

Jamie pointed, jabbing with his bloodstained finger.
"See — unbuckled! There — and there! The shirt-of-mail open.
Undone. Of a purpose. By Saint Bride — he left him undone!
That he might do . . . this!"

There seemed little doubt that this was so. The chain-mail shirt
opened down the back, and here was only fastened at the neck by
one toggle, instead of all the way down. And the steel back-plate
of the cuirass which covered it was loose at the left side, its leather
straps unbuckled. It was the armour-bearer's task to fasten both,
as he dressed his lord. And only the armour-bearer could have
known that neither *was* fastened, and that a dirk, driven in and
down sidelong, would meet no resistance from plate- or chain-
mail. The thing was clear to all. The Earl of Douglas had not
fallen in fair fight, but had been murdered. And by his own
trusted servant.

Moray straightened up, set-featured. "Take him to his tent," he
ordered. "Find the man Bickerton. We will deal with this anon."
Until his elder brother, Dunbar and March, appeared on the

scene, Moray was senior commander. "Now — there is much to do. Get the men to order. Marshal the prisoners. Succour the wounded. Discover how it goes with my brother. And with Buccleuch. And Keith the Marischal. My lords — to your tasks. St. Clair — see you to the prisoners. Hepburn — rally our men into their companies. Ramsay — down to the haughs, to my lord of Dunbar . . ."

Keith the Marischal rode up. "Where is my lord of Douglas?" he demanded. "The English horse are in our camp. Ravaging it. They were more than double our strength. We tried to hold them, but could not. They drove us back, right from the ford. Under Matthew Redman. Now they rob our camp . . ."

"So long as that is *all* they do!" Moray panted. "They do not follow you, to attack us here?"

"I think not. They seek booty . . . But — where is Douglas?"

"Douglas is dead. Slain. I command meantime. My lord of Crawford. Take sufficient men, and go attend to this Redman . . ."

Jamie Douglas paid no attention to all this. He was now bending over his fallen friends, removing helmets, loosening armour, Lundie aiding him. Will Douglas was already sitting up, head in hands, rocking back and forth. Simon Glendinning was alive, breathing stertorously. Robert Hart's eyes were open, but wandering, blood dribbling from open mouth. At least none were dead — yet.

A runner came from the Redeside meadows to say that all fighting had virtually ceased there, with the Scots pursuing the fleeing foe. Elsewhere there appeared to be pockets of resistance, but only that. There was still no word from the high ground.

With the aftermath of the battle beginning to be brought into some sort of order and discipline — although a fairly large proportion of the victors appeared to be out-of-touch and chasing Englishmen eastwards — Jamie and the chaplain supervised the careful transportation, by prisoners, of their three friends back to the ravaged camp across the dean. There they found no sign of Redman's cavalry, nor of Lindsay's, though the place was in a sorry state, tents down, gear strewn everywhere, horses running around loose. In one of the re-erected tents they laid the wounded esquires. Lundie, like most clerics, was trained in caring for the sick. He thought that Glendinning would survive. Will Douglas had been little more than stunned. But Hart was grievously hurt and had lost much blood. He doubted whether he would survive till morning.

That young man did, in fact, die without regaining consciousness, just as dawn began to break. Only then did Jamie Douglas allow weariness to overcome his sorrow and anger, and he slept, still in his blood-spattered shirt-of-mail from France.

The sun rose on a scene and situation full of contradictions, of desolation, ruin, the groans of wounded and the smell of blood. The Scots had won a major victory — but there was little of elation in their camp. The death of the country's greatest soldier and most respected leader overshadowed all, even the humbler men-at-arms and mosstroopers recognising that something more than just a great noble had been removed. Those who knew most of the national and political situation in Scotland were the most concerned. And a great many had loved and admired the Douglas as a man, despite his rather stolid and unforthcoming manner, and mourned him truly. There were others to mourn, too — although in fact the Scots losses were extraordinarily light, all things considered — little more than one hundred dead, though four times that number wounded, most not seriously; whereas 1,800 English dead were counted on the various battle-grounds, and the wounded and prisoners amounted between them to another thousand. They had made a clean sweep, almost, of the English leadership, with not only Hotspur and his brother captured but the Seneschal of York, Sir Ralph Langley, Sir Robert Ogle, Sir Thomas Walsingham, Sir John Lilburn, Sir Thomas Abingdon, Sir John Felton, Sir John Copland and many another distinguished knight. As against this, few prominent Scots were lost, though many were injured or somewhat battered. But, strangely, Sir James Lindsay of Crawford was a casualty, at the last. One of his men, who had ridden back into camp soon after daylight, told the extraordinary story. Lindsay and his company had managed to clear the Scots camp of the plundering cavalry under Redman, Captain of Berwick, and had thereafter chased them, and, burdened as they were with the Scots spoils, had caught up with them in the Kirkwhelpington vicinity about eight miles to the south-east, with Redman no doubt heading for Newcastle. There had been another fierce, if lesser battle, which the Scots had eventually won, Lindsay himself defeating and disarming Sir Mathew Redman. He was heading back to Otterburn with his prisoners and recaptured booty, when in the dawn light had seen a host moving southwards towards them across Kirk-whelpington Common, which they took to be the main Scots force — but which in fact proved to be the Bishop of Durham's fresh army of some 10,000. Lindsay and his party had been captured, in turn, and Redman released — and so far as he knew, this survivor alone had escaped to tell the tale.

This news, of course, upset the Scots leadership in more than distress at the loss of the Lord of Crawford, important as he was. If the Bishop's large force had been only eight miles or so away at dawn, he could be a deal nearer now. And though he would be aware of Hotspur's defeat, and presumably the warier, the Scots were in no state to engage in a new battle with a fresh army of 10,000. Especially as Neville's force might well also now be near at hand. The Earl of Dunbar and March, now in command, sent off Pate Home and his scouts with urgent instructions, and ordered an immediate preparation to march. They were, after all, only some fifteen miles from the Scots border at Carter Bar.

In all this stir, Jamie Douglas was not concerned. Only little rested, he was busy on his own, searching the camp and questioning. John Bickerton was nowhere to be found; none had seen him since the early stages of the battle.

Jamie was summoned from his fruitless quest by Dunbar himself, almost ready to move off but delayed by the difficulties of coping with so many wounded, the construction of horse-litters proceeding apace. Batches of prisoners, wounded and cattle—which no Borderer would consider leaving behind—were being despatched westwards up Redesdale all the time, in long convoys, the severely injured in improvised litters or hammocks slung between two horses.

Jamie found the Scots leadership assembling in an open space. The Earl of Douglas's body was there in the midst, wrapped in his own standard now, and standing beside it his two sons, Will of Drumlanrig, looking very wan, and Archie of Cavers, between tears and a silly grin, clutching the Percy pennon instead of his sire's banner. The corpse of Rob Hart lay beside that of his lord. Simon Glendinning stood shakily at the other side, supported by Richard Lundie. Jamie was directed to stand beside them. Sir Harry Percy, and sundry other English notables not seriously wounded, stood behind, just a little apart from the ranks of the Scots lords and knights.

Dunbar, flanked by his brother Moray and the Lord Maxwell, stepped forward, clearing his throat. "My lords, friends and esteemed foes," he began, a little uncertainly. "We are here to do honour. First, to James Douglas, who lies here. A noble man. A stout friend. A puissant and worthy foe. In him, Scotland has lost much, its greatest fighter and most able councillor. We proclaim that loss. Scotland will mourn him long."

There was a prolonged murmur, part growl. Dunbar was no orator, with a thin and reedy voice unsuited for outdoor heroics; but what he had said so abruptly touched all.

Into the murmur another voice spoke, a voice much more assured, yet with that incipient hesitation of delivery and pronounced burr. "I, Harry Percy, would crave your permission, my lord, to add my word of praise, of honour. The Douglas was the fairest flower of your fair land. I, and all my people, mourn him little less than do you. But he died, as he lived, in honour. On an honourable field. May I do as well!"

If some breaths were caught at that, most were not, and there was a swell of approval. The Scots leaders had decided that nothing was to be gained by announcing to all and sundry that the Douglas had been murdered. It would serve his name and memory nothing. It would not be forgotten by those who knew; but some things were better handled discreetly, it was felt.

"I thank you, my lord Percy," Dunbar acknowledged. "I would expect no other word from one of your renown. It was a well-fought fight, and none who took part will forget it. Or its cost. For many died, beside the Douglas. We honour them all, Scots and English both."

Again the tight-lipped murmur.

"Aye." Dunbar coughed. "And now we have an especial token to pay, in honour. Last night, certain young men played a noble part much in advance of their years. They supported the Douglas — that was their duty. But they did it passing well. And when he fell, they carried him forward as he had commanded, dying and dead, to the forefront of the battle, where he would ever be. They held him up, and his standard above him, and cried his slogan as encouragement and example to all. And when, hard-pressed, they must lay him down, they guarded his body to the last, fighting above it like . . . like ancient heroes!" Even the Earl's reedy voice was vibrant. "One lies dead, here, before us, with his lord. One is wounded, all are hurt."

There were cheers now, unrestrained.

Dunbar held up his hand. "Hear me. Of these young men, one is in holy orders, Richard Lundie from North Berwick, chaplain. Him we must leave Holy Church to honour. Of the others, three are Douglases — William of Drumlanrig, Archibald of Cavers and James of Aberdour. The last is Simon Glendinning, son to Glendinning of that Ilk here present. He who died is Robert Hart, from Douglasdale. I say to the four who may, step forward to the side of him who may not!"

Eyeing each other doubtfully, the four paced, shuffled or limped out to stand directly beside the corpses, Lundie with them, aiding Glendinning. "Kneel," the Earl commanded, drawing his sword. He stalked over to them. "I do hereby welcome these four into the most honourable, worthy, valiant and lofty estate of knighthood," he announced, his voice squeaking a little, with emotion. "Well and truly earned on that field where the honour is doubled — the field of battle. William Douglas, I dub thee knight, young as you are." And he brought down the great blade on the lad's shoulder. "Be thou good and true knight unto thy life's end. Arise, Sir William. And you, Archibald, younger still, who bore your standard to victory, with your sire dead at your feet—arise, Sir Archibald, and be thou good and true knight unto thy life's end."

The boy's gulping sobbing sniff was heard by all; and evoked no single grin nor remark.

"And you, James Douglas of Aberdour, namesake and chief esquire to your puissant lord — the most valiant of all, I am assured. Be thou good and true knight until you rejoin the Douglas! Arise, Sir James."

"Amen!" Jamie muttered — the only one who remembered the due form of what was, in fact, a religious ceremony.

"And Simon Glendinning, who fought on wounded — be thou good and true knight until thy life's end also. Arise, Sir Simon."

Richard Lundie said the Amen for his swaying, dizzy charge, raising him to his unsteady feet again.

95

"And you, Sir Priest, I cannot knight. But I would shake you by the hand!" Dunbar added, reaching out. Then he turned to the body lying beside that of the Earl. "Robert Hart," he jerked, swallowing. "You were one of this knightly band. I would not now hold you apart. You cannot kneel nor rise — but I can still dub you knight. Rest in peace, Sir Robert Hart, and serve your master still, if you may."

A sigh arose, like the breakers on a long shore.

"This I have done," Dunbar ended, "because I believe that James, Earl of Douglas would have had it so." He raised sword on high. "Now, my friends — enough! We march for Scotland, without more ado. My lords — to your places, in column. Sir Harry Percy and his captor, Sir John Montgomerie, will ride with me. Trumpeter — sound the March . . ."

*   *   *

The Prince-Bishop may have been only a few miles away, with his large force; but he evidently preferred to keep that distance from the retiring Scots. No doubt refugees from Otterburn reaching him did not understate the numbers and capacities of the victors. At any rate, the invaders were not attacked on their fifteen-mile march to Carter Bar, although a discreet distance behind the Bishop's people were reported as keeping pace, as it were, seeing them off. By mid-afternoon the Scots had crossed the March and were back in their former camp at Southdean, unmolested. Pate Home sent word that the Bishop had halted his main array at Ramshope four miles from the Borderline, sending forward only a token force to the lofty pass-like junction of the two kingdoms above Catcleuch. Clearly there was to be no attempt at rescue of the Percys and other notables, humiliating as this must be for Hotspur.

The Scots leaders had hoped that there might be couriers from the Earl Robert of Fife and the western invaders, indicating progress or intentions; but none such appeared, although first Douglas and then Dunbar had sent messengers across country to keep the main army informed. There was only minor debate now as to whether any move should be made to join the other force. At this stage, with the Douglas dead, so many wounded and prisoners to see to, not to mention thousands of cattle to be suitably disposed of, there was no enthusiasm for prolonging the expedition. Not only the Mersemen, mosstroopers and other Borderers found home beckoning. The break up of the eastern force commenced.

Jamie Douglas was nothing loth. He had had sufficient of war and invasion, hero as he now found himself to be considered. Normally he would have been highly excited, elated, at his almost unbelievable elevation to the rank of knighthood, something he could scarcely take in, as yet. But any such exultation was at present effectively damped down by his sorrow over his hero's death, and his seething anger at the murderer. He desired no further distracting adventures, meantime; he had but one ambition — to avenge his late master.

The next day, then, only the rump of the host rode northwards, although with most of the leadership still intact. They went by Jedburgh, Ancrum and over Lilliard's Edge to Tweeddale where, at Melrose Abbey, under the three isolated peaks of the Eildons, the Trimontium of the Romans, they laid to rest the body of James, Earl of Douglas — Moray, his brother-in-law asserting that he had once expressed the wish to be buried there, where the great Bruce's heart, which he bore represented on his shield, was also interred. Sir Robert Hart they also buried, beside his lord, in a ceremony which brought tears rolling down many a rough and unshaven cheek. They passed the night at Melrose, the monks giving skilful attention to the wounded. And next morning, as they were about to resume their northwards march, couriers at last arrived from the Lord Robert's force. They declared that this also was on its way home, the messengers having left it at Carlisle. They had had a successful expedition likewise, it seemed — although they had not got so far south as Lancaster. But all to the north of that they had harried and laid waste in traditional style. They had had a brush with the Lord Clifford, to his disadvantage—Sir William Douglas of Nithsdale, Archibald the Grim's gallant son, having apparently challenged the Englishman to single combat, in true chivalric fashion, and been curtly rebuffed. With huge booty they were now crossing back into Scotland unpursued, in high satisfaction — although, of course, mourning the death of the Earl of Douglas. Robert of Fife ordered that the late Douglas's force await his arrival, wherever it might be. No reasons for this were given.

The Earl of Dunbar and March, who hated all Stewarts on principle — and was moreover on his own territory here — was not prepared to comply. He declared that all who wished to take their departure might do so, and rode off himself to his own castle of Ercildoune in Lauderdale, with a selection of prisoners for ransom. But he left his brother Moray with what remained of the force, to await the others.

Jamie seized the opportunity to take his leave. With a group of young Douglases, including Sir Will of Drumlanrig, he set off up Lauderdale also, on business bent. He had ridden southwards a youth; he rode northwards very much a man.

VI

WITH SOUTRA MOOR behind them, and the head of Lauderdale, the travel-stained and battle-scarred group of young men gazed down over the lovely spread of East Lothian, all green pastures barred by the golden rigs of harvest, dotted with demesnes and manors and castles, their villages and hall-touns, to the far blue haze that was the smoke of the fires of Haddington, its capital. Out of it all rose the isolated and abrupt humps of the Garmyleton Hills, Traprain and North Berwick Laws and the soaring Bass, like leviathans from a verdant sea, whilst beyond stretched all the silver-and-blue mirror of the isle-strewn Forth, to the distant cliffs and strands of Fife — surely one of the most fair and fertile prospects in all Southern Scotland, from these Lammermuir heights.

But the horsemen were not concerned with prospects, save as they related to a certain locality.

"You cannot see it from here," young Patrick Ramsay of Waughton declared. "It lies just behind West Garmyleton Hill, yonder, on the edge of Aberlady Bay. You can see part of the wide bay — but not Luffness. Twelve miles? Thirteen? There, east of

Garmyleton, is my father's house of Waughton, also vassal to Lindsay. Five miles east from Luffness." Ramsay, about Jamie's own age, was an extra esquire of Sir James Lindsay's, at a loose end now with his lord captured.

"He may not have returned to his home." The new Sir Will voiced, not for the first time, the doubt that beset them. "Would any of *you* do so? With every man's hand against you? He may have fled deep into England."

"Every man's hand may not be against him. In Scotland," Jamie said levelly. "He may come home to acclaim and reward, the Judas!"

"No! Never that! You are saying . . .?"

"I am saying, Will, that it may not have been merely spite, ill-will, which turned Bickerton assassin. Would a blow from a mace, by chance, serve for that? As all declare? I say that he may have planned his treachery long before. But waited his opportunity. When it might pass undiscerned. If I had not seen that dirk . . .!"

"But why, Jamie—*why*?"

"There are those who do not love Douglas, in Scotland. Who fear Douglas power. Who would bring that power down. Are there not? Some who might welcome this vile deed. Who might possibly have devised it. Some not so far from the Throne!"

"God! You mean . . . the Wolf?"

"The Wolf, perhaps. It could be his style. Or the Lord Robert himself. I trust him little more than his brother. I swear neither will shed a tear for their good-brother, our dear lord!"

Silent now, the young men rode down from Soutra Hill into the green plain of Lothian.

They went by Hundebie amongst the foothills, past Keith the Marischal's castle and through the great Wood of Saltoun to the Tyne, which they forded at the village of Samuelston. Then, keeping well to the west of Haddington, they began to climb over the skirts of the Gled's Muir and up the gentle green slopes of Bangly Hill beyond, till they stood on the summit of the West Garmyleton ridge and could look down directly over the coastal levels around the great V-shaped bay of Aberlady and the woodlands of Luffness at its apex, a bare three miles now. It was late afternoon and the scene was peaceful and very fair.

The Lindsay castle of Byres they passed, like that of Garmyleton to the east — for all this land was Lindsay territory — but they did not halt. At the church and hospice of St. Cuthbert at Ballencrieff, however, they did pause to enquire whether any of their comrades from the English expedition had returned — for churchmen tended to know all that went on in their area, and these were no doubt in fairly close touch with the Carmelite monastery at Luffness little more than a mile away. But the friars here knew nothing of any recent travellers of significance; indeed asked young Ramsay, with whom they were acquainted, for any news of John Bickerton, whose father they seemed to respect. Keeping their own counsel, the party rode on.

Circling the undrained marshlands of Luffness Muir, where cattle grazed knee-deep in the part-flooded meadows of the Peffer Water which flowed into the bay nearby, they came at last to the major Lindsay stronghold of Luffness Castle, rising islanded in a strong position on a sort of tongue of firm land between the Peffer, the bay and the marshes. Here towered a great and massive redstone keep of five storeys, topped by a parapet and wall-walk with bartisans and machicolations, within a large curtain-walled enclosure with circular flanking-towers at each corner and a gate-house to the east. The monastery lay a quarter-mile to the south-west, on the same tongue of firm land. To the north the sea glittered, with the tide almost full over the shallows of the bay.

Now that they were here there was some debate as to procedure. The newcomers could not hope to rush this great castle. If Bickerton had indeed returned, he would presumably hold it against all Douglas visitors, he was its keeper, after all. Guile, on the other hand, was unlikely to gain them entry. It was decided that they should remain hidden in the trees at a short distance, and only Ramsay ride forward alone, to enquire. He was known here, and no Douglas; and one young man would not seem to constitute any great threat.

However, he came back in only moments, to say that the castle stood open, the drawbridge down, the portcullis up, the gates wide, no sign of special caution or alarm. It looked as though Bickerton had not come home.

Considerably deflated, the party rode over the drawbridge timbers, through the pend and into the wide courtyard enclosure, amongst clucking poultry. Servants wheeling dung from the stables gazed at them interestedly — but only that. A wench with a pail, dimpled, giggled and lingered.

At something of a loss, the vengeance-seekers reined up and dismounted. A thick-set, stooping elderly man appeared at the arched doorway of the keep. He eyed them doubtfully, but civilly enough.

"A good e'en to you, my young friends," he greeted. "How can I serve you, at Luffness? I'd say that you have ridden far. And show signs of war." Will of Drumlanrig was not the only one who still wore bandaging. "My son? Do not . . . do not tell me that you have come . . . to give me ill tidings? Of my son . . .?"

Jamie frowned. "I am Douglas of Aberdour," he jerked. "I . . . we come from England, yes. From Redesdale. Your son is John Bickerton, sir?"

"Aye. I am John de Bickerton, tenant of these lands. My son, who keeps this castle in my stead for my lord of Crawford, is not with you? He is not . . . dead, young sir?"

"No. No — would that he . . ." Jamie restrained himself. "Sir — we had looked to find your son here. He, he left the field. Before us. Before all. At Otterburn, in Redesdale. Four nights past. He has not come home?"

"Why should he, friend?" The older man looked from one to the other, warily now. "What is this, of leaving the field? What field? He was with the Earl of Douglas. Armour-bearer. Was there a battle? If the Earl fell, why should John come home betimes?"

"Because he slew him, sir! Stabbed him in the back! That is why," Drumlanrig burst out. "John Bickerton slew my father."

"Slew . . .?" The old man stared. "What folly is this? Are you out of your wits, boy?"

"No! The folly is otherwise, sir. I am Will Douglas of Drumlanrig — Sir William! And your son killed my father, the Earl. Miscreant . . .!"

Others of the Douglases joined in then, in a chorus of accusation and fury. It caused the older man to step back into his doorway in concern, and his servants to move closer, wondering. But it also had the effect of calming Jamie Douglas, oddly enough. He held up his hand.

"Quiet! Quiet, you!" he exclaimed. "This will advance us

nothing." He turned on Bickerton. "You, sir — how did you know that the Earl of Douglas had fallen?"

"Eh? Did I say so? I but said *if* the Earl had fallen. No more. Else his armour-bearer would not leave his side, surely? I meant no more than that."

"Yet it was strangely said. As though you . . . knew!"

"No, no. I swear it. Here is all some sorry mistake. My son would never do what you say. You err, young sirs. You have been misled . . ."

"I saw it, with my own eyes. Saw your son's hand strike, dirk held. At the height of the battle. Armour and shirt-of-mail unfastened. At the back. I was his chief esquire. At your son's side. No mistake, sir. Save that I *saw* — who should not!"

"I'll not believe it," the old man said. "Not John. Not my son."

"Your son, yes. So we think to find him here, in this castle."

"You will not find him here, I tell you. Come search, if you will. There is none here but my wife and daughter."

"We will, yes, to be sure. For found he must be."

All were for pushing into the keep, but Jamie ordered some to remain outside, to search the stables, byres and outbuildings. His knighthood, and the experiences of the last days, had given him an authority unknown previously.

They went over the castle, from lowest pit and vaulted basement to topmost tower and caphouse, and found nothing. Some unhappy and bewildered women watched them, wringing hands and protesting; but there were few men about the place, Lindsay having taken almost all away with him on the expedition.

Jamie had to admit defeat. He made some sort of apology to Bickerton's wife, but in stilted fashion, before they mounted and rode away.

They had barely crossed the drawbridge before the great gates clashed shut behind them, and they heard the rumble of drawn bars. Then the portcullis clanked down into place. Bickerton senior evidently intended to suffer no more intrusions. Even as they gazed back, Ramsay spoke up.

"What kind of horse did Bickerton ride?" he asked.

"Lastly, a tall grey, with dark dappling on legs," Jamie answered. "A good animal. Why?"

"No matter."

"Then why ask, man?"

"I but found a beast strangely stalled. When you were searching the keep. Behind the yard. In the base of one of the angle-towers. A mare stalled. Not in the main stables — apart. No stall at all, indeed — an icehouse for keeping fish and meat, I'd say, with a doocot above. It was a blue roan, with a white left knee. I had a notion that I had seen the beast before, somewhere."

Jamie drew a quick and audible breath. "A blue roan with a white knee? Left knee — and mare! My lord had such as his third horse. A gift from the Lady Isabel. It was with us, at Otterburn!"

They stared at each other, silent now — until they all began to speak at once.

Out of much angry debate and clamour, they came to a decision. Clearly they would not be let back into Luffness Castle—nor could they force their way in to such a strong place. But, if they kept a discreet watch on its gates, day and night, they might either gain entry, or grab John Bickerton if he ventured out. He could not remain shut up somewhere indefinitely. But they would require many more men for such a round-the-clock watch. Ramsay could bring some from Waughton, fairly quickly. But not sufficient. Jamie declared that he would get Douglases from Tantallon. It was only some eight miles away, and he had to go there anyway. The Countess Isabel had gone there when her lord set off for the expedition — it was her favourite seat, by summer seas. He would have to go break to her the news of her husband's death — to his sorrow. Meantime, the rest of the party must stay here on watch, well hidden. Ramsay could also fetch food and drink from Waughton.

Jamie rode away eastwards, along the shallow Vale of Peffer, Will of Drumlanrig at his side. That youth was still not fully recovered of his hurt, and his stepmother's house at Tantallon was as near to a home as he knew.

*   *   *

It was near to dusk when they came to the mighty castle of Tantallon, the impregnable Douglas fortress on the cliffs east of North Berwick, compared to which even Luffness seemed modest. There was no other castle in the land quite like it in design. It consisted, in effect, of merely a simple and long hugely high wall, like part of a city's ramparts, crowned by the usual parapet and wall-walk, which cut off a thrusting small peninsula of the cliffs. Three tall towers rose therefrom, one at each end and one in the centre, the latter a gatehouse-tower very large and strong, almost a keep. No fewer than three deep and wide ditches and their associated banks protected this long frontage landwards, in addition to the steep and narrower moat, water-filled, which lay immediately below the walls, from neck to neck of the peninsula. And seawards the cliffs dropped sheer in dizzy precipices to the restless waves. Offshore a mile-and-a-half the stupendous rock of The Bass soared abruptly from the tide, stark and awesome, the cloud of screaming seabirds a perpetual halo round its lofty head.

The drawbridge under the great central tower was raised for the night when the two young visitors arrived; but the guards had been watching their approach and the bridge was lowered for them promptly enough on the shouting of their identity — both well-known here, of course.

Once through the long dark cobbled pend below the gatehouse-tower, it was as though they had entered a different world. Here was nothing of fortification, grim strength or beetling threat. Suddenly all was light and delight, peaceable domesticity, colour and space — indeed, spaciousness was the dominant impression, with the sky the most evident feature. For although there were minor and subsidiary buildings within the vast curtain wall, these were of no great height and extent and at the sides only, stables, kitchens, storerooms, a chapel. But all the wide centre of that cliff-plateau was vacant, right to the precipice-edge, save for grassy lawns, flower-beds, rose-bushes, winding paths, arbours, a well. So lofty were the cliffs that from here the sea was only visible at a major distance and it was the sky and the wheeling birds which took the eye until the very lip was reached. Then, suddenly, the endless hush and sigh of the creaming waves on the reefs and skerries far below added a new dimension.

Two ladies strolled in that fair green pleasance in the cool of the August evening, and a boy with them. At sight of the dismounting newcomers, the lad came running.

"Jamie! Will!" he cried. "You have come back. How did you fare? Did it go well? I wish I could have gone. My lord would not take me. Though he took Archie, who is not much older than I am. Where is he — my lord?"

Will began to speak, but Jamie gripped his arm tightly.

"He is not here, my lord," he said carefully. "We have come alone. The expedition had . . . its successes. We won a battle. But . . . we must pay our duties to the Countess. And to your lady-mother . . ."

"A battle? You fought a battle? Against the English? And *I* was not there! Tell me, Jamie. You, Will . . .?"

"My lord Earl — the Countess first. Both Countesses. You would not have us fail in our respect?"

"Oh, if you must!" The fair-haired, delicate-featured twelve-year-old shrugged. He was George Douglas, Earl of Angus.

They moved over to the ladies, Jamie's feet reluctant indeed. They bowed.

"Will! And Jamie!" Countess Isabel welcomed them warmly. "I joy to see you back. Safe. But, Will — are you hurt? Not sorely, I hope? You have not brought my lord with you? Shame on you both!"

"No, lady," Jamie said, and swallowed. "I am sorry."

The other woman laughed. "Do not look so concerned, boy!" she said. "I do not doubt that the Lord James did not seek your agreement!" She was a somewhat older woman, but still handsome, bold-eyed, lively, a foil for the more gentle Stewart princess.

Jamie drew a deep breath, his eyes on the Countess of Douglas. "Madam," he began. "My lady—I come bearing ill news. To my sorrow. My lord, my good lord . . ." He stopped, unable to go on.

"Jamie!" The Lady Isabel took a step forward. "Do not say . . .! Oh, God — do not say it! Are you telling me . . . telling me that my lord . . . that my lord is . . .?"

He nodded, dumbly — although he had rehearsed what he should say to her times without number these last days.

"A-a-ah!" A long, shuddering sigh broke from her trembling lips. And turning abruptly, she hurried away from them towards the sea side of the garden.

Will began to blurt out the dire story to the Countess Margaret. But Jamie went slowly after his mistress. He did not go right up to her, where she stood, shoulders heaving, at the cliff-edge and staring out to sea, but waited perhaps a dozen yards back, silent, desolate.

At last she turned and came back to him, drying tears with her long flaxen hair, seeking to control her lovely features.

"Tell me, Jamie," she commanded. "I am myself again. I can bear the worst, now. How . . . how did it befall?"

"The worst is very ill, my lady. It makes sore telling. My lord was slain in a battle. A great battle which he won. In Redesdale in Northumberland. Against the Percy. But . . . he was not slain in fair fight. He was murdered. Stabbed in the back. By his own armour-bearer, John Bickerton. Murdered by that *dastard*!"

Horrified, speechless, she gazed at him.

"He had left his armour undone. And so could dirk him. From behind. I saw him — saw the dirk. So evil a thing . . . !"

"But why, *why*?" That was a wail.

"None know, lady. He . . . Bickerton, thought himself affronted — but I believe it more than that. None would slay his own lord for the like."

Again the Countess turned away, and once more Jamie Douglas waited silent. At length, when she did not speak, he began to talk quietly to her back, telling her all, the entire extraordinary story of treachery, hate and heroism, and of battle won by a dead man — although he did not emphasise the part he himself had played.

In time, tight-lipped but in command of herself, the Countess Isabel allowed him to lead her indoors, to her own boudoir in the castle — and even thanked him for his care and thought for her.

Later, as they ate, with the Lady Isabel sending a message that she had retired for the night, Jamie sought the other Countess's permission to send men to Luffness to aid in the apprehension of Bickerton — and found her co-operative. She was a very different creature from Isabel Stewart, spirited, almost fiery, out-spoken, heedless of convention. She had lived here for long, by courtesy of the Earl James, for she had been his father's mistress, although she had lands of her own in Angus. The two Countesses were good friends, however peculiar their relationship.

So a group of Douglas men-at-arms and servants were sent riding through the night to Luffness, with explicit instructions. Only then did Jamie follow Will to bed.

In the morning he was wakened by the Countess Isabel herself coming to his chamber in the east tower — to his minor embar-rassment. She was heavy-eyed and pale — but, he thought, the more beautiful for it. He had always admired her greatly, with something almost like awe, not only as his master's wife and the

King's daughter, but for a calmly serene quality and unfailing kindness — not least towards himself, whom she had always befriended, unaccountably to his own mind. If tenser than he had ever known, she was now self-possessed again, and lucid. She came to kiss his brow, before sitting on the end of his bed.

"Jamie — or Sir James, as I hear you are now to be styled — I am come to thank you," she said, with a quiet control which was palpable. "For all your goodness and duty towards my lord and myself. Your kind thought. Your last service to him. Your coming here. I am much in your debt — and would be more so."

"I am yours to command, my lady. Always."

"Scarcely that, Jamie. You are now a knight — and something of a hero I hear. A laird likewise, with your own lands of Aberdour. You are no longer my lord's esquire — nor any lord's esquire. But a man of some substance. Your own man — although but eighteen years. What do you purpose, Sir James?"

"My lady!" he cried. "Do not speak so. I am not other than I was. I am James Douglas, who was my lord's leal servant. Now I am yours, so long as you need me,"

"Not servant, Jamie — but friend. And I need you. Yes, need a friend, I think. A stout and leal friend. As I have never needed one before. Will you be my good knight and support, Jamie Douglas?"

"To be sure I will!" he exclaimed, sitting up in bed, forgetting his nakedness. "And gladly, joyfully. But, my lady — why speak so? Of need? You, Countess of Douglas, and the King's daughter, can have the pick of Scotland's lords and knights for your support. What need have you of such as myself?"

"You think so, Jamie? Think again, then. Have you thought at all, my dear? I am the King's daughter — one of many. But . . . have you thought of the King's *sons*? My brothers, God help me! Think you they will cherish the widow of Douglas, sister or none? And my father is but a shadow, a helpless old man, half-blind, and scant protection for me or for any."

The young man swallowed. "He is still King of Scots."

"So they tell me!" She shrugged. "So much for the King's daughter! And what of the Countess of Douglas? Who will be *Earl* of Douglas now, Jamie? Have you thought of that, also?"

He frowned, biting his lip. "I . . . I do not know. I had not thought, no. To me, there was but *one* Earl of Douglas . . ."

"Aye, lad — to me also. But it behoves us now to think differently. Had I had a son to James, or even a daughter, all would have been otherwise. But our child died, as you know — and I have borne no more. Not through lack of will. So there is no heir to all the Douglas power, their lands and wealth. James had no brothers. No clear heir — but there will be hands outstretched to grasp and grab, of that you may be sure. And I in the midst, a weak woman! Now do you see why I need a leal and honest knight in my support, Jamie? Even at eighteen years!"

Appalled, he gazed at her. "I had not thought ..." he muttered.

"I *have*," she said calmly. "I have spent the night thinking. Do you see that as strange? The sorrowing widow? Should I not have been mourning my dear lord? Not thinking thus. But I shall have years to mourn him, Mary pity me! I must needs think *now*. Plan. Enquire. Discover. And I need help."

"My help is yours, lady. Now and always."

"Dear Jamie! But — what did you intend? What think to do? Now, that you are your own man. You must have had some notions?"

"None, no — beyond serving you. All these past years I have been servant to my lord as page and then esquire. Since I was eleven years and I left my father's house for yours. I have no other thought, save to avenge my lord's murder, on that assassin Bickerton. This I have sworn." He stirred restlessly under what blankets still covered the lower part of him. "I should be on my way now, my lady. Back to Luffness. We have trapped him, I believe. And must needs spring the trap. Ramsay and the others await me. I must go ..."

"Bickerton, that foul wretch, can wait, Jamie. Meantime. Let the others deal with him," she said. "They are sufficient, surely at Luffness? I need you. Forthwith. If Bickerton is penned in Luffness castle, he will not escape."

He looked doubtful. "And I must ride to Dalkeith Castle. To see my father. He will look for me ..."

"It is thither I would have you take me, Jamie. For Sir James — save us, you are *both* Sir James now! A confusion. Sir James of Dalkeith, your father, is one of the wisest men in this realm, forby a Douglas. And trustworthy. He will advise me. A member of the Council, he will know what to do. What is best. Today, Jamie — for the tidings of my lord's death will cover the land swiftly. Douglas's death will set the tongues wagging and the agile wits leaping. Grasping hands will move fast, I prophesy! I must move fast also, if I would save what I can."

"As you will, my lady. Allow me to rise, dress and eat, and I shall escort you to Dalkeith."

"I thank you. But — can we not have done now with this of my lady? You are a knight, now — and my friend."

"And you a princess, madam."

"As to that, it signifies little. In especial, now! When we are alone, at the least, Jamie, call me by my name. Isabel. In token of true friendship. I want a true knight to my support, not a servant. Can you bring yourself to do that, Sir James Douglas?"

He nodded wordlessly.

They rode for Dalkeith, leaving Will with the Countess Margaret and the Earl George. It was nearly a score of miles to the west, near Edinburgh, in the Esk valley. They had to pass the vicinity of Luffness on the way, and Jamie took the opportunity to visit his little beleaguering force, now almost thirty strong and with Ramsay very much in command. It was difficult, he said, to keep them all out-of-sight of the castle all the time, and maintain constant observation. The main gate remained shut and the drawbridge up; but a postern-gate to the west was opened now and again momentarily, and servants used this to come and go, especially down to the little haven and boat-strand on the bay shore, where there were fishing-boats. Ramsay's men were watching this like hawks, naturally, lest Bickerton should seek to escape by sea. The castle's occupants were acting very warily—so almost certainly they realised that they were being held under scrutiny. Fortunately the Carmelite monks of the monastery were being helpful. Richard Lundie had had an interview with the Prior before proceeding home to North Berwick, and had been assured of cooperation in the apprehension of Bickerton. For the monastery was a Lindsay foundation, and with their lord a prisoner in England, the monks were anxious that his interests should not be prejudiced. On Jamie's suggestion, the Countess called on the Prior in person, to inform him that she would do all in her power to obtain Sir James Lindsay's release from the Bishop of Durham, possibly in exchange for one or more of the Douglases' own distinguished captives — after all, Lindsay was son to the Lady Egidia of Dalkeith. In return, all Lindsay vassals and supporters must give every assistance in bringing the Earl of Douglas's murderer to justice.

They rode on westwards through the Garden of Scotland, as some named Lothian, from Seton onward becoming almost wholly Douglas lands.

Dalkeith Castle was not a mighty fortress like Tantallon, nor yet a major stronghold like Luffness; but rather a kind of palace, although in a strong defensive position, as befitted the seat of the wealthiest of all the Douglases. Large and with extensive ramifications, it stood in wide parkland on the peninsula where the North and South Esks joined, its town lying a little way upstream, no mere castleton this, but a burgh of barony to rival many a county capital.

The new arrivals found the place in something of a stir, with its lord preparing to ride forth — and the Lady Egidia with him, for she, the King's sister, was not the sort to be left at home in domesticity when anything was toward, and especially now when her captive son was to be rescued, by one means or other. Clearly something *was* toward today, with an air of excitement evident everywhere. Of course the Earl of Douglas's death was now known on all hands; and it was recognised that there would inevitably be changes in the land. And with Lady Egidia concerned for her son, everyone else had to be concerned also.

Sir James of Dalkeith welcomed the Lady Isabel with warmth and sympathy, and his son with real pride and affection. But there was no denying that he was an anxious man — and not too greatly in connection with James Lindsay. He expressed his sorrow, shock and horror at the Earl's murder, and his deep concern for and loyalty to the widow. But that his concern went further and deeper than that he did not seek to hide. While expressing due satisfaction at the victory of Otterburn and the successful outcome of the entire English expedition, he who was statesman rather than soldier, had other preoccupations. If his favourite though illegitimate son's heroics and knighthood did not gain quite as full acclaim as they might have done in other circumstances, Jamie had no complaints to make. At least his younger and legitimate brothers, like Johnnie, were duly impressed.

The Lady Egidia seemed much more indignant that her son had allowed himself to be captured than worried about his state.

It seemed that even before he got back from his raiding, the Earl of Fife and Menteith had called a meeting of the Privy Council for next day, 18th August, at Linlithgow — the Earl Robert, not his father the King, and at Linlithgow not Stirling. This haste was alarming to the Lord of Dalkeith. In theory, of course, it could be said to be a result of the success of, and necessary adjustments occasioned by, the English expedition; but there was no such great hurry for that. Equally, in theory, the Earl Robert had no authority to call any such Council; he did so in the monarch's name — but clearly had not consulted his father in so doing from Carlisle. Almost certainly there was other reason for the meeting — and it would be strange if it was not connected with the death of the Earl of Douglas.

Sir James, senior, suggested that the Lady Isabel and Jamie ride with him and his wife to Linlithgow, another score of miles to the west.

They rode in style, suitable for the richest man in the kingdom, with a large retinue of knights, vassals and men-at-arms — rather more, Jamie felt, than were necessary for mere attendance at a Council meeting. But he did not question his father's motives. Despite the style, the ladies chose to ride saddle-horses like the rest — Stewart princesses tending to be of the kind to eschew horse-litters and other femininities. As they went, the older man amplified some of his disquiets.

"Isabel, my dear — have you considered fully what changes this sorry death may bring to your circumstances?" he asked, gravely if kindly.

"I have, yes. Though how fully, I cannot say. That is why I have come seeking *your* advice, my lord."

"Aye. And you will require advice, I fear. The most powerful earldom in Scotland is fallen vacant, with no sure heir — and there will be many seeking to improve on the situation. You, as Countess, may well be either a target to aim at or a hindrance to be brushed aside."

"That I realise. I have said as much to Jamie here."

"Whoever is Earl of Douglas can control great manpower, see

you. Greater than any other soever in the realm. Who *needs* great manpower, in especial, think you?"

"My royal father needs it — but is not like to want or use it! His sons my brothers, are . . . otherwise!"

"So think I. But they cannot be Earl of Douglas, any of them. And, praise God, you are their *sister* — and even his present Holiness at Avignon cannot grant dispensation for brother to marry sister! So they, at least, must plan otherwise."

The Lady Egidia hooted. "God — I would not put even that past my nephew Alex!"

The Lady Isabel bit her lip. "I think, my lord, we must discern one from another," she said, a little breathlessly. "John needs men, and strength, yes — but he would not stoop to gain it by ill means. That I am sure. David is not concerned greatly with power and riches. Walter is — but he is young and foolish, a babe compared with the others. So we are left with Robert and Alexander."

"Aye — and a sufficiency, these two, by the saints! They have always looked on Douglas with envy."

"Yes. Think you one or other arranged the murder of my husband?"

There was a shocked pause. Even the Lady Egidia, woman of the world as she was, stared at this blunt and terrible suggestion from her pale but lovely niece.

Dalkeith cleared his throat. "My dear — I think that you should put such thoughts from you. They are . . . dangerous."

"No doubt. But I shall find out. Jamie here as good as hinted at it. Others may think similarly. He considers that some small slight, as between lord and armour-bearer, was scarcely sufficient cause for planned murder. Bickerton left my lord's armour part unfastened — and only he knew it. To repay a hot word and a chance scratch from a mace? I think not."

The older man shook his head. "It is passing strange, yes. But the other . . . is scarcely believable. One thing is certain—if it was so, we shall never learn the truth. That I'll swear!"

"Perhaps we shall, my lord," Jamie put in. "I believe Bickerton is hiding in Luffness Castle, despite his father's denial. We have the castle surrounded, watched. When we have the wretch, we will make him talk — that *I* swear!"

His father eyed him sidelong. "You might be safer lacking his information, lad. Folk who will slay once, will slay again!"

"You would have me to fail in avenging my lord's murder?"

"The Earl of Douglas, God rest his soul, would not have you to follow him to the grave, I think! As you might, thus."

They rode in silence, for a while.

"You clearly believe that this shameful deed was more than just a young man's resentment, my lord," the Lady Isabel said, at length. "We have thought of two who might have conceived it. Of these, I would say that my brother Robert would be the one, rather than Alex. He is the plotter, the colder villain. Alex would slay, yes — but would likelier do it with his own hand! He is a rogue—but the more honest rogue, I think! He would strike down whoever got in his way — but with his sword, where Robert might use poison!"

None commented on this elaboration on her assessment of her princely brothers.

"But — there could be others, could there not? Who might have subborned Bickerton? Who could seek to gain by James's death. Who, think you, will win the earldom?"

"I cannot believe that any who could possibly become Earl of Douglas could do such a thing. For they would have to be themselves Douglases — and it is inconceivable that any such would plan the death of their chief. But I agree that others could seek to *use* a new Earl of Douglas for their own ends, his power and influence. And so might possibly have done this. But again — who is placed so to use him? Or gain by the using? Other than one of the royal house?"

"It would have to be a very great noble," Jamie put in.

"Aye. But which? There are not many of sufficient power and stature to be able to play in such a game, to profit by it. Who are not Douglases or Stewarts. Dunbar? Moray? Or, or . . ."

"Say it," his wife snapped. "Or Lindsay! There are no others of sufficient stature. With Mar and Angus in women's hands. And Fife, Menteith, Carrick, Buchan and Atholl held by Stewart. Sutherland, Caithness, Ross and the Isles take no heed for our Lowland concerns. Which leaves Lindsay! He was there. And it was my son's vassal who did the deed. But I swear that James had no part in this! He is no saint — but this is not his style. And he admired Douglas."

113

"I, too, would swear that Sir James Lindsay knew naught of this," Jamie declared. "As also my lords of Dunbar and Moray. These all were friends."

"I agree," the Countess said. "We need consider none of them. But there is one, perhaps, whom you have overlooked. Not of quite the same stature, no — not an earl or a great lord. But an ambitious man of an ambitious house. No friend of my family — but linked to the Crown nevertheless. Sir Malcolm Drummond of Cargill. Whose aunt was second queen to King David, and his sister Annabella wife to my brother John. He is married to my dear lord's only sister, the Countess of Mar. He has not claimed the title of Earl of Mar—but he is acquisitive, and might be waiting to do so. If he was to claim also the earldom of Douglas, in his wife's name, he could become the most powerful man in this kingdom!"

"Whe-e-ew!" Dalkeith whistled, turning in his saddle to look long at the princess. "Malcolm Drummond! *That* I never thought on. But it is true. The Countess Isobel of Mar, whatever else, will inherit much by her brother's death. Not the earldom, I think — but wide lands. The unentailed lands of Douglas. Or most of them. Drummond I have never liked — though that may be but prejudice. You have sharp wits in that bonnie head, my dear! Drummond was not in this late expedition?"

"No," Jamie said. "After winning his tourney at Stirling, he went back to Kildrummy, they said. His wife's castle in Mar."

"And Bickerton? He was not at Stirling, I seem to remember. *You* acted armour-bearer to Earl James, there?"

"Yes. Bickerton was not at Stirling."

"So it seems the less likely that Drummond should be concerned."

The Lady Egidia took up the inquisition. "You said, James, that Isobel of Mar will inherit most of the *unentailed* lands of Douglas. But what of the entailed lands? Who gains them?"

"Whoever becomes Earl gets Douglasdale. And part of Ettrick Forest, I believe. But the major part of the landed heritage goes to Archie. Archibald of Galloway. The lands were entailed on him back in '42, by the Earl William, Earl James's father, a cousin, although illegitimate. After James himself, and his heirs. That entail, so far as I know, has never been altered. James leaving no direct heir-male, it will stand, I think."

"Archie the Grim! And will he become Earl of Douglas also?"

"Not necessarily. Others might have as good a claim. And be legitimate! Archie was only a natural son of the Good Sir James, Bruce's friend."

"So! Here we have another possible assassin — Archie the Grim!"

"Never! Archie is leal of the leal, I'd stake my life on that! Leal to Douglas."

"But a friend of Robert Stewart. And that nephew of mine has few friends. Lord — what a tangle!" The Lady Egidia leaned forward to look past her husband at the Countess. "My dear, in all this sorry roll of suspects, do not let it escape your notice that there is another who could have a claim to the earldom of Douglas. And so could become even richer and powerfuller than he is now — James Douglas, Lord of Dalkeith! Do not forget *him*!"

"Egidia, my heart — I find your humour too *Stewart* for my taste!" her lord said coldly. "I pray you, curb it. For Isabel's sake, if not mine."

They rode on in silence, with more than enough to think about.

VII

THE LITTLE GREY town of Linlithgow beside its loch, a few miles inland from the narrow Forth, midway to Stirling, seethed like an anthill disturbed, that evening, with much of the Scots western army encamped around it, the handsome brown-stone Palace on the ridge above the loch occupied by the princes and lords; and most of the houses of the burgh itself taken over temporarily by clerics and lesser nobility and gentry. Newcomers were arriving all the time; indeed Dalkeith's party finished the journey in company with the entourages of the Abbots of Melrose and Kelso and of the Lord of Borthwick. Jamie and his father were immediately struck by the fact that the army was here, and had not been disbanded like the eastern force. Moreover, that large numbers of lesser lords and lairds, Stewarts in especial, who had no connection with the Privy Council and had not been with the English expedition, were coming in also.

"I do not like this," Dalkeith said. "What are all these for? They can only be here because they have been summoned. And since the Earl Robert of Fife is in command, *he* must have summoned them. And that man never does anything without good reason. Or, leastways, without *definite* reason!"

"The Lord Archie of Galloway will, no doubt, tell us what's to do," Jamie suggested.

But it transpired that the Lord of Galloway was not in fact present. He had left the army after it recrossed the Border northwards, with his son Sir William, for his own castle of Threave, near Kirkcudbright. He was expected for the Council, nevertheless.

Bonfires were being lit on all the gentle hill-tops around Linlithgow as they rode up the quite steep causeway, past St. Michael's Kirk, to the Palace. It appeared that tonight was to be an occasion for celebration, festivities, gaiety — little as the Earl of Fife was apt to be associated with such manifestations normally. Presumably it was to celebrate the successful outcome of the English expedition — although the Douglases at least found it scarcely suitable or tactful, with mourning for the kingdom's greatest soldier more fitting. So far as Jamie could ascertain, the western thrust had produced no great achievements anyway; a few skirmishes, a number of not-very-important prisoners and hostages, and some thousands of head of English cattle, were hardly sufficient to account for such large-scale rejoicings. All the dramatics had, in fact, been with the eastern force.

The Dalkeith party's reception at the Palace was not enthusiastic; but then the Earl Robert had never been an enthusiast. He expressed formal condolences with his sister on the sad death of her husband; but that was all. He was more forthcoming towards Dalkeith himself, briefly almost affable indeed — although he eyed his aunt with distaste. Unlike some of his brothers, he was not a lover of women, not even much of a liker. Jamie, needless to say, he ignored. The Earl David of Strathearn was much more friendly and sympathetic towards his sister — but appeared to be as little informed about the reasons for the Council-meeting, and the allied rejoicings, as were the newcomers. Robert told him nothing, he complained. As for the Lord Walter of Brechin, he was drunk as usual, with his whores, and in no state to inform, sympathise or even recognise anyone.

The Palace, though large, was crowded already. Small and inadequate accommodation was found for the Lady Isabel, and better for Dalkeith and his wife; but Jamie had to find quarters where he could in the town, eventually teaming up with some Nithsdale Douglases in the stables of a hostelry. His new knightly status cut little ice in Linlithgow, it seemed.

He did gain some information from his new companions however. According to them, the victory fires and festivities were not only to celebrate the Northumbrian and Cumbrian invasions, but their own earlier victory in Ireland under Sir William of Nithsdale, at Carlingford, their destruction of the English fleet and their taking of the Isle of Man on the way home. These, taken in conjunction with the western thrust almost to Lancaster, were considered to be much more strategically and politically important than the fight at Otterburn — which was, after all, little more than a personal feud and bicker between Douglas and Percy. In token of this, when Sir William, the Flower of Chivalry, arrived with his father, on the morrow, there was to be a great merrymaking, and the announcement of the King's bestowal of the hand of his youngest daughter, the Lady Gelis, on Sir William, in royal approbation. Archie, Lord of Galloway, was also to be honoured in some fashion, it was thought.

Jamie Douglas, lying on straw in that inn's stable, knew a smouldering resentment on behalf of his dead lord, and against the gallant William of Nithsdale and his father. But though he was suspicious enough to perceive a Stewart wedge being driven shrewdly between the main stems of Douglas, he did not recognise that the iron point of that wedge had already penetrated his own mind.

All the following morning and forenoon new arrivals poured into Linlithgow. Sir John Montgomerie of Eaglesham escorted his illustrious captive, Hotspur, treated by all with great respect. The Earls of Dunbar and Moray came, grumbling, but brought with them other important prisoners, by request — although Sir Ralph

Percy was too sorely wounded to travel further. The Lady Gelis appeared, gay and colourful, with a bevy of her ladies, from Dundonald in Ayrshire, where her royal sire had retired. Archie the Grim, his legitimate son Sir Archibald, Master of Galloway, and the illegitimate but renowned Sir William, rode in in fine style, with a large following, with the chief of the Johnstones and the Lord Maxwell with them These at least paid immediate respects to the bereaved Countess. Sir Malcolm Drummond came from Tayside, and a host of Stewarts from Bute, Renfrewshire, the Lennox, Menteith, Fife and Berwickshire. Two notable absentees however were Earl John of Carrick and Earl Alexander the Wolf. Presumably these had ignored their brother's summons.

The Council was held at noon on the 18th of August, in the lesser banqueting hall of the Palace. Despite the huge concourse assembled at Linlithgow, only a very few were Privy Councillors, of course, so that not more than a score could attend the meeting. The remainder and the women could only wait on events.

Jamie, attending on the Lady Isabel, went with her to call on the Lady Gelis — who had been allotted much superior quarters than those of her elder sister. The young man was less than happy at the prospect. For although he still was hopelessly under the spell of the younger woman and longed to be in her company, the thought of her forthcoming union with William of Nithsdale was like a knife in his breast, he told himself; and close contact with her now would only turn that knife in the wound. Moreover, he felt that this public betrothal was somehow all part of a deep plan to denigrate the memory of his late master and to split the house of Douglas — and, knowingly or not, Gelis Stewart was lending herself to it. He admitted, however, that he might be a little prejudiced.

The two sisters met in a little rush of affection. For although one was an elder daughter of the King and the other the youngest, with fourteen years difference of age, they had always been good friends.

"My dear, my dear!" Gelis cried, and impulsively threw her arms round Isabel. "My heart bleeds for you! My very dear — how cruel, how cruel! I am desolate for you. In your great loss. What am I to say? James — so grievous a blow, so noble a lord!"

"Say . . . say nothing, Gelis sweet," her sister got out. "What is there to say?"

"Isabel, my heart, my brave one . . . !"

They wept on each other's shoulders.

Highly embarrassed, Jamie looked away, looked at the other young woman in the upper tower chamber, Mary Stewart, one of the King's bastard daughters and principal of Gelis's pretty throng. She looked as though she too was going to burst into tears. Clearing his throat, he strode over to the window to stare out at the loch. He should never have allowed himself to be brought here.

Presently out of much sniffing and swallowing and broken words, he heard the Countess congratulating her sister on her forthcoming marriage, saying, in a rush, what a splendid and gallant bridegroom she would have, and how she always had known that her heart was set in that airt. It was not every princess who was permitted to wed the man of her choice. And so on.

Mary Stewart came over to stand beside the young man, tears apparently quickly swallowed, a dimpling, warm-eyed, lively piece, not so beautiful as Gelis but markedly good-looking for all that, in person as in feature. But then, the Stewart women were nearly always good-looking. This one had a very notable bosom, which rose and fell close enough at Jamie's side, and under his regard, to be distinctly affecting.

"So much sorrow and joy in one small chamber!" she murmured. "Stewarts and Douglases! Think you women should so seek marriage? Might they not do a deal better lacking it?"

Startled, he raised his eyes from breasts to face. "I . . . I do not know, Mistress Mary. Have not thought greatly. As to marriage. For women."

"I dare say not. Men seldom do, I think. And yet — you were born out-of-wedlock, were you not? As was I !"

He cleared his throat. "Aye. So you are not a princess, Mistress — and I shall never be Lord of Dalkeith !"

"True. But we may live the happier — who knows? And bastardy does not seem to have done you much other dis-service, Sir Knight !"

"I, ah, did naught to deserve knighthood," he assured. "I but did my plain duty."

"That was not the tale as I heard it, Sir James! But have it as you will. Men have been knighted for less than doing their duty."

"Jamie Douglas!" That was Gelis calling now. "Come — allow that I mark your advancement to new estate, in fitting fashion." And as he approached, and bowed, she reached up, took his cheeks between both hands, and kissed him full on the lips. "There, Sir Knight — another accolade! As well deserved, it may be! Heigho — I have always wanted to do that — to one of the best-looking young men in my father's realm!"

"My, my lady. I . . . I . . ." Jamie was stammering, flushing hotly, when his lips were closed by another smacking kiss, this time from the girl Mary, a hearty salute the impact of which was by no means lessened by the strong and well-defined pressure of two prominent breasts against his chest.

"I did not dare before, but now I may!" that young woman declared, laughing breathlessly. "For is not every true knight vowed and bound to cherish and serve all ladies in their need?"

"The price you pay, Jamie! For feminine admiration," the Lady Isabel said, smiling away her tears. "As well that you are *my* assured knight, is it not?"

"Tell us," her sister commanded. "Tell us how you did it, Jamie. How you did aid the Douglas to win his last battle. How you bore him forward. Isabel, my heart, will be but proud to hear it again, I vow!"

"I have not truly heard it once, yet! Only the bare facts."

"There is naught to tell," he protested. "After, after my lord was stabbed by, by . . . after he was stabbed, he *ordered* that we do it. *He* was the hero, not us. Ordered us to carry him on, dying or dead. To hold him up, to shout his slogan, to keep his banner above him. That none might know him fallen, friend and foe alike. And when we might no longer bear him onward for the English swords and axes and spears, we laid him down and fought above him. We could do no other. Here was no deed worthy of knighthood . . ."

"Yet three of the six fell, did they not? On top of the Douglas? And Rob Hart died?"

"So not only did a dead man win a battle, but a man was knighted, dead?" Mary said.

"Oh, I wish that I could have seen that sight!" the Lady Gelis cried.

A choked-off sob from Isabel turned them all — and Jamie chewed his lip as the others went to seek comfort their sister, proclaiming their thoughtlessness.

He made an effort, and changed the subject. "You, Lady Gelis, should seek your tales of heroes not from me but from your Sir William," he said. "All declare *him* to be the true hero. That his battles were those that mattered. That our sallies against the Percy were but by-play!"

If there was a slightly sour note behind that, Gelis did not seem to detect it. "Oh, I will have it all out of him, yes. I long to hear it. But I have scarce seen him. Robert and the others have been so busy making much of him. And now they have him into this Council. A great honour for so young a man, I have no doubt. Ah, well — my time will come. I have waited thus long — I can wait a little longer."

"And what of the King of France, lady?" Jamie surprised even himself by bringing that out. "He waits also, does he not?"

"Why, let him wait, Jamie! I never wanted him. He is fat, they say — and slobbers! Lacks something in wits, I have heard. He has my picture — let him bed with that, if he likes it so well! I would not exchange Will Douglas for any king or emperor! Indeed, there are other Douglases I'd sooner wed than any monarch, if the truth were known!" And she dipped a mocking curtsy.

Confounded, he blinked and flushed again, wordless.

Mary Stewart, laughing, took his arm. "She but would make sure of *some* Douglas or other, lest Sir William be now grown too great to look at her! But come, Sir Jamie — I warrant these two have matters to discuss between them fit only for princesses' ears! Let us bastards go walk a little by the loch and feed bread to the waterfowl. And you can tell me how you broke into Newcastle town behind a herd of stolen cattle!"

"You know of that . . .?" he wondered.

"Ah, we know of many things, sirrah — more than you think. Who knows, I might even tell *you* some!"

"Come back shortly, Jamie," the Countess told him.

Uncomfortable, in that the young woman did not release his arm, even when going down the winding turnpike stair — which occasioned not a little bumping together and close contact in the process — and on amidst the idling, strolling, laughing throng in the great quadrangle and out in the terraced pleasance beyond,

Jamie was not very forthcoming at first; but his companion chattered away inconsequentially for both of them. It was not until they were down skirting the reedy fringe of the loch, where the coots scuttered and the mallard launched out in quacking protest, that she changed her tone and tune.

"Tell me," she said, "do you know much of Sir William of Nithsdale? How he lives? What are his . . . ways? As a man — not a hero? Or a lover, perhaps! You are kin to him, in some degree, are you not?"

He looked at her, warily. "So distantly as not to signify. But I *know* him a little, yes. Less well than does the Lady Gelis, I'd think!"

"Perhaps. She knows one side of the man, yes. But there are other sides which a woman may not discover easily *before* marriage! Something of a drawback!"

"No doubt. But it is late in the day, is it not, to think of that?"

"It is not new thought of. But there is a matter the Lady Gelis would know more of. And on which Sir William has not spoken. One appropriate that you and I should consider, bastards both! We have heard that Sir William has already a bastard son. Where, and by whom, we have not yet learned. Have you heard of this?"

"No. But it is not so strange, surely? Many men have, by his years. And he is a natural son, himself."

"Oh, to be sure. Men are ever very generous with their seed, we women have discovered! Perhaps you, likewise? But this matter is more delicate than some. For, from what we have heard tell, Sir William is sufficiently concerned for this child to settle property upon him. So it seems that it is not just some milkmaid's get, to be made into a forester or a falconer. Yet he has not declared it to his bride-to-be. You will perceive the problem, Jamie? The mother! The Lady Gelis is not seeking to lay blame — she could scarce do so, coming from *our* family! She would happily accept such a child, see to its rearing perhaps. But the mother is a different matter."

"I see that, yes. But I know nothing of this. Have not heard of child or mother. Your informant, who knows so much — surely he could tell you more?"

"That is the rub. For the tale came to us less than directly. By second mouth, or third. At Court, you know how it is. We do not even know if it is true. Save that it sounds too particular to be wholly contrived. The Lady Gelis would wish to know the truth. And hopes that you might learn it for her."

"So! I am to play spy on my kinsman?"

"Scarce that. Just to discover, if you may, whether the tale is true or false. She is entitled to know that, is she not?"

"She could ask Sir William."

"Not the easiest question on this happy occasion! All the realm will be lauding Sir William of Nithsdale and his royal bride. And he has not told her of this. If it is untrue . . .! Delicate, as I say. You agree? And Gelis conceives you her friend."

"Aye," he said, heavily.

"You do understand, Jamie? This must be secret. There are none so many we can trust. If there *is* a woman whom Sir William cherishes sufficiently to settle lands on her child, she must be of at least lairdly rank. Yet he professes faithful and undying love for the princess! To start married life with such a hidden mistress could be . . . trying!"

"Very well. I will see what I may discover."

"Do, Jamie. We shall all be grateful. For I, too, am devoted to my sister's interests." She squeezed his arm. "The Lady Gelis's quarters will be open to Sir Jamie Douglas at any and all times!"

He cleared his throat as comment to that.

"Now, alas — we may be required by our betters . . ."

The Council-meeting ended sooner than might have been expected for so evidently important an occasion, and the members came out looking distinctly bemused, where they were not scowling — save for some few, who seemed gleeful. Dalkeith, Dunbar, Moray and indeed David of Strathearn, were amongst the blackest-browed. Archibald the Grim, for once, managed to look uneasy and undecided, his son William equally doubtful.

The Lady Isabel was not long in repairing to the Dalkeith's chamber, Jamie with her. They found his father stamping the floor and haranguing the Lady Egidia — which was not like that equable and moderate individual. He promptly turned on the newcomers.

"It is not to be borne!" he declared. "The man is insufferable! It was no Council but a . . . a presumption, an effrontery! He treated us all like bairns before a tutor. Hectored us, would hear no contrary view. All was decided, arranged — we were there but to be *told*! The King's Privy Council!"

"And you bore it like sheep?" his wife asked.

"We did not. But your precious nephew allowed no vote, over-rode all. In his cold, sour fashion. He is to be master in Scotland."

"He has been the power behind my father for long, now," the Countess pointed out.

"Aye. But now it is much more than that. He is to be Governor of the Realm. That is to be his style. As good as Regent. To take over all the functions of government, on your royal father's behalf."

"But . . . can he do that? Is it possible?"

"He says that it is with the King's consent. It will require the confirmation of a parliament. But that is to be called shortly."

"And will he gain that confirmation?" the Lady Egidia wondered. "Robert is not loved in the land. And does not Douglas sway sufficient votes in any parliament to check him?"

"Douglas! Well may you ask! The man is a devil. Cunning. He has waited until now to bring this forward. Planned all. It is all clear now. Why he agreed to the English invasion — which surprised me, I will admit. Why he went with it, unlike himself as this was. He comes home a victor — although *he* gained no victory! Advances Will of Nithsdale as the realm's hero, and gives him his sister to wed, amidst public rejoicings. And splits Douglas in twain! That is Robert Stewart!"

"If Douglas is so weak as to allow Robert to split it!"

"That is the devil of it! Whether or no *he* caused the Earl's death, it plays into his hands. Removes the undoubted leader and chief. He could never have done this with the Earl James living. But now he as good as confers the earldom on his friend Archie of Galloway."

"But even he cannot do that, can he?" the Lady Isabel cried. "Even in his father's name?"

"No — God be thanked! It requires a due process, of law. And earldoms fall to be confirmed by the King in *parliament*. But Archie has the entailed lands — he had the papers there, on the table, to prove it, the Earl William's testament. That is why he went to Threave, from Carlisle; to fetch them. And he is in the running for the earldom itself. I did what I could. I protested. I put in claims for the earldom — to ensure that it was not settled out-of-hand. For myself. And for young Angus, who is a half-brother, though illegitimate. But Archie himself was illegitimate. Drummond put in a claim on behalf of his wife, as we guessed he would. Myself, I do not desire to be earl. But the claim had to be laid. So Douglas is indeed split — which is what Fife desired and planned."

"I esteemed Archie a true man, and no fool," his wife said. "He will not wish this to damage the Douglas power. For though he is friend to Robert, he does not love us Stewarts — makes no secret of that. He might well be the best Earl of Douglas, forby!"

"Agreed. I do not contest that. But not if he is in Fife's pocket."

"Robert is a plotter, yes. A shrewd and hard man. But he is not a man of action, James. No warrior . . ."

"That is why he needs Archie and young William of Nithsdale. They are."

"If he *needs* them, then the power remains. With Douglas."

"He has begun to whittle it away already — and Archie did not seek to stop him. Fife has himself assumed the position of Chief Warden of the Marches, in Earl James's room, a position that has been Douglas's for generations. It gives him additional great power, in the Borders in dealing with the English. It is damnable!"

"Robert had all his plans laid, then," the Countess said levelly. "This was not all contrived in a day or two. And none, or little, was possible while my lord lived! I think that we need look no further for his murderer."

They eyed her with varying expressions, silent.

A knock at the door heralded a servant to announce the Lord of Galloway and Sir William Douglas of Nithsdale to see the Lord of Dalkeith. Archibald the Grim strode in, followed by his son. "James—it is necessary that we speak . . ." he began, in his harsh, strong voice; and then noticed the Countess, and paused, to bow jerkily. "My lady Isabel! My dear lady— I am sorry. Desolated for you. A tragedy. I deeply feel for you."

"I too, lady," Sir William added, bowing more deeply. He had a musical voice, in contrast to his father's. "That your loss is the realm's loss can be scant comfort to you now. All true men grieve with you."

"All *true* men, no doubt, my lords!" That was very cool.

Askance, they eyed her, and transferred their bows to the Lady Egidia.

"We were speaking of you, Archie," Dalkeith said, less than cordially. "And that travesty of a Council."

"Yes. To be sure. I reckoned that you might. That is why I am here."

"Sent by my lord of Fife?"

"Curse you, James — no man sends Archie Douglas! Stewart or other! Now or ever! Mind it, will you?" He paused, and nodded briefly to each of the ladies. "Your pardon. But Sir James should know me better. We have been acquainted, friends, for sufficiently long."

"That is what I thought, Archie. Until today!"

"Why should I change, man? Today? Because of the earldom, think you? For myself, I care nothing to be Earl of Douglas. Lord of Galloway is sufficient for me. And now I have the entailed lands. Enough. And am an old man, getting . . ."

"Yet you let your friend Fife claim the earldom for you."

"Aye. Since I could not stop him. Nor could I say that I would refuse it man. I have as good a right as any. But, see you, James — this is no matter for bickering over, you and me. Or any. You could have a claim, yes. Young Angus, yes. Others perhaps. But are claimants' rights all that is concerned? I think not. That is why I have come to you." The great stooping eagle of a man strode about the room. "What is the Earl of Douglas? What different from other earls and lords? Power, I say. Douglas power. Man-power. Not wealth — you have the most of that. Not lands or name — save insofar as these command men. It is being able to put a dozen of a thousand men in the field, horsed and armed, that makes the Earl of Douglas different from others. Can you deny it?"

Dalkeith shook his head.

"What then? This power. The Earl must be able to *use* these men if he is to be a power in the land. Able and ready. That means he must be a soldier, a fighting-man. I say that is the heart of it. Are you that, James? Could you command ten thousand men in the field? Could the boy Angus? Could the Lady Isobel of Mar, or her Drummond husband? Or any other who could make a claim? *I* can. And my sons after me. That is why I let the Earl

Robert make that claim for me. I, and no other, can hold the Douglas power together today. And so held it must be, for the weal of this realm."

Into the pause, his son spoke. "I believe that my lord is right. Our Douglas power is great — but it could vanish like snow off a dyke, lacking a fighting leader. You must see it, sir? You are greatly respected, trusted. But would armed men flock to your banner? And if they would not, where is the vaunted power of Douglas?"

Dalkeith cleared his throat. "I, or other, as Earl, could call on my leal supporter and friend the Lord of Galloway to lead my host in the field!"

"Aye, but it is not the same thing, my lord . . ."

"I would do it," Sir Will's father said, "but as Archibald of Galloway would all of Douglas rally to me? Galloway and the south-west, yes. Douglasdale possibly. But what of Ettrick and Teviotdale? What of Lothian and Clydesdale? Of Kilpatrick and Lochleven? Of Abercorn? And all the rest? Would these all gladly follow a Gallowayman who was not Earl?"

"Archie is right, James," his wife said, quietly. "If you would retain the real power of your house, Archie had best be Earl of Douglas. And if Robert is to be contained, that Douglas power will be needed!"

"But Archie is supporting him! Douglas power will be used to *aid* Stewart, not contain him!"

"Not so, James," Galloway denied. "I think none so ill of Robert Stewart, unlike so many! But my support for him is not final, unchangeable. Still less so if I was Earl. I support him now because I see him as strong, and would see him stronger. For the realm's sake. This kingdom must have a ruler, James, a governor. You have said so yourself. It has not had that, in truth, for long. My regrets towards your ladyships, but the King has not ruled the land for years. And when a king does not rule, others must, or there is confusion, anarchy. Scotland needs a Governor, and a strong one."

"Perhaps. But . . ."

Sir William spoke up again. "Have you considered the other choice, my lord? If the Earl Robert does not take the rule? Someone must, and will! And who is next in line — since it is sure that the Earl of Carrick will not — the Earl Alexander. Again, with these princesses' forbearance, since I speak of their brother and nephew — would you have the Earl of Buchan ruling Scotland?"

"God forbid! But the Earl John of Carrick *is* the heir to the throne. And a man of sensibility and judgment. Not strong, perhaps — but with the support of the Earls Robert and David — to which he is entitled, but has never had — he could rule well, honestly, whilst his father lives. In preparation for when His Grace dies."

"No avail, James," Galloway said. "You know, as do we all, that Carrick has not the stomach for it. As in the earldom of Douglas, the Kingdom of Scotland requires a strong hand, not a hesitant one. Ever has done. Carrick would not serve, and could not. Alex the Wolf *would*, and might — to our cost! I say we must support the Earl Robert in this pass."

"Even though he may have contrived the murder of my husband to gain it?" That stark question dropped into the heated discussion like a douche of icy water.

"Robert? Murder . . .?" Galloway got out, staring. "What is this? What are you saying?"

"I say that though my lord was slain by the hand of this wretch Bickerton, his was not the *mind* behind it. Would some small slight suffered days previously provoke such cold-blooded assassination? Robert has planned this present entire assumption of power and government? He could not have done it with James alive. Therefore he assumed James dead! I believe he subborned Bickerton to do it."

"Christ God! No — I cannot believe that."

"Who, then?"

"I do not know. But — not Robert. He would not stoop to murder. Of his good-brother. His own sister's husband!"

"Has he ever shown me any love? Affection? Shown any his love and affection! His wife? His son Murdoch? Save perhaps to yourself, my lord! You are his friend. But even with you, I think, Robert will drive a hard bargain. His support for you will not be without price, I swear! You will find that out, one day."

Sir William's quick indraw of breath was obvious to all.

The Countess looked at him. "Something occurs to you, sir? Part of the price? Since you are to become another good-brother of Robert's, you would be well advised to walk warily!"

"It is not that, Lady Isabel," the younger man said. "I had just remembered . . . Tantallon!"

"Sakes, yes — that I also had forgotten! In all the rest." Dalkeith exclaimed.

"What of Tantallon, my lord?"

Dalkeith and Galloway exchanged glances, almost guilty glances. "It is part of Robert's price, I suppose. For supporting Archie's claim — although he gains on every hand, anyway. He is requiring Tantallon Castle to be handed over to himself, he told the Council. For his own use, Isabel. To be *his* property."

"But he cannot do that!" Most of them had probably forgotten the presence of the youngest member of the party, who had sat silent, watchful throughout, not raising his voice in the company of his elders and betters. Now protest burst from Jamie. "Tantallon is my lady's home — which she and my lord loved best!"

Tantallon was in an especial position. The barony of North Berwick belonged of old to the Celtic Earls of Fife. It was the southern end of their ferry across Forth to Fife — as Earlsferry was the northern. The first small castle of Tantallon was theirs, built to protect the ferry-passage. When the Earl William's father desired to build a large castle there, for some reason he did not buy the entire barony, but only leased the old ruinous tower and its ground — why, was not known. Perhaps the then Earl of Fife would not sell. So Fife still owned the ground and superiority — and when the Earl Robert gained the Fife earldom in gift, he must have learned this. And now he sought to resume possession. It was, after all, one of the fairest houses in the Kingdom — and the strongest!

"That is unworthy — even of Robert!" the Lady Egidia declared.

"Yes. But . . . lawful!"

The Lady Isabel drew a long quivering breath. "So! I am to be homeless as well as husbandless! And friendless likewise, it would seem! Am I to have nothing, my lords — nothing? The earldom given to whoever can serve Robert best. The entailed lands to Galloway. The unentailed lands to Isobel of Mar and whoever else may claim them. And now Tantallon, my home. What of the Countess of Douglas, my lords? What is left for this wretched woman, chief princess of Scotland?"

Unhappily the men gazed at her tense loveliness.

"No doubt provision, due provision, will be made," Sir William said.

"Something will be done, my dear," Sir James assured.

"To be sure," Sir Archibald agreed, heavily.

"Ah, I thank you! So kind! And think you that you can affect Robert? My lords, you are but babes to my brother!" the Countess rose. "Jamie — escort me hence, I pray you. I require better counsel than I shall gain here, I think." Proudly she swept towards the door — which Jamie leapt to open for her. But before she passed through, she turned and spoke in a rather different tone. "My friends — consider well. If this is how Robert commences his reign as Governor — beware! *I* am paying, first — but you all will pay before the end! I say — God preserve our land, from Robert Stewart!"

Outside, she took the young man's arm. "Jamie — go find my brother David, and bring him to my chamber. He will like none of this, I swear!"

"Yes. To be sure. But . . . the Earl of Strathearn is scarcely a strong man for you to lean upon. I cannot think that he will avail greatly in this pass . . ."

"Then I must be strong enough for both of us — with your support, Jamie. He is still the King's son, as much as Robert is. And tomorrow we ride to see the King! My father is still King of Scots, however feeble. His royal signature and seal is law. We ride for Ayrshire, Dundonald. And I would have David to ride with us."

"Ayrshire? But . . . I must go to Luffness, Lady Isabel. To see to Bickerton . . ."

"Bickerton can wait. He will not escape. Besides, others can attend to him. I need you, Jamie. I need *somebody* I can trust, close by me."

"Very well. But will you not see the Lord Robert himself, before you go? He may prove less harsh . . ."

"Never! I shall never seek anything from that man, save vengeance! For I am a Stewart too, I'd remind you! Go, now . . ."

Earl David of Strathearn proved sympathetic, indignant at his brother and some comfort to his sister in that he offered her a home at his own castle of Auchterarder, would later find a house for her on his broad Perthshire lands somewhere. But he would not come with her to Dundonald — not meantime. He had to return to Strathearn forthwith. His wife was poorly—and of course he had not seen her since he left for the English expedition. Why did Isabel not come with him, to Auchterarder? She would gain little or nothing from the old man at Dundonald anyway, he said. She thanked him but insisted that she must see her father. Perhaps later she would come to Strathearn. Clearly David was not going to oppose his brother actively.

That night in his stableyard accommodation in the town, Jamie Douglas, by discreet questioning of his Nithsdale companions, learned the gist of the story of Sir William's bastard son — and it seemed to be no secret, in fact. The mother had been the pretty daughter of a small Kirkpatrick laird near Closeburn in Dumfriesshire, who about five years before had died giving birth to the child. The young father had been sorely distressed, and had insisted on taking full responsibility for the boy, as a sort of penance, giving him his own name of William Douglas. No doubt all this would be explained to the princess in due course.

Before they set out next morning on their sixty-mile ride to Ayrshire, Jamie sought out Mary Stewart in Gelis's quarters of the Palace, and retailed this information. It was well received, since it put a much kinder light on the bridegroom-to-be, indeed a somewhat romantic one, which did his renown but little harm. Jamie was uncertain whether to be glad or sorry. Mary's reaction towards himself, like that of her mistress, was positive however, and indeed almost heady for a young man.

In something of an emotional turmoil they left Linlithgow for the west, the Countess, Jamie and his tail of three.

VIII

B<small>Y THE HIGH</small> moorlands of the Upper Ward of Lanarkshire, upper Clydesdale and Strathaven, they came to the long valley of the River Irvine at Loudoun Hill, where Bruce and Wallace had both won victories not so long before, and eventually, in the eye of the sinking sun to Kilmarnock, where the hills sank to the coastal plain and the western sea spread golden before them in gleaming molten glory. Four miles nearer the sea, the castle of Dundonald soared out of the green levels on its rocky hillock, a massive thick-walled hold, far from palatial, smaller than Dalkeith and not so strong as Tantallon or even Luffness, but the King's favourite home, where the best years of his life had been spent before the problems of being first High Steward and then monarch descended upon a simple, friendly, unambitious man really unsuited to be either.

The King maintained little or nothing of a Court here, no style nor circumstance, well content to be little more than the Laird of Dundonald —although inevitably there was a chamberlain, chaplain, secretaries and a fairly large guard. Even his illegitimate sons all lived in finer style than this.

The old man was unaffectedly glad to see his eldest daughter, even though he was preparing to retire for the night when they arrived with the dusk. He had always been fond of his bed, and nowadays spent an increasing proportion of his time therein, with a notable capacity for sleep. But whenever Isabel began to mention the reasons for her visit, he waggled a hand in the air.

"Not just now, lassie — not just now!" he quavered, all but pleaded. "I knew you would be wanting something, to have come all this way. But I'm right tired, Isa. The morn — we'll see about it the morn. I am for my bed. I'm an auld man, mind . . ."

His daughter sighed. "Yes, Sire — as you will. But you are still King of Scots, and my father. And it is family matters that bring me here. Tomorrow, I must have the attention I am entitled to, as your daughter."

"Aye — the morn, Isa. I'm right vexed for you, mind, losing your man, lassie. An ill business. Aye, right vexed." He leaned forward, peering from those bloodshot eyes at Jamie. "And who's this laddie you've got? Do I know him?"

"This is Jamie Douglas — now Sir James. Natural son to Dalkeith. Knighted by my lord of Dunbar after ... after that terrible battle. He was esquire to my husband. Now is my true knight."

"Ooh, aye. Douglas, you say? There's a wheen Douglases. Over many, maybe. Over many Douglases and over few Stewarts for the Crown's weal! Forby, mind, I've made as many Stewarts as I could, in my day!" That came out in a little spurt of spirit. "Aye, well — I'm away to my bed. I'll see you the morn, Isa."

"Yes, Father. Sleep well."

"A good night, Your Grace."

But in the morning there was no sign of the monarch, nor any summons to his presence. Fretting, the Lady Isabel waited until nearly noon; and when still her father did not put in an appearance, she told Jamie to come with her. She was going to beard the old and weary Lion of Scotland in its den.

"Not me, Isabel!" he protested. "Not into the King's bedchamber. I cannot go there. Forby, this is no matter for me, between you and His Grace."

"No — I want you with me, Jamie. I have my reasons. Your presence will help me. Come."

They made their way up to the monarch's rooms on the second floor of the keep. Two guards stood at the ante-chamber door, but the princess swept past them without a glance. Within, a secretary sat at a table with sundry papers, quill and ink-horn, and another guard stood at an inner door.

"Countess," the secretary said, rising and bowing. "His Grace is not to be disturbed."

"Perhaps not by you, sir. But *I* shall see him."

"But ... no, my lady! His Grace is ... occupied. His royal command ..."

"His command to you — not to his daughter. I shall see my father. Stand aside, sirrah!" This to the guard, peremptorily. "Come, Jamie."

A blast of hot air met them as they passed through the inner doorway, for although it was a muggy August day a large fire

133

of logs blazed in the wide arched fireplace. The King was sitting up in a huge fourposter bed, with a stained and threadbare cloak around him and a woollen nightcap on his white head. Nearby, an elderly monk sat and read aloud in Latin from a large illustrated volume.

"Och, Isa! Isa!" the monarch wailed. "You shouldna . . . you shouldna . . ."

"Sire — I did not ride across the breadth of Scotland to kick my heels in your waiting-chamber! I have important matters to deal with, and will not be put off further."

"Aye — but I'm busy the now, Isa. Hearing Holy Writ, no less!"

"Holy Writ has kept these thirteen hundred years, Father. It will keep an hour longer! Moreover, if I recollect aright, it declares somewhere a father's duty to his children! Sir Priest — leave us."

The chaplain hesitated, recognised realities, and bowed himself out.

"Och, lassie — and you were aye the gentle one! Biddable . . ."

"I am no longer your gentle, meek daughter, Father. I am a woman hardened, Countess of Douglas and first princess of this realm. And I needs must fight for my rights — since it seems none other will do so for me, save Sir James, here."

"Robert will see to it, Isa. Ask Robert. He's the one for seeing to things. He's to be the Guardian or Regent or some such. He'll see to all "

"Robert is the last one to go to, Sire — since it is Robert who assails me. Why, oh why, did you give him this power? Delivering your realm into his evil hands!"

"Hech, hech, lassie — say not so! You must not speak so ill of your brother, I say. It's not right. Robert has wits . . ."

"Wits, yes — of a sort. Wits to look after Robert Stewart and care not who else suffers. I believe he it was who had James murdered. So that he could be quit of the Douglas power — or some of it. Which might curb his own. He offers the earldom to Archibald of Galloway, to gain his support. He will break up all Douglas lands, allotting them to whom he will. Save to me, Countess of Douglas! He takes the office of Chief Warden of the Marches, for himself. It has always been a Douglas office. And he takes from me even Tantallon, my house, for his own. All this within days of James's death."

The King's mouth had fallen open at this recital. He shook his old head helplessly. "No, no, Isa — you have it wrong, I swear. Robert wouldna do the like of that."

"He has done it — and in *your* name, Sire! All is now done in your name, by Robert. As though you were dead, and John likewise. So I have come to you, the King. You are that still. And he can do little or nothing *against* your expressed will and royal command. You must assert your kingship — or not only I but all Scotland go down in ruin."

"But, lassie — that is *why* I let Robert take the rule. I'm auld and done — and I canna see right. I canna read papers and the like. Forby, my belly pains me. Who else can I turn to, girl? Johnnie will take no hand in things. Och, he can read the papers fine — but that's all he'll do. You know Johnnie. He should have been a monk! And Alex! Alex I can do nothing with — nor ever could. There's a devil in Alex, I reckon. Davie's well enough — but he lacks all purpose, the lad. Like Johnnie. He's aye wheenging about this or that, but he never *does* much. And young Wattie! He's but a headstrong laddie, aye drinking over much. When he's older, maybe, he'll serve. But no' now. And I canna set John of Bute, above his lawful brothers — though he's got a good head to him. Others likewise . . ."

"If you will not rule yourself, Father, you could appoint a *Council* of Regency. Jamie's father, Dalkeith, suggested it. Like the Joint Guardians who followed Wallace — the Bruce, Comyn and Bishop Lamberton. Three. Two others to keep Robert in check. Perhaps Traill, Bishop of St. Andrews, my lord of Dunbar, or Dalkeith himself . . ."

"Robert would not have it, Isa. He would not."

"If you commanded it, signed and sealed it, he would *have* to."

"He would not. He'd make me unsign it, lassie. Robert's right masterful." The old voice quavered away.

Helplessly she looked at him. "Oh, Father! Will you do *nothing*! You, crowned and anointed lord of this realm!"

"I canna, Isa. I'm . . . I'm not myself. I'm sick and tired and needing my sleep. You should not come troubling me."

She took a long breath, and spoke in a different voice, almost sternly. "Well, Sire — if you will do nothing for the realm God gave you, I must see that you do something for *me*, your daughter. I must be provided for. I must have my share of the Douglas lands. I demand my jointure annuity be paid to me — three hundred merks each year from the Customs of Haddington. Also the barony of Ednam, at Kelso, settled on James and myself on our marriage — if James could retake it from the English! Which he did. These at least I must have."

"Ooh, aye, lassie — if these are yours, you shall have them. Robert will not keep them from you . . ."

"He must not be allowed to! You have a secretary in the next chamber, Father. He shall make a writing of it. Jamie — fetch him. With paper and ink."

"But, Isa — there's no need . . ."

"Go, Jamie. And bring the priest too, as witness."

So the clerk and monk were brought in; and the Countess Isabel, in firm clear tones, dictated something like a charter to the effect that the King's Grace hereby confirmed to his beloved daughter Isabel Countess of Douglas the annuity granted to her and her late spouse of three hundred merks or £200 Scots paid from the customs of the burgh and port of Haddington; plus fullest possession and all rights in the barony, manor, mill and multures of Ednam in the shire of Roxburgh. And that thereafter the said Countess Isabel's due share or terce in the unentailed lands of the earldom of Douglas were to be allotted to her freely, all sheriffs of counties wherein lay the said lands to make disposition thereof on pain of royal displeasure.

The spluttering quill laboriously set all this down in good Latin, Isabel took it and the paper and put them on the bed before her father.

"Sign," she said, and as he held back, she took his trembling, mottled old hand and guided it into some sort of signature.

"Robert'll not like this," the grandson of Robert Bruce, the hero king, complained. "He said *he* was to do all the signing now."

"He is not Governor of Scotland yet! Not until your parliament confirms it, Sire. Sir Monk — pray witness His Grace's signature here. And you, Jamie, below. Sand it, Master Secretary . . ."

The King crouched further down in the great bed, turning his face away from them all. "Leave me, now. I'm tired," he said

136

thickly. "You're not like my Isa, any more. I . . . I wish I was dead, just!"

For moments she gazed down at the wreck of a man and a monarch, and her eyes filled with tears. She was, in fact, still the gentle, biddable Isabel Stewart, and every word spoken and move made that noontide had been screwed out of her with the most painful resolve and distress. When her father still did not raise his bleary glance to her, abruptly she turned and almost ran from the overheated bedroom, clutching her paper. Bowing unhappily towards the bed, Jamie sighed, and followed.

Going down the twisting turnpike stair within the thickness of the walling, he caught up with her, and perceiving her bent and shaking shoulders he took her arm.

"Do not grieve so, Isabel," he faltered. "He is not himself, as he said. He forgets — and will forget. He will not hold it against you. And it had to be done."

She twisted round, sobbing, and buried her face against his chest, gripping him tightly. "Oh, Jamie, Jamie — what am I to do?" she mumbled. "All, my whole life, is fallen in ruin about me. I have nothing left, nothing! Not just lands or castles but, but . . . I am alone, now. I had so much, so much. With James. And now — nothing. Not even a father, or brothers. All gone. And I must needs harry that old broken man — for this! A wretched paper scratched by a clerk!"

He held her, while the paroxysm of grief and shame ebbed, and gradually she quietened. He even stroked her fine golden head. At last she straightened up, blinking away her tears. "Dear Jamie — you are good, kind. How would I do without you? Forgive me, a weak, silly woman. I promise that I shall not weep on you again! See, take this paper and keep it safe for me — a paper I hate myself for, God knows!"

"Will it serve?" he asked. "Can it gain you what it says? If the Earl Robert wills otherwise?"

"We must make it serve. Robert is not yet Governor in *law*. And the King's signature *is* law. We must work fast to gain what it says. Before the parliament. A parliament requires forty days to call. We have that time, only."

"The parliament will do as the Earl Robert says?"

"I fear so. Almost certainly. Since it is the King's appointment. And he will not change it — you can see that. With no Earl of

Douglas to rally those against. And Archie of Galloway supporting. I fear there is no hope. In forty days Robert will be master of Scotland, in law as in fact."

"So what do we do? Now?"

"We go see the Prince and High Steward of Scotland! John, Earl of Carrick and heir to the throne, no less!" She grimaced. "He is little stronger than his father, an old man before his time. But at least he will not hide in his bed, I hope! And he has power — if he will use it. Robert will not want the heir to the throne publicly against him. We go to Turnberry."

"Do not look for too much," the young man said.

*   *   *

Turnberry, chief seat of the Earldom of Carrick, and the Bruce's birthplace — his mother had been the Celtic Countess of Carrick in her own right — stood on the coast some ten miles south-west of Ayr. Skirting that town and the smaller burgh of Maybole, capital of Carrick, the little cavalcade was trotting south-westwards through the low green hills and whin-clad braes near to the Abbey of Crossraguel, when a peremptory trumpet-blast turned them all in their saddles. A colourful and glittering body of horsemen had crested a long grassy ridge behind them, presumably come from Maybole. Shouts followed, most obviously directed at themselves.

"Unmannerly ruffians!" the Princess said. "Ride on."

The thunder of hooves behind them, and more trumpeting, made Jamie uneasy. "Perhaps we should wait?" he suggested. "They are many more than we."

"No! In Scotland, the King of Scots' daughter does not wait for anyone. Especially in Carrick! Draw your sword, Jamie."

"Is that wise, my lady? Four against forty?"

"Not to *fight* them. To show that we will not brook brigandage against honest travellers on the King's roads."

Reluctantly Jamie and his trio unsheathed their weapons.

The sight drew a prolonged yell from their pursuers. Coming on at the gallop, they were not far behind now.

"Dod — fetch them to me!" High and vital above the rest, an authoritative voice prevailed, bell-like, assured, its sharp clarity like a woman's. "Bring them here."

A big hulking man, roughly dressed but superbly mounted, detached himself, with seven or eight others, from the main party which had drawn up about seventy yards back, and spurred forwards.

"Steel, heh?" this individual bellowed. "You seek a bout, cocksparrow?" And he whipped out his own blade in a lightning flourish. "Jump, laddie — jump!" he hooted laughter as Jamie jerked back in his saddle to avoid the flickering point an inch from his nose. "Mistress — hide your pretty boy in your arms, lest I collop and skewer him for my supper! And these cattle with him."

"How dare you, sirrah . . .!"

The large man, contemptuously ignoring Jamie now, swung on Lady Isabel and grabbed her bridle. "I dare mair'n that, my bonnie birdie!" he cried, and leaning over, threw a great arm around the Countess and lifted her right out of her saddle to set her before his own. He started to slobber kisses on her shrinking, jerking person.

Jamie slashed sideways with his sword at one of the others who had grasped his own bridle, and the arm went limp as the fellow yelled. In the self-same movement the weapon lunged directly at the back of the man. Dod's thick, red neck. Somehow he prevented the point from actually driving in deep, so that it only nicked a scarlet cut in the bristly roll of flesh, partly aided by the man's turn of head at his colleague's shout. Blood flowed, but only slightly, staunched as yet by steel itself.

"Unhand the Countess, animal!" Jamie cried. "Or this point drives home! And you others — one move, and you will need to bury this oaf!"

Whether it was the blood, the commanding tone so unexpected, the mention of the word Countess or the self-evident fact that they had an expert swordsman to deal with here, there was an immediate and flattering reaction on the part of the attackers, a sort of momentary freezing of motion and sound over the entire scene. Jamie raised his glance — although his sword-tip remained steady, indenting the fleshy back-neck.

"Does he die?" he called towards the group waiting at a distance. "Or do you, whoever you may be, come make amends to the Lady Isabel?"

There was a distinct pause, in strange contrast to all the previous vehemence and activity. Then a single rider trotted on from the colourful throng.

At first they thought that it was indeed a woman, despite the clothing, so light a figure bestrode the magnificent black. But then they perceived that this was a boy, not even a youth, slender, straight, assured, sitting the huge horse as though born to it and dressed richly in the height of fashion. To call this child — for he could not have been more than eleven or twelve years — good-looking was an understatement; he was, in fact, beautiful, of feature as of person, with great lustrous eyes, heavily-lashed, long fair hair wavy to his shoulders, with a slender gold band holding it in place around a brow that would one day be noble. A sword hung at his side and a dirk at his hip — but neither were drawn. Instead he carried in his hand a quite substantial riding-whip of stock and thong.

"You are bold, Sir Swordsman!" this apparition called, in that high and flutelike voice as he approached. "I like bold men — so long as they are not *too* bold for their own good! Did you say *Lady* Isabel, sir . . . ?"

"He did, nephew!" the Countess declared, pushing back the silken scarf which she wore over her head when riding and which, though somewhat disarranged by the man Dod's attentions, still had partly obscured her features.

"Christ God — Aunt Isabel!" the boy exclaimed. "By the Mass — here's a turn! And a joy, to be sure — aye, a joy indeed! My dear Aunt!" And his trill of melodious laughter rose sufficiently joyous for any.

"Joy, child! Do you call being assaulted and mauled by this . . . this brute-beast of yours a joy? Or being chased like gipsies by your unruly horde!" She wrenched herself out of the big man's now lax grasp as she spoke, and slid to the ground, flushed, angry — her proud beauty remarkably like that of the boy.

She was, as it were, just in time. With a hissing crack the whip-lash streaked out to fall right across the face of the unfortunate Dod in abrupt savage punishment. Snaking back, it slashed again and again and again, on face, head, shoulders, wrists.

"Hog! Stirk! Fool! Fool, I say!" the beautiful boy spat out, as he belaboured his servitor in a quite extraordinary exhibition of vicious and sustained vehemence, improbable even in a grown

140

man. "Cur! Creature! How dare you . . . so treat . . . a Stewart!" he snarled.

The hulking giant sat crouching but still under the rain of blows, not even raising an arm to protect his face — although his horse reared and sidled.

"Enough, David — enough!" the Countess cried, quite quickly. "Have done boy — of a mercy! This is too much. Unsuitable. Especially when *you* so ordered it!"

"Ah — you think so, my dear Aunt? Very well — if you say so." Following up a final slash with an elaborate bow from the saddle, the lad beamed an angelic smile on her. "So, my lady Countess — I hope that I see you well? Despite my lord's sad death. All grieve for you, I am sure." He was panting only a little from his punitive exertions.

"Thank you," she answered, very coolly. "Jamie — this is the Lord David, son and heir to my brother the Earl of Carrick. David — Sir James Douglas of Aberdour. To whom you owe most profound apology."

"Sir — I grovel at your feet!" the lad cried, with the sweetest smile imaginable, and something of a flourish. "If my oafs offended you they shall pay for it, believe me! I know not where Aberdour is, but welcome you to Carrick. We Stewarts must ever make Douglases welcome, must we not?"

Distinctly warily, Jamie eyed this remarkable and precocious sprig of the royal tree — who presumably one day would be his monarch, a notion apt to give pause. "I thank you, my lord," he said carefully. "I trust that I have not damaged your servant. But Douglas tends to look after its own! Even in Ayrshire!"

"To be sure." The youngster laughed happily. "Care nothing. Dod will mend his ways — and watch heedfully for Douglases in the future, I swear! As do I. But . . . there are many bands of rogues roaming the land, see you, robbing, burning, slaying. Irish scum in the main, broken men from the Irish wars — but insufficiently broken yet, by God's eyes!"

"And did *we* look like broken Irish scum, David?" the Lady Isabel demanded. "Even at a distance?"

Laughter tinkled. "Save us, Aunt — but you might have been! They steal good horseflesh. They much trouble the good folk of Maybole. I have three here that I am going to hang." And he turned and pointed back to the main mass of his band, where certain bound and battered individuals sat slumped in the midst.

"Hang . . .?" the Countess echoed.

"Why, yes. I could have done it at Maybole, but conceive that they will hang more prettily at Turnberry! I like to keep our gallows-tree there well stocked, you see! It serves a useful purpose."

"Indeed! And your father . . .?"

"Oh, Father concerns himself otherwise. He studies chronicles and verse and the like. Myself, I write some poetry, mind — but I seek not to neglect my other duties!" Again the joyous laughter. "But come, Aunt — and Sir James. It *was* James? I will escort you to my father and mother. They will be much pleasured to see you. As am I. We can hang these creatures afterwards . . ."

Isabel and Jamie exchanged glances, as he assisted her back into her own saddle.

They came in resounding style to Turnberry, therefore, on its green terraces above the bay-scalloped shore. It was a great sprawling establishment, more of a fortified township than a castle, a community of miscellaneous buildings within a lofty and extensive perimeter wall, in the old Celtic patriarchal mode rather than any Norman-type feudal fortress, although there were sundry later castellated works, towers and barracks, erected by the English invaders during the Wars of Independence. The place now had an afternoon rural quiet about it, as of a village dozing in the early autumn sun, with leisurely harvesting going on in the surrounding rigs and fields. But the young Lord David soon changed all that. Obviously he was very much the master here, sending everybody about their business in no uncertain fashion. He brought the visitors to the long central hall-house with its attached chapel, which formed the centre-piece of the entire establishment; but could find neither parent here, even in the chapel where apparently his father spent much of his time. Racing off, in a sudden reversion to more typical boyish energetics, he presently hallooed them to follow him into a most pleasant orchard and rose-garden, contrived within the walling, where the ground fell in gentler shelves towards the beach in a south-facing enclave. Here, in an arbour facing out over the blue plain of the sea, he brought them to Annabella Drummond, Countess of Carrick, sitting at her needlework.

"Mama, Mama — see whom I have found for your delight!" this surprising juvenile called. "Aunt Isabel of Douglas, no less. Come all the way from Lothian. And Sir James Douglas of Aber-somewhere. Is this not a joy?"

The tall, calmly Junoesque woman, of a serene and quiet loveliness, rose to greet them, clearly pregnant, the future Queen of Scotland. She smiled slowly but warmly, and came forward with a sort of gentle deliberation — which was indeed how she did all things.

"My very dear Isabel," she murmured. "The dearer for your great loss. My heart aches for you." She opened her arms wide for her sister-in-law.

Watching them embrace, interestedly, the Lord David turned to Jamie. "Are women to be envied or pitied, think you, Sir James?" he asked speculatively.

"Eh . . .? Sakes — I do not know! That is scarce something for *us* to decide."

"You think not? I would not wish to be a woman, of course. But there are some things they do better than we do. How old are you, sir?"

"I shall be nineteen at Yule, my lord."

"Not very old," the young-old prince remarked. "I thought not." There might have been a certain criticism implicit in that. But the issue was not pursued, for the Countess Annabella spoke over Isabel's shoulder.

"Sir James — forgive us. I bid you welcome to Turnberry. We shall talk later. Davie — look to Sir James's comfort and refreshment."

"Yes, Mama. Where is Father?"

"With Abbot Colin, I should think. At Crossraguel. When you have attended to Sir James, have my lord informed, Davie."

"Yes. Come," the boy said. But as they were passing out of the orchard he addressed Jamie confidentially. "Are you much in need of rest and refreshment, Sir James? Or would a tankard of ale or wine serve you meantime? You see, I think that I will hang those three Irish *before* I go get my father. You will wish to watch the sport, no doubt?"

Jamie swallowed. "Thank you — no! But . . . *can* you do this? Yourself? You — hang men! Without trial . . .?"

"To be sure. No need for any trial. They were caught in the act,

143

inflagrante delicto indeed! Rape and robbery. At Myremill. They hang. And better before my father comes. Kinder. He has over-soft a heart — and would suffer as much as they, I swear! I seldom tell him of such matters. Do not say that *you* are of a like kidney? And you a swordsman, clearly? Unlike Douglas, I think!"

"I prefer my sport ... otherwise! And despite what you say, I would counsel you to refer the issue to the Earl of Carrick before you do anything more, my lord."

"Nonsense!" The youngster laughed. "We do not trouble father with the likes of this. But, come — you shall have your refreshment, Sir James. Each to his taste!"

Later, drinking wine and munching bannocks alone in the vast cavern of the great hall under the smoky hammer-beam rafters and thatch, Jamie listened to prolonged cheering from somewhere not far off. He did not doubt but that it signified the successful exercise of justice on the part of the second heir to the throne.

When Limping John of Carrick eventually arrived from nearby Crossraguel Abbey, that he was pleased to see his sister was not in doubt. But his gladness was nevertheless overlaid, clouded, by the sort of wariness and mild alarm, mixed with apology, which had become the man's general reaction to life, as though he knew well, from sad experience, that even the simplest and most modest of pleasures fell to be paid for by demands which were either painful, distasteful or quite beyond him. It was, admittedly, easier when his beloved wife was present — for then he could push all on to her calm and capable shoulders. And the lad Davie undoubtedly saved him from much troublesome decision.

No specific discussion of the Lady Isabel's problems took place until after the evening meal in the hall, with sixty or seventy present, and Jamie sitting at the end of the dais-table with the Lord David and the three Carrick daughters, Margaret, Mary and Elizabeth, aged ten, nine and seven respectively. Thereafter, with the children dispersed again, and the Earl John muttering about time to be going to the chapel for prayers, the Lady Annabella steered the adults firmly into her own small music-room which opened on to the orchard, and where they could watch the sun sinking over the jagged mountains of Arran to the north-west. Jamie would have excused himself, but Isabel held him close, clearly desiring such small support as his presence might offer.

Once started, she poured out her troubles in a flood. Her brother listened with sympathy but still more manifest and growing discomfort, sighing a lot, shaking his head, and fidgeting. His wife was less demonstrative, quietly intent; but at the end, when she had given her lord ample opportunity to groan, spread his hands helplessly and bite his finger-nails, the Countess Annabella it was who expressed a practical reaction.

"It is clear then, John, that your brother Robert must be countered in some measure, for Isabel's sake, but also for the realm's likewise. Robert is an able man, but he need not be permitted to rule all at his own devices. We must contrive otherwise."

"Counter Robert!" her husband exclaimed. "How can we, Anna — how can we? I canna do anything with Robert — nor ever could. You know that. He never heeds me, goes his ain gait."

"Yes, my dear. But there are ways in which he can be curbed. Until he be Governor."

"Not by me."

"By the King, your royal father's writ, John. If I understand it aright, and from what Isabel says, until the Governorship is confirmed by parliament, it is not valid in law. And the King can order undone anything done in the interim. Is that not so?"

"Aye, but . . ."

"Moreover, only the King or his Governor can summon a parliament. Robert cannot yet do this, without your father's signature. Such signature then, my heart, is *your* strength and weapon. On Isabel's and the realm's behalf. We know that your father is as wax in Robert's hands. But you must keep him from signing the necessary summons for a parliament. Prevent it until your sister's affairs are decently settled."

"How can I do that, Anna? Even if he heeded me in the matter, the moment Robert came stamping down to Dundonald with his papers, my father would sign. You know he would."

"In Dundonald he might, yes. In Turnberry, he might heed his eldest son the more."

"Eh? Turnberry? You mean . . .?"

"Bring him here, John. He is a sick old man, and not like to live long, I think. You are his eldest son. Bring him into your house, whether he would come or not. We shall look after him. I shall

145

nurse him well. And guard him from Robert's servants, as all others. Robert will come in person, in time, yes — but we can keep him from seeing his father alone. It will all delay the day. A parliament requires forty days calling, does it not? Six weeks. If we can delay even one month, in the summons, it will put it off until mid-November. A little longer and we shall be into Yule — no time for a parliament. Mid-winter, with the fords and passes closed and the roads impassable, will not serve, since but few could travel the country to attend. Parliaments are never held in mid-winter. So it would be spring . . ."

"Annabella! How clever you are!" Isabel cried. "I swear I had not thought of that! The longer we can delay, the better. Meanwhile Jamie's father Dalkeith, with Bishop Trail, Dunbar, Moray and the rest, can seek rally the forces of good, of moderation."

"My brother Malcolm would help."

Her sister-in-law blinked, and found no comment. After all, Sir Malcolm Drummond was one of the possible suspects in the murder of the Earl James. This could hardly be hinted at here.

The Earl John provided a suitable if involuntary distraction by getting up and limping about the little room, dragging that right leg — the leg which indeed might be held as partly responsible for much of Scotland's present woes. For until the age of eighteen, John Stewart had been a stalwart enough young man, not exactly excelling at tournaments and field sports, but a fair enough performer. He had even led one or two minor military expeditions with some success. Then, at a hunt, a Douglas horse — and Jamie's own uncle's horse — had lashed out a hoof and shattered the youth's knee-cap, turning the High Steward's heir at one blow into a cripple for life. And worse than the physical was the mental effect. Suddenly John Stewart became inadequate, and grew ever more so. For a leading Scots noble, especially an eventual heir to the throne, to be incapacitated from sitting a horse properly and all that that implied, from sword-fighting, hunting, archery, and manly sports, as well as from going to war — especially with the brothers this one had — was utter invalidation. Only a man of the strongest character and will-power could have overcome such handicap.

"You make it sound simple, Anna," he objected now. "But my father will not *want* to come here. And if come he does, we canna

146

keep Robert from seeing him. Robert is masterful. He will order all from the chamber, see you . . ."

"Robert cannot order you, the High Steward of Scotland, to do anything, John. Especially in your own house. You must stand up to him, in this — to your *younger* brother. Isabel will stay with us here. And she, I doubt not, will not bow to Robert's commands! She will support you . . ."

"To be sure I will. We could have Gelis here also. Until she marries. She little loves Robert. Even brother David might come. Never fear, John — you will not be left to outface Robert alone. And meantime, with your support, I shall take all lawful steps to save what I can of the Douglas heritage. With the King's signed paper I have, and the High Steward's backing, surely even Robert will be able to do little — until he is confirmed Governor."

"You are over-sanguine, lassies, over-sanguine . . ."

So it was decided, however doubtful and unhappy the Earl John. Isabel would spend the winter months at Turnberry — she was as well there as anywhere, in the circumstances; and this area was really home to her, for she had been brought up mainly at Dundonald. Moreover, Gelis would be summoned home to her father's side also; and since Nithsdale was just over in the next county of Dumfries-shire, she should find no fault with that. With Tantallon having to be vacated, the Countess Margaret of Angus and her son would have to move out, and should be invited to come to Turnberry also. The Angus Stewarts were only distantly connected with the royal house; but she was a strong-minded woman and would make a stout ally against Robert. With the King clearly weakening, and at seventy-three not likely to live long, the heir to the throne must inevitably become the focus of much manoeuvring and positioning — however little he liked the prospect. The Stewart women would, as it were, hold these two feeble but essential cards in their slender hands, hold them close. Robert of Fife and Menteith was not master yet.

Jamie Douglas would go east again, shortly, with a varied mission — but mainly to bring back the Lady Gelis Stewart to her father's side. He was distinctly uncertain as to his feelings in this matter; not that that would be allowed to weigh in any balance soever.

147

IX

WITH THE LEAVES already beginning to curl, crinkle and mottle with autumn — here, with the salt winds off the North Sea, they did not achieve quite the brilliant scarlets and gold of the inland trees — Luffness Castle glowed a mellow rose-red in the declining September sun, so very different a pile at the edge of so different a bay. Jamie was surprised and concerned to find no guard keeping watch on it, no sign of Richard Lundie or young Ramsay, nor even the Tantallon Douglases. The place looked quietly normal, with the harvest being led in from its fields to the adjoining farmery buildings and stackyards. Reluctant to present himself at the door again to face old Bickerton, he rode round to the Carmelite Priory in the demesne, established by the Crusading Sir David Lindsay, one-time Regent of Scotland a century earlier who, dying of a fever on his way to the Holy Land, had arranged for his body to be brought back home by dispossessed monks from the monastery on Mount Carmel, these being given land at Luffness to set up a new establishment.

He found the brown-and-white habited brothers at vespers in their chapel above the long snaking quarry which ran down to the shore, and from which the stone for castle and priory had been hewn, a pleasant quiet place now under tall old trees, with a yew-enclosed little graveyard adjoining and fish-ponds nearby. Here Jamie waited patiently, listening to the sweet singing coming from within the chapel. He wondered, amongst other things, how the lord of this fine barony was faring as a captive in England — whether perhaps he had already been ransomed. It would undoubtedly be best for the entire Bickerton business to be cleared up before he returned.

The singing ended. When the monks came out, he approached Prior Anselm, an elderly, gentle man, bastard uncle of Sir James Lindsay himself. To him he put his questions.

The old man eyed him sombrely. "So you do not know, young man?" he commented, shaking his grey head. "There has been shame committed here, at Luffness. Murder. Four days ago. My lord of Crawford would be sore affronted. Young John Bickerton may have done ill, in England — I know not. But he should not have been murdered."

"Murdered! Bickerton? What do you mean?"

"I mean, sir, that that unfortunate young man lies there." He pointed to a spot just outside the square of dark yew trees which marked the graveyard, where six feet of newly-turned earth scored the green sward. "He was hiding in the castle, as you know. Four days back he ventured out, rashly — by the postern to the boat-haven. He was seized by your waiting men. And then that young man Ramsay, from Waughton, came up and dirked him, there before them all. A most vile slaying — a man held and defenceless. Without opportunity for confession or absolution. Whatever his fault, this was shame and evil, against the laws of God and man. We buried him there, outwith our holy acre, his old father sorrowing. We dared not place him in consecrated ground . . ."

"Ramsay did that? Why? Why?"

"I know not. Vengeance. Misplaced vengeance . . ."

"But it was not for Ramsay to take vengeance. He was not one of the Earl of Douglas's men. He is a follower of Lindsay's. Bickerton was to be taken, and questioned as to why he slew the Earl. I must see Ramsay forthwith."

"I fear that you will not, Sir James. He is gone from Waughton, none knows where the very next day, in guilt, no doubt. An evil business, my son . . ."

Jamie went and looked down at the grave of John Bickerton, tight-featured, before he rode on from Luffness.

At Tantallon he found the Earl Robert's men already taking possession, the Countess Margaret in a white-faced fury, with what amounted almost to a state of war existing between the Fife men and the Douglas retainers. The Countess, of course, had no legal right to remain there; but it had been her home for long. Earl James's father, Earl William, had installed her there as his mistress — although she owned large lands elsewhere as Countess of Angus in her own right and widow of the Earl of Mar. Earl William's lawful wife, James's mother, had queened it at Douglas, Drumlanrig, Cavers, Liddesdale, Ettrick, Abercorn and the other Douglas castles, but left Tantallon to her rival — although, indeed, that was no correct description of their relationship, for they remained good enough friends, being in fact sisters-in-law, the Countess of Douglas being the sister of the deceased Earl of Mar and bringing that earldom to her husband the Earl William when her brother died. It was a peculiar and involved situation, but the arrangement seemed to suit all parties. When his father died, Earl James allowed the Countess Margaret to stay on at Tantallon with her child, his half-brother; but he often stayed there himself also, with Isabel, who loved the place. There had been room enough for all, anyway, and the two Countesses got on very well. Now, all was to be changed.

Jamie had no difficulty in persuading the Lady Margaret and her son to go to Turnberry, especially as part of a scheme to counter the machinations of Robert Stewart. A fiery creature when roused, she would have travelled to the ends of the earth to do just that, she declared. She had been refusing to budge, for the Fife men: but clearly that could not go on indefinitely. She had many Angus houses she could have retired to; but Turnberry represented positive action. She gave orders for immediate packing.

Jamie questioned the Douglas men-at-arms who had been at Luffness, and who had returned here when their vigil there had so abruptly ended. But he learned no more than Prior Anselm had told him. Two of them had been at the postern when Bickerton had been apprehended, presumably on his way to escape by boat from the little haven. They had taken him in triumph to where the rest of the party were gathered — and there and then, without warning or consulting other, Ramsay had snatched out his dirk and knifed the man they held. Afterwards he had cried vengeance and declared that this was a murderer's due deserts. Master Richard Lundie had been there, and was much upset. He had had them take the body to the Priory. Then they had all dispersed, Ramsay the first to go.

The next day, while the Countess was still packing up her goods and chattels, Jamie rode into North Berwick to see Lundie. He found the young chaplain, son of a small laird on the outskirts of the town, still much distressed at having been the witness of a cold-blooded slaying, so very different from blood-letting in the heat of battle — indeed inclined to blame himself for not having been able to prevent the attack. But it had been so swift, so totally unexpected, all over in a moment.

"There was no provocation then? No words passing between them? To account for Ramsay drawing on Bickerton?"

"None. The others had just brought Bickerton up, ungently but no more. I was asking them how and where they had taken him, when Ramsay pushed me aside, no word spoken. I only saw that he had a dirk in his hand when it flashed down on Bickerton's unprotected breast. He . . . he went on dirking him, Jamie, till we dragged him off. But by that time Bickerton was as good as dead. His . . . his throat cut. Blood . . ."

"He cut his throat?"

"Yes. After he was down. After many stabs. Neither had spoken a word. Afterwards he said it was just punishment. It was a terrible scene, Jamie. A taste of hell, no less!"

"Aye. But — you said something there, Richard. That neither spoke a word. Could that be what was behind it all? That nothing *should* be said! That Ramsay, for his own reasons, wanted Bickerton's tongue silenced at all cost? That he had intended all along to silence him thus?"

"But why? Ramsay surely had nothing to do with Earl James's death. He fought bravely enough at Otterburn. In *Lindsay's* array."

"I believe that somebody paid Bickerton to slay our master. Might not the same pay Ramsay afterwards to ensure that Bickerton revealed nothing? No names. And now Ramsay has gone none knows where!"

"The blessed saints! Who? Who, Jamie?"

"That I mean to discover, if I may — God helping me! It must be one who will much profit by the Earl's death. Someone very powerful."

"Or someone who hated him."

"Perhaps. But — think you not that all this has the marks of cunning and greed and calculation, rather than hatred and anger? I think of three. First, the Earl Robert Stewart, who I conceive to be capable of any infamy. Secondly, Sir Malcolm Drummond, married to our lord's sister and only near lawful kin. And thirdly, Sir Archie the Grim himself — who is like to be third Earl of Douglas."

"Oh, no! Not he — not a Douglas!"

"I hope not. But he had more to gain than any other — save the Earl Robert. And he is the Earl Robert's friend."

"That I cannot believe, Jamie. He is a hard man, but noble enough. A great warrior, not a back-hand killer. A true Douglas. Might it not be, rather, the Lord Alexander — the Wolf? He is an evil man — and often quarrelled with our Lord James."

"He has been in the north all this time. He could scarce have arranged it all. Especially this last. Besides, this I think has little of that man about it. He would slay and murder and cheat, yes — but he would do it *himself*, not use others at long range. No — I think his brother Robert is the more like. If we could but trace a link between him and Ramsay . . ."

Next day, Jamie, now with all the Tantallon Douglas men-at-arms as tail, escorted the Countess of Angus and the young Earl George to Dalkeith, on their way to Turnberry. There were some forty of these stalwarts, well armed and mounted, and in default of other master they were glad enough to attach themselves to the young knight who had been their lord's chief esquire. Presumably they were really the Lady Isabel's men now — if she had the wherewithal to pay them. But meantime Jamie was well content to use them in her name — and found his status the more greatly enhanced.

At Dalkeith, he explained to his father the situation at Turnberry and the opposition developing against the Earl Robert's designs. Also, of course, the death of Bickerton, which might or might not be related. Dalkeith was interested, but doubtful. He did not see any coalition of women, however spirited, defeating Robert Stewart; and the King's and Carrick's contributions he dismissed as valueless, save insofar as the royal authority could be utilised. On the subject of Bickerton, he agreed that it had almost certainly been a silencing killing — but drew the self-evident lesson that any further enquiry would therefore be highly dangerous and best left alone.

His son kept his own counsel.

That evening, he and his father and brothers with Uncle Will of Mordington, discussed the national situation long and earnestly. The older man saw matters from a slightly different angle, more concerned with the maintenance of the power of the house of Douglas than with the mere policy of countering the Earl Robert. After much thought, he told them, he had come to the conclusion that Archie the Grim was the key to the entire situation. He was satisfied that he was honest, strong and able, if irascible, and the best man to be Earl of Douglas. Moreover, he could have more effect on Robert Stewart than could anyone else. The country had to be governed, and with a strong hand, not allowed to drift as it had been doing for too long. Robert Stewart could undoubtedly provide that strong hand, for he also was an able man, if less than honest. If he could be steered, influenced, pushed towards the good, his evil tendencies restrained, the realm might well do none so badly under his Governorship. After all, but for the accident of primogeniture, *he* might well have been the heir to the throne instead of John. He might have made a passable King. Archie of Galloway was a possible bridle to curb and guide the Earl Robert, in the realm's interests as well as those of Douglas. Therefore he, Dalkeith, was prepared to offer Archie his support, and try to sway other Douglases to do the same. And in return he would seek Archie's aid and cooperation in a policy of containing Robert Stewart. This by no means need run contrary to the Turnberry developments. Indeed, if they had Archie's cooperation, anything done there would be much more likely to be effective.

It was Jamie's turn to be doubtful. But he was so very new to politics and statecraft, so recent a recruit to the ranks of knighthood, and so comparatively humble a member of this family, that he must needs defer. His father, however, sufficiently accepted the validity of his doubts and questions to suggest that he should accompany him on a visit he had planned to pay to Threave Castle in Galloway, to see Archie. They would go the very next day, and would travel so far on the way with the Countess Margaret, then leave her in the Cumnock area, to continue on to Turnberry, whilst they turned southwards for Galloway. Jamie could return to Turnberry and the Countess Isabel's service thereafter.

This was accepted as a sound programme, the urgency doubted by none. It appeared that the Earl Robert was intending to have a parliament at Edinburgh in the first week of November, and planning, as a popular spectacle to enhance the start of his regime, to have the marriage of his sister Gelis and Sir William of Nithsdale at the same time. Any contrary moves would have to be made quickly.

It was a major cavalcade that left Dalkeith next morning, for its lord usually travelled in style as a matter of policy. With the Tantallon Douglases they made a company of over two hundred.

Even such as the young Lord David of Carrick would think twice about assailing these travellers. They rode in cheerful, colourful fashion, with even mounted musicians to while away the tedium of travel, Douglas of Dalkeith being one of the very few Scots lords rich enough or sufficiently old-fashioned to indulge in such conceits — although he did it to maintain the prestige and image of the house of Douglas as much as anything else. The Lady Egidia came along too, determined to be involved in whatever went on, and with perhaps some part to play at Turnberry as the King's sister; and she and the Countess Margaret made a lively chattering pair. Also, Sir Will of Mordington was a hearty extrovert, of very different character to his brother. Jamie indeed felt the almost holiday atmosphere to be unsuitable. But perhaps all his recent responsibilities and commitments were making him too sober-minded, old before his time — for he was basically a high-spirited young man.

He rode with his three brothers, all younger than himself, the legitimate James and Will and the bastard Johnnie — and though he would hardly have admitted it, even to himself, he was not a little pleased to note the new respect all three accorded him. Even though he had been the eldest — and their father never made any real distinction between those born in wedlock or out of it — he had always been very much aware of his bastardy. But now he was promoted, the only knight amongst them, something of a hero, and deeply involved in current affairs. Moreover, he had a tail of over forty men-at-arms who trotted behind *him*, not part of their father's following, most respect-inspiring. So, even though Jamie felt that music and laughter were somewhat inappropriate in the present state of affairs, with his master so recently murdered, the realm in crisis, not to mention the implications of the Bickerton business, he was not altogether displeased to be riding so gallantly through the golden autumn forenoon.

They followed the south-eastern slopes of the green Pentland Hills, crossed into the Upper Ward of Lanarkshire at Dolphinton and traversed the high moorlands beyond, ever with the lofty isolated cone of Tinto beckoning them on. From there onwards they were in Douglasdale, which was accepted as running from Tinto Tap to Cairntable, tall summits fifteen miles apart, with the Douglas Water threading the low ground, the fair and fertile land from which they all took their name. Fifty miles from Dalkeith they halted for the night at Douglas Castle itself. The great fortress — another which had been partly razed and then rebuilt and enlarged by the English occupiers in the bad years at the beginning of the century — was held at present only by its keeper and a small garrison; but these hastened to welcome and provide for such distinguished Douglas travellers — and Jamie that night occupied his own old room in the south tower, which had been allotted to him when he was the Earl's page and then squire. The earldom possessed a score and more of castles; but though Tantallon had been the Earl James's favourite house, this was the seat and centre of all. Just who owned it now was still to be decided.

The following morning they rode on out of Douglasdale and over the shoulder of Cairntable, by Muirkirk and more heathery watershed, to Cumnock, with the Ayrshire plain beginning to spread wide before them. Here they left the two ladies and the young Earl of Angus, with half Jamie's tail as escort, to proceed on westwards another twenty-five miles to Turnberry, while the main party swung southwards through the hills to Dalmellington and the Doon valley, which they followed up to Loch Doon, scene of some of the Bruce's early adventures, and so over another watershed to the south-flowing Ken and into Galloway. Riding hard now, with music and singing a thing of the past, they reached the river Dee by dusk, and Threave Castle amongst its marshes as night fell, weary but satisfied. The Douglases could still cover eighty miles in a day when so they chose.

The Lord of Galloway was not at home, but was expected back the next day from a justice-ayres visitation, with his son and heir Archibald, in Wigtonshire. Meanwhile the visitors were entertained by Joanna, Lady Galloway, now an elderly handsome dame inclining towards stoutness but once a noted beauty, heiress of the rich and powerful Morays of Bothwell, whose hand Archie, in his young and dashing days, had fought five knights for in succession, in single combat. She had brought him the great lands and castle of Bothwell and also the hereditary office of Pantler, or Butler, to the King; and this Threave Castle had been largely built from her money. It was an unusual fortalice, rising from a sort of island in a widening of the Dee where the river spread almost into a loch, amidst marshlands, a safe and mighty place, approachable only by water — with a zigzag under-water stone causeway for knowledgeable horsemen, an exceedingly tall and massive square keep within a walled and towered enclosure built to the exact shape of the island. All its stables, farmery, mill, brewery and castleton necessarily were some little way off, on the 'mainland', which had its inconveniences; but for security it was all but impregnable, not quite so strong as Tantallon but nearly so.

When its lord returned next day, he welcomed his guests in his gruff, jerky way, warmly enough, but bluntly wanted to know why they had come. His old friend Dalkeith did not make a habit of visiting him, nor indeed stirring far from his own domains — especially not, as it were, in force like this. Had he come to challenge him for the earldom?

It was not until considerably later, in the privacy of his personal chamber at the top of the keep, that he got his full answer. With his son Archibald—Sir William was still sweethearting in the Stirling area with the Lady Gelis — he was closeted with Dalkeith and Mordington and Jamie, stalking long-legged about the floor like a restless crane, frowning and puffing, whilst his friend and distant kinsman held forth. Archibald, Master of Galloway, listened very differently, a quiet, thoughtful, unsmiling man in his mid-thirties, well aware that though his heir he was not his father's favourite son.

"So Robert Stewart must be held," Dalkeith wound up. "He has his virtues, no doubt, and is capable of rule in this land — if kept within bounds and not allowed his head. But he is untrustworthy, unscrupulous and secret, and could serve both the realm and Douglas mighty ill if let and allowed. Already has done, it may be. You are closer to him than most — for he has few friends, as you well know, Archie. With your help, I believe, he can be held and guided aright."

The other snorted. "Guided where, man? I do not know that I could guide Robert Stewart anywhere. But if I could — where? Who chooses the direction? Not I, 'fore God!"

"There are many who would aid you in that, Archie. Many of them Douglases!"

"Oh, aye — we could look after our ain! But think you Robert Stewart would accept that? Douglas control?"

"It would not be done so bluntly. The Privy Council is there to advise the ruler — if the ruler will heed its advice. As has not been done for long. Douglas, I think, can still sway a majority of the

Council. So it can be the Council's guidance you press on the Governor. He will not always heed you. But it could make the difference between tyranny and honest government."

"You are naming Stewart tyrant before he has so much as taken office, James! I say that you misjudge him. I think not so ill of the man as you and many do. What makes you so sure that he will act the tyrant?"

"What he has already done. Since Earl James's death. Whether or no he had anything to do with that slaying. He immediately assumes the rule. Takes to himself the Douglas office of Chief Warden of the Marches and Justicier of the South. Seeks to divide up the Douglas patrimony. Grasps Tantallon for himself and excludes the Countess Isabel from her rights. All before he is even confirmed in office . . ."

"All this seems more hurt to his sister Isabel than to the realm at large. Or even to Douglas."

"And you would allow him to mistreat the Countess of Douglas, your chief's widow?"

"Not so. But I would not turn the realm upside-down over a Stewart family quarrel."

"You would not turn that quarrel amongst Stewarts to Douglas advantage, Archie?" That was Sir William of Mordington.

"Ha! And there we have the meat of it! You want me to weaken Stewart that Douglas may gain? The old ploy!"

Dalkeith frowned at his brother. "That is not my intention — although Douglas can be, *must* be, a useful halt on Stewart power. Else we are all like to suffer. I fear that we shall have great power abused — what we have seen already but a warning. Nor are the fears only mine. The Stewarts themselves dread the future — and are taking steps to counter it. Jamie — tell my lord."

The young man cleared his throat. "At Turnberry, my lord, the Countess Isabel, the Countess Annabella of Carrick, the Countess Margaret of Angus and the Lady Egidia, are all of one mind. They will do what they can to delay the Earl Robert's rise to supreme power . . ."

"A confederation of women! What can *they* do, boy?"

"I believe, my lord, more than you might think. The future queen, two princesses and the Lady Angus, have much influence. And they hold the King."

"Eh? The King? What is this?"

"The Earl John by now should have His Grace at Turnberry. They will cherish him there. Others may join them — the Earl of Strathearn, the Countess Marjorie of Moray, the Lady Gelis it may be. Surrounded by these, the King will be the less likely to sign what the Earl Robert puts before him. The summons for a parliament, and the like."

"I see. Yes, I see. But Robert will not be long in putting that bees' byke to rights! They will not keep him from his father."

"No. But they can keep him from being alone with His Grace, they declare. Which may serve."

The older man stared at him, from under shaggy, beetling brows.

"You see it, Archie?" Dalkeith said. "My *wife* does, I assure you! And she lacks not shrewdness. She was not to be left out of it. Robert Stewart needs his father's signature to gain supreme power, in calling the first parliament. The old man is weak, yes. But with these close around him . . ."

"And what do you want of me?"

"That you will aid us — and them. Urge moderation on your friend. Help delay the parliament. To give time for moderate men to rally, for moves to be made to secure our positions."

"And why should he heed me?"

"Because he *needs* you, Archie. He has few friends, as I have said. And the support of the Earl of Douglas could be important indeed."

"But I am not the Earl of Douglas."

"Not yet. But you could be. I could hope, *will* be."

"Ah! So that is the way of it?"

"Yes, my friend. With *my* support, and that of other Douglases I can sway, Earl Robert can have you appointed to the earldom — as is his desire. The Lady Annabella, I swear, could persuade her brother, Malcolm Drummond, not to make any claim on his wife's behalf. And Margaret of Angus make no claim for her son."

"And the price I pay for all this?"

"No more than you might choose to pay anyway, Archie. No more indeed than your simple duty, I think. To take the lead and uphold the name and power of Douglas. And, where necessary for the weal of the realm, to help restrain Robert Stewart. As his friend, this would be in his own best interests, to be sure."

"You make it sound mighty simple, James. And this was what you came to Threave to put to me?"

"It was. And I charge you, Archie — do not dismiss it lightly."

There was silence in that upper chamber for a little. It was Jamie who, greatly daring, broke it.

"My lord of Galloway may be loth to become Earl of Douglas and then to run counter to the Earl Robert," he suggested.

They all eyed him doubtfully now.

He did not realise that he was frowning almost as blackly as Archie the Grim. "If the Earl Robert can perhaps have one Earl of Douglas slain, who was in his way, might not he do likewise with another?"

"Curse you, boy!" That came out in a great explosion from their host. "Mind what you say in your betters' presence. Jumped-up puppy! How dare you!"

Jamie sat his bench tensely. "I meant no offence, my lord. I but would point out the danger . . ."

"Danger! To *me*. It would take more than Robert Stewart to endanger Archibald of Galloway! God's wounds — who do you think I am! I was leading armies when Stewart was a babe at breast — and a sickly one!"

"Forgive me, my lord. I . . . misjudged."

"Aye, you did! Watch your callant tongue, in future. Forby, there is no reason to believe that he had aught to do with the Earl James's death. *That* is dangerous talk, see you! I'd counsel you to watch your tongue there also, boy. Or you might find it short-ened!"

"Yes, sir. Like, like John Bickerton's has been shortened!"

"Bickerton? Is he taken, then?"

"He is dead, my lord. Stabbed to death before he could utter a word from that tongue! By Ramsay of Waughton — who is now none knows where. Silenced, sir."

The breath came from Archie the Grim in no explosion this time, but in a long exhalation. "Is that so?" he said slowly. He started to pace the floor again.

"It obliges one to think, Archie," Dalkeith put in quietly.

"Think, aye. But who did this thing? Not Robert Stewart, I'd swear!"

"Who else fell to gain greatly by the Earl James's death?"

"*You*, sir!" That was the Master of Galloway's first contribution to the conversation, as he looked at his father. That man's bark was eloquent as it was wordless.

"We can think of only Malcolm Drummond, other than the Earl Robert, who would so gain. And yourself, Archie, as Archibald here points out," Dalkeith added. "And Drummond has been all the time in Perthshire. There could be something in what Jamie says. As to risk, danger . . ."

"Bah! Danger! Are you all out of your wits? Do you think fear of a dirk would prevent me from becoming Earl of Douglas?"

Archibald Douglas looked at Jamie, and smiled thinly. "*I* think there are wits here sufficiently sharp!" he murmured. "But I conceive this, this compact a good one, sir. I would say agree to it."

"When I require your counsel I'll ask for it, sirrah!" his father jerked. He jabbed a finger at Dalkeith. "If I accept this thing, James, I shall be no slave to your Council. Or to any soever. I shall use my own judgment."

"I should expect no other."

So, without any further actual undertaking, the matter was agreed, and what could be a decisive step taken in Scotland's journey.

A hawking was planned for the morrow, in the great Dee marshes; and a hunt for the day following — whereafter the Dalkeith party would return whence it had come.

X

DESPITE HIS AWARENESS of the situation and its implications, Jamie was unprepared for the state of affairs prevailing at Turnberry. It had become a household of women, and masterful women with strong personalities, each used to having her own way and controlling large establishments. Although they were united in the policy which brought them there, in other respects they were less so, and harmony was scarcely automatic. Moreover, the Lady Annabella was the only one who was not a Stewart, but was mistress of this castle and would one day be Queen; yet was accepted as distinctly inferior by those who were born royal — which now included the Lady Elizabeth, fourth daughter of the King and wife of Sir Thomas Hay of Erroll, the High Constable. Fortunately Annabella Drummond was a woman of quiet dignity and serenity and though as strong-minded as any, did not display it habitually. She indeed was the peace-keeper and catalyst. Her lord kept himself out of sight as far as possible, spending most of his time at Crossraguel Abbey — and very little with his father, immured at the top of a tower and approachable only via a single, narrow turnpike-stair. For all the impact *he* made on the establishment, King Robert might hardly have been present, well content to stay in his bed, with his confessor and clerk to minister to him when he was not pleasantly dozing, no trouble to anyone and glad when his daughters and sister found it unnecessary to attend upon him. Young Lord David, unfeignedly pleased to see Jamie returned, confided that he would positively welcome the appearance of his Uncle Robert, or his Uncle Alex, or anyone else who would deliver him out of the hands of all these women, male and female.

Inevitably Jamie was much in the boy's company, for there was little for him to do in the Lady Isabel's service, in these circumstances, and escape from the castle precincts became something of a daily preoccupation. Unfortunately, he found that he was expected to act as something of a controlling influence on this precocious child, at least by his mother — for the Earl John appeared to have given up all attempts at restraint, if he had ever made any. Needless to say, David Stewart's main reaction to Jamie Douglas's representations and chidings was amusement and enhanced extravagances. He did not so much resent the young man's tentative strictures as invite them, challenge them, enjoy them. Indeed, he seemed to both admire and pity his companion, adjudging him painfully out-of-touch with the realities of life, and taking upon himself the onus of widening that experience. In this quest, Jamie was led hurtling about the countryside, usually at the head of a large cut-throat band, looking for trouble in whatever shape it might offer itself, allegedly seeking out law-breakers, disturbers of the King's peace, petty oppressors, remiss payers of feudal dues and the like, but in fact stirring up the desired disharmony and turmoil for the satisfaction of putting all drastically to rights. Nothing pleased David Stewart more than a hanging, a beating, a ducking and the general chastising of wrong-doers, multiple if possible; or a burning or demolishing of offenders' premises. All in the name of justice, feudal or royal, of course — his father's name. He was on the young side for personal rape, but was always interested in seeing women's reaction to stress and punishment, especially if deprived of their clothing. His men were allowed a long rein — but were notably careful to keep an eye on their young lord throughout all activities, alert for any sudden change of mood or withdrawal of approval; for he could be as devastating towards his own minions as towards their victims. Jamie by no means enjoyed these expeditions, and did all he could to tone them down. He sought, wherever possible, to divert his young host's energies towards the hunting field, fowling, exploratory voyages by galley to Arran and the Stewart island of Bute, archery and athletic contests, horse-racing and the like. The boy had never had anyone with whom he could compete and identify on, as it were, equal terms, with only sisters, and no friends of his own age and status. Now he had an associate, a companion who, although not of his own rank, was of the superior status of knight and who had actually proved himself on the battlefield, and as such was worthy of youthful approval. Gradually Jamie's influence began to tell.

But before all this developed, that other and anticipated development on the national scene began to evolve. Two days after Jamie's arrival from Threave, a messenger from the Earl Robert came riding to Turnberry, via Dundonald. In fact, it was Sir John Stewart of Bute, bastard brother of the princesses, probably the King's favourite child and most popular member of the family generally, a genial, darkly handsome and capable man. He brought a paper for the royal signature — the summons for a parliament to be held at Edinburgh on 4th November. Surprised not to find the monarch at Dundonald, he had come on in haste — since there was some urgency.

Sir John was not long in being apprised of the situation — and found himself escorted upstairs to see his father by the entire regiment of ladies, who then remained in the bedchamber throughout the interview. After initial surprise and mild protest, when the King waved away the paper and refused to sign, rheumy old eyes darting from one daughter to another, John Stewart took it all in good part; but he emphasised that his half-brother of Fife would certainly take a very different attitude. He was only a courier, a messenger, with no responsibility beyond the carrying of the summons. He would have to send word back to Robert at Doune Castle, whom he feared would be very angry. After all, the King had *agreed* that Robert should be Governor, and this parliament only necessary to confirm it, a mere legal formality. He imagined that Robert would come in person, and swiftly.

At his aunt's and sisters' urgent request, he agreed to delay sending his own report to the Earl Robert for two or three days more — since every day counted. It was now turned mid-September, and by another week it would be too late to give the necessary forty days' notice for a parliament by 4th November. Postponement would therefore become inevitable. For his own skin's sake, Sir John told them ruefully, he would betake himself on to Rothesay, the main Stewart castle on Bute, of which he was hereditary keeper, and stay there meantime, leaving some unfortunate servant to be the bearer of the tidings to Doune. But he wondered whether the ladies knew just what they were doing?

Ten days passed after the departure of Sir John, ten distinctly anxious days at Turnberry — although the anxiety by no means transmitted itself to the Lord David, who was in the highest of spirits and kept Jamie fully occupied on a variety of ploys. On the ninth day there was an excitement. When out on a sea-fishing competition — one of Jamie's suggestions — in Maidenhead Bay, the boy was aroused by the sight of a column of smoke rising from a hilltop inland; and nothing would do but that they all must pack up this stupid fishing at once and return to the castle for horses and men. Shouting orders to this effect to the other boats involved, David revealed that he had, of his own authority, arranged for beacons to be prepared on prominent view-points, to be lit as warning of the approach of the Earl Robert's party, from the east. It would not do if the Earl of Fife was not properly met and escorted to his brother's house.

Jamie's doubts over-ruled, they hastened up from the boat-harbour to the stables, calling for men, mounted and were off north-eastwards, a smaller company than was the boy's usual, about a score strong. Some four miles on, under Mochrum Hill where the beacon was now but a smouldering heap, they were able to see a cavalcade approaching.

"A Stewart banner," the boy pointed out, presently. "Blue and gold. At least he does not ride under the Lion Rampant — yet!"

"True. But see you the other flying beside it?" Jamie asked. "Blue and white, with gules for difference. That is the Red Heart of Douglas, for a wager."

"Your friend Sir Archie of Galloway with him?"

"I would think not . . ."

As they neared, it became evident that there were women in the oncoming company, quite a number of women. And the Earl Robert was no lover of the opposite sex and unlikely to travel so encumbered. David groaned.

"More of them!" he said.

But Jamie's heart thumped. That tinkling laughter sounding across the hillside turf he would know anywhere — Gelis Stewart. And . . . others. "Your Aunt Gelis, my lord," he exclaimed. "And Sir William Douglas of Nithsdale. Not the Earl Robert, at all."

"Jamie! Jamie Douglas!" a cry rang out. "Here's joy! Ha — Jamie!"

The Lord David glanced at his companion sidelong. "My Aunt Gelis seems more concerned for Jamie Douglas than for her nephew!" he said. "And I see you flushing, do I not? Here's joy, indeed!" And his own laughter was as musical as the young woman's.

Belatedly the rest came. "And young Davie! Grown almost into a man! I scarce knew you, Davie."

"We cannot all be Douglases!" the boy returned. "Welcome to

164

Carrick, Aunt Gelis. At least, you are the prettiest of them! Is she not, Sir James?"

Fortunately any reply to this was unnecessary in the general greetings as they came together.

Gelis leaned over in her saddle to kiss her nephew — and then leaned further to grip Jamie's arm impulsively. "How kind to come to meet us!" she said. "How did you know that we were coming?"

David laughed again. "Ask Sir James, Aunt," he advised.

Jamie cleared his throat. "We did not *know*, Lady Gelis. For sure. But my lord's beacon, the smoke yonder, made it . . . a possibility. A signal. The Lord David was on the watch . . ."

"How clever! I thank you both. Will — this is my nephew, the Lord David of Carrick. Who will one day be liege-lord for us all, God willing. Sir William of Nithsdale, my betrothed . . ."

"Another Douglas hero! I' faith — where would we be without them? How fortunate you are, Aunt Gelis — two of them!"

Sir William considered the boy warily. "*I* am the fortunate one, my lord," he corrected. "And the more so if I win your regard. As Sir James seems to have done."

"Sir Jamie wins wherever he turns, I swear! Ask Aunt Isabel!"

Jamie, frowning a little, sought to cut this short. "The Countess Isabel will be happy to see you, Lady Gelis. As will the Countess of Carrick and the other ladies. You have come . . . to aid them?"

"I do not see my coming aiding any, Jamie. But Isabel besought me. And, and . . ."

"My father added his persuasion," Nithsdale added, significantly.

So this was the first-fruits of Archie the Grim's compact — a hopeful sign. "All aid will be required, I think," he said gravely.

He was assessing the value of Sir William's presence — who was, after all, something of a protègè of the Earl Robert's, and partly beholden to him for Gelis's hand — and turning his mount's head westwards again, when his thigh was jostled a little by another, as a horse sidled close, and a voice spoke quietly.

"So very sober, Jamie! Such weight on these young shoulders! Where is the smiling lad who was esquire to Douglas?"

He turned to find Mary Stewart's comely features near, and none the less attractive for being flushed with riding into the autumnal wind. Despite her concerned tone of voice, her eyes were dancing.

"I am sorry," he said. "Sorry if I seem heavy, dull. I have matters on my mind, yes. Problems . . ."

"To be sure. But she is betrothed to Sir Will, and there's naught to do about it! You must needs content yourself with lesser game, Sir Knight."

He darted an alarmed glance around lest any other should have heard. "No!" he jerked. "You mistake. It is . . . quite otherwise. Nothing of that sort. Problems laid on me. The Countess Isabel. That of the Earl Robert. And now this Lord David. His mother seeks my aid in curbing him. It is difficult . . ."

"He seems a knowing child!"

"Too knowing! He is a devil! But likeable also, in some fashion. He greatly lacks his father's hand."

"So Jamie Douglas must act father, in place of the heir to the throne? Father to a devil — though not yet himself, himself . . . !" She let that go. "I can think of a better part for you to play, at your age, Jamie."

"And you so old and wise, yourself, Mistress Mary!"

"I am older than you by a full six months! Yes, I asked your brother Johnnie. Besides, women are always older than men at our age."

"You tell me so? You scarce look it, I vow! All lightsome fairness and winsomeness." His glance was drawn down inevitably towards her prominent bosom, by no means negatived under her riding-habit. "And, and grace of form."

"Ha — that is better!" she approved, reaching out to pat his arm. "No problems with Mary Stewart, at least! Remember that, Jamie, will you?" He looked at her thoughtfully for a long moment, and then nodded, with a sort of decision, but unspeaking.

The Lady Gelis looked back over her shoulder. "Mary — what are you muttering to Jamie? Watch her, Jamie — for she is a scheming minx! You would be safer riding by *my* side, I vow!"

"Would I, Princess? I do not think that I am safe with any of you! Unlike Sir William, perhaps."

"Stewart women are no man's safety," Nithsdale gave back. "But we Douglases never learn, do we? We are but moths to their flame."

"Nor do the Stewart men ever learn it, I swear!" David put in. "My Uncle Robert, now — think you *he* will learn?"

That silenced them—for the Earl of Fife was no character to joke about, at any level.

As they rode on, Mary spoke again, low-voiced. "All is well now, between these two, Jamie. Over the child. Gelis told him that she knew of it — saying nothing of you. And he explained all. He was relieved to, I think. They will care for the boy, both of them. Instead of being a stone for stumbling, it may become a blessing."

"I am glad."

She considered him. "I believe that you are. How strange a man is James Douglas!"

So they returned to Turnberry more companionably than might have been anticipated. There the coming of the new arrivals cheered all at the castle greatly — save perhaps its lord, who saw every addition to his household as only portending further trouble. Gelis's presence was important for their project — but Will Douglas's could be more so, in the circumstances. And Gelis's young ladies were a colourful and cheerful boon to any company — even though with one accord they all spoiled young David Stewart deplorably.

Jamie Douglas found himself in a highly unsettled state.

It was the following noontide that the smoke-signal rose again from Mochrum Hill, and archery, with the young women competing, was abruptly dropped forthwith, at the Lord David's command, he insisting that Jamie should come with him. William Douglas preferred to stay where he was, sensibly, and this would have suited the younger man better. But the boy was as imperious as he was impetuous. The Earl Robert must be met and welcomed. They left the castle behind them in a state of excitement — with the young Earl George of Angus, a quiet, retiring lad, despatched to Crossraguel to fetch back the Earl John.

The welcoming party discerned the newcomers in much the same area as they had met the Lady Gelis's party the day before — and again the Stewart colours waved at its head, although on a much larger banner and unsupported by other. Young David grinned cheerfully.

"Look not so glum, Sir Jamie!" he cried. "My Uncle Robert

will not eat you! Nor me, either. Come!" And he spurred onward, into a gallop.

The company they approached in such headlong fashion was a large one, with fully a score of gentlemen besides five times that number of men-at-arms. It drew up, nevertheless, in an approximately defensive posture as the Turnberry party of about forty came pounding on. Though Jamie would have reined back considerably, he was unable to do so without being over-run by their tail, which was being waved and hallooed on by the Lord David, as though at a stag-hunt. Arrows pointed at them from the drawn bows of mounted archers following their line of approach, they thundered up, and in a wide circle rode right round the stationary cavalcade, the men yelling "A Stewart! A Stewart!" The complete circuit made, the boy pulled up his black rearing on its hind legs right in front of the tight group of staring gentry, and doffing his velvet bonnet with a flourish, bowed extravagantly from the saddle.

"Who are you who come to Carrick in force and unannounced?" he cried. "Even under the Stewart colours? Welcome if you are friends. Beware, if not!"

As the astonished and indignant notables spluttered, the thin and so slightly impedimented voice of Robert Stewart was raised. "Insolent!" he said. "I am the Earl of Fife and Menteith. What is the meaning of this, this outrage?"

"Ah — Uncle Robert, is it? I am David of Carrick, your nephew. You should have warned us of your coming, should you not?"

"I do not require to warn any of my coming, boy. I am the Great Chamberlain of Scotland and Governor of the realm."

"You say so, my lord?" Another laughing bow. "Then I welcome, in my father's name, my lord Chamberlain, who has strayed from his chambers to Carrick! But scarcely as Governor — since there is none such, I understand, until parliament in its wisdom so agrees. Am I right, Uncle?"

The Earl Robert was neither eloquent nor glib-tongued, unlike his nephew, however agile his wits. He stared in cold disapproval now. "Insolent!" he said again. "Remove your rabble, boy — I would proceed. On the King's business."

"Ha — the King's business, is it? That is different, Uncle," the boy allowed, smiling dazzlingly. "Come — I will conduct you to

168

His Grace's presence. If he will see you. For he is sickly, these days. Taken to his bed. But if His Grace cannot see you, my father will serve, no doubt. To conduct the King's business."

His uncle sought for words. "Boy!" he got out. "Are you so great a fool as you sound? This is intolerable! I need none to bring me to my father's presence. In especial, such as you! I speak with the King's voice — and do not forget it. As for your father . . ."

"My father will be King before long, my lord. And I heir to his throne. I would remind all here, likewise, not to forget it!"

There was an appalled silence as men eyed each other and looked from still-faced ice-cool uncle to brilliant beautiful nephew. Undoubtedly the thought that shared alarm in most minds was that here was a very different son from father, a difference which Scotland would have to reckon with.

The Earl summoned his dignity. He shrugged, spoke a word to his closest companions — who barked appropriate laughter — and then urged on his horse.

The Lord David caracoled his mount around, and reined over to his uncle's side. "Back!" he said briefly, with an authoritative flick of his slender hand to those who flanked the Earl. And, after a momentary hesitation, these did pull back — for he was, after all, the King's senior grandson and third in precedence in the kingdom, outranking anyone present. As he drew alongside, he waved over to Jamie to take the place of the dismissed riders at the other side of the Earl. "This is Sir James Douglas of Aberdour," he informed.

His uncle did not so much as turn his head. "I am acquainted with the young man," he said shortly. "And I do not seek his escort — nor yours!"

"Ah, but it is our pleasure. Is it not, Sir James?"

Highly uncomfortable, Jamie mumbled something incoherent.

"You do not often honour us with your presence, Uncle," the boy went on. "Indeed, I cannot recollect you being at Turnberry before."

He got only a grunt in response; but continued to make ostensibly polite but essentially barbed conversation all the way back to the castle, betraying no least awareness of the hostility he had so successfully generated. Jamie marvelled at the sheer ability of the lad, quite apart from his brazen effrontery.

But at Turnberry Castle, of course, the situation changed dramatically. The Earl Robert could ignore young David with his father, mother and aunts present — and these were less expert and successful in dealing with him. From the moment of arrival, he adopted an air of complete mastery and command, the chill assumption that all would fall out as he intended. He was curt with his brother, still more so with his sister-in-law, looked disapprovingly at his three sisters, but strangely enough paid a certain wary heed to his Aunt Egidia and the Countess of Angus, older women both, and formidable. Will Douglas he was formally cool towards, clearly indicating that he found his presence there unfortunate. After the initial greetings, and some brief introductions of his gentlemen, he crisply announced that he was going to see his father, and at once. He intended to return to Dundonald that evening.

Everybody looked at the Earl of Carrick.

That reluctant protagonist evidenced more than his usual unhappiness. "Maybe you'd better not, Robert," he said. "He's, he's not well, mind. Sleeping. Not himself. We had to bring him here ... for his health."

"Nonsense, man. Where is he?"

"Och, Robert — he's not just fit to see folk. He's up in his room . . ."

"God's eyes, man — I have come all this way to see my father on business of state! The realm's affairs must go on — or have you forgot? We cannot all hide ourselves away, reading poetry and mumbling prayers! Take me to my father, John — and then I will relieve you of my presence. Which I find is scarce welcome here!"

Helplessly the Earl John looked at the others, and moved slowly towards the door.

His brother, following, waved to certain of his gentlemen to accompany him.

Immediately the ladies moved into action. In a rustling phalanx they hurried after the two princes, all six of them — and inevitably, the non-royal visitors had to hold back to allow these precedence. As the Countess of Angus, last of them, passed through the hall doorway, young David took swift charge. He held up his hand against the group of his uncle's attendants.

"You will wait here, my lords and gentles," he ordered. "We

cannot have His Grace's chamber of sickness throng with folk. A family audience only." There were protests, pointing out that the Earl Robert had commanded them to follow him; but he was peremptory. "In this house, sirs, my royal father or myself give the commands. Sir James — come with me. Sir William — entertain these gentlemen *here*." And grasping Jamie's arm, he drew him out and slammed the door behind them.

"My lord — not me!" Jamie protested. "I have no place in this."

"Aunt Isabel said to bring you," the boy assured, gurgling appreciative laughter. "Did you see their faces? Is this not a notable ploy? As good as a play-acting."

"I fear it will be no play-acting. The Earl Robert is not to be played with, see you. Others have discovered that. I urge that you walk more warily, my lord — even you!"

But the boy was already racing up the twisting turnpike stairway, hooting his scorn.

They caught up with the panting women near the topmost landing, and pressed on into the King's bedchamber behind the Lady Angus as the chaplain and clerk were expelled. Jamie squeezed himself into an inconspicuous corner of the over-crowded and over-heated room, but David pushed forward to the bedside.

The monarch was already in a state of alarm and distress, a protective arm across his brow as though to ward off a blow. He was mumbling a general protest — and none there paying the least attention.

"I will not have this, John!" the Earl Robert was saying sternly. "I insist on seeing my father. Alone. Have this, this crowd removed from the room. Forthwith. It is unseemly. Disgraceful."

"I canna do that, Robert," his brother said. "They're his bairns, the same as we are. And his sister. Besides — they'll not go!"

"They will go," the other declared grimly. He turned. "All of you — leave this chamber. At once. I would speak with my father alone. On the realm's business."

Nobody moved.

"Fools!" he jerked. "Bairns and women! Out, I say — and quickly."

"Robert — you will speak to *me*, at least, more respectfully!" the

Lady Egidia declared. "You will not order me out of my brother's presence."

"Nor me! Nor me!" That was a chorus.

Belatedly the Earl turned to his father. "Sire — command this, this rabble to leave your presence. A royal command."

"Och, Robbie — I canna do that," the King moaned. "They're my bairns — and not doing any harm. But . . . but I'd fain see you *all* gone. I would so!"

"I have come a hundred miles to see you, Sire. On important business."

"Aye, well. Another time, Robbie. Not the now. Later, see you. I'm not well . . ."

The Earl Robert's lips tightened to a thin band. "Very well, Sire — if that is your royal will." He drew out a folded paper from his doublet. "Just sign this document, and I will be gone. And the others with me, I think!" He looked round. "Have the clerk in, with his ink-horn."

The monarch wagged his white head, and would not touch the proffered paper, eyes darting from one to the other of his visitors. "I'm no' for signing papers the day, Robbie. I'll no' can hold the quill."

"I will guide your hand, Sire."

"No, no — I tell you, not today."

"Sire, the business of your realm must go on, whether you are well or ill. You are King of Scots, do I have to remind you? *I* do your work for you, not these idlers! And have done, for long. I cannot do it without your royal signature. The seal I can have affixed. But this signature I require. If the realm's business is to continue to be transacted. It will take you but two moments." He looked round. "Where is that clerk?"

"He's gone, Uncle Robert," the Lord David informed him. "Down the stairs."

"Then go fetch him back, boy. With his quill and ink-horn. Quickly."

"Shall I, Father? Mother?"

As John Stewart bit his lip, his wife answered for him. "His Grace says that he does not wish to sign anything, Davie. Not today. So there is no need to fetch pen and ink. Is there, my lord Robert?"

"*I* say, fetch it!" the other snapped.

Again none moved, save for the King who sank lower in his bed and sought to cover his red eyes.

"Blood of Christ God!" the Earl cried, driven into unwonted vehement wrath. "Have you all lost what little wits God gave you? This paper is to call a parliament of the realm. I have already sent it to be signed, as is my right — and have had it returned to me unsigned. How dare you! How dare any of you hold up the calling of a parliament? Part of the kingdom's right and duty. This could be named treason!"

"Can the King commit treason, Robert? And his heir? Or his heir's heir?" That was the Lady Isabel, her voice quivering, but strong enough. "Our royal father does not consider that a parliament is necessary at this time. Nor do many who advise him. Your paper will not be signed."

The murmur of agreement from all around left her brother in no doubt but that this was the case. He drew a long breath.

"Very well," he said. "If this is your bairns' plot. Think you it will serve you aught? I have another paper, at Doune. Duly signed by the King. Appointing me Governor of this realm. I shall not fail to govern the realm, I assure you. With or without parliament called. Until parliament meets. I am master of this land — and you will all discover it! When parliament does meet it will confirm my appointment — only that. And I am Governor whether parliament confirms or no."

"But is that not unlawful, Uncle Robert?" the boy asked interestedly.

The other ignored him. "I warn you all — you are playing with fire. When your foolish fingers are burned, do not come greeting to me!" Folding up the paper, he put it back in his doublet. "Sire — I do not congratulate you on your present advisers. I'd counsel you — change them! You would be better back at Dundonald, likewise. Where I am going now." And nodding curtly to his father, he turned, and pushed his way through the press of them to the door, and out.

There was a throbbing silence when he had gone, until the Lord David's gleeful crowing.

"A victory!" he cried. "A notable victory. He has not got his signature that he came for, and cannot have his parliament. We have him beat!"

None of the others were quite so sanguine.

A sort of sob from the bed drew all eyes, and brought Gelis impulsively to grasp her father's hand. But he withdrew it fretfully and burrowed lower in the bedclothes.

"Go away!" the King mumbled. "Go away — all of you. Let me alone, will you. I wish, I wish I wasna here." And he sought to draw the covers over his head.

After a moment or two, with one accord they all moved to the door — some even remembering to turn and bow as they went out.

XI

THE CONCENTRATION OF accomplices could not remain at Turnberry indefinitely, especially once the Earl Robert had returned to the east and the immediate tension was relaxed, although even David Stewart was not so optimistic as to believe that they had heard the last of the matter. But there would be no parliament in November. Sir William Douglas was the first to go — although only over into Dumfries-shire, to his house of Gilmour in Nithsdale from whence he could visit Gelis in half-a-day's riding. The Ladies Egidia and Marjorie had to return to their respective husbands and households. The Countess of Angus and her son stayed on for the time being, but she said that she must proceed to Angus to collect rents and deal with affairs before the winter set in.

Lady Isabel herself decided that she must make a few visits to specific places and persons in order to seek salvage what she could of her inheritance and rights while still she might — this being, after all, one of the reasons behind the plan to delay the parliament and Robert's assumption of complete power. The Lord of Dalkeith had said that he would act for her, do what he could; but that was scarcely sufficient. And it would be wise to go sooner rather than later, not only on account of the weather for travelling but in that Robert would surely be unlikely to stage another descent upon Turnberry immediately. She would go almost at once, then, in the first days of October, and seek to be back within the month. Gelis was well enough content to stay and help Annabella sustain and strengthen the Earl John's feeble will-power meantime; Turnberry was much the nearest royal house to her betrothed's home.

The Lord David, restless and chafing at being left alone with the women — for of course Jamie Douglas was to escort his mistress on her journey — pleaded vehemently to be allowed to accompany them; and it was a marked change for that autocratic juvenile to be pleading instead of commanding. But he obtained no encouragement and was told that his place most certainly was to remain at Turnberry supporting his mother and acting for his father where possible. Jamie added his own recommendation — namely that the boy should be available to act escort for his Aunt Gelis when she rode abroad; since, as he would be the first to admit, escorts for ladies were entirely necessary in Carrick.

"Ha — that from the practised knight-errant and escorter of ladies, Sir Jamie Douglas!" the other exclaimed. "Shall we change places, then? You stay here and squire my Aunt Gelis, while I escort my Aunt Isabel on her travels? I think you would prefer that? But would your kinsman, Sir William?"

They were walking together along the shore-line where the castle gardens came down to the sea, a favourite promenade of an evening. These two were much in each other's company, the boy clearly finding Jamie more to his taste than any other in the castle; the young and gentle Earl of Angus, who was his own age, he despised utterly. It would not be accurate to say that they had become friends; there were too many differences of outlook and background, as well as of years, for that. But they had developed an understanding and companionship, and possibly a sort of respect — however wary on Jamie's part. He eyed the other sufficiently warily now.

"I am the Lady Isabel's servant," he said stiffly. "As I was her husband's. I go where she goes."

"How splendid for Aunt Isabel! She finds that to her taste, I vow! But do *you*?"

He frowned. "To be sure I do. The Lady Isabel is kind and true as she is fair. And she needs aid. She has been sorely misused. Such service as I can render her, I do so gladly."

"No doubt. And she will find your service welcome — since you are a good-looking fellow, are you not? Well set-up and dark enough for any woman. Women like dark and personable men, I am told! One of the best-advised young men about the Court, one lady named you!"

"My lord — I would be grateful if you would not speak in these terms. Of the Lady Isabel and myself. It is unsuitable. We are princess and servant . . ."

"Yet the princess approves Jamie Douglas's various parts, as escort, I swear! I have watched her. And noted that she *disapproves* of my Aunt Gelis's approval of the same parts!"

Jamie halted. "Lord David — I must ask you not to speak so. Or I must leave you. You are wholly in error, talk of matters you know nothing of. The Lady Gelis is kind towards me only as she is towards all."

"I would not judge you a fool, Sir James! Nor yet blind. But . . . nor am I! My aunts find Jamie Douglas agreeable to their tastes — or some of them do, for I have over-many aunts! And that does not exclude my bastard aunt, Mary! Who, I think, would fight either of the others for you, if need be! Tell me — is it pleasing to you to be so approved by women? Or a weariness? Myself, I find it trying, at times."

Jamie swallowed and shook his head helplessly at this impossible but all too percipient stripling. "I do not know of what you speak, my lord," he said shortly. "Nor wish to know. If we are to walk further together then I request that we speak of other things."

"Heigho — do I touch you so shrewdly? Very well, Sir Knight — as you will." The boy pointed. "That ninny, there — playing with my sisters like any bairn. Why is he not to be Earl of Douglas instead of your Archie the Grim? Who is himself a bastard. This of bastardy — what means it? In such matters?"

The young Earl George of Angus had come into view amongst the tidal rocks, with the three young Carrick girls, evidently collecting little crabs and starfish in the pools.

"I cannot tell you for sure," Jamie admitted. "In law, a bastard does not inherit title or lands. He can win them, but not inherit them. But if there is no lawful heir, it can be arranged. By special destination I think is the way they say it."

"George Angus is a bastard. Son of the Countess of Angus in her own right. But also of the Earl William of Douglas. If he can be Earl of Angus, why should he not be Earl of Douglas also, now that his half-brother Earl James is dead? None are so close as he."

"I do not rightly know. He *could* be, I think. And one day might wish to be. But there are two reasons that come to me. The first, that to be chief of Douglas is an especial position—as all know. It is not the oldest or most senior, but it is the most powerful earldom in the land. Since the Comyns were put down by the Bruce. It fields ten thousand men. *That* is the reason. It is meet, and necessary, that Douglas should have an earl who is strong, a warrior, a grown man of proven ability. No child. Second, the realm, the Council, parliament, your uncles, would not wish Douglas any *stronger*, I think! Angus is a great earldom too, though it lacks the Douglas manpower. But it is rich and controls wide lands. Add Angus to Douglas and many would consider it too much for one man. Especially Stewarts! So Earl George is not considered. Perhaps wisely."

"Wisely! If I was my Uncle Robert I would take and cherish this . . . this bairn! Make him Earl of Douglas and Angus both. Then hold him fast. Make him my servant, to use as I would. And so have the power of Douglas and Angus and Stewart combined. I think my terrible uncle, whom all so fear, is something of a fool! Do you not agree, Sir Jamie?"

The other stared at this great-great-grandson of the Bruce, and wondered anew what sort of monarch Scotland was going to have in a few years' time. The era of weak kings appeared to be moving towards its end. Rounding another little headland of the shore-line, they perceived three women strolling back towards them on the green machair just above the beach—the Ladies Isabel and Gelis and their half-sister Mary. They themselves were walking on the sand and shingle of the strand itself, and Jamie would have continued to do so, even edged a little seawards perhaps and raised a hand to salute from a distance. Not so David Stewart. He headed straight for the ladies, determinedly.

"My dear Aunts!" he cried. "Well met. I have been offering to change places with Sir Jamie here. To act escort for you, Aunt

Isabel, on your travels, while he squires Aunt Gelis. But he pretends to have none of it! Is not this a pity?"

Jamie looked black as any Douglas, and the women exchanged glances.

"It seems to me an excellent exchange," the boy went on. "I am penned here at Turnberry all my days, like a stalled ox. Or, not an ox, perhaps — but stalled, at least!" He laughed, and winked. "I never get opportunity to see the country — which one day I am to rule, after all. My father takes me nowhere — would go nowhere himself if he might. Whereas Sir James is for ever riding abroad. Moreover, he would, I swear, better entertain Aunt Gelis in the absence of her betrothed, than would I! And Mistress Mary also, of course! Do you not all agree?"

"Not so, Davie," the Countess told him. "We have spoken of this already and decided otherwise. You would make a very good guard against thieves and robbers, I have no doubt. But I require Sir James for other services than that."

Her nephew grinned wickedly. "Aye — I feared as much! Indeed, I said so to Jamie, did I not? And I *am* on the young side for such services — and moreover, your brother's son! Ah, me! But we could both come, could we not? When my presence was uncalled for, I could successfully absent myself."

"Davie — I do not think that I like your tone of voice. You, you lack respect for your elders."

"Ah, my aged Aunt! I would not name you elderly — yet. Three times *my* age, yes — but barely twice Sir Jamie's! And what, after all, are years? My father, and his royal sire, are both babes compared with myself! Even this Douglas here, I sometimes think, has the simplicity of a bairn! Especially where women are concerned. And I swear you all trade on it!"

"Davie — enough! We will have no more of this," the Lady Isabel exclaimed. "You will keep your flyting tongue better curbed when speaking to me."

"And to me," Gelis agreed. "And when speaking of Sir Jamie, too."

"Ha — yes! Sir Jamie. You hear that, my friend? How they support you, seemingly, these princesses. At the expense of one who will one day be your liege lord—and theirs! Be warned, my simple friend. They will make you pay their price . . ."

"Nephew!" Stepping forward, the Countess grasped the boy's

arm, quite sharply, and tugged him round. "Come with me. We shall have a word together you and I! Gelis—I think that you should come also."

"It is high time," her sister asserted, nodding, and took the other arm. Over his shoulder, the irrepressible Lord David glanced back. "At least we leave you with the best endowed, Jamie — to my mind. You will thank me yet!"

Jamie, holding back with Mary, watched the trio walking over the sandy greensward of the machair towards the castle. "That boy is a handful, i' faith!" he got out. "I never knew the like. He has a tongue like a whiplash — and a mind as quick!"

"I have not failed to notice it," the other admitted.

"Where he gets it, God knows! With his quietly strong lady-mother and his humble saint of a father . . ."

"Perhaps that is it, Jamie. His father may be a humble saint, but he is little of a man. David has had to act the man, for his quiet mother. And not all the Stewarts are spiritless! Alexander was something of this sort, when young, perhaps — though lacking such wits. And the Drummonds lack not for fire — as Queen Margaret Logie taught all!"

He shrugged. "Who knows? But I find David hard to bear with. There is no handling him. And yet, not always. At times, he can be a very good companion. And in a fight, I'd sooner have that boy at my back than many men I know."

"Still fathering him, Jamie!" She paused, and laid a hand on his arm. "See you — he talks much nonsense, and hurtful non-sense. But he is sharp, and there is some truth behind his fleering words. I think that you might be well advised to heed it, Jamie."

"Which of his follies and insults should I heed?"

"What he hints about my royal sisters. This is difficult to say, for I love them both dearly. But . . . they would both use you, Jamie, I think. Not only as a loyal and trusty servant, but as, as a man! A personable and even desirable young man." She stopped, swal-lowing, as though she perhaps had said too much.

He frowned. "The Lady Isabel is my mistress. I am her knight. Of course she will use me — as is *my* desire. As for the Lady Gelis, she is kind — that is all. *She* has never used me — even though I would serve her gladly!"

Mary shook her fair head at him. "Jamie — is that boy right, then? *Are* you a simple bairn, in some things? Do you not know when you are being used? By women!"

He smiled. "I would have thought that it would scarce pass my notice! You now, Mistress Mary — I would not fail to notice if *you* were using me kindly! Or otherwise."

"I wonder! One day, perhaps, we shall see! But . . . do you not see what I mean? What that insolent nephew of mine was meaning also? Isabel needs a friend and helper, yes. A man she may rely on. But she finds you more than that, I warrant. Tell me that she has never put herself into your strong arms? Or perhaps wept on your broad shoulder?"

He coughed. "I have sought to comfort her, to be sure. When she was sore troubled. Over my lord's death. It is my simple duty. She was always kind to me — before my lord was slain. I believe that it was through her good offices that he chose me as his principal esquire . . ."

"Exactly!"

"What mean you by that? She stood friend to me. Should I not stand friend to her, now that she needs me?"

Mary Stewart drew a long breath. "Jamie — believe me, I would not turn you against my sister even if I could. And she *does* need you. But in the ways of women, I think you are little more than the babe Davie said. You are not yet twenty. Isabel is thirty-five. Almost old enough to be your mother. For you to be accepted by all as too close to her could be no good thing for you. But that is what folk will say. She is an attractive woman still — and attracted by you, clearly. And a widow. With strong passions, however seemingly gentle. We Stewart women were always like that. I think, perhaps, you might yet be wise to take young Davie with you on your travels, as he suggests!"

"No! This is a great foolishness. You misjudge the Lady Isabel, Mary. Shamefully. She is good and kind and has been much ill-used. I am her knight, and shall remain so — so long as she will have me."

"As you will. Perhaps once away from Gelis she may be less . . . heedful!"

"Gelis? Dear God — what is this you are at now? What has the Lady Gelis to do with it?"

"That you need ask such question proves you an innocent,

Jamie! For long you have made sheep's eyes at Gelis, we all know. You are scarce clever at hiding it! Not only you, I agree — most of the men at Court are like to do the same. But you, you have a *longing* in your eyes, at times. And Gelis, being Gelis, and a Stewart, plays on it. For she is fond of you also—oh yes, no question of that. If Sir Will had not come along first, older, a great hero, knighted and with an inheritance ...! But we Stewarts can be generous with our affections! Look around you! So to some extent Gelis encourages you — which is less than kind, perhaps. And Isabel sees it all too clearly. And, and resents it. And so acts accordingly."

Bewildered he huffed and puffed. "But this is crazy-mad! Women's tattle grown monstrous! It is not true. None of it. Like some play-acting, making much out of nothing. I swear, you it is Mary who plays the bairn now. You must be simple indeed, to believe all this!"

"You think so, sir? Simple, lacking in wits to have *told* you, perhaps! Doing my poor self no good in your knightly eyes! But — at least you have been warned. Whether it will preserve you remains to be seen."

They had come to the castle gatehouse. Briefly she laid her hand on his arm again. "Forgive me, Jamie, if I have hurt you in this. I, I meant well."

Stiffly he bowed to her and hurried away to his own quarters.

*   *   *

They left next day, without David Stewart but with a jingling escort of Tantallon Douglases, heading east by south. They were making for Ednam, across on the other side of Scotland, on the edge of the Merse near where Teviot joined Tweed north of Kelso the barony, English-held at that time, granted by King Robert to Earl James as dowry for his daughter Isabel, on their wedding — if the Douglas could capture and hold it. A somewhat doubtful dowry, as the bridegroom had observed at the time — caring not, since he was five times as wealthy as the Crown anyway. But he had made a point of taking and holding Ednam, or more properly Edenham, nevertheless — and surely no property in Douglas possession was more properly the Countess Isabel's now. Gelis accompanied them as far as Castle Gilmour in Nithsdale, any excuse to see Sir William a good one. With Mary present too, for that first day, Jamie was distinctly distant and aloof towards all three ladies, stiffer than he knew — and the kinder they seemed the stiffer he grew. Mary at least had no cause to grumble.

The Countess's party did not linger at Castle Gilmour but left quite early next day, due east now. Jamie, without actually forcing the pace, pressed ahead smartly, glad to stretch himself after the constrictions of Turnberry — and Isabel seemed by no means averse. She was a good horsewoman and physically fit. They rode up the fast-flowing Mennock Water, through the high, steep Lowther Hills, with only sounds of baaing sheep and yittering curlews to compete with the hollow drumming of their horses' hooves. Through the green jaws of the Mennock Pass they trotted, after a long climb, to Wanlockhead, and then down the east-flowing Elvan Water beyond, to Elvanfoot — no country for lingering in, anyway, empty, inhospitable. Now they were in the upper Clyde valley, still deep in the shouldering hills, Lindsay of Crawford country, only a few miles south of Tower Lindsay. It occurred to Jamie that Ramsay of Waughton, son of a Lindsay vassal, might just possibly have come here to escape the consequences of his crime; but the Lady Isabel was not in favour of going to see, declaring that there was nothing that they could do about it if he *was* there. She was, oddly enough, much less concerned over the murder of Bickerton than was Jamie, averring that the wretch had merely got his deserts.

After resting their horses in a meadow of the Clyde, fifteen difficult miles behind them, they started another long climb over the high watershed of southern Scotland, where the west-flowing Clyde, the south-flowing Annan and the east-flowing Tweed all rose from a single mountainside, using the old Roman road to take them across the lofty bleak moors to near the head of Tweed, eight more peat-pocked, broken miles. In late afternoon, mud-spattered, weary but thankful to have the worst over, they turned down that stripling river, their way more or less uncomplicated and straight-forward from now on. Another eight miles and they halted at lonely Oliver Castle for the night, to a kindly welcome. Oliver of that Ilk was a vassal of Douglas, and two of his sons had been at Otterburn.

Isabel had stood the gruelling test and pace well, and Jamie found himself to be proud of her, his stiffness of manner replaced by mere stiffness of joints. The emotional strains of recent days faded into tired good companionship.

Next day's riding was comparatively easy, drove-roads following Tweed all the way, north and then east, by Drumelzier, Lyne, Peebles and the northern edge of the Ettrick forest, Traquair, Elibank and Yair, to the confluence of Ettrick and the greater river, all in Douglas country now, forty miles. Another five and they came to fair Melrose, where emotion of a different sort took over. Here, of course, the Earl James was buried, and his widow — and to some extent Jamie also — was preoccupied with grief and memories. Abbot Bernard, their host, was kind, thoughtful, refraining from discussing the matter of the handsome tomb the Countess had ordered to be erected until she raised the subject herself. Arrangements were thereafter made for a chaplain's fee to be paid for all time coming in order that perpetual prayers and masses should be offered for the soul of Earl James Douglas. This had all been proposed and outlined previously; now it was finalised — in the hope that the Countess's revenues would in fact be such as to stand the cost, which included the eventual building of a new side-chapel.

They spent all the next day, Sunday, at the lovely red-stone abbey under the green Eildon Hills, a bitter-sweet interlude in which the monastic peace and quiet regimen, the chanting of the monks and the mellow tolling of bells, was mixed with sad memories, hurt and resentment at what lay behind it all. True peace of spirit was more than even Melrose could offer them.

But mourning, of the passive devotional sort, was not really in the Stewart nature — for which Jamie was thankful — and on the Monday morning they rode on, in a drizzle of rain now, by Leaderfoot and Smailholm to the Eden Water at Nenthorn, and so to Ednam, where the gentle green hills finally died away and the great fertile plain of the Merse spread towards the distant sea — which seemed indeed none so distant that noon-tide, with cold rain driving in from the east and a grey curtain over all. They were only four miles from the Borderline at Carham.

The small stone tower of Ednam, within its courtyard, had been burned so frequently by the English that it had finally been left abandoned. But the thatched steward's house nearby, surrounded by the barony's hamlet of cottages, was reasonably roomy and probably more comfortable than would have been the tower. Dod

Ormiston the steward, a big, burly, red-faced Merseman was much put about by the unprecedented necessity to entertain the Countess of Douglas in his house, but rallied nobly and, aided by his sonsy wife, provided excellently well. Jamie was a little ashamed to find himself relieved that their quarters here permitted little of privacy. Despite himself, Mary Stewart's absurd warnings were having their effect, and he was on his guard against any unsuitable intimacies.

They had three days of typical east coast chilly thin rain, which hampered their survey of the barony inevitably. It was a bigger property than either of them had realised, comprising a rough triangle with two-mile sides, and a three-mile base where the Eden Water flowed into Tweed, almost touching the abbey-burgh of Kelso on the south and reaching within a mile of Birgham village on the east. Within this area were many farmsteads, two corn-mills a lint-mill, a tannery, a brewery and much pasture heavily grazed by good cattle. The rents, multures and vassalage from all this should amount to a goodly sum, and Ormiston confirmed the fact. He also informed that he conveyed the whole, in cash and kind, quarterly to the Abbot of Melrose — an item Abbot Bernard had omitted to mention during their conversations. It seemed that the Earl James had granted the whole revenues of this barony to the abbey as a token of piety — along with how many another, who could tell? It was a side of his character and behaviour unknown to wife or esquire.

Much exercised by this revelation, the visitors left the steward in no doubt as to procedure in future. Expensive if creditably secret piety might be all very well for the rich and powerful Earl of Douglas, to ensure his warrior's soul's entry into eventual bliss; but his deprived widow would have to rely on a more humdrum behavioural virtue, and Holy Church must get along without her jointure-house and barony's revenues. Jamie had some unkind epithets for the so kindly Abbot of Melrose, with whom they had so recently been discussing the financing of side-chapel, tomb and chaplaincy.

From Ednam they rode a short day's journey northwards across a corner of the Merse, by Eccles, Fogo and Duns, to Evelaw Tower high in the southern skirts of the Lammermuir Hills, another small Douglas lairdship which had been alienated, for debt, to the Abbey of Dryburgh, but which the Earl James had repurchased a few years previously — and which therefore could by no means be considered as part of the entailed lands of the earldom. Here they found the indebted vassal, John Douglas, an elderly soured man, still in control as tenant. He was in turn instructed where to send his rents and dues in future. Compared with Ednam, Evelaw was a poor place; but it had 10,000 acres of high hill pasture, and the wool of its sheep-flocks, exported from Berwick-on-Tweed to the Low Countries, produced sizeable revenues annually. The bare and draughty little tower was a comfortless shelter, and the Lady Isabel slept that night in a chilly garret which no princess certainly had ever previously occupied, while Jamie had to make do with a blanket on the hall table.

Their next call was a deal more civilised, no less than the royal burgh and sheriffdom of Haddington, some twenty miles across the grassy heathery Lammermuirs northwards and down to the plain of Forth, where their business was with the Abbess Margaret, who oddly enough farmed the royal burgh's customs, and those of its port of Aberlady. In the Cistercian nunnery a mile east of the town she was shown the Countess's letter with the King's signature confirming his daughter in the customs and revenues. Unenthusiastically, the distinctly masterful Mother Superior agreed that it seemed she must pay the Lady Isabel the dues in future — less of course her fair percentage for collection thereof, which naturally fell to be greatly increased from what it had been owing to the general difficulties and uncertainties of the times. The Countess was quickly out-manoeuvred by an obvious expert, and though Jamie sought to haggle he was not long in admitting a measure of defeat. Lady Isabel would be fortunate to net even half of the customs duties, he reckoned, royal edict or none.

Nevertheless, he considered that their tour of inspection had been well worth-while, an estimated average of £600 Scots per annum being more or less assured — no princely income for a princess admittedly, but a deal better than had seemed likely a few months before. Harboured carefully — if he could persuade any Stewart so to behave — it ought to serve to keep his mistress in modest comfort. But not to pay for extravagances such as a tail of Douglas men-at-arms, to be sure. That was a different problem. However, there were still one or two other sources of possible revenue to be investigated in due course.

Leaving Isabel at the nunnery next day, low with her feminine monthly troubles, Jamie took the opportunity to ride the five or six miles northwards across the Garmyleton Hill to Luffness and Waughton, to see if there was any news to be gleaned as to the whereabouts of young Ramsay. In this quest he drew a total blank; but was interested to discover that Sir James Lindsay himself was back home at Luffness Castle, having been not so much ransomed as exchanged for the wounded Sir Ralph Percy. He was somewhat on the defensive over the behaviour of his two vassals, Bickerton and Ramsay, though of course deploring their deeds. He could add nothing by way of explanation or exoneration. But he was clearly shocked at the entire situation, sympathetic towards the Countess Isabel and prepared to see the Earl Robert as principal villain of the piece. In any eventual power-struggle he almost certainly could be looked upon as an ally of Douglas. He assured Jamie that if he could discover Ramsay's whereabouts, he would — and would take steps to get the truth out of him. He also congratulated Jamie on his knighthood, declaring it to be well-earned — and indeed treated the younger man with the respect due to an equal, not a little flattering in the circumstances — not that the Lord of Crawford and Luffness was yet thirty, himself.

The day following the travellers proceeded from Haddington the fifteen miles to Dalkeith, to report to Jamie's father and to seek his advice as to further moves on the Lady Isabel's behalf. They were warmly enough welcomed, and approval was expressed over what they had achieved; but there was something, just something that was not quite right; and Dalkeith was a little restrained about what should be done next. On the wider front, he informed them that the Earl Robert was proceeding steadily, but meantime fairly discreetly, to gather all power in the kingdom into his own two hands, preparatory to parliamentary confirmation. Archie the Grim was seeking to exert a restraining influence, as agreed; but the man's progress was inexorable notwithstanding. Robert Stewart was going to rule Scotland—nothing was surer. Perhaps he would do it better than they feared—since someone must. It behoved all who could, therefore, to look out for their own interests.

And those of such as could not do so themselves, his idealistic son added — to his sire's non-committal grunt.

That evening the Lord of Dalkeith summoned Jamie, alone, to his private sanctum in the west tower of the castle, a circular room lined with books and parchments and charters and genealogies, indicative of Dalkeith's wide range of interests. Many an hour the boy had spent in this chamber, unlike any of his brothers, who had shunned it — although it had been the romances in the main, which surprisingly were to be found there, well-thumbed — rather than the more serious works, which had been apt to attract him; his father, who clearly had catholic tastes in reading, only mildly censorious. Tonight he seemed a little preoccupied to say the least, less at ease than was his usual with his favourite bastard.

"Jamie," he jerked, rather abruptly, after some markedly casual remarks far from typical of the man. "I want a word with you, lad. A . . . a word for your own good. Sit you — sit down, a God's name!"

Warily son eyed father. "Yes, my lord."

"Tcha, boy — do not my lord me! This is a serious matter, see you. You will pay me due heed."

"Do not I always, Father?"

"Aye. Well. This is it, then. For your own good, lad, as I said." He coughed. "There is talk, see you. Ill talk. Who set it about, I know not. But I hear tell of it from more airts than one. Of you and the Lady Isabel. It must stop, boy. It is folly, I know — damnable folly. But . . . it will not do."

Jamie felt himself flushing hotly. "What must stop, sir?" he asked, demanded.

"Do not speak so to me, sirrah! Remember your place, boy. I, ah, I mean that this ill talk must be stopped. And quickly. Once and for all."

"There is no truth in it."

His father peered at him from under down-drawn brows. "No? You deny it — yet I have not said what the talk is! You have known of it, then?"

"You said it was . . . of the Lady Isabel and myself, sir. Ill talk. There is nothing that is wrong between us. I am the Lady Isabel's servant, as I was her lord's. I am her knight, her protector. It is a knight's duty to protect helpless ladies, is it not? I seek to aid her in her affairs. That is all."

"Aye. Worthy, very worthy. But she is an attractive woman — and you are a man now, Jamie. I was wed two years before I was your age. Folk *will* talk."

"Some folk! Must we needs heed them? The Lady Isabel is kind, good, fair — but she is old enough to be my mother, almost."

"I am relieved that you recognise it, lad. But such talk, in Court circles, could do you harm — do her harm also. For she is a princess, remember, and one in a difficult position. Precarious — aye, precarious is the word. No ordinary woman. And one the Earl Robert has discovered cause to consider his enemy, sister as she is. Archie says that he blames all the trouble with the King on her — and on you! Scarce an enviable position for a young man of barely nineteen years."

"So we know now whence the talk stems!"

"Perhaps. But the talk must be stopped, for all that. It is entirely necessary for my name, and the name of Douglas."

"Sir Archie has not forgiven me for what I said at Threave, I think. That if he became Earl of Douglas he might have cause to fear the Earl James's fate."

"Tcha! Archie has more to consider than your laddie's haverings! He wishes you no harm — indeed only good. Hence these steps we must take. For your good and hers, Jamie."

"Steps . . .?"

"Aye. We have decided on it. The Lady Isabel must marry again. And quickly."

"But . . . but . . . dear God — how can this be? You cannot mean it? Truly? Marry . . .!"

"It is the only way, boy. She needs a protector, yes — and not a mere youth, but a man of substance to provide the King's daughter with what she requires. A man in whose name and state she will be secure again."

"And where will she find this paladin, sir? And, and at short notice?"

"We already have him. I have sent for him to come see her. Tomorrow. Edmonstone. Sir John Edmonstone of that Ilk."

"Edmonstone! That, that lumpish Lothian lairdie! Johnnie Edmonstone, who hunts and drinks and sleeps and does naught else! To wed the Countess of Douglas!"

"Watch your tongue, boy! How you speak of your elders and betters. Sir John is a sound man, honest, and of good ancient lineage. Ninth of his line. Moreover, he is a vassal of my own.

Under my superiority he holds large lands. And his mother was a Douglas. He has been widowed these five years. He will serve very well."

"But . . . she can scarcely know the man!"

"That is small matter, in a marriage of this sort. We have chosen carefully, never fear. He is rich enough to provide for her every need, of respected name and standing to be her second husband — but of rank sufficiently below her own to leave her, the King's daughter, free to live her own life as she wishes. And it will keep her within the Douglas camp, so that our own protection can be called upon, if required."

"She will never wed Edmonstone — Isabel Stewart!"

"I say she will. And gladly. It answers most of her difficulties, can you not see? She can make of the marriage what she will, much or little. Edmonstone is a good-humoured man and scarce lusty. He will not trouble her if she does not wish it. Besides, she requires Douglas support. Without our backing the Earl Robert would quickly bring her down — as she knows full well. She will do what we say."

"I wish you well in the telling her, my lord! She is a Stewart, remember!"

"Ah — that will come better from her aunt! My wife, another Stewart, should be telling her even now! And making the position clear, I hope."

For a little there was silence. "What does Edmonstone get out of this?" Jamie asked, at last, dull voiced.

"Why, some enhancement of standing, wed to the King's daughter. Certain further lands from myself, to aid him in his extra expense. And the castle and barony of Tulliallan, in Perthshire, from Archie. Though this is partly to have his support in his claim to the earldom of Douglas."

"I see. All is thought of. Save for the Lady Isabel's desires! And myself, to be sure. What of me, sir, in all this?"

"You, lad, will be much advantaged. Once she is wed, the talk will cease. You will see. And the Earl Robert will have less cause to judge you as in his road. Which is important, Jamie — whatever *you* think. You are too young to be making an enemy of the most powerful man in the land."

"I was not too young to fight my good Lord James's enemies, by his side. At Otterburn. I shall not cease to fight them because he was murdered."

"Vengeance, lad—there speaks the voice of vengeance. Too expensive and too dangerous a voice for an eighteen-year-old in this Scotland! Forget the past and Earl James Douglas, my boy — and think of the future of Sir James Douglas of Aberdour! That is a father's counsel — and command!"

"Yes, sir." Jamie rose. "Have I your lordship's permission to retire?"

"Aye." His father sighed. "Go, then. But ... God give you a head as well as a heart, lad. Go use it, of a mercy!"

Jamie went straight to his own bedchamber. He had no wish to have to speak with Isabel Stewart, or anyone else, that night. His mind in a turmoil of conflicting emotions, he lay on his bed and stared up at the four-poster's canopy for hours before he slept.

* * *

In the morning, when the Lady Isabel came down to break her fast, he found that he just dared not meet her eyes. And yet she seemed almost as though nothing had happened, a little thoughtful perhaps but cheerful enough and still apparently on good terms with her host and hostess. It was as though nothing important had been decided and she, at least, had not had anything like a disturbed night.

Jamie did not see her alone until nearly noon, when the chill November rain ceased and they might walk down to the Eskside in the watery sunlight. He blurted it out as soon as they were out of hearing of the others.

"This, this of marriage, Isabel! This folly, this impertinence! What is to be done? And John Edmonstone — that clod! What is to be done?"

"Why, marry the man, Jamie! What else?" she replied, shrugging. "I have little choice in the matter, it seems."

"But ... but ..." He stared at her. "You would *do* it? Wed Edmonstone?"

"Why, yes — if I needs must. There are many men I'd sooner *not* marry than Sir John, if marriage it is to be. And it seems to be necessary. I have feared this must come, for some time. Princesses must have husbands, they tell me — and husbands who are not over-ambitious for power and who will not embarrass the Crown. Sir John Edmonstone fulfils these requirements. And he is a civil enough man, genial, kindly they say, well thought of . . ."

"But he is a drunken boor. Lives only for his hounds and his hawks and his flagons!"

"So much the better for me! I have learned that the best virtues in a husband are such as bespeak the least trouble for the wife! I do not seek, and shall not find, another Lord James. You, dear Jamie, had you been but ten years older . . .!" She took his arm and squeezed it. "But, alas—ifs and buts will serve me nothing. I must have a husband of name, lands and substance, to protect my *own* name and substance. If I can gain such a one who will not trouble me unduly, then I am fortunate. Or so I am assured!"

Jamie bit his lip. She kept her hand on his arm.

"I understand that Edmonstone Castle is not strong but comfortable — and in need of a woman's hand. A bare three miles from here, so we shall be close neighbours. And Douglas will continue to support my cause."

He could not bring himself to look at her, despite the pressure on his arm, for disappointment in her. Somehow she seemed to have failed him, become less than herself, less than the mistress he had delighted to serve, the Princess-Countess. Johnnie Edmonstone . . .!

"And myself?" he got out, looking away across the river. "What becomes of me? You will need *me* no more, I think. And James Douglas will never serve John Edmonstone!"

"Jamie, my dear!" she cried, turning to throw her arms around him. "I will ever need you. You are my valiant knight — and must always remain so. If you will. Of course Sir James Douglas will never serve Sir John Edmonstone — you, knighted on the field as hero! Sir John will be but a husband, a *second* husband — you remain my true knight and friend, Jamie. I would not wed him were it to be otherwise — that I swear."

Glancing hastily around him to see that they were not observed, he managed to disentangle himself. "John Edmonstone may see it differently."

"John Edmonstone will heed my wishes — or do without Isabel Stewart as wife!"

"My father, likewise, may have other notions . . ."

He got no further regarding his sire's probable doubts, the drumming of hooves, many hooves, on the castle approach drowning his words. A hard-riding party of about fifty were beating across the parkland, to thunder over the drawbridge — a bridge Jamie had scarcely ever seen raised. A large Douglas banner, differenced with the white lion of Galloway, fluttered at their head.

"Archie the Grim!" he exclaimed. "The other marriage-maker! And in haste it would seem. Why, I wonder? Not wedding-bells, I warrant, to bring *that* one hot-foot, to Dalkeith."

By mutual consent they turned back to the castle postern.

It was not, indeed, any thought of weddings or reputations which had fetched the warrior Lord of Galloway from Linlithgow that day, but much more serious matters. He came to inform his friend and colleague Dalkeith that Alexander Stewart, Earl of Buchan and Lord of Badenoch, had at last elected to issue out of his Highland fastnesses, where he acted Justiciar and Lieutenant of the North, to take a hand in affairs of the South — and a high hand at that. They had all begun to forget Alexander the Wolf, something Scotland could never afford to do for long.

XII

THE FIRST THEY knew of the trouble, at Turnberry, was the actual clamour at the castle-gatehouse just at daybreak of a dull November morning. The Earl of Carrick was still at his devotions, with his wife and children, in the castle chapel when Pate Boyd, the steward, came urgently. It was perhaps significant that it was not to the Earl his master that Boyd tiptoed but to young David Stewart, kneeling at the end of the line before the candle-lit altar.

"My lord," he whispered hoarsely. "Visitors. Fell strange visitors. Seeking entry."

"Visitors? At this hour?" David did not trouble to lower his musical voice, despite the priest's intonations. "What insolence is this? Who comes to the High Steward's door before sunrise? Tell them to be off, before they are taught better manners."

"I canna do that, lord — I canna. It is my lord Earl o' Buchan, he says. Your lordship's ain uncle." Boyd looked over towards the Earl John, who, head bent, was either too deep in his devotions to hear or preferred not to do so.

"Buchan! My Uncle Alex? The Wolf!" The boy stared. "God be good — what brings *him* here? From his Hielands. You are sure, man? It is not some impostor . . .?"

"He shouted it loud enough, my lord — right lordly and strang. And a wild pack wi' him, Hielantmen a', by the looks o' them. He'd have me to lower the drawbridge there and then, and no' keep him waiting. But I didna. I said I maun needs ask . . ."

The youngster rose from his faldstool, and caught his mother's eye on him. He smiled to her, with a small wave of his hand, reassuring, assured, strangely so to come from one so youthful. He turned and went out with the steward, while the priest's voice droned on uninterrupted.

"Why, in God's name were we not informed, man?" David demanded, once clear of the chapel. "None should be able to approach Turnberry unannounced. Even my uncles. They must have been seen coming here. Someone will suffer for this!"

"Aye, my lord — but it's my notion that they have come frae the beach. Come by sea. There isna a horse amongst them."

"Sakes — the sea! Uncle Alex! Well, now. And with a pack of Hielandmen, you say? This is . . . peculiar." David paused. "Pate — send a man up to the topmost tower. All the shore can be seen from there. See if there are boats, ships — galleys perhaps. It will be well to know."

"Yes, lord. But — what can it mean?"

"We shall see. But, if Uncle Alex comes visiting, he might well choose to come by sea. From his Lochaber, down through the Isles. And none would know. Which might be his desire . . ."

They came to the gate-house and David Stewart slowed his pace to stroll out unhurriedly on to the parapet wall-walk. Before him, across the water-filled moat, in the thin drizzle of chill rain off the Firth of Clyde, a crowd of men stood waiting, huddled in wet plaids and cloaks, a strangely silent, watching, menacing throng, strange in their ragged tartan clothing, their curious wary

193

tense-seeming stance, their absolute quiet, and the fact that two splendid banners flapped above them damply in the blustery westerly breeze, both gold and blue, one showing the fesse checky of Stewart, the other the yellow sheaves on azure of the earldom of Buchan.

The boy had hardly shown himself, with Boyd, before a tall figure stepped out from the crowd, wrapped in a plaid like the rest but different from all others in the long, silver-gilt shoulder-length hair of his bare head, as in his commanding presence, a spectacularly handsome, splendidly-made man in his early forties. He raised his powerful voice.

"Where is the Earl of Carrick?" he demanded. "My brother. I sent for him. Lower this drawbridge. I have stood waiting here over-long already. Down with it, I say. I am Buchan."

"Ha, Uncle — and I am David Stewart, your nephew. My father, the High Steward, is at his devotions. As is suitable at this hour. No doubt he will welcome you anon. Meantime it falls to me to do so, all unworthily. Thus early in the day!"

"Then let us in, boy. Get the bridge down. I am not used to standing at doors."

"To be sure. It will take only a little time . . . when I have given the order."

"Saints of mercy — then give it, sirrah!"

"Oh indeed yes, my lord of Buchan. If you *are* my lord of Buchan! We have not met, have we? You are ever in your far Highlands, I have heard tell. You must agree, sir, that I have to be sure that it is my father's brother who comes chapping unannounced at our door before sun-up of a winter's morning. Before I open up. The merest precaution — like the swords I perceive beneath your company's cloaks. How do I know that you are the Earl of Buchan, sir? It is an odd hour for visiting, is it not?"

"God's blood, boy — have you taken leave of your wits? Or have you none? Would any man in my father's realm *say* that he was Buchan if he was not?"

"As to that, sir, I know not. Men have strange ambitions. But no doubt you can think of some means to identify yourself, to my satisfaction?"

"*Your* satisfaction!" Suddenly and surprisingly the big man down there burst into loud laughter, slapping his thigh — and in so doing revealing that he was clad in chain-mail under the enveloping plaid. "Lord save us — your satisfaction!" he shouted. "Boy, I like you — on my soul I do! But this of identity — you scarce sound like your father's son. My brother Hirpling Johnnie Stewart's brat!"

Boyd at David's shoulder, was speaking now, low-voiced. "Six Hielant galleys beached on the boat-strand, my lord. Big boats," he reported. "More men, forby. Hundreds. Hech, hech — had we no' better lower the brig? You canna keep yon one out . . ."

"Not him, perhaps, but *them*!" The boy clenched his slender fists, but the features he turned back towards the visitors were as sunny as ever. "I rejoice that I find favour in your eyes, sir," he called. "But I shall still require my father's permission before I may lower the drawbridge. Far be it from me, however, to keep my uncle standing in the rain — if such you are. Will you come round to a small postern we have in the wall, where but one at a time may enter? The Sea Gate we call it. Just yourself my lord. And I can take you to my father."

"The Fiend take you — no, I will not! Alexander Stewart does not go creeping to back doors like some whipped cur! Damnation, boy — I was *born* in this house. Enough of this, I say. I have come to see my royal father, the King's Grace, who I hear is held here. Would you, or any, dare stand between me and the King, you insolent cockerel?"

"There are orders for the protection of His Grace's person, sir. You would not have it otherwise, I swear? I will go . . ." David Stewart paused as a shuffling step sounded at his back, and turned to find his father peering anxiously past him down the bridge-end.

"Och, Alex — it's yourself," the High Steward of Scotland said. "Man, man — it's you? Here's a surprise — a right surprise. Alexander, by all that's wonderful . . ."

"Alexander perished with the cold and needing his breakfast, Johnnie," the other gave back. "That brat of yours will not have me inside. Does not know his own uncle when he sees him. Have down this bridge and let me in, a God's name! I've come to see you. And my father."

"Yes, yes, Alex — to be sure. Boyd, man — have the bridge down and the portcullis up. We must not keep my lord of Buchan waiting."

"Father," David said urgently, beneath his breath. "Have a

195

care. He has a large force of Highlandmen with him, come secretly by sea. We do not want all that rabble of savages in here."

"Nonsense, Davie — we cannot keep my brother out. We cannot keep him from seeing the King."

"Bring him in at the Sea Gate, then. Alone . . ."

"No, no. Not my own brother, Davie. That would not do. Alex is none so ill as he's named. Boyd—let down the bridge, I say."

And so the Wolf of Badenoch strode into Turnberry Castle, a vigorous, commanding figure, all large laughter and bonhomie now, although his fine but curiously colourless grey eyes glittered with other than benign good-nature. And in behind him flooded his Highlanders, silent, wary and armed to the teeth.

Slapping John of Carrick on the back to the extent almost of knocking him over, his brother was loud in greeting. When he turned to his nephew he appeared to have forgotten all offence and patted the fair head, not altogether unlike his own, with avuncular approval, declaring that here was a fine spirited gallant who would one day, God willing, make a fine spirited king. And when, presently, he came into the presence of the Countess Annabella he was polished gallantry itself, bowing, kissing her on both cheeks, admiring with frankly masculine appreciation whilst retaining her hand in his own. As for the Lady Gelis, just down from her bedchamber, he took her in his arms and kissed her comprehensively lingering on her lips in no mere brotherly salute and then letting a knowledgeable hand stray over her bosom speculatively. Alexander Stewart it seemed, loved them all and bore no grudges.

He shared breakfast with them, in a small chamber off the hall, while his multitudinous followers were being fed in the main apartment — and being eyed askance by the castle retainers. Since the former spoke only the Gaelic, there was no communication between the brothers' entourages; indeed most obvious mutual suspicion. But Alexander made up for any stiff uneasiness, even if John did not, being excellent company, affable and amusing.

"Now to our respected but burdensome parent, Johnnie," he announced, when he rose from the table.

"Eh? Och, Alex, he'll scarce be awakened yet. It's early enough for an old, sick man . . ."

"Tush — he has nothing to do but lie in his bed all day, has he, man? Unlike myself. And you, to be sure. As well now as later. I am in something of haste to be on my way, see you. Much as I would wish to linger in such peerless company."

"You ... you are not biding then, Alex? You are for off again ...?" His brother quite failed to disguise the relief in his voice.

"I fear so. This is but a call in passing, as it were. I am apt to have much to see to when I venture out of my northern fastnesses, Johnnie. I cannot let my business wait overlong on an old bed-ridden man's sleep."

"He is your monarch, as he is mine!" the elder brother reproved, although less than decisively.

"So he is, on my soul — so he is! So I'll up and pay my best respects, without further delay. Lead the way, nephew."

"You do not wish to trouble him with, with papers and the like?" Carrick put to him unhappily, eyeing his womenfolk.

"Papers? God — no! I leave papers and the like to Robert." Alexander hooted a laugh. "I heard how you had cheated Robert of his precious paper about the parliament. A notable ploy — excellent. Now — I'll see my father." That was crisp.

The other shrugged. "Davie ..."

They climbed the winding turnpike stair in file, with young David well ahead, his uncle close behind and then a lengthy gap before the slower limping and panting heir to the throne, followed by his wife and sister. At the King's lofty quarters, the Earl of Buchan entered the ante-room, swept aside the protesting friar and clerk and marched straight into the royal bedchamber without so much as a knock, like a gust of sea breeze.

"Ha, Sire! Father — here is your prodigal!" he called out loudly. "Awake, awake — here's no occasion for sleeping. It is not every day that you see your son Alex, Your Grace of Scotland!"

"Eh? Eh?" The monarch peered up from the bed in alarm. "Guidsakes, guidsakes ... is it ... is it yourself, Alex? It's Alex, is it? I canna, I canna see right ..."

"To be sure it's Alex. Your favourite son, is it not? Come all the way from Badenoch to see you. God — it's hot in here."

"Alex — aye, it's yourself. I can hear it's you." The old man reached out a trembling hand — and touched a cold chain-mail sleeve. "Och, guidsakes — what's this? What's this, Alex? Mail, aye link-mail. You're, you're clad for war, Alex! What's this, eh?"

"I came by sea, Sire. From far Lochaber. And when a man sails your western seas, by the powers, he does well to wear mail, with your grandson Donald of the Isles around! You should keep him in better order, I say. Or let me do so!"

"Och, Alex — he's headstrong. Like yourself, mind — aye, like yourself. And I canna do all I'd like. I'm no' well, lad — no well . . ."

"We'll get you better, never fear. That is why I am here."

"Eh? Na, na, lad — there's no betterment for me, I fear. It's ower late for that, Alex. My days are numbered. Numbered, aye . . ."

"All our days are numbered, Father — even mine. But you'll have many yet, I wager. I'll see to it. I've come to take you in hand. Over-much lying abed and sleeping. We will have you on your feet again — the King of Scots! Never fear, Sire."

Something like a sob came from the bed.

A quiet voice spoke from behind. "What mean you, my lord? When you say that you have come to take His Grace in hand?" That was the Countess Annabella, who with the others now stood near the foot of the bed.

"Just what I say, my dear good-sister. My father needs a change. Of air and of company. He has had too much of women's cosseting, too much of being treated as though he was a-dying! You mean him well — but he is being coddled into his grave! I have come to take him into my care, for a while. And he will do the better, I swear."

"No! You cannot do that. It is out of the question."

"Alex — you'll not mean it? You jest, cozzen us . . .?" his brother gasped.

The other ignored them. "Sire — come with me to Rothesay. To your own house there. You ever liked the place. Away from women's pampering for a space — lest they smother you in their too-kind thralldom. You are the King — a man! With a realm to rule. We'll make a man of you again. At Rothesay."

The monarch had crept further, deeper, into the bed-clothes. He was staring up in horror, shaking his white head wordlessly.

"Alex — do not be a fool!" the Lady Gelis exclaimed. "Are you mad? Father is sick. And of great age . . ."

"Are you coming, Sire? With Alex. A change from Johnnie."

"No-o-o!" That was a wail, quavering, agonised.

"I say that you are!" His son bent swiftly to grasp the old man, bed-linen and all, and snatch him up in strong arms. King Robert had been a large man himself, and was still no light-weight; but Alexander Stewart was strong, six feet three inches in height and powerfully built. Bundling his parent in the blanketing, he swung around. "Out of my way!" he cried, and marched for the door.

Although Carrick held out imploring hands to stop him and the two women stood in his way, Buchan pushed past them all unheeding. Only young David Stewart actually sought physically to halt him, hurling himself bodily at his striding, burdened uncle, to try to bring him down by grasping him about the legs. The other raised knee and foot and lashed out, kicking the boy violently across the floor to crash against the arras-hung stone walling, heavily. Reaching the door to the ante-room, he again raised foot to smash it open with his booted heel and so stamped through, past the gaping, hand-wringing clerk and friar.

"Open that door, fools!" he cried, and so authoritatively that the clerk hurried to do so even as he gabbled pleas and incoherencies.

Down the winding corkscrew stairway son and father descended, at anything but a careful pace.

The Ladies Annabella and Gelis were now at Alexander's heels, trying to halt him still. But there was little that they could do, in the circumstances, since they could not win past to get in front, and he ignored entirely their ineffective efforts at obstruction. Shaken and dizzy from his head's contact with the bedchamber wall, David only made up on them as his uncle reached the hall doorway — and the hall of course was full of the Highlanders, who came to crowd round their striding master at once, precluding any rescue attempt.

Not yielding up his precious burden to any, Alexander Stewart pushed on, within his circle of now grinning clansmen, across the hall and out into the courtyard, making for the gatehouse-pend; and though many of Carrick's servitors and retainers stared in amazement, none was so bold as to seek to interfere — even when young David's voice rang out in urgent command. The Highlanders now produced naked dirks from under their plaiding.

Out they swept, unimpeded, through the gatehouse-passage, over the echoing drawbridge timbers and off down the wet slippery track to the beach and the waiting galleys. If the King of Scots protested, it was from under smothering blankets.

The Wolf of Badenoch seldom left his upland fastnesses for purely social occasions.

II

XIII

THE GREAT ABBEY-CHURCH of Holyrood was packed to the
doors, and the noise emanating therefrom could be heard
even at the foot of Edinburgh's Canongate and no little way
up the steep green slopes of Arthur's Seat to the south — which
would scarcely please the mitred Abbot. It was an odd situation,
really, for more than the Abbot and his monks; for parliaments in
Scotland were not usually attended by hundreds; indeed seventy
or eighty was normally considered a good turn-out. But here was a
rather special parliament, this April noontide of 1389. It was the
first for many a long day, and called in highly significant, not to
say irregular, and dramatic circumstances; it was only very doubtfully constitutional, since it did not, in the end, have the King's
written authority as summons; and it was being held, unusually,
here in Lothian, for the very good reason that the Earl Robert did
not dare hold it anywhere further north or west — for here, where
Douglas influence was paramount, he could rely on sufficient security, a highly important matter, with his brother Alexander
south of the Highland Line. Edinburgh town was as full of
Douglas minions and supporters this day as was the Abbey itself of
their betters. Archie the Grim had seen to that. Moreover, the
occasion was abnormal, and the church packed, because for the
same security reasons, not only the parliament's members were
present but hundreds of spectators also, something new in procedure. If a high proportion of these onlookers were named
Douglas, that was only to be expected in Lothian — and of course
they had no voice nor say in the debates or votes, however much
noise they made at this preliminary stage. But at least they ensured

that few others would interrupt and perhaps seek to dominate the proceedings. It had been a bitter decision for the Earl of Fife to take; but confronted with the situation engineered by the Earl Alexander of Buchan, he had little choice.

Jamie Douglas had an excellent position and viewpoint, sitting beside the Lady Isabel Edmonstone — although she never called herself that — and her husband, in the high clerestory gallery on the south side, where the April sunlight shone in warmly from above the crags of Arthur's Seat in dancing mote-clouds. The smell of humanity was very strong. Annabella Countess of Carrick, now recovered from an unfortunate miscarriage, and her son the Lord David Stewart, sat nearby; also the Lady Gelis, the Lady Marjorie of Moray, the Countess of Mar, the Countess of Angus and the young Earl George, and other notables linked with the royal house. Below, in the chancel, the members of the parliament itself sat or stood — for there were insufficient stalls for all — and there sundry familiar figures could be picked out, such as Jamie's father, Sir James Lindsay of Crawford, Sir John Montgomerie of Eaglesham, Sir Will Douglas of Nithsdale and many another Douglas, Sir Malcolm Drummon of Stobhall, Sir Walter Scott of Buccleuch and so on, amongst all the bishops, mitred abbots, lords of parliament, sheriffs and representatives of royal burghs. The nave of the church was full of the less privileged onlookers, standing close as herrings packed in a barrel.

Sir John Edmonstone, not a commissioner of parliament, a big, burly red-faced man whose bullish manner was redeemed by a simple almost childlike smile — though this could deteriorate into a braying laugh — was trying to identify all the commissioners below and decide who were in the Earl Robert's pocket, who in Archie Douglas's and who might vote against both. He was not very good at it, lacking insight and judgment. Often he irritated Jamie — and no doubt his new wife more so — but basically they all got on a lot better than the younger man had anticipated. He had misjudged the man, indeed, for he was in truth honest, good-hearted, even-tempered and undemanding. Also predictable, which can be a help. He now declared loudly that the churchmen were the doubtful entity — one could never be sure of clerks, slippery as eels. Save that few of *them* would be apt to be in the Wolf's camp, at least . . .

A trumpet-flourish quelled these assessments, like the noise generally, and the earls of Scotland filed into the chancel to take up their positions in the choir stalls. There were only five of them present, for there were gaps in the august total of fifteen meantime. Countesses in their own right, such as Mar, Athol and Lennox were represented by their nominees; minors such as Angus and Sutherland could not sit; and the royal brothers now accounted for five, Carrick, Fife and Menteith, Buchan and Strathearn — and David of Strathearn had died suddenly, in allegedly mysterious circumstances, only two months before, leaving a daughter of ten years. So, since Alexander of Buchan was not honouring this assembly with his presence, and Henry of Caithness—who was also Earl of Orkney and considered himself a Norseman — did not deign to attend, there were represented only Dunbar and March, his brother Moray, Ross — who was the Earl Robert's son-in-law, and Carrick. This last's role as heir to the throne being unprovided for in parliament, he sat merely as senior earl — but his modest, limping entry was quite overshadowed by the simultaneous arrival of a resplendent figure in full Highland panoply, who drew all eyes and considerable exclamation, Donald, Lord of the Isles, son of the King's eldest daughter Margaret. The Earl Robert's success in coaxing this almost legendary potentate to his parliament preoccupied all present, and most were still talking about it when another trumpet-blast heralded the appearance of Master John Peebles, Bishop of Dunkeld, Chancellor of the realm, in richest episcopal canonicals, with behind him the sober spare figure of Robert, Earl of Fife and Mentieth. At the same time, by a side-door, Archie of Galloway slipped into his place as a lord of parliament, lower in the chancel.

The Chancellor, bowing to all, took his seat in the throne-like chair behind the table set before the high altar, Earl Robert positioning himself on a bench a little way aside, but facing the assembly. It was the Scots usage for the monarch to preside in person over his parliaments, taking a full part in the debates, the King in Parliament being no idle formula. When he was not present, the Chancellor was in procedural charge; otherwise he acted as something between secretary and working chairman. Peebles was a big, old stooping man, thin-bearded, with an unctuous voice but shrewd little eyes. He now raised all to their feet, opened with a brief Latin prayer, waved all to their seats again but remained standing himself, and went on, almost without pause and in the same sing-song voice, to announce that by God's will and the King's royal authority, this ninth parliament of the reign, duly called and constituted, was hereby in session.

A voice from the back of the nave interrupted him to declare that it was not duly called but most unduly, and indeed was no true parliament.

Amidst the general stir and exclamation, the Bishop went on unmoved, as though he had not heard, not so much as raising his eyes from his papers on the table. He read out that their business, of grave import for the realm, had been much delayed by ill-disposed persons interfering in the due processes of summons, and in especial seeking to influence and counter His Grace the King's royal will in the matter. It would be most necessary for parliament to take the necessary steps to ensure that such infamous, indeed treasonable, activities were nullified, brought to an end and their perpetrators duly punished.

Dead silence greeted this announcement. Some eyes were raised towards the royal ladies in the clerestory gallery, nobody looked at the Earl of Carrick, and most present were carefully non-committal. The Wolf of Badenoch might not be present, but he cast a long shadow, and none knew for sure who might be in his pay and service.

The Bishop went on. "My lords and commissioners — before proceeding to the general business of this parliament, it is entirely necessary that His Grace's expressed will relating to the rule and governance of his realm be made effective, belated as this must be. The King's Grace has nominated and appointed to be Governor of the Realm, in his royal name, with all and full powers and authority so to rule, the Lord Robert Stewart, Earl of Fife and Menteith, Great Chamberlain of the kingdom and Chief Warden of the Marches. It falls to this parliament, the first assembled since the King's pronouncement — which I here hold in my hand, duly signed and dated the 8th day of September last — to confirm and homologate that royal will. Does any present so move?"

"I, Archibald of Galloway, so do." That was brief, but swift and clear from mid-chancel.

"And I, James of Dalkeith, second," Jamie's father added quietly.

A tremor of excitement ran through the great church, as everywhere men exchanged glances, smiled, grimaced or otherwise recognised realities as distinct from sentiments and prejudices. If the whole power of Douglas was being placed behind the Earl Robert, then parliament, like most of the rest of the realm, would not say otherwise — meantime. Up on the clerestory, however, a high and musical laugh rang out, mirthful, unconstrained but somehow shocking in those circumstances, drawing every gaze. The young Lord David Stewart of Carrick smiled down beatifically on all, and then glanced along the gallery to his left.

"You hear, Sir Jamie?" he called, clearly. "You hear?"

At the gasps from all, Bishop Peebles banged his gavel on the table. He opened his mouth, then shut it again almost with a click. Even the Chancellor could hardly shout 'silence' at the second heir to the throne, especially when his father sat there, head bent, unmoving. Instead, he cleared his throat and said hurriedly,

"The motion is moved and seconded. Is there any contrary motion?"

In the hush that followed, with many breaths held, Jamie stirred uncomfortably. "That was ill done," he muttered, to the Lady Isabel. "He is Satan itself, that boy! But then, it is *all* ill done, I say!" And he gestured down to the chancel below.

She shook her head. "I know not. We can but trust your father and Sir Archie. We must."

"You do that," her husband agreed.

Another voice was speaking down there, a voice which made all the others sound slightly harsh and jerky, speaking in the softly sibilant lilt of the West Highlands. "I, Donald, do not offer any contrary motion, my lord Bishop," the Lord of the Isles observed mildly. "I but make support of my grandsire's expressed will — so long as it is exercised for the weal and benefit of the realm in *all* its parts and peoples. Which exercise it will be my concern and duty to see carried out hereafter, whatever — as the good God is my witness!"

That also set tongues wagging and heads nodding. If Donald of the Isles, almost an independent prince who practically controlled the entire West Highland seaboard and the Hebrides, like Douglas, supported the Earl Robert, then any opposition was going to be cramped and limited indeed. It escaped the recognition of few that all the Wolf's great territories of Lochaber, Badenoch and Highland Moray were flanked by those controlled by Donald of the Isles. Yet the soft-spoken Highlander, who so seldom interested himself or intervened in Lowland affairs, was giving plainest notice that his support was conditional on his own interests being served, and that he could and would withdraw it at will.

The Chancellor coughed. "I, ah, thank you, my lord," he said, a little doubtfully. He glanced sidelong, quickly, at the Earl Robert, as though for a cue. Receiving none from that stern-faced, ice-cold individual, he drew a hand over his mouth, and added, "I say again — is there any contrary motion to that proposed and seconded?"

If any had come prepared so to move, they could scarcely fail to recognise the inutility of anything such now. Any small and feeble vote would be worse than none at all. There was a heavy silence.

"Very well," the Bishop said, obviously relieved. "I declare that this parliament confirms the expressed will and command of the Lord King Robert in appointing the Earl Robert of Fife and Menteith as Lord Governor and Guardian of this realm of Scotland, during the King his pleasure. Let all men, high and low, heed, accept and note well, else at their peril." He turned, and bowed low to the Earl Robert, vacating his chair.

The other rose, nodded and stalked forward, to seat himself without hint of ceremony in the Bishop's place, pushing aside the papers on the table — the Chancellor hastily gathering these up and standing aside. There was no cheering, no demonstration of any sort, any more than on Fife's part. Undoubtedly few there felt what was done was any occasion for celebration.

Robert Stewart stared levelly out over the assembly for long moments. Then he jerked his head at the Chancellor. "Continue," he said, shortly, his first word spoken so far.

Peebles coughed again. "Yes, my lord Governor." One of his papers fluttered down at the far end of the table. He seemed less assured than heretofore. "Ah . . . the next business. Aye, the next business is that of the French treaty. His Grace of Scotland's compact with His Grace of France expired before Yule last. It should have been renewed, but required parliament's confirmation, likewise. Our King's letter might have served, but such was not sent — for reasons known to all. My lord Governor sent his own letter of intent. It is now required that this parliament should confirm full renewal of the treaty. It is suggested, for a period of three years. On the same terms. Such accord being necessary in order to ensure the mutual defence of both realms against the aggressive designs of the King of England. Is it agreed?"

"I so move," Walter Trail, Bishop of St. Andrews, the Primate, called.

"And I second," Sir James Lindsay added. "I have been lately tasting of English hospitality, and can confirm the need for education in that nation!"

There was a cheer for that, on all sides — the first sign of enthusiasm in the gathering.

The Chancellor took this as implying no contrary motion, and went on, "Further to this, His Grace of France has, in his good pleasure, newly concluded a truce with King Richard of England, in the hope that this will further limit the Plantagenet's war-like designs. None set great store by this, but King Charles did seek to have this realm of Scotland included in the truce, as good ally should. But King Richard would have none of it, and we are excluded. Wherefore my Lord Governor is minded to apply some persuasion." He looked up from his papers. "My lord of Galloway will speak to this."

Sir Archie rose. He was not much more of an orator than was the Earl Robert — and scowled the more blackly in consequence. "I have little to say," he jerked, resentfully. "Richard Plantagenet needs a lesson. Added to that we gave him at Lancaster and Otterburn. To bring him to sign a truce with us. He has newly appointed the Earl Marshal of England to be Chief Warden of the Marches. In place of Hotspur — who is still aiding Montgomerie build his new Polnoon Castle."

This drew a general laugh. It was an open secret that Sir Harry Percy's ransom money was being used to erect a handsome new fortalice at Eaglesham for his captor, Sir John Montgomerie; and that Hotspur was not to be released until the work was more or less complete.

"Richard has ordered his Earl Marshal to prosecute offensive warfare and rapine against our Borders with all vigour," Sir Archie went on, warming a little to his task. "Therefore, I say — and the Earl Robert says — let us strike first. This Marshal has taunted that he would meet us on any fair field, were our numbers twice his own. Let us show the Englishman, and his liege lord, that the Scots are better neighbours when seated at a treaty-table than when threatened with rapine and war! How say you?"

There was, of course, a great and continuing shout of acclaim. That sort of talk, however far short of eloquently delivered, could always be relied upon to arouse a Scots audience. But there was a questioner, nevertheless — the said Sir John Montgomerie, Lord of Eaglesham, when he could make himself heard,

"That would make better sense, Archie, if it was not broadcast to all the world in advance, here in this church," he observed conversationally. "Last time, we kept it secret, and took them by surprise. Now, I warrant their Earl Marshal will know of this in two days' time. And take steps."

There was some murmuring of agreement from the older compaigners.

"Let him," Galloway declared. "That will serve us well enough, Johnnie. So we considered. We have heard that he plans an attack on Annandale. This news will perhaps make him less eager to attack meantime. To look to his defences, rather. He cannot know when we will come, nor where. Let him sweat over it, I say!"

That was accepted. No vote was required to confirm this strategy.

"My lord Governor," Chancellor Peebles resumed, "further to this matter, if it is necessary to assemble large numbers of men-in-arms, then certain steps will require to be taken to aid in it. As all will recognise. Foremost, there is the matter of the earldom of Douglas. That earldom can, and should, field a greater number of men than any other. But at present owing to the lamented death of the late and noble Earl James, it stands in disarray. It is, moreover, right and proper for the weal of the realm, that this issue of the earldom be resolved. It is a matter for this high court of parliament. The Earl James of Douglas left no direct heir. It falls for a new earl to be appointed with His Grace's royal consent — as exercised by the Lord Governor — and with the agreement of this parliament. And, to be sure, that of the House of Douglas itself. Who will speak to this matter?"

"I will." Sir James of Dalkeith rose. "And I speak, not only for myself but for all of the name of Douglas. We declare, represent and advise that Sir Archibald Douglas, Lord of Galloway, heir of entail of the earldom lands, should forthwith be appointed, accepted and confirmed as 3rd Earl of Douglas, in the room of the late Earl James, of noble memory."

"This I support . . ." Sir William of Mordington, as nominee in the parliament for the young Earl of Angus, jumped up to second; but his voice was drowned in the great shout of agreement from the ranks of Douglas present, both members of the parliament and spectators. The applause went on for some time, the Chancellor making no attempt to halt it. Earl Robert sat inscrutable.

When it could do so and be heard, a single voice was upraised. "I demur, my lords," Sir Malcolm Drummond of Stobhall cried. "I do demur. My lord Chancellor, you erred when you said that the Earl James left no direct heir. No direct male heir, perhaps. But he left a lawful sister, the Countess of Mar, who is my wife. In her name I demur. She is the rightful Countess of Douglas. When the Earl William, of Douglas and Mar, died, she heired his earldom of Mar. Now that her brother the Earl of Douglas has died, leaving no lawful child, she heirs this earldom also. So I claim, my lord Chancellor."

"H'mm." Peebles cast a quick glance at the Earl Robert. "Does, does any support that claim?"

"I protest!" Sir Archibald of Galloway exclaimed, rising. "No woman shall lead Douglas! This is understood. It has all been considered. God's eyes — will your wife take ten thousand Douglas lances into battle, man?"

"The Countess can appoint her captain to do that, my lord."

"*You*, Drummond? You?" That was a snort. "Think you one single Douglas blade would follow you to war!"

"Damn you, Douglas . . ."

"My lords, my lords!" the Chancellor quavered. "Of a mercy — address the Throne, the Lord Governor, I'd mind you. I bid you to curb your tongues."

Dalkeith rose, pressing Sir Archie down to his seat, probably the only man in the realm who might do so. "My lord Governor — permit me to intervene," he said, quietly, soothingly. "There are, I submit, two points relevant to Sir Malcom Drummond's claim. One is that while an only female child may be accepted as heiress to an earldom — as is not infrequently the case — a *sister* is in a different case. There is no such ruling. It *could* be so, lacking a better claim. But in this instance there *is* a better claim. As has been said, the earldom of Douglas fields the largest fighting force of any in this land, and it is only suitable that a man, and a soldier, should control it. Such was foreseen by the Earl William himself, the Earl James's father, who forty years ago entailed the earldom lands on Sir Archibald as next heir to Earl James and any lawful son of his. This, to ensure proper and strong rule of the earldom. I myself, my lords, who might have claimed the earldom, I accept that decision of the Earl William, and with-draw any claim, in favour of the Lord of Galloway."

Loud and prolonged Douglas applause, and angry gestures towards Drummond, left that man in no doubt as to how any vote would go. He must have known all along, of course; and therefore was only making this demand as a formality, or for other advantage or bargaining power.

"My claim, on behalf of my wife, stands," he said, with some dignity, and sat down.

"Do you wish it put to the vote, my lord?"

"Since that would be without effect — no."

"Very well. I declare that this parliament accepts and confirms Sir Archibald, Lord of Galloway, in the earldom of Douglas — which lord now to step forward before all."

Sir Archie, puffing and snorting in his own sort of embarrassment, rose and came stamping up the steps to the table before the altar, amidst loud plaudits. He could be seen to be carrying in one hand a clearly heavy weight that gleamed brightly golden. Coming to the side of the table he halted, and bobbed his grizzled head — he was never much of a man for bowing. Then he held out his golden burden to the Earl Robert, who rising, took it — and required both hands to hold it. Even then it part-fell to the table with the weight, unrolling, and proved to be a magnificently-wrought massive shoulder-belt of close-linked golden chain. This, after a little awkward fumbling, the Governor managed to put over his friend's head and one shoulder, where it hung down on the left side, the recipient half-crouching his great height to facilitate the business. He had never looked grimmer.

"In the name of the King's Grace, I belt you earl," Fife said levelly, thinly. "Stand, Archibald, Earl of Douglas."

Straightening up, the other nodded again, looking as though he might speak, changed his mind, and turning, stamped down the steps again — although this time he made for the earls' stalls not to his own former seat. Less ceremony and display could scarcely have been shown by either principal. Yet nothing more significant had taken place in Scotland for long.

But if Archie the Grim was no play-actor he quickly demonstrated that he was far from averse to action of a more practical nature. No sooner had he sat down, next to the Earl of Moray, than he was on his feet again, whipping off the golden earl's belt and tossing it aside.

"My lord Governor," he grated, "I, Archibald, Earl of Douglas, do declare and inform that Sir Malcolm Drummond of Stobhall, in the name of his wife, Isobel, Countess of Mar, has wrongfully and unlawfully taken possession of certain lands belonging to my earldom — to wit, the northern parts of the Forest of Ettrick — these three months past, and moreover takes and holds the revenues and rents thereof, contrary to all right and custom. These lands have long been part of the entailed property of the earldom of Douglas. I demand his, and her, immediate ejection therefrom, compensation and restoration of revenues to be made. Moreover censure to be passed on the said Malcolm by this parliament." He sat down, amidst uproar.

What the Chancellor could not thereafter achieve in the way of order and silence, young David Stewart, up in the gallery, did without apparent effort. His silvery laughter, high enough to be heard above all, rang out again, with its own dramatic effect.

"My poor Uncle Malcolm!" the boy cried, in mock sympathy. "Fallen amongst thieves, Border thieves! Seek you a Samaritan speedily, Uncle! I suggest my other uncle, Alexander of Buchan!"

Appalled, alarmed, outraged or merely intrigued, the company stared — all save the Earls of Carrick and Fife. In the ensuing hush, the latter tapped the table with one knuckle, a small sound but somehow more pregnant with meaning than the Chancellor's gavel; and the former sank his greying head between his hands, shoulders hunched.

Drummond, biting his lip, rose. "My lord Chancellor," he said, "my wife took possession of those lands in token. Token of her claim to the earldom — which I have here put forward. As was surely just. No single oxgate of land has been given or offered to her out of the vast lands of Douglas. She, the only lawful close kin to the late Earl. His bastards have received the great properties of

213

Drumlanrig and Cavers. It is inconceivable that his sister and true heiress should receive nothing. So this land at Ettrick was taken in token. Will you censure her for that?"

Peebles coughed. "In that these lands are entailed in the earldom, yes," he answered. "This was meet and proper for censure. Some, some other lands might have been chosen."

Dalkeith stood, and quickly, ever the smoother of the way. "My lords — the Chancellor is right. Some other lands *should* have been chosen. For this token. It is true, as Sir Malcolm declares, that the Countess of Mar should not be denied some due portion of her brother's lands and wealth. But there are other lands, more personally held. I say that some such may be decided upon, for transfer to the Countess — some suitable lands. I offer my word upon it. And, I make sure, the new and noble Earl of Douglas will concede likewise." He looked hard at Archie. "That this issue may be equitably resolved."

Drummond and the new Earl glared at each other. Then the former inclined his head. "I accept my lord of Dalkeith's undertaking. In the name of my wife," he said. Undoubtedly this was what his hopeless claim to the earldom had been made for.

Earl Archibald frowned, but shrugged. "So be it — so long as censure is passed on this ill deed." As an afterthought, he added, "That the King's law be upheld."

Relievedly the Chancellor nodded vigorously. "The law, yes. The law. In that this was contrary to law, it is most meet for censure. This parliament must indeed pass censure. I so declare. No need for further debate. May we proceed to the next business, my lord Governor?"

A curt nod from the throne.

"Yes, then." The Bishop made great play with his papers. "We now come to a more grave and lamentable matter, my lords. As must be known to you all, a notable and heinous wrong has been perpetrated in the realm, in that our liege lord King Robert's royal presence has been rudely invaded and his sacred person seized upon and apprehended. By . . . by persons of note. Who, I say, ought to know better, my lords. His Grace even now is in a state little short of captivity, to the shame of this his kingdom, parliament and people. It is entirely necessary that due steps be taken to right this great wrong, relieve our liege's unhappy situation, and, deal with the offenders." That came out in something of a spate. The Bishop, in an unenviable situation himself, looked up. "The Lord Walter of Brechin to speak to this."

The stir aroused by this ominous challenge was enhanced as everywhere men peered about them looking for the King's youngest son, whose presence in the church was not obvious. No sign of any response to the summons to speak was forthcoming.

Boyish laughter from the gallery *was* forthcoming however, once more. "Seek the nearest whorehouse!" the Lord David advised blithely.

Unhappily the Chancellor looked at the Earl Robert.

That man smoothed a hand over tight mouth. "Call on the Earl of Carrick," he said.

"Ah, yes. My lord Earl of Carrick — will you speak to this matter of the seizure and holding of your royal father, the King's Grace?"

The Earl John raised a protesting, trembling hand. "No! No, I will not!" he got out. "I cannot. Not me. I . . . I cannot condemn in others . . . what I myself have done. God pity me — I cannot!" And jumping up from his stall, he turned and stumbled over to the vestry door, and out.

Up in the gallery the Countess Annabella rose quietly and made for the nearest stairway, while her son raised his all too clear voice helpfully.

"Uncle Robert — you must needs do your own dirk-work your own self, for once."

There were moments of tense silence. The Lord David had, as was quite usual, exactly the rights of it, of course. In any move to condemn and take parliamentary action against one of the King's sons, none who was not himself a prince of the blood could dare take the initiative. Alexander the Wolf still held the King bedbound prisoner in Rothesay Castle, issuing threats and defying his brother Robert and all who might support him. He was demanding, in his father's name, all sorts of appointments, privileges and powers. The Lord Walter, lined up for the task, had failed to appear. The Lord John had refused and was gone. The Lord David of Strathearn was dead. Which left only the Lord Robert himself, able to speak. That prince's reluctance to do so was self-evident. Robert Stewart always used others as mouthpiece and sword-hand both. Although every motion hitherto considered had been at his instigation and devising, all knew, he had not had to

215

enunciate or speak to any. Now he found himself in a corner, and his distaste was daunting to witness. Looking at none but considering his own fingertips, he spoke.

"A kingdom may lack a king, but must still be governed. His Grace my royal father is sick, old — but still, under God, our sovereign lord. He has appointed me to govern, in his name. In despite of this, Alexander, Earl of Buchan has elected unlawfully to abduct and constrain His Grace, holding him fast and preventing him from signing papers, issuing writs and doing other needfuls for the governance of the realm. Such is treason." He paused, letting that dread word make its own impact. "Treason. And the penalty for treason, by whomsoever, is death."

There was a still longer and shocked pause, made nonetheless tense for the even, unemotional tone in which that had been enunciated. Not for long, not since the Baliol aftermath of the Ward of Independence, had anyone suffered death for treason in Scotland.

Robert Stewart leaned back in his chair, eyes upturned now to the stone-groined roof. "I am now Governor, appointed and confirmed, and require no longer His Grace's signature for any action of rule I may take. Let all note well. But I am a merciful man. And sensible that my brother's folly is more to blame than is his sin, for he was ever headstrong. Therefore, whilst I condemn his action as treason, I do not seek his death. This time." Another lengthy pause. "But penalty there must be. Sanctioned by this parliament. I declare that Alexander Earl of Buchan is no longer a fit person to be Lieutenant of the North and Justiciar North of Forth. I therefore pronounce his removal from these high offices under the Crown, and from all revenues and emoluments therefrom. And I nominate in his place the Lord Murdoch Stewart of Menteith, as one who may be trusted to sustain faithfully the duties and responsibilities of these offices. The Earl of Buchan to be seized and apprehended so soon as may be. And the King's Grace to be enlarged forthwith to the freedom of his own house of Dundonald, or wherever else he may elect." That was as lengthy a speech as anyone could recollect that man making.

The clipped cold voice was, as it were, bitten off sharply, and the speaker closed his eyes. Apart from chuckles from the gallery, none thought fit to comment.

"Thus . . . and thus!" David Stewart observed. Clearly he now considered himself to be the voice of the silent majority, a voice that none would find easy to silence. "This to be the way of things! And Cousin Murdoch is a ninny! Uncle Alex will eat him! Unless yonder Heilantman takes a hand? Eh, Cousin Donald?"

Despite themselves, everyone present had to admit the uncanny shrewdness of this precocious juvenile who one day should be their King David III. Mere spectator and with no right to raise his voice, he was yet holding a sort of balance in this charade of a parliament — and the only one who was. All eyes turned more or less involuntarily towards the large and colourful figure of Donald of the Isles — who smiled gently but held his peace meantime. All eyes save the Governor's that is, which remained closed.

When the lack of comment or reaction began to become embarrassing, the Chancellor recognised that his was the responsibility again. "My lords — we have heard the Lord Governor's decision and, h'm, merciful pronouncement, on this matter. Does any wish to speak to it?"

"Move acceptance," the Earl of Douglas jerked, shortly.

That should have been all there was to be said, in the circumstances, with Douglas and Stewart lined up together. But as young David had reminded them, there was a third and very relevant force to be considered here. It was all very well to talk of depriving the Wolf of Badenoch of his offices of Lieutenant and Justiciar of the North, virtual ruler of the entire North-East of Scotland; but quite impracticable to remove his power as such, whoever bore the titles, unless with the full and active cooperation of the man who ruled the North-*West* — Donald, Lord of the Isles, whose territories marched with the Wolf's for hundreds of wild and mountainous miles. That potent individual now rose to his impressive height.

"I do agree, my good lords, that my uncle the Earl of Buchan is sorely at fault in laying violent hands on my grandsire the King," he said, sighing sorrowfully and shaking a noble head — the jaw-line strength of which much belied the mild and gentle manner. "May I not suffer for so admitting? *Auribus teneo lupum!* But then, if you consider it, my friends — *homo homini lupus!*" he added, for further confusion. For this was no untutored if picturesque barbarian, as the Lowlanders were apt to name all Highlanders, but possibly the most highly-educated man in that assembly, the churchmen included, a graduate of the University of Cambridge, a poet of some renown, a historian, and with it all one of the greatest warriors in the land and certainly the most feared captain of galleys on the Western and Irish Seas — some would say pirate. "I would but remark that it is less difficult to condemn the Earl Alexander's activities than to enforce his better behaviour, see you. More than motions of parliament are necessary, whatever. Even when seconded by the most puissant Earl of Douglas."

The new earl scowled, but warily.

"The Lord Alexander, my uncle, hearing your lordships' strictures and threats in Rothesay Castle, has only to take one of the many galleys always moored at that quay, place His Grace of Scotland therein, and sail for one hour, to Cowal or two hours to Kintyre, from that Isle of Bute, and he is quite beyond your reach. Not beyond *my* reach, my lords — for these are in my domains. But beyond yours. Do you not agree? Thereafter he may travel by land, or in his galley if so he wills, up through the Suderies and Lorn to Loch Linnhe and his own lands of Lochaber and the North — where not only you, but I myself, may not touch him at all. You will take my point?"

None, not even the least knowledgeable in geography, failed to do so.

"So, my lord, you require Donald's aid in this matter. No? But to help you effectively, Donald also is requiring *your* aid, in some measure. North of Lochaber and the Great Glen is the large earldom of Ross, whose present lord, my cousin's husband, sits here. This earldom marches, all to north and west, with the Lord Alexander's northern territories. But . . . can it be used against him? My lord of Ross will forgive me if I say that he is scarce a soldier! Moreover, he is not even a Gael, a Highlander, being of the Lowland house of Leslie, whose father but *married* the Lady Euphemia, daughter of the last true Earl . . ."

Alexander Leslie, Earl of Ross, jumped to his feet. He was a mild young man, and no warrior indeed, but he could scarcely sit still under this attack, however genially framed.

"My lord Robert," he exclaimed, to his father-in-law, "I protest! The Lord of the Isles has no call to abuse me. I have done him no hurt . . ."

The Earl Robert pursed his thin lips, but said nothing.

"My good cousin — I do not abuse you," Donald assured,

almost kindly. "I but remind this parliament that to prosecute action, successful action, against your uncle, and mine, all powers in the North must be wielded, and wielded strongly. You, Cousin, are scarcely a wielder of the sword, and your earldom of Ross, which could be a bulwark against Badenoch and Lochaber and Braemoray, is not. I say that, meantime, it should be in more swordly hands — or part of it. For the realm's weal."

There was considerable indrawing of breaths.

Donald addressed himself to the chair again. "My Lord Robert, as you and all know, the late King David, for his own purposes, forfeited my kinsman, the last true Mac-an-t'Sagairt Earl of Ross, William, and bestowed the earldom on his *second* daughter, Euphemia, married to Leslie, ignoring the elder daughter, my wife Margaret. Which Countess Euphemia, her first husband dead, is now the wife of the same Earl Alexander of Buchan, although deserted by him. Her son, Alexander Leslie, my lords, sits here as Earl of Ross. I know naught to his disfavour — save that he lifts no hand against the Earl of Buchan. I, who I say *should* be acting Earl of Ross in the name of my wife, the elder sister, would do so, and could, since my lordship of the Isles makes one with much of the Ross territories. In especial Skye, which island was unjustly taken from my father and given to Ross and which the Countess Euphemia took as her portion on her second marriage, and is now ruled by Alexander of Buchan. The Isle of Skye is mine of right, my lords. I say now, give Donald back the Isle of Skye, and in his wife's right, control of the western territories of Ross, meantime — and you need fear no more from Alexander of Buchan. If not . . . *incidis in Scyllam cupiens vitare Charybdim!*" Bowing, he sat down.

The young Earl of Ross half-rose to his feet, chewed at his lip and sat down again, silent. This was beyond him, he recognised. Only the Earl Robert, his father-in-law, might deal with the mighty Lord of the Isles — and the Earl Robert it was who had invited the man here, no doubt knowing the consequences.

Men eyed each other. This then was the price of the Islesman's unaccustomed journey south and his further co-operation, the Isle of Skye and control of much of Ross. The Governor must have offered him inducement to come — therefore this might well be Robert Stewart's own policy against the Wolf. In which case, it would stand, nothing surer. The boy David had already spelled it out, had he not? No contrary or protesting voice was raised, then, in all the Abbey-church.

The Chancellor looked uncertain, but got no help from the Governor. "How say we to my Lord Donald of the Isles?" he asked.

When still Robert Stewart did not speak, Dalkeith rose. "I move that the Lord Donald be granted the Isle of Skye and control of the western lands of the earldom of Ross, meantime, during the pleasure of parliament and the assent of the King's Grace, through his Governor," he said. "The Earl of Ross's interests to be sustained, and compensation granted."

Fife's nod was almost imperceptible — but the Chancellor perceived it.

"Very well. If none controvert it, that is agreed. The Lord Donald's requests granted meantime, the Earl of Ross's interests to be upheld and maintained by parliament."

The Wolf of Badenoch was a useful scarecrow, if nothing else.

Seeing the Governor yawn, the Bishop spoke briskly, relievedly. "This session must draw to a close. Tomorrow at noon another session will deal with matters of sheriffdoms, allocation of customs duties, royal burghs, wapinschaws and the like. However, there is one other item which would seem to be best considered today — since it refers to another earldom, that of Strathearn. Unless, my lord Governor, you would prefer it to be held over. Until the Lord Walter of Brechin might be here to speak to it?"

"No." Robert Stewart presumably having abandoned all reliance on his youngest brother, and committed himself to advocacy once, if need be could do so again. "I will speak," he said, if acidly. He raised a minatory finger. "My brother, whom God rest, David, Earl of Strathearn, died two months past. He left but one child, a daughter of ten years, the Lady Euphemia Stewart. The earldoms are the prime support of the Crown. It is not meet that they should remain in the hands of females of tender age, who can nowise render the Crown due aid. Since this is a royal earldom, I advise that the said Euphemia of Strathearn should wed, and forthwith. I advise that Sir Patrick Graham, brother to Sir David Graham of Montrose here present, a knight of proven worth, be selected. He can be relied upon to uphold and manage the earldom for the benefit of my piece and for the good weal of the realm. I *inform* parliament. But this being a royal fief, I do not require its confirmation by any." Without altering his level and factual tone, and making no pause, he went on. "My lord Chancellor, you may prorogue this session." He rose, and without a backward glance, stalked from the chancel.

Into the surge of excited clamour that arose on every hand, Jamie Douglas added his contribution. "Saints of God — did you hear that!" he exclaimed. "The man is beyond all! I say we have raised a monster to rule over us — and will tell my father so."

"Hush, Jamie," the Lady Isabel warned. "If it is so, you must watch your words the more."

"I care not. All, all was a mockery, I say! Even that last. If Strathearn is a royal earldom, it should have gone to one of his father's other sons. The Lord Walter had first claim. But he does not trust Walter of Brechin to do as he tells him — so he weds this wretched child to one of his own vassals of Menteith, Graham, who *will* do as he is told. So Strathearn becomes another earldom to add to Fife and Menteith. Which will be the next . . .?"

"Ha, Sir Jamie — so now we see what a parliament means!" the Lord David interrupted, pushing forward — and certainly not lowering that resounding voice. "Was it not an enlightenment? The true voice of the King's subjects assembled — as issuing from the lips of my Uncle Robert. Every voice that spoke was his — save perhaps Cousin Donald's. Your own father's, no less. And your Sir Archie's. Where stands Douglas now, heh?"

Jamie swallowed his own seething doubts, necessarily. "Sir Archie is now Earl of Douglas. And as such, he will speak otherwise than in a parliament, to be sure. You will see . . ."

"When I hear him speak otherwise than with my uncle's words, I will believe you!" The boy stared round at them all, as they waited to descend the narrow turnpike stair from the clerestory. "That, then, was a parliament, my friends! God's blood — it will be different when I am King — that I promise you!" And he thrust his way through the press to the stairway.

XIV

T HE SCOTS WERE riding southwards again through the rolling English countryside, armed for war and in superficially
gallant style — yet all so differently from that last and truly
gallant occasion, at least so far as Jamie Douglas was concerned.
Perhaps he was prejudiced, comparing the leadership but poorly
with that of the other. He was loyal enough to the new Earl of
Douglas, of course — although, to his mind, Archie the Grim was
but a poor successor to the Earl James. But that hard-bitten
character was not in fact in charge today, the Governor himself
being in command, despite the fact that over half the 12,000
horsemen involved in this adventure were Douglases or their
vassals. It was the first major display of Douglas strength under
the new regime, and all wrong that the overall commander should
have been Robert Stewart.

Jamie himself was relegated to a very minor and inconspicuous
position. Not only was he not up in front in the personal train of
any of the leaders; he was not even in the hundred-strong Dalkeith contingent, the command of which had been given to his
legitimate brother James, specially knighted for the occasion by
the Governor — part of the price for the Lord of Dalkeith's support at that parliament. Jamie got on very well with his half-
brothers; but James was a year and more younger than himself,
something of a scatterbrain so far and totally inexperienced in war
and military matters. The next legitimate brother, William, was
his second-in-command, although no knight and barely seventeen.
Jamie had preferred to attach himself and his own small 'tail' to
the joint company of his former colleagues-in-arms, Sir William
Douglas of Drumlanrig and Sir Archibald Douglas of Cavers, the
bastard son of the Earl James. These three young Otterburn
knights, still with an aura of the heroic about them, however little
regarded by the present leadership in Scotland, rode together well
down the long column, at the head of some three hundred men-at-
arms, Jamie's contribution being ten of his own, ten of the Lady
Isabel's former Tantallon men, all she could afford, and a score of
her husband's retainers, Sir John Edmonstone himself not being of
a warlike disposition.

This expedition was unlike the Otterburn one, in other ways. It was differently routed, adopting an invasion course midway along the Borderline but trending ever towards the west. This was because the English Earl Marshal, the Earl of Nottingham, acting Chief Warden, whose challenge the Scots were hereby accepting, was not on good terms with the Earl of Northumberland and the Percys, who considered the Wardenship to be hereditary in their house and Harry Hotspur's present unfortunate absence in Scotland no reason for installing strangers. In consequence Nottingham found it politic to make his base at Carlisle in the west, avoiding the Newcastle-Alnwick Percy country. The Scots were not exactly heading for Carlisle, it being no part of their policy to assail fortress cities. The strategy was to strike down the centre of the country and then cut diagonally across, behind and below Carlisle, making for the Gilsland Gap, in the Haltwhistle Fells, and so into the Upper South Tyne valley, constituting a dire threat to sundry unprotected areas and thus, hopefully, drawing the Earl Marshal out of his Carlisle Castle, to meet them in the open field. At Lanercost they would be within seven miles of the vital Gilsland Gap — which surely Nothingham would never allow them to take and exploit.

Jamie's part of the Scots host heard little of tactics or policy. But they trusted the Earl Archie to keep the Governor right on strategy, for he at least was a seasoned campaigner. They would have been happier however, had his son Sir Will of Nithsdale been present; for his father, at sixty-four, might be less vigorous and adventurous than once he had been, and the expedition was already somewhat depressed by rumours that the whole enterprise was really only something of a gesture, no serious fighting being envisaged, the object being to bring pressure to bear on King Richard Plantagenet to include Scotland in his peace-treaty with France. Unfortunately Will of Nithsdale was not with them, he having departed immediately after the parliament on a semi-diplomatic, semi-chivalrous mission to the Prince of Danzig who was organising a Crusade against the Saracens, and at the same time seeking to re-negotiate the harbour-dues of the great port in favour of the Teutonic Knights—which could gravely affect the trade of the many Scots merchants exporting to Poland. Sir Will was said to have left the Lady Gelis six months' pregnant. Jamie and his friends were not alone in thinking that a warrior of

Nithsdale's renown might have been better employed on this expedition than in traipsing off to Danzig.

They were beginning the gradual descent into the broad Vale of Irthing, south of Bewcastle, when scouts sent back word that they were in touch with light enemy forces just north of the great Roman Wall. This was presently amplified with news that there were further forces at and behind the Wall itself, larger than seemed likely for mere patrols out from Carlisle. The Scots array halted. It could mean that the Earl Marshal had already moved out to oppose them, better informed than they had given him credit for. Caution, it seemed, was advisable.

They moved forward again, more slowly. But with Lanercost Priory coming into sight from the last modest heights before the Wall and the Irthing, they were halted again. They could see for themselves, without scouts' reports, a large body of men drawn up under flags and banners on a hilltop site to their half-left, less than a mile away.

The mighty Hadrian's or Picts' Wall, stretching from coast to coast, here followed the Irthing, on the higher ground of its north side. Although superficially broken down and breached, it still constituted a prominent and formidable barrier, reinforced at fairly regular intervals by mile-castles and turrets, minor forts of considerable strength. These tended to be set on heights, and the highest in this area, where the ground rose fairly abruptly to a sizeable hill, had been chosen as stance for this large waiting force, or for the centre and hub of it, for the Wall and flanking fortlets were obviously manned also.

It represented a poser for the Scots leadership, which had not for a moment anticipated that the old Roman defensive system would be used in modern times. They had not expected the enemy to thus stand prepared for them, and in a purely defensive posture, as seemed to be so. A score of miles within England, the English Earl Marshal, who had been challenging the Scots for weeks, might have been expected to be rather more assertive. To attack this fortified hill, and the massive Wall itself, would be almost as costly a business as besieging the walled city of Carlisle. None doubted that here was Nottingham himself, for the Leopards of Plantagenet were blazoned on a great banner.

There was much debate as to what should be done. The hotter, younger spirits urged an immediate and direct assault, first on the flanks, then from behind where the ascent was less steep. The Earl Archibald advised that they seem to ignore the entrenched enemy, swing off before them eastwards for the Gilsland Gap, as originally intended, leaving the English high and dry on their hill or forcing them to come down and follow, when they could be attacked on lower ground. But the Earl Robert would have none of either proposition. The one was much too dangerous and liable to defeat; the other ran the risk of them being cut off from Scotland. Who knew what the Marshal might have arranged? Let them all remember that they were here to make a demonstration, not to court defeat and disaster.

The Scots army seethed with frustration. This was not the way the Douglases, at least, went to war. But the Governor was coldly adamant. And so long as their new Earl deferred to him, they could do nothing. Camp was set up on the hillside opposite and in full view of the enemy. Trumpets challenged them from the Roman heights.

Presently, although the Earl Robert would indulge in no undignified shouting-match, the Earl of Douglas, under only his own Crowned Heart banner, rode forward with a large group of his supporters, Jamie included, to as near the Wall and hill as they dared, to remain outwith arrow-shot — for nothing was more certain that those ramparts would be lined thickly with English bowmen. Here, below the central fort, they blew trumpets in return, and eventually a party of notables came a little way down the slope towards them. Since these brought a Leopard flag, presumably they included the Earl of Nottingham, Earl Marshal of England.

The Earl Archibald, who did not enjoy shouting any more than did his friend, had brought a herald to do it for him.

"In the name of the high and mighty prince, Earl Robert of Scotland, Governor of the realm; and of the noble and mighty Earl Archibald of Douglas, Lord of Galloway, we ask if we have the honour to address the excellent and renowned Earl Marshal of England, acting Chief Warden in room of Sir Harry Percy presently prisoner in Scotland?" this functionary called.

After a moment or two the reply came, sufficiently clear. "I am John of Nottingham, Earl Marshal, yes. And I am Chief Warden of these Marches — but not in the room of any, especially not of the captive Henry Percy. I demand to know what does the

Lord Robert Stewart and the Earl of Douglas, with an armed host, on English soil?"

Archie muttered to the herald, who shouted again. "They are here at your lordship's invitation. You besought them to come and cross a lance with you and yours, saying that wherever you found any Scots you would give them battle, and more potently than did the Percy at Otterburn."

The response was immediate. "I am rejoiced, sir, that these Scots are come to show their mettle. As distinct from raiding farms, burning churches and raping women, as is their usual. By all means let them now prove their worth and ability in war. We are most ready. Make your onset my Scots friends. We await you."

Amidst an outburst of disbelief and abuse the Scots eyed each other. The man was inviting them to assail a strongly fortified position behind which he and his force sheltered. It was inconceivable. Was this English chivalry?

The herald began to interpret this righteous indignation, when the Earl Archibald pushed him roughly aside.

"My lord!" he cried — and he had quite as loud a voice in fact as had the herald, with noticeably more rasping harshness. "You cannot truly mean what you say? Surely between knights of name and renown, a fair fight is the only way to resolve differences? Yet you enclose yourself in a fort and ask us to assail it with lances and swords! Or did I, Douglas, mishear you?"

"Ha — is that the new-made Earl Archibald?" Nottingham had a fine carrying voice, though slightly and proudly nasal. "I greet you well. But if you have failed to come provided with due and proper weapons, am I to blame? When visiting England you should come better prepared, sir."

"Damn you — we came prepared to meet knights and men of honour, in answer to challenge. Not hill-top forts and skulking defenders!"

"You invade our kingdom and yet would pick your own battle-ground, my lord? Surely not. Come up here, sirrah, and see how we skulk."

Cursing, the Douglas sought to change his tone. "My lord — you cannot mean that you are content to sit behind those ramparts and do naught?" he demanded. "No true knight could hold up his head after such cravenry. In especial the Earl Marshal of England. Come down, sir, with many or with few and let us settle our scores in fair fight, as honest men should."

When he was vouchsafed no reply at all, swearing, he tried again. "See you — we Scots are 12,000. I know not how many are you. But bring down 5,000 and we will field 4,000. Or bring 500 and we will field 400. Any five against four. Can I say fairer?"

Silence from above.

One last throw. "Englishman," Archie shouted, "if you be indeed knight, or man at all, I, Archibald Douglas challenge you to single combat. I conceive you to be a deal the younger. Choose you the weapons. Let it be an honest trial of strength."

"Not so, old man!" came back the haughty rejection. "I, of the blood of kings, do not cross swords with Border cattle-thieves."

Archie gulped, swallowed, but still found voice. "Because you know better Englishman! But you will not then refuse to fight the Governor himself? The Earl Robert Stewart, the King's son — you of the blood of kings."

The listening Scots drew quick breaths. This was tempting Providence with a vengeance — for nothing was more sure than that the Earl Robert would not indulge in any single combat. But they need not have been anxious.

"No, sir," came the reply. "I represent here His Grace of England, King Richard. In his name I fight no such childish contests. If you think to defeat us, try you! If not, then I command that you leave His Grace's territories forthwith, without further hurt or harassment to this land. I have no more to say to you." And turning about, he led his party back up the hill.

The Scots burst into wrath and scornful denunciation; but that was all that they could do.

Later, however, the argument waxed hot and furious. Those for direct assault on the line of forts had gained many more adherents. Douglas himself still advocated an outflanking move towards the Gilsland Gap. Others suggested a surprise dash on Carlisle itself, now presumably left only partly defended. But the Governor would have none of it. Surprisingly he was not displeased with the outcome here. According to him it was a moral victory, an English defeat on their own soil — and without a life lost for the Scots. They had demonstrated that they could march into England without let or hindrance, and put the Earl Marshal's forces on the defensive, helpless. This would not be long in reaching King Richard's ears — and he would read the due lesson. Possibly they had achieved all they set out to do.

Extraordinary as this attitude appeared to his fellow-countrymen, Robert Stewart held to it — and in this new dispensation his word stood as law.

In mid-afternoon, then, despite resentment almost amounting to revolt, the camp was struck and the Scots turned to face north again. But before they could move off, the Earl Archie insisted on riding back to where he had hailed the English previously. This time nobody came down to speak with him although an arrow or two winged over, to fall well short. He was accordingly forced to bellow the louder.

"Englishman — you named Douglas cattle-thief, and the Scots ravagers and burners. I promise that you will regret those words! I will make them true, see you. All the way back to Scotland. Your folk here will curse your name, Nottingham — curse you. I swear it!" He reined around, shaking his fist.

It is to be feared that the Earl of Douglas redeemed his promise, that July day and the next — for the Scots did not return as they had come, the direct way, but headed north by east over the fells to the North Tyne valley, where there were much richer pickings in the Barrasford, Wark and Bellingham areas, cattle-country which they despoiled with a ruthless thoroughness, burning, looting and ravishing at leisure, knowing well that there was unlikely to be any danger at their heels. The sky darkened with the well-known smoke-clouds, the cattle-herds grew and grew, their dust and lowing protest seeming to fill the Middle March. The Governor did nothing to stop it — probably recognised that he could not do so, with 12,000 angry and all but mutinous troops under commanders almost as disappointed and thwarted as their men.

Jamie Douglas rode homeward as discontented as the rest, but with the added depression engendered by what might have been, the recognition that this was all a grievous downfall, a degeneracy and blot on Scotland's escutcheon. Also the recognition that Archie the Grim would never be another Earl James, and that the high zenith of Douglas pride, power and prestige was past. He feared greatly for Scotland hereafter under this new and ignoble regime. As for the cattle-reiving, he was not against it on principle — of Border stock he could hardly be that. But he deplored the violence and savagery which now went with it, and which should not have been sanctioned by the nobles. He allowed none of the men under his control to take part in excesses — but that was a mere drop in a loch.

It was not that he was wholly committed to the chivalric code, now declining throughout Christendom. He recognised its follies and contradictions, its outdated arrogances and preoccupation with personal fighting valour as against the well-being of the majority. But he greatly endorsed the noble ideals of knighthood, and the disciplines these imposed — and was young enough to try to apply them wholeheartedly. And what he had seen around him on this expedition, on both sides, he felt to be the negation of knighthood.

Another part of Jamie's trouble was that, for the first time in his life he was at odds with his father. He believed that Dalkeith had made a grave mistake in coming to terms with and then actually supporting the Earl Robert, letting down the Lady Isabel in the process. Always he had greatly respected his father, believing in his judgment, wisdom, integrity. Now he was less sure of all three. Perhaps the preference shown to his legitimate brothers in this unfortunate raid rankled more than it should.

At any rate, back in Scotland unpursued, Jamie did not return to Dalkeith but went straight to Edmonstone, a significant gesture. There dire news awaited him. The Lady Isabel had gone to Dunfermline to be with her sister Gelis. Sir Will of Nithsdale was dead, slain at Danzig, vilely.

Within the hour Jamie was on his way to Fife.

XV

THE PALACE OF Dunfermline stood back a few miles, on the rising ground, of the north shore of Forth, in Fothrif, the western division of Fife, beside the large and wealthy abbey where the Bruce and his queen were buried. It was an ancient place and had been one of the favourite seats of the old Celtic kings, Malcolm Canmore's in especial. Here the present monarch had been brought on his release from the Wolf's clutches at Rothesay. Donald of the Isles had surrounded the Isle of Bute with his entire fleet of hundreds of galleys, as only he could do, and the Wolf had quickly understood the realities of the case and slipped away in a small boat, by night, for the far north, leaving his royal father to be collected by the Islesman. The Earl Robert had had him brought to Dunfermline, as being conveniently near to his own Fife castle of Falkland, where he could keep a close eye on him in future, lest anyone else sought this short-cut to power in the land.

Jamie and his twenty men crossed the Forth at Queen Margaret's Ferry, and reached the grey town of Dunfermline, crowding around the twin eminences of palace and abbey, as the sun was sinking behind the Ochils to the north-west, on the first evening of August. To his surprise he was welcomed by the jangling cacophony of the bells of the abbey and of the other churches and chapels. He was more surprised still when, on enquiry, he elicited the information that the Governor himself had arrived earlier that afternoon, from the South, and this joyous pealing was to signalise his great victory over the Earl Marshal of England, near Carlisle.

At the old rambling palace, part of it half-ruinous, Jamie, avoiding the finer quarters where the Earl of Fife might be looked for, found his way to the princesses' chambers in the ancient east wing. Here he discovered Mary Stewart in sole charge, who greeted him with a hug and a warm kiss.

"Jamie himself—back from the wars!" she exclaimed, with undisguised pleasure. "Safe and unhurt, too, God be thanked! Here's joy, Jamie — and we could be doing with some, I swear, here at Dunfermline."

He snorted, with scant appreciation of her fine welcome. "Unhurt! Would God some of us *had* been hurt! Then we might at least have been able to hold up our heads, like men. Not hang them, like cheats and cozeners!"

"Sir Jamie Douglas hanging his head in shame? I'll not believe it!" she cried. "Besides, you won another victory, did you not? Hear those clanging bells — which I would to God would stop ...!"

"Those bells are as great a fraud as the rest," he told her. "There was no victory. Not even a battle or a skirmish. Nothing. Not a sword was drawn or a lance couched, save against the English countryfolk on the way home. It was all a folly, from start to end. The English would not fight, and sat in their forts behind stone walls — and the Earl Robert was scarce keener. So he turned back without a blow struck. He never intended that there should be any true fighting. A demonstration, he named it. He would allow no move further into England — and our new Douglas earl yielded to him. We turned tail, unblooded, and came home — assailing only farms and villages and reiving cattle. And for that, your precious half-brother rings Dunfermline's bells."

She stepped forward to put a finger against his lips. "Hush, Jamie — in this house speak not so. I love Robert little better than do you — but I do not shout it aloud in his own palace! That one has ears and eyes everywhere — spies. And he mislikes you sufficiently already."

"I care not . . ." he began. But his voice faltered and faded. She had come very close to him, to touch his lips, and the sheer power of her vivid femininity literally took his breath away. Mary was not really beautiful, like her half-sisters Gelis and Isabel, but she was lovely, warm and so much woman that a man was roused, challenged and yet to some extent disarmed, inevitably. Or Jamie Douglas was, at least.

He drew back, in sheer self-defence, changing his tone when he could. "But . . . but I did not come here to talk of the Governor and his ill ways," he said. "I had tidings at Edmonstone, and so came . . ."

"Aye, came in haste seeking your two princesses!" She finished for him. "Ever their fond knight! And my warnings unheeded! Well, Sir Knight, they are both presently dining with the said and unbeloved Robert. He summoned them to his table — a modest banquet to celebrate his victory, see you. So you must needs put up with me meantime, my friend and fellow-bastard!"

"Not so," he objected. "Or . . . I mean . . . No. You mistake me. I came to find out, to discover. What ill befell Sir Will of Nithsdale. I heard only that he was slain. And how it is with the Lady Gelis . . .?"

"To be sure. I have a shrewish tongue, Jamie. It is a bad

business. We got the word the very day you rode South. Sir Will was basely slain. At Danzig. Set upon by bullies, in the street, and stabbed to death. It is said hired by the Lord Clifford. Though . . ."

"Clifford? You mean the English lord from Carlisle?"

"The same. He was in Danzig also for this Crusade folly. It seems that in the previous raid on England, when you were at Otterburn, in the West array Sir Will came up against Clifford somehow, who miscalled him pirate and assassin. Over the Isle of Man campaign. Clifford had certain interests in Man. Sir Will challenged him there and then to prove his words in fair fight or single combat, or to retract them. But Clifford refused. So they met again in Danzig, and Will repeated his challenge before all. And again Clifford would not. But that night, hired bullies way-laid Will in a dark lane and did him to death — presumably that there be no more uncomfortable challenges. So Gelis, ten months wed, is a widow — and expecting a bairn in eight weeks' time."

"Dear God — how dastardly a deed! Clifford! I will not forget that name!"

"If Clifford it was. I suppose that Sir Will might have had . . . other ill-wishers."

He brushed that aside. "What sorrow for the Lady Gelis, what pain and hurt. Hurt for Scotland also, for he was a notable soldier. We have not many of his like."

"And yet, you did not greatly love him, I think, Jamie?"

"I admired him, esteemed him. Was it necessary that I should also love him?" That was a little stiff.

"Perhaps not." She smiled.

"How is Gelis? How does she bear this great blow?"

"Well. Bravely. But, she is a Stewart — and she is angry too."

"Aye. And with cause. Like her sister. Both widowed, and by assassination. An evil fate indeed."

"That thought has not escaped them both. As you will discover."

"Both husbands Douglases. And two of the realm's finest leaders, fighters. Is there a curse on Douglas? Or is it on Stewart?"

"I think not. I do not believe in curses. Save human ones, such as my brothers Robert and Alex! And perhaps young David? Although he may grow out of his accursedness — who knows?"

"You make the Stewarts sound sufficiently accursed!"

"Not the women, I hope?"

"No," he agreed. "Not the women. But — now *you* it is who talk dangerously. No?"

"No doubt. Let us go walk in the orchard then, Jamie — where none shall overhear our . . . indiscretions!"

Warily he eyed her. But he felt that he could scarcely refuse—nor particularly wanted to.

So they went strolling along the avenues of fruit-trees which sloped down into the glen of Pittencrieff below Malcolm's Tower, in the cool of the August evening, she with her rounded bare arm tucked in his, he very much aware of the pressure and motion of a shapely breast against his side. They made a handsome pair, for other strollers of the Court — but sought private ways in the interests of security. Mary did most of the talking, but despite her warnings about precautions and the like, they spoke little that was particularly significant or controversial. Indeed much of the time they did not speak at all, and this was undeniably pleasant — for the man, at least. He recognised that he was by no means at his best in making conversation with young women. Yet he liked their company, some more than others. After he had left such, he could always think of a hundred witty and devastating things he could have said, but had not.

Although they did not speak incessantly, perhaps Mary Stewart learned more than she wanted to know about Jamie Douglas than in other more talkative sessions.

They visited Queen Margaret's Cave, but unfortunately it was already occupied. Whereafter they sat decently in a rose-arbour, slightly cramped as to space but uncomplaining — until the midges drove even the stalwart Mary into retreat, she being scarcely clad for midge-resistance. Jamie was suitably concerned and helpful about brushing the creatures off.

Soon after their return to cover, the two princesses came back from the banquet, early, and there was quite an emotional scene as they welcomed their knight-errant with more embraces and kisses — and Jamie, ill at ease, wishing that Mary had not been standing there in the background smiling gently. That they were both glad to see him, despite a certain preoccupation, was obvious; and though Isabel naturally was the more demonstrative, Gelis was far from backward, with unshed tears in her violet eyes as she greeted him. Oddly enough, although he instantly blamed himself fiercely for it, his fine sympathy for her was distinctly eroded by a sort of offence at her so evident state of pregnancy. Unfair and ridiculous as this was, it was somehow basic, elementary — and he was still only nineteen, after all. The feeling of her great belly pressed against him as she threw her arms around him undoubtedly displeased. He sought to keep his eyes studiously on her face thereafter — not with entire success.

The subject of Sir Will's death, although in all their minds, was not mentioned at first, as though deliberately. Instead they spoke of the fraudulent victory at Lanercost, the humiliations of the Douglases, the declining health of the King, and the Lord Robert's probable intentions in the immediate future. Jamie in fact wondered at the Governor inviting these two so uncooperative sisters to his table here, and the sisters, exchanging glances, agreed hurriedly that this certainly represented very much a change in tactics. Perhaps he felt the need of some superficial royal family support, now that David of Strathearn was dead, he had for the moment alienated the Lord Walter, the Earl Alexander was in open revolt, and the Earl John eyed him ever the more askance. The Stewarts at present could scarcely be called a united family; but it was probably necessary for Robert to try to preserve an illusion of concord as far as possible. Isabel, biting her lip, said that she hated her brother more than ever, but that Gelis and she could not wholly abjure and renounce his company meantime, unfortunately. The King was undoubtedly sinking fast, and in duty bound, as well as in their own interests, they could not abandon him wholly to Robert's sour ministrations and manipulations.

Jamie accepted that, of course. When, after a curiously uncomfortable interval of silence, he felt bound to raise the subject of the assassination in Danzig, stiltedly expressing sympathy and revulsion, he was unprepared for the reaction. It was as though a dam had been breached. Both princesses burst out in exclamation of pent-up feelings. In a babble of incoherent and jumbled assertions, they vied with each other in completely confusing as well as embarrassing their hearer — who was unable to get the gist of their hot accusations, save that once again their brother Robert was the target. Clearly they had been bottling this up all along.

234

But quite quickly they recollected their dignity, and Isabel, presumably recognising her sister's priority in this, fell silent, while Gelis spoke, more quietly but still tensely.

"I should have known, have guessed," she said. "I blame myself. He has been ill disposed towards Will, ever since Turnberry, when we came between him and our father. Will had but little to do with it, but *I* had, and Robert has not forgiven me. He never forgets—and he is a man who will strike a woman through her husband. Moreover, Will had opposed him in more than one matter, since. I should have guessed, when *he* was chosen to go on this mission to Danzig, that he might never come back."

Jamie stared. "But . . . but . . ." he floundered. "What are you saying. What is this . . .?"

Isabel took up the charge. "Who sent Sir William to Danzig? Robert — he only. His father, Sir Archie, did not want him to go. He would have had him with him on this planned raid on England. Robert sent him, for his own purposes."

"But Mary said that it was the Lord Clifford who slew him. Or planned it."

"Clifford takes the blame, yes. No doubt Clifford hired those evil bravoes," Gelis said. "But who was behind Clifford?"

"The man Bickerton slew James," her sister added. "But we believe that Robert it was who caused Bickerton do it. He could as readily have arranged it with Clifford. Robert never soils his own hands."

James shook his head. "Clifford is a powerful English noble. He would scarce act assassin for the Earl Robert. Go all the way to Danzig . . ."

"He could have been bound for Danzig and this great Crusading gathering anyway. Robert is ever well-informed. If he learned of it, what more simple than to send a secret courier to Carlisle and suggest this? After all, Robert was with the western array when Sir Will and Clifford exchanged words. He knew Clifford would bear resentment — and was a craven into the bargain. The man he needed."

It was all possible, certainly — but somehow even Jamie, loathing Robert Stewart as he did, could not quite bring himself to believe it.

"You have not taxed him with it? The Governor?" he asked.

"What use in that? He would deny it, and we could prove

nothing. And then he would be the more on guard against us, menacing us the more."

"On his guard . . .?"

"You do not think that we shall not seek our vengeance? And rely on *your* help to gain it, Jamie!"

He shook his head. "Do we not need proof before we seek vengeance? You say yourself that you could prove nothing. And your brother is not the man to leave proofs lying for folk to find. Since Otterburn I have managed to learn nothing, of either Bickerton or Ramsay. No single word. My lord Governor is a clever man, and if he is also what we fear he will not easily be discovered. Not that I can credit this of Clifford and Sir Will . . ."

"Why do you say that?" Gelis demanded. "You believe that he planned the Earl James's death. If he can murder one good-brother, he can murder two. Three, indeed, perhaps . . ."

"Three?"

"It could be. Not good-brother, but brother itself. He could have slain David. David of Strathearn."

"Oh, no . . .!"

"Why not? None knows of what David died. He ailed and died suddenly, without warning. His wife believes that it was poison. Who should poison David of Strathearn? He was a gentle man, without enemies. Who, then, gained from his death? Only Robert. He immediately took the child Euphemia into his own guardianship, and has now married her, bairn as she is, to his own vassal Patrick Graham. So he has the great earldom of Strathearn firmly in his hands — to add to the others. I say that we are dealing with Satan Incarnate!"

Jamie looked from one to the other of the women. This seemed to him to be a sort of hysteria — no doubt caused by Gelis's pregnant state, allied to shock over her husband's death. But Isabel nodded grimly. Mary shook her head, and half-shrugged. He sighed.

"I do not know. We cannot tell. We would be wise. I think, not to seek to go too far, or too fast, in this. All is but supposition, see you. We should hold to our course meantime, I say. Bide our time. Make no rash moves, to give him cause to suspect us . . ."

"What do you conceive us to be doing, Jamie?" Isabel was almost sharp with him. "Why are we living under this roof? Why

236

did we sit at his table, eating his meat which all but choked us? Is that rash, unwise? Think you we need telling that we deal with a viper?"

"Forgive me. I spoke unthinkingly, Princess." Abruptly he sought to change the subject. "Lady Gelis — how shall you do now?" he asked. "Where live? How contrive your affairs? If there is aught that I can do to aid you . . .?"

"I may need call on you yet, Jamie. Meantime, I shall contrive by learning from Isabel. Who has trod this road before me! At least I will have this child." She patted her stomach. "Will's child. In this, to be sure, I am blest. I have the young William, also. For though he is bastard, he is Will's son likewise, and a proper child. I shall continue to rear him, as Will would have wished. And one day, perhaps, one or both will avenge their father!"

Jamie had nothing to say to that.

*   *   *

Jamie Douglas would have preferred not to remain at Dunfermline Palace for long. The atmosphere he found little to his taste. It was impossible to avoid the Earl Robert's presence entirely, and that self-contained individual, although he did not actually order the young man to leave, left him in no doubt that his company was not welcome. The quite large entourage which attached itself to the Governor — it could hardly be called a Court, since he seemed to exist quite independently of it, indeed ignored it most of the time — took its cue from him nevertheless, and in the main treated Jamie as a sort of leper. Only in the princesses' quarters was he welcome — but these were so poor and restricted that he found lodging, amongst the men-at-arms, in the little town. Moreover, the King was very ill, and this produced its own sombre but tense reaction — for all recognised that the end could not be very far off, and that there were bound to be great and fundamental, not to say alarming, changes in the state of affairs in Scotland thereafter. What would happen in the new reign was anybody's guess — but Lady Gelis at least was convinced that Robert Stewart would seek the death of the Earl John and so gain the Crown for himself. Indeed so sure was she of this that she sent off one of the Tantallon men as messenger to Turnberry, to warn her eldest brother of his danger.

Had it not been that the princesses urged him to stay, Jamie would have been off in a day or two, about business of his own.

But to get away from the palace and its hostile aura for a little, he decided to pay a visit to the barony and lairdship his father had so generously settled on him — Aberdour. He had been there only once before, content to enjoy its modest revenues from afar. But this seemed a suitable opportunity to inspect it, especially as there was an old-standing dispute anent certain revenues connected with it and the Abbot of Inchcolm, which would be better cleared up if he could discover the facts. Since Aberdour lay only some seven miles to the east, along the Fife coast, he suggested that it would make a pleasant excursion on a warm August day for the Stewart ladies, a break from the palace and its strains. But Gelis decided that in her condition she could not risk horse-riding; and Isabel, after agreeing to go, the previous night, announced that her royal father's state of health that morning was such that she ought not to leave his side. Mary, however, appeared to have no such scruples, and said that she at least would keep Jamie company. He, as usual, was uncertain if this was altogether wise; but he could hardly refuse her, especially as Gelis decided that her half-sister and companion deserved an outing and that it would do her good.

So, seeing no need for an escort in the circumstances, they left Jamie's own tail of ten behind, to trot off companionably through the pleasing and fertile Fothrif countryside, well-tended church-lands in the main, by Pitreavie and Letham to the sea at Donibristle, and so along the scalloped shoreline of reefs and skerries and headlands, linked by sandy small bays. It was a day of heat-haze and little colour, with the Forth's islands seeming to float in flattened outline above the surface of the gently-lapping sea. Jamie pointed out Inchcolm, the closest inshore of these islands, on this north side, as the site of the abbey whose abbot was in some way involved in the controversy over revenues — though he was unsure of the details. Mary declared that she had met the Abbot of Inchcolm, and liked him little — he lived most of the time, it seemed, not at his island monastery, but in some style, with his crony the mitred Abbot of Dunfermline, two princes of Holy Church. They could see the square tower of the abbey, for the island was only a mile off shore from Braefoot Point of Dalgety Bay.

Mary Stewart appeared encouragingly concerned about his revenues from the Aberdour barony, asking sundry businesslike not to say searching questions such as he had scarcely expected from a young woman, especially one of the King's bastards.

They came, just before noon, round a long and broken headland of skerries and low crags, to a wider and more open bay than that of Dalgety, or rather to twin bays separated by a grassy tongue — though not quite twins either since, oddly enough, that to the west had a golden strand and that to the east a silver. White sands are highly unusual on the east coast of Scotland, however common on the west, and this of Aberdour was renowned, Mary duly admiring it. Behind the strands, on the higher ground but under the green Cullalo Hills, towered the quite massive square keep of a medium-sized castle, with nearby on one side a circular stone doocot and on the other the gables and traceried windows of a fair-sized chapel.

"So that is your inheritance, my lord of Aberdour!" the girl said.

"A small barony, much neglected," he admitted. "But . . . it might be restored and improved."

"What I was thinking my own self," she agreed.

Aberdour Castle, on closer approach, proved to be a tall and fairly rude oblong tower of four storeys and a garret, its thick walls surmounted by a parapet and wall-walk, rising to the east of a courtyard with subsidiary lean-to buildings, all on an eminence above the Dour Burn — and in a poorer state of repair than had appeared from a distance. The steward, whom they found ensconced in what had been the priest's house of the chapel of St. Fillan, was apologetic. The place was not in good order, no — but his instructions from my lord of Dalkeith had been to spend as little upon it as might be and send all possible monies accruing to Dalkeith for the young master's benefit. The young master conceded, rather shamefacedly, that he had indeed been glad to accept all revenues thus produced, without any great enquiry as to how obtained. The responsibility undoubtedly was his. He asked what, in fact, these revenues of his comprised?

The steward, who seemed an honest if somewhat garrulous individual, revealed that the rents of the farmeries and holdings, plus the multures of two mills and the salmon fisheries and harbour dues — all received in kind, of course, but sold for the best prices obtainable at Dunfermline market — constituted the main revenues. But the oyster-fishing in Whitesands Bay was becoming increasingly valuable, and accounted for the slow but steady rise of the late years. If only half of it all was not having to be handed over to the Abbot of Inchcolm each quarter, the barony's affairs could be said to be in a reasonably healthy state. But Holy Church was hard, hard, to the last groat, ever at him . . .

It was Mary who interrupted him. "I have met the Abbot of Inchcolm, and like him but little," she said. "What is this matter in dispute?"

Like a flood released the complaint poured out. "It is a right iniquity, lady," the steward said earnestly. "An auld story, but nane the less ill, for a' that. It was forty years back, when my grandsire was steward here. This barony then was the Mortimers'. You'll mind, sir, this was before your faither's faither bought it. The Lord Alan de Mortimer was the last o' his line. His son died before him, leaving but a lassie. Years before he died, with the son still living, he gave a bit charter to the Abbot o' Inchcolm yonder, leaving him a moiety o' the revenues o' the parish o' Dalgety — o' which this barony is the main portion — on condition that he and his heirs and successors should be given place o' burial before the high altar o' the abbey church o' Saint Colm yonder . . ."

"And were they?"

"They were not, lady. The son was killed in foreign wars, his corss God kens where. And when the Lord Alan died, in 1350 it was, and his corss in its coffin o' lead was being ferried oot yonder to the island, some o' thae ill-disposed and black-hearted monks tipped it oot, over the side, to sink in the sea." The steward's stubby finger pointed south-westwards across the bay. "See you yon bit, between Braefit Point and the island? Yon's still ca'd Mortimer's Deep, and nae fishermen will net there, by God!"

"But why, man? Why throw the body out?" Jamie demanded.

"Why? For that they wanted the jewels and gold to be buried wi' the corss. A gold belt he wore, they said. And his lady's jewelled crucifix. None kenned then — but one o' the oarers told o' it a year after. He was one o' thae serving brothers, and was put out o' the abbey for some trouble wi' the abbot. He told the Lord Alan's daughter, and she found another oarer to vouch for it. But the Abbot denied it, would hae nane o' it. On oath . . ."

"So you are saying that the conditions of the charter are unfulfilled and therefore void?" Mary took him up eagerly.

"Neither this Alan nor his heir were buried in the church, and there were no other Mortimers? So the grant of this — what did you name it? Moiety, yes. This moiety should not have to be paid?"

"Aye, lady — you have it. And a moiety is a full half, mind! The Lady Jean Mortimer said then, and we have aye said since, that nae moiety is due, and the charter forfeit."

"The monks must do more than just deny it, surely?" Jamie said. "If the body is not in the sea, where is it?"

"Och, they say it's in its place, right enough. In its bit coffin in the kirk. Under yon muckle slab. They've aye said that . . ."

"You mean buried?"

"No' just buried, no. There's a bit arch in the wa', up in the choir. To the side o' the altar. A stone coffin, just, wi' this muckle slab o' stone carved like a knight lying on top. The Lord Alan had it carved for himsel'. They say that the corss is in there—as it should be. I say it's no'. Nor the gold or the geegaws."

"Then here's a simple matter," Mary declared, laughing. "Let us go and see. Out to the island. Look under this slab, this stone effigy. If the bones are there, and the jewellery, we are satisfied, and you continue to pay your moiety, Sir James. If not, then you know where you stand."

"Och, they'd no' let you, lady—they would not. No' in the kirk . . ."

"Why not? Sir James, here, is the lord of this barony of Aberdour. That barony has long been paying large dues for right of sepulture in the abbey church. The barony has surely the right to inspect its leasehold! He could be concerned for his own future burial! What say you, Jamie?"

He grinned. "It seems an excellent ploy to me. And perchance profitable I confess, I'd not have thought of it. But since *you* have . . ." He turned to the steward. "Can you find us a boat to take us out to the island?"

"I can that, sir. My ain bit boat's doon at the haven. It's a fine flat sea. I'll oar you oot mysel', wi' my son. Aye, wi' pleasure, sir. God kens, I'm sweer to see under yon slab!"

So, leaving the horses, they strolled down to the little harbour, the steward's husky son, Tom Durie, about Jamie's age, less tall but more heavily built, hurrying after. Mary was in great spirits and holiday mood, finding it all a pleasing adventure. Steward

Durie and his son were clearly much more impressed by her than by their new-found laird.

The row out in the small boat was enjoyable — although undoubtedly it could be much otherwise in different conditions, Inchcolm often being stormbound it seemed. The two Fifers pulled strongly, scattering the rafts of crooning eiders and sending sooty scoters scuttering off right and left, patterning the glassy surface with their busy feet. Further out, gannets from the Bass Rock were diving hugely for fish, dropping from great heights with uncanny accuracy, masters of air and water both.

As they neared it, Inchcolm proved to be a fairly rocky island about half-a-mile in length, cliff-bound to the east, green to the west, kidney-shaped, the two halves all but separated by a low isthmus — over which, the steward said, the winter seas often surged, making it two islands indeed. The abbey, with its church, monastic buildings, chapterhouse, outhouses, farmery and gardens and even small patchwork fields, was on the western and lower half.

There was a jetty at the isthmus, where they landed, watched idly by two serving-brothers in their black Augustinian robes as they fished from nearby rocks. Mary skipped ashore gleefully, with skirts kilted up.

"They will not put me off, a woman, from this so holy island, will they?" she wondered. "They will have to carry me, screaming, if they do."

"I think it will not come to that," Jamie told her. "I would have my knightly and baronial say, first!"

Even mock-anxiety was unnecessary, however; for having climbed the track from pier to abbey gatehouse, and passed the untended porter's lodge, all seeming to sleep in the warmth of the August mid-day, the first person they saw was a woman, who answered their continued knocking at a door — and a cheerful, plump and bold-eyed woman at that, far from over-dressed above the waist and as approximately monastic-seeming as was Mary Stewart.

"We seek the Abbot of this place, mistress," Jamie said. "I am Sir James Douglas of Aberdour and this is my steward."

"Hech, hech — the laird, is it?" she exclaimed, with a whinnying laugh and a sketched curtsey. "Braw, young sir, braw! As the lady'll no' contest, I jalouse!" Another laugh. "Auld Durie I

ken — aye, and young Durie something better! Eh, lad?" That
was added with a chuckle that sounded significant, and set the
young man flushing. "But you'll no' find the Lord Abbot here,
young sir — Durie could ha' tell't you that. It's Dunfermline toun
for the likes o' him. But I could bring you to Master Ramsay, the
Prior, if that will serve your Honour?"

"*Ramsay*, you say?" He paused. "Yes, mistress — the Prior will
do very well. I thank you."

She led them through a succession of rooms and along corridors,
rich with smells of cooking, stacked with victuals, stores, wines and
the like. In the large refectory, set for a meal, two elderly monks
dozed. In the inner courtyard, surrounded by the arcaded cloister-
walk, with a fountain playing in the midst, a portly man sat in a
chair beside it, open-mouthed and fast asleep.

"Father Prior!" the woman declared, gesturing. She strode
forward, to shake the sleeper vigorously. "Wake up, wake up!" she
cried, with scant deference. "Here's no way to greet the quality, I
declare. The young laird o' Aberdour, nae less. And a bonny
leddy, forby. Aye, and auld Durie, the big stot . . . !"

"Eh? Eh?" The stout cleric started up in alarm. "A mercy . . . !"

"Do not fret yourself, Master Prior," Jamie soothed. "It is a hot
day, and we intrude. I am James Douglas, seeking your aid. But
hurry there is none."

"Ah. Yes. To be sure, Sir James. It is . . . we are honoured.
In this poor house. If you had sent me word . . ."

"No need for that. Since I seek only a very small service. I wish
to see my barony's burial-place in your church. That is all."

"Oh!" Prior Ramsay had a face rather like a seal; and now the
round eyes popped even more prominently. "Burial-place . . .?"
he faltered.

"Yes. Burial, interment, sepulture — name it what you will. In
the choir of the abbey-church here. We would inspect it."

"But . . . sir, my lord — that is *Mortimer's* tomb. Sir Alan de
Mortimer. Scarce yours . . ."

"It was paid for, and still is being paid for, out of the revenues
of my barony of Aberdour, Master Prior. It was Mortimer's
once — but it is Douglas's now. Or would you have me to withdraw my revenues?"

"Ah no, sir — no! Not that. Not to be thought of. But — this is a
matter for the Lord Abbot, not for me. I have no authority . . ."

"Then I shall speak with your Abbot — later. But now we are here, we will see the tomb."

"Not now, Sir James — not now. See the Lord Abbot, first. At Dunfermline ..."

"I shall do no such thing. We have come out to this island, and we shall see what I have been paying for. A moiety of my barony revenues, no less. You say that you have no authority to discuss the issue — therefore you have no authority to prevent me from seeing it, either. Do you take us there, Master Prior—or do we go look for ourselves?"

Muttering, the stout man girdled his robe about him and led the way across the courtyard to the north side, where rose the church, with its tall square battlemented tower. Church and monastery had been founded by Alexander I in 1123, when he had been driven ashore here in a storm whilst crossing Queen Margaret's Ferry, and had been forced to shelter for three days and nights, until the gale abated, in the cell of a hermit, living on shellfish and the milk of the Columban anchorite's cow. The King's fright, on this occasion, resulted in this oddly-sited abbey of the Augustinian canons.

Opening the door into the church nave, cool and lofty in pillared stone, Prior Ramsay crossed himself elaborately and spoke in exaggeratedly hushed voice.

"Your lady, Sir James, must abide here, by the door."

Jamie shook his head and refused to whisper. "No, Master Prior — she will remain with us."

"But ... but it is forbidden, sir. In our Order ..."

"The woman who led us in would be forbidden to your house by your Order, likewise, I think? Moreover, this lady is the King's own daughter, the Lady Mary Stewart, and she bides at no door in her father's realm!" He promoted her to the title of lady, as though she had been legitimate — and she squeezed his arm.

The cleric's eyes popped again, and he made awkward obeisance. He hurried forward into the church without more ado. The Duries, father and son, looked further impressed.

The chancel or choir, at the east end of the long building, was directly under the tower, up three steps. Here, the feature that they sought was readily apparent. To the left of the altar, inset in the walling, was a wide arched niche or alcove, with the recumbent effigy of a knight in full armour, life-size, shield on breast and sword at side, feet crossed at the ankles to indicate that he had been on Crusade. There was another niche and effigy on the opposite side, likewise, but this was carved in clerical robes with a crozier—an abbot. The Prior, genuflecting towards the altar, pointed.

"The Mortimer tomb, Sir James. And Princess."

"The *Aberdour* tomb," Jamie corrected, stepping forward for closer inspection. "Handsome. But then, it should be, for £150 Scots each year, should it not?"

Their guide murmured something indeterminate.

Jamie stooped to peer at, and then to try to lift the massive sculptured lid—whereat the Prior cried out in agitation, and indeed grabbed the younger man's arm.

"No, no, sir! I pray you — do not touch it."

"Why not? I desire to look inside. I pay for a sepulture, not just an effigy, Sir Prior. I must see its state. Stand back."

"No, Sir James — no! This is sacrilege! The property of Holy Church. You may not touch it. Without, without my Lord Abbot's permission. None may."

"Has he ordered so, Master Prior? The Abbot?"

"Yes. Yes, indeed."

"Why should he do that, tell me? Did he guess that someone would come looking? Or is he afraid of what maybe found therein?"

"No, no, sir. But all within the choir is holy, sacrosanct. Not to be touched by unconsecrated hands . . ."

"*You* will help me lift this stone cover then, Prior. Moreover, my hands are consecrated after a fashion, for I have taken knightly vows. You will not deny the validity of the knightly order?"

"No. But . . . I cannot, I cannot, sir. Cannot permit this." The cleric turned away, however, to go kneel before the altar, wringing his plump hands.

Jamie, ignoring him, jerked his head at the Duries, and nothing loth, they also stooped to help him lift the massive lid. But though it moved slightly, their fingers could gain insufficient purchase. Only a narrow crack appeared beneath, and closed again as their pressure relaxed.

"We need bars. Of iron. It would snap my dirk-blade . . ."

"Spades," young Durie suggested. "They hae a graveyard here. They'll hae spades."

"Go find some, then."

"No-o-o!" That came in a groan from the altar, as the Duries hurried out.

"Do not distress yourself, Sir Prior," Mary said, soothingly. "We will do no hurt to anything. Merely raise this slab and look inside. See the state of the, the, the remains. See what space remains. We shall replace all as it was."

The other burst into gabbled Latinities.

The Duries came back with two spades. Also two serving-brothers, whom they had evidently recruited, and who gaped at all, and crossed themselves for safety's sake.

"Ah — helpers," Jamie greeted them. "Come, friends — aid us with this lid."

"You will not! I forbid it!" Prior Ramsay exclaimed, turning his head though still on his knees. "I ... I ..." He seemed as though he might be considering more drastic commands, but thought better of it, and returned to the comforts of Latin.

"You lift, all," Mary said, taking one of the spades. "I will put the blades in."

The three men stooped to their task, and into the opening crack between lid and coffin the young woman deftly slipped the spades. Then, with the leverage, it was a simple matter to raise the effigy-carved cover. Save for some scuttling spiders, the space beneath was entirely empty.

"What did I say!" old Durie exclaimed. "Nae corss. Nae gold nor jewels either. Nor ever has been. Devil-damned monks!"

"Sir Prior — come you here and see this emptiness. You others likewise — as witnesses!" Jamie invited. "Neither Sir Alan de Mortimer nor his gold is here. As we feared."

Ramsay held back. "It ... it is long," he quavered. "Many years. Half a century. All has decayed away. Dust, no more. Dust and ashes. *Requiescat in pace*."

"There is not even dust here, man. And bones do not decay away, in a dry place, in fifty years or a hundred. Nor do gold and jewels! Mortimer is not here, nor ever was, I vow. Tipped into the sea, in Mortimer's Deep, and his golden belt and crucifix stolen. Douglas has been paying for a fraud for thirty years!"

The cleric was up and plucking at his lower lip now. "I know

246

nothing of this," he protested. "I have been here but eight years. My Lord Abbot but a dozen. There has been some mischance . . ."

"Mischance, yes. One does not cozen Douglas, with impunity! Even Holy Church! This mischance will fall to be righted."

"Thirty times £150 is a notable mischance!" Mary observed, judicially. "I make it £4,500 — although, it may be my summing is wrong? And the Lady Mortimer's heirs, before that, may be interested!"

The Prior let out a strangled wail. "Saint Colm and Saint Bridget — save us! Saint Augustine, our founder, protect us, come to our aid! Mary Mother of God, hear us . . . for we are a poor and humble house, lacking in the world's gear . . .!"

"You say so, sir? I have seen no sign of it," Jamie told him. "I think you prosper most genially, on this isle. And will scarce notice the loss of my £150 each year."

"Ah, no, sir. You have not seen. Broke buildings. The wreckage of storms. Timbers wormed. Dykes fallen. Salt winds killing the apples . . ."

"Then if you are so poor, where do all the revenues go? Mine, with the rest? Perhaps your Abbot, in his fine town-house in Dunfermline, could tell us? And will! Now, we shall leave you, Master Prior, and return to that good town." Jamie paused. "But before we go, I have a small matter to ask of you . . ."

"Anything, sir — anything!" the other said earnestly. "Our poor house is at your service. And the Princess's. If you will tell my Lord Abbot that I, that I . . ."

"Sought to prevent us from looking into yonder tomb, sir? Surely, I shall tell him so, never fear. But my question is this. I think that I heard that your name is Ramsay?"

"Indeed yes, sir. Joseph Ramsay."

"I am interested in the name of Ramsay, Prior Joseph. And it is no common one in these parts. The Ramsays of Dalwolsey are renowned. In Lothian, not far from my father's house. But few others, I think, save at Waughton near to Haddington, vassals of Lindsay . . ."

"Waughton is the line I come of, Sir James. An old house, somewhat decayed, but honourable. Ramsay of Waughton is my cousin-german."

"Ah — he is? Then, Master Ramsay, perhaps you can give me tidings of his son Patrick, my one-time companion-in-arms?

We fought side-by-side at Otterburn. I have been seeking him . . ."

"Pate? You know young Pate, Sir James? A good lad, a fine lad — if headstrong a little, perhaps. But no ill to him. And like to do great things. He was here, to be sure, not long since . . ."

"Here? Pate Ramsay — on Inchcolm? Do not tell me that he was thinking to turn monk — that one!"

"No, no — the saints forbid! He was but biding here a while, with me his father's cousin. Lying quiet, I would suspect, after some youthful escapade! He did not confide in me—but he is a spirited lad. As you will know."

"Spirited, yes. That is true. So he was here? Small wonder I could not find him! And now — he is gone again?"

"Yes. Near a month now."

"But not home. There was no word of him at Waughton."

"No. I think that he headed into the north. The Highlands. On great affairs." That last was said with a sort of knowing pride.

"Great affairs? Patrick Ramsay?"

"To be sure. We Ramsays are well thought of, see you." The cleric nodded portentously. "Twice whilst he was here, on the island, he went to Falkland. Twice. Aye, and once to St. Andrews . . ."

"To Falkland! Why? Did he say why?"

"Falkland is my brother Robert's house," Mary mentioned. "But — a town, besides."

"Yes, Princess—the Governor's castle. What he did there, he did not say. Some privy matter." The Prior sighed, clearly regretful. "But he was concerned in some ploy, I swear. For he had money to spend — as I have never known him to have. And a fine horse he came back with. He stabled it with this Durie." The steward nodded confirmation. "Good new clothes, besides . . ."

"I see. So whatever he did at Falkland, whoever he saw, it was profitable."

"Profitable and important, yes. And at St. Andrews, he went to the castle, I do know — the Bishop's castle."

"M'mmm. You think, on the same ploy?"

"Belike. He went to St. Andrews between the two visits to Falkland."

"But it was not to Falkland nor St. Andrews that he went,

finally? You said that he headed northwards. Into the High-lands."

"North, yes. He told me that he was travelling on a long journey. That he required good horseflesh. Much siller. And a sharp dirk — for he was going amongst Hielant savages."

"He had ever a sharp dirk! But . . . amongst Highlandmen? For why?"

"He would not say, Sir James. Save that he would do well out of it. For he conceived the Bishop more generous than the Earl Robert! That is all he said."

"He said that? Generous. The Bishop? And he *named* the Earl Robert, in this? The Bishop of St. Andrews, he meant?"

"I cannot tell what he meant, sir. Or which bishop. He would tell me no more."

Jamie and Mary exchanged glances, hers distinctly mystified.

Try as he would, the young man could get no more out of the Prior. Ramsay was, in fact, a simple man, not notably intelligent; and almost certainly all that he knew had been wormed out of him.

They left the abbey, then, amidst pleas to be merciful, generous, understanding, to be good and faithful members of Holy Church, and to think well of the future of their immortal souls.

They went back down to the jetty. But there, as the Duries were preparing to aid them into their boat, Mary demurred.

"The day is young yet," she pointed out. "Whilst we are here, I would wish to see the rest of the island. Who knows, I may never be here again. Our friends can wait. Fish, or sleep, or row back to Aberdour, and then return for us. No? And we shall make a round of this rock in the silver sea, and discover its secrets. I have ever had a notion for islands."

Jamie found nothing really wrong with this suggestion; and old Durie said that he and his son would go back to the mainland and return in two or three hours with a flagon of wine, some cold fowl and bannocks with honey. The two monkish fishermen were still where they had left them.

As they strolled off southwards to climb the quite steep ascent to the modest clifftops, the girl took Jamie's arm.

"It has been an interesting day, has it not?" she said. "Is it always thus when Jamie Douglas takes the air?"

"I would say that *you* it is who gave the day its spice," he told her. "I would not have thought of coming out to this island to see that tomb."

"No. You do not care greatly for such things, do you, Jamie — moneys, revenues? For gear and goods. But they are important, also. We Stewarts are perhaps over-well aware of that! But if you will not look to your own interests, someone else must! We have made a start today. You must keep it up, see you."

"You mean in refusing to pay this wretched Abbot of Inchcolm his £150 each year? I shall certainly pay no more of that. So that I shall be that much the richer. For which I have to thank only you . . ."

"I mean far more than that, Jamie Douglas. That is a mere nothing, as I see it — although it may double your yearly revenue. I was not wholly playing the foolish woman with that fat Prior when I spoke of thirty years of wrongful payments. I say that you must claim back from the Church your due moneys. Scarce the total, of course — I cannot conceive of you winning £4,500 from the coffers of Holy Church. But a large sum should be demanded, nevertheless. For false assessment. In amends and repayment. We will have Sir Jamie Douglas a rich man, yet! Although I suppose that your father might claim some of it?"

"Lord — this is folly, Mary!" he protested. "You dream! £4,500 is a fortune . . ."

"Yes. Are you not fortunate, then? But I must warn you, Sir Knight — you will become the target for scheming women! With all that in your coffers, they will be after you, like wasps round ripe fruit! Even, perhaps, king's daughters!"

"Oh!" he said, looking at her sidelong. "I . . . ah . . . umm."

"Yes. So you are warned, my friend. Once more! Keep all such at arm's length — and keep your siller to yourself!"

He conjured up a laugh. "The warning I note. But the need I doubt. For this I swear — I will get no penny of your £4,500 out of Holy Church. None can hold on to their siller better than the churchmen. This Abbot will scorn me. I can hold back the £150 each year — although they will try to gain that, too. But to get money *from* them — never! You do not know churchmen, I think!"

"Which is where you are much wrong, Jamie. I do. Notably

one. *I* think that you have not considered this as closely as I have done, in my so feeble woman's head! Inchcolm Abbey has its Abbot, yes. Who is no doubt all that we say. But he is not supreme. Inchcolm, and Dunfermline Abbey likewise, come under the supreme authority of the metropolitan diocese of St. Andrews, the greatest and wealthiest see in the land. And who is in charge of the revenues and moneys of that diocese? The Archdeacon. And who is Archdeacon of St. Andrews, and right-hand of the Primate-Bishop? Who but my own favourite brother, *full* brother, son of both my mother and my father, Thomas Stewart! You have it now?"

He whistled soundlessly.

"So very soon we shall go and see Master Thomas. I would have wished to go, anyhow. He will not come to Dunfermline, I think, for he does not love Robert and keeps his distance."

"But ... but ... even so, Mary, the Church will not pay out large moneys. However much your brother may regard you. Bishop Trail, the Primate, will have other notions."

"Perhaps. But even Bishop Trail will not wish to offend too greatly the Lord of Dalkeith's son. Nor his Archdeacon, the King's bastard. He will, I think, wish to seem at least fair. Moreover, we have a strong card to play. In that gold belt and crucifix amissing. Theft by fraud Holy Church may belittle — when done by itself. Theft by secret stealing is another matter. They will wish this kept quiet, I swear — and must needs pay for it!"

He gazed at her, astonished, part-admiring, part-askance.

"So, you see — those riches may be within your grasp, Laird of Aberdour."

"I do not know what to say," he got out. "To you. Who have contrived all this. Whether to thank you, or, or ..." He swallowed. "None other that I know could have done it, that is certain sure."

"There you are wrong, Jamie. Many others could — made otherwise than yourself! However, let us agree that neither of my sisters Isabel nor Gelis could. For this is not princess's work — despite the title which you gave me to yonder Prior! Mind it. And do not thank me until you hear that siller jingling in your pouch." She pointed, with her free hand. "Now, since climbing cliffs and teaching high-minded knights their business is tiring work, I suggest that we go sit on yon grassy shelf for a space.

Watch the gannets dive. We have earned a rest, have we not?"

He could not deny that. Just below the cliff-edge there was a ledge above the sheer drop to the waves, and here, between sea and sky, they sat themselves down. The ledge was deep enough for safety, but sufficiently constricted by ribs of rock that they must sit close together. It was very warm, such breeze as there was, from the west, not penetrating here where they faced east, down Forth. Mary threw off her riding-doublet, and after a little, the man did likewise.

"This of St. Andrews," he said. "Why did Patrick Ramsay go to St. Andrews?"

"Do not ask me," she told him. "I did not understand all of that. What you were at, seeking out. This Ramsay was the man who stabbed Bickerton, was it not?"

"Yes. He came here to hide, it seems — and an excellent place. But from here he made these visits to Falkland and St. Andrews. Falkland I can understand — since I conceive him to be in the pay of the Governor. But St. Andrews . . .?"

"Perhaps Thomas may be able to tell us. Save that, if this Ramsay was on Robert's business, Thomas would be unlikely to be concerned."

"It is all most strange. This of going on a long journey, into the Highlands. Why? And talk of a bishop. The Bishop, he conceived, might be more generous than the Earl Robert, he said. Is this Bishop Trail, the Primate? Although, as the Prior said it, I thought it more as though the bishop he referred to was in the Highlands. Where he was going. Did not you?"

She shrugged. "I do not know. See you that gannet? The splash it made. They are very large birds . . ."

"Yes, yes. But this bishop. It is important, Mary. You must see it . . ."

"Perhaps, Jamie. But . . . none of it was very clear to me. Did you reckon that it meant so much?"

"Would that I knew what it meant! For I would seek out that Ramsay to the uttermost end of Scotland! Is he indeed in the Earl Robert's service? If so, why send him into the Highlands? Since it seems that somebody did — with money, new clothes and a fine horse. And a bishop at the end of it, perhaps? There are none so many bishops north of the Highland Line. Moray, Ross, Argyll and the Isles. These three, since Caithness and Orkney are scarce Highland. Argyll is west, not north. So we have Moray and Ross. Ross is far away. Moray, then? What might the Governor want of the Bishop of Moray that he must needs send such as Pate Ramsay as messenger?"

"Who knows? Such a great edifice to build out of so little, Jamie." Mary did not sound very interested. "How do the gannets dive on moving fish? From so great a height? Surely the fish will have swum on . . .?"

"I know not. It is a wonder. But — this of Ramsay. The secret, I think, must lie at St. Andrews. We shall learn nothing at Falkland or Dunfermline, I swear. But at St. Andrews . . ."

"Very well. We shall go to St. Andrews, and soon. As I said. But, now . . ." She yawned prettily, and leaning back, closed her eyes.

At least he had the sense not to go on. He watched the gannets, and gradually the frown of concentration eased from his dark brow. A vessel under full sail was tacking up-Firth between Inchcolm and Inchkeith.

Presently, with no further remark from Mary, he turned to look at her. She lay back, one firmly-rounded arm outflung towards him, fingers loosely curled, eyes closed, lips slightly parted. She breathed softly, regularly, flushed with the sun, tiny beads of perspiration on brow and upper lip. And as he had been all but overwhelmed, the first evening at Dunfermline, by her vital femininity, now, in a rush he was again by her naturalness, her frank unconcern, her seeming trusting helplessness there at his side. She appeared to have dropped straight off to sleep, uncaring for his presence. The linen bodice she wore under her doublet was part open, and anyway did little to hide the full shapeliness of her person.

Leaning on one elbow, he considered her, rather ashamedly at first, as though somehow he stole what he should not. But most clearly she had cared little in this respect, or she would not have lain back thus. So perhaps he was entitled to his gazing. Whether he was or not, he gazed his fill, something he had never done nor had had opportunity to do before with any woman, watching the gentle movement of her breathing, the rhythmic rise and fall of the rounded bosom, the faint pulse beating in the hollow of her throat, the sweep of eyelashes on cheek, the tiny occasional twitchings at the tip of her nose. He was strangely moved, as well as physically stirred.

Indeed, he was more moved and stirred than he realised. For without actually being aware of it, he had moved ever closer to her, identifying with the warm vitality of her, until his face was close enough to the girl's to feel the regular little puffs of her breath against his skin — and found it a delight.

Then, suddenly, her eyes were open and she was gazing into his own, long, steadily, untroubled, until most naturally her hand came up and gently pressed down the back of his head so that his mouth bore down on her own. Their lips met and gradually stirred, then became eager, questing.

"Jamie! Jamie!" she murmured into his mouth. "It has taken you long, long!"

He did not now waste time nor breath nor tongue in answering her, not in words, at least. His hands found employment to match his lips and he all but sobbed at the rich feel of firm breasts and the thrust of hard nipples. Her arms were round him now and holding him fast — and despite his ever-present doubts, it was all the most natural development in the world.

It continued that way, and the August afternoon stood still for them.

When at length they reluctantly moved on from that ledge on Inchcolm's cliff, it was hand-in-hand, slowly, in a companionable silence. Now and again they smiled to each other, that was all.

The Duries had to wait longer than they expected for their passengers.

XVI

JAMIE HAD HIS interview with the Abbot of Inchcolm Master John Dersy, two days later, in much finer quarters than the princesses occupied, in a wing of Dunfermline Abbey, to which the Abbot had just returned, hawk on wrist — and as the younger man had anticipated, got little or nowhere with the smoothly arrogant prelate. He admitted nothing, conceded no whit, deplored Sir James's sacrilegious descent upon his abbey without his permission, declared the revenues of Holy Church inviolate and scoffed at any suggestion of compensation. Jamie kept his temper, stated his case clearly, made no threats. He did declare, however, that the Aberdour-Dalgety moiety would no longer be paid. The Abbot pronounced this to be unthinkable, impossible, and murmured about higher authority and the dire penalties which the Church could impose against its intractable sons. On that note the interview ended.

A few days thereafter they rode to St. Andrews, quite a major journey of nearly forty miles, across Fife from south-west to north-east. The old King had rallied again somewhat meantime, and the Lady Isabel decided that on this occasion she might accompany Jamie — and indicated that, in the circumstances, there was really no need for Mary to go, since she could equally well make all necessary representations to the Archdeacon Thomas, her brother also. But Mary was determined, and since she was Gelis's lady-in-waiting, not Isabel's, she found no call to accede — especially as Gelis encouraged her, for some reason. Jamie was uncertain whether to be disappointed or relieved — anyway, he had no least say in the matter.

The weather was less kind to them, being dull and grey; but it did not rain and they made good time riding across hilly Fothrif and the fertile Howe of Fife, this time with an escort befitting a princess. Once they were started, the two half-sisters were good enough friends, and Jamie rode between them without the feared discomfort and with only occasional pangs of disloyalty when he found himself riding sufficiently close to rub knees with Mary rather than with his mistress the Countess-Dowager. Moreover she was, he reminded himself, the wife of Sir John Edmonstone, after all.

The journey took them most of the day, and an early evening sun came out at their backs to light up the spires and towers and pinnacles of the ecclesiastical city on the edge of the restless sea, the wide ocean here and no longer the Firth of Forth. It seemed a fair place as they gazed down from the heights of Magus Muir, with a host of proud and prominent buildings, the great cathedral and Bishop's castle dominating all. There were literally scores of religious edifices in this the ecclesiastical metropolis of Scotland, churches, chapels, priories, monasteries, nunneries, seminaries, hospices, colleges and shrines, with a large population to staff and support them. Here the Primate, Bishop Walter Trail, held sway, every second man in the street was monk or priest, and the sound of chiming bells was seldom absent.

It was a walled town, and the travellers hastened to win through the gates before they might close at sunset. Within, the main streets were broader than in most cities — although there were narrow wynds and lanes between — and the buildings of consistently superior architecture. This was a community where wealth was not in short supply.

The castle stood above the shore on a small cliff, many-towered in warm red sandstone. They had some difficulty in getting past the porter's lodge and gatehouse, for Bishop Trail was from home and the Archdeacon was, it seemed, out hunting still on Tent's Muir. However, identities were established and they were allowed inside; and soon afterwards Master Thomas Stewart and a cheerful, notably unclerical-seeming company arrived, all hooded hawks and slavering, tired hounds, loud in praise of an excellent day's sport.

Jamie was surprised to find Thomas Stewart a young man, only a few years older than himself. He had assumed that to be an archdeacon would require more mature years, forgetting that this was Mary's full brother and therefore likely to be not so very different in age. He was good-looking, stylish, with no hint of the ecclesiastic about him, in dress or manner. He welcomed his sisters warmly and Jamie genially.

A deal better fed than they would have been at Dunfermline, at length they found themselves alone with their host in the east tower of the castle. Mary wasted no time in introducing the subject of the Inchcolm tomb and payments. Any notion that the Archdeacon Thomas might prove unsympathetic, difficult or even particularly cautious, was quickly dispersed. In fact he shouted with laughter, slapped his knee and appeared to find the entire story much to his taste. He was not, evidently, in the least shocked at the monastic theft, fraud and treatment of the departed, nor was he surprised nor put out by Mary's claim on Jamie's behalf, for compensation for years of moneys paid out under false pretences. Without hesitation he agreed to see what he could do to ease matters along.

Jamie, at least, felt that this was all too easy, too casual altogether, and in consequence little likely to come of it.

"Can this Abbot be made to pay?" he asked. "Unless he can be forced, he certainly will not. He made that very clear to me, even talking of penalties of the Church against me should I persist."

"Ah, I doubt if *you* could make John Dersy pay a groat," the other laughed. "But we here can squeeze him somewhat, in various ways. He is an unpleasant knave and I rejoice at opportunity to bring him down a notch or two. Leave John Dersy to me."

"How much will you get out of him, Thomas? For Jamie?" Mary demanded. "I say it should be a great sum, many hundreds of pounds, thousands indeed. That Abbey has been defrauding the Mortimers and the Douglases for thirty-five years. That is £4,500 mis-spent."

"Sakes — so much! But you were ever greedy, my dear Mary!" her brother accused. "A glutton for what you wanted! I fear that we cannot reach for such great treasure as that. But some solatium we should achieve for you."

"How much?" she insisted. "Do not cozen us, Thomas. How much, think you?"

"A plague, vixen — how may I tell? As yet . . ."

"Sir James should accept no less than £2,000!" Mary asserted crisply.

"Mary . . .!" Isabel exclaimed. "Have you taken leave of your wits?"

Jamie swallowed. No such figure had been mooted. He would never have suggested any such vast sum, and well pleased with a fifth of it. He stirred uncomfortably.

"Heigho — ever the same Mary Stewart!" the Archdeacon chuckled. "That would be a mountain of siller, girl! I fear even *our* treasury would look askance at that. What will Sir James do if it is not forthcoming?" That was interested, easily conversational.

"Why, at the next Privy Council, or parliament, one of the Douglas lords, Sir Jamie's father perhaps, could announce the secret theft of gold belt and jewelled crucifix by the canons of Inchcolm and require their restoration, with due penalty and penance by the said abbey. And, to be sure, due solatium, as you call

257

it. Our brother Robert will be anxious to retain the goodwill of Douglas, I think — since he needs it. I say that it would be less expensive for Holy Church to pay now!"

Her sister at least looked shocked. "You cannot threaten and assail Holy Church so, Mary! Like — like some common merchant!"

"I can, and will. Or Sir Jamie can. Why not? The Church is not above the law. And even the Church's law says Thou shalt not steal!"

Her brother shook a rueful head. "You should have been the man, and Archdeacon of St. Andrews, sister!" he said. "I vow you would have set all by the ears! But you, Sir James — I fear for you! With this one at your heels. She requires a strong hand. Are you so equipped? I, for one, never could master her. Who are these great moneys for? You — or Mary? If you let her get a grip on them . . .!"

"Pay no heed to him, Jamie. A brother's blethers. But at least he clearly believes that there will *be* great moneys to be gripped! We will hold him to it. Perhaps you should offer him some small . . . encouragement?"

"Mary — enough!" Isabel commanded. "You have a wicked tongue. Enough of this. I say we should pass to the other matter . . ."

"So long as Thomas remembers to do his utmost — if he would save his Church trouble!" the irrepressible younger woman put in.

"Other matter?" Thomas Stewart groaned elaborately. "Do not tell me that there is more? A further claim on the long-suffering Body of Christ?"

"No. Nothing of that sort," Isabel said. "A more important matter. Which in some measure concerns me also. Concerned with the death of my husband. Jamie will tell you."

"We seek to learn, sir, what one Patrick Ramsay was doing at St. Andrews a month past, or six weeks? When he came here on some . . . ploy."

"Patrick Ramsay, you say? Ramsay? Should I know? Who is he? This is a large town, Sir James, with many folk, much coming and going. Should I have knowledge of this Ramsay?"

"I had hoped that you might, Sir Archdeacon. Or at least

258

recollect the name. For he came *here*, we are told. To this Bishop's castle. On some seemingly secret mission."

"A month ago? I know no Ramsays, save Neis Ramsay of Banff in Angus. But he has not been here . . ."

"A young man, sir. Younger son to Ramsay of Waughton, in Lothian. Biding for a time on St. Colm's Inch. Come here to see the Bishop, we believe . . ."

"Ha! St. Colm's Inch, again! I reckon I have you now, yes. A young man came here, some weeks past, from Inchcolm Abbey. Though not from Abbot Dersy, I think. To see Bishop Trail. I had naught to do with it, nor him. Did not know his name. This was your Ramsay?"

"Yes. Do you know, sir, what was his business with the Bishop?"

"M'mm. I do, yes. But that business was, shall we say, privy."

"You cannot tell us? Even some small word of it? It is . . . important."

"Important, yes. That is why I am reluctant to speak of it. Save to, to . . ." He looked at his sisters.

"Can you speak of it to *us*, Thomas?" Isabel asked. "For if you can, there is naught, I swear, that we would not wish Jamie to hear. He is my very good friend and leal knight. As he was my husband's . . ."

"I know how Sir James won his knighthood," her brother nodded. "But — this matter has naught to do with the death of the Earl of Douglas, Isabel."

"Are you sure?" Jamie said. "I think that there may be some link in that ill chain."

Thomas Stewart stared closely at him. "How much do you know, Sir James?" he demanded.

"I saw Bickerton of Luffness, the Earl's armour-bearer, stab my lord in the back at Otterburn — and believe that he was set to do it by someone much more important. We sought to take Bickerton, at Luffness, to make him tell all. But this Ramsay reached him first and slew him before he could talk. Most certainly to close his lips for ever. Murder, of a set purpose. I have been seeking him since, to learn who paid him to do it!"

"We believe that it was our brother Robert," Isabel added factually.

The Archdeacon's handsome and mobile features had turned very still, set.

"On Inchcolm we learned that this Ramsay had been hiding there, on the island. After the murder. The Prior is his father's cousin." Jamie went on. "Whilst there he twice visited Falkland — this before the Earl Robert's recent expedition into England. He gained at Falkland money, a good horse, new clothing. And came here to St. Andrews Castle. And then left, to travel North, in the Highlands. Telling his cousin that he believed that the Bishop would be more generous than the Earl Robert!" He paused. "There seems to be proof, therefore, of a link between the Governor and Ramsay. But . . . we need more than that."

Stewart drew a long breath. "What makes you believe that Robert was behind the Earl James Douglas's murder?" he asked. "Even for Robert, it seems a, a long step!"

Isabel answered him. "He misliked James. He had most to gain by his death. Within days he was grasping at James's properties and offices. And he got the power of Douglas into the hands of his friend, Archie of Galloway. Moreover, who else could have done it? Only one or two could, or would. And such we think to have ruled out."

"So-o-o! Robert is a hard and harsh man. But . . ."

"Gelis believes that he also is behind the slaying of *her* husband. In Danzig . . ."

"God's eyes! This is too much . . . !"

"Yes, too much," Mary agreed. "I think that folly. The delusions of a woman stricken and pregnant. Poor Gelis, she has siezed on this. But I say it serves our present quest nothing."

"Aye so would say I. But what *is* your present quest?" her brother asked. "For I cannot see any link between the murder of Earl James and this mission of the man Ramsay to Moray."

"Ha — to Moray!" That was almost a chorus from his three hearers.

Jamie answered him. "We do not seek a link, necessarily. What I seek is Patrick Ramsay. I must see him. Get the truth from him. I have taken a vow on it. Wherever he has gone, I will follow him — to Moray, or further. He closed Bickerton's lips; I will open his!"

"To prove Robert guilty? Suppose you do so, man? What then? What can you do, any of you, against Robert? He rules this land now, all-powerful. He can bend all to his will. What will it serve to prove that he did this deed? You cannot bring him to trial. No court in the land could try the Governor, no tribunal heed you. And he will deny all. You but beat your fists against a wall."

"Somehow, sometime, we will find a way of being avenged," Isabel said levelly. "Tell us, Thomas — was this mission of Ramsay's on Robert's concerns?"

He nodded.

"I was sure of it!" Jamie exclaimed. "Ramsay *is* in the Governor's pay, then. Even though his present employ is naught to do with the Earl James's death. Or other concern of ours."

"I shall believe that when I hear what it is, Thomas," Isabel said.

Her brother shrugged. "You are determined," he sighed. "But it is in truth a *family* matter. Of the Stewarts. If you care not that Sir James hears it, and promise secrecy, I suppose that I may tell you, since you are sisters of both concerned." He paused. "Robert is in fact, seeking to force our brother Alexander of Buchan's hand. He has a subtle mind, has Robert, and he has conceived a scheme whereby he may perhaps win advantage on two scores. It is to do with Alex's wife — whom he has not lived with scarce since he married her seven years ago. He wed Euphemia only for her great lands and titles, for she was Countess of both Ross and Buchan, Lady of Skye, Badenoch and Lochaber. Alex got the earldom of Buchan, and Badenoch and Lochaber, with her — but not Ross, which went to her first husband's son, Alexander Leslie, the present Earl and Robert's good-son. Since when Alex has deserted his wife, to live mainly with this Mariota de Athyn."

"Euphemia is well quit of him, I say!" Mary observed.

"No doubt. But that is scarce the point. What signifies is that Euphemia could be said to be denied of her conjugal rights. Robert has seen an opportunity here. If the marriage could be said never to have been consummated — and there are no children of it — then, with Euphemia's agreement, the Church could proclaim it null and void, however Alex objected. In which case his earldom of Buchan, and other lands he gained, could be taken from him, his power utterly ruined. All came to him through Euphemia—Skye, Lochaber and the rest."

"Ha — Donald of the Isles!" Jamie exclaimed.

261

"Exactly. Our nephew Donald could find his position much affected, if these great lands all reverted to Euphemia."

"But is this not folly?" Mary broke in. "We all know Alex. At first hint of this, he would go straight to the Countess Euphemia, take her and consummate their marriage there and then, for all to see, whether she would or no! Then there could be no decree of nullity."

"To be sure," Thomas nodded. "Hence present secrecy. Alex must not learn what is afoot until the trap is set. If you could think of this, Mary, so could Robert! And has done, to some effect. He has sought an order of Holy Church from the Diocesan — that is the Bishop of Moray, Alexander Barr — and backed by the whole power of the College of Bishops as represented by the Primate here, commanding Alex to take up co-habitation with his lawful wife, deserting the other, under penalty. This is why your man Ramsay is acting secret messenger, why he came here with Robert's text, to gain Walter Trail's agreement, and now is in Moray, conveying it secretly to Bishop Barr for ratification. And to gain Euphemia's signature, at Forres."

"But ... but ... what will that serve?" Jamie cried. "The Wolf — the Earl of Buchan, will no more obey such bishops' order than he will give up the earldom and lands. He will pay no heed, and cannot be turned out by force, in those fastnesses."

"Save perhaps by Donald! But that is true, Sir James. Save that, I think, you have not duly noted that phrase I used. Under penalty. That penalty is not fully stated in the first order — lest Alex perceives his danger. All that will be declared is under penalty of £200 payment. But the true penalty is, in fact, excommunication for disobeying the command of Holy Church. Excommunication, swift and final. And being ratified by the Primate, the Pope will confirm it without doubt."

"Will excommunication greatly trouble the Lord Alex? He is scarcely a religious man!"

"God's death, it ought to! Religious or not. For an excommunicate forfeits all rights in law, in state as well as Church. He becomes as good as dead before the law. So Alex would be unable to contest forfeiture of his earldom and lands, unable to claim any rights soever, his hands tied. Not his sword-hand, perhaps — but if he reverts to the sword he becomes a mere outlaw and brigand, with all who value their immortal souls ranged against him. Including, of course, Donald. So says Holy Church."

They stared at him.

"Robert has planned all this? Against his own brother!" Isabel said.

"He has. Alex has defied him, and is too powerful. He is the only man who might challenge Robert's rule, the next prince in succession—since John will challenge nothing. That Alex could never do, as excommunicate."

"It is clever," Mary conceded. "For Alex will scorn and ignore the order — before he knows of the excommunication. And then, no matter if he does go back to his wife and consummates the marriage, it will be too late. For he will have no rights in this, either."

"Precisely. The Church will not accept an excommunicate's cohabitation as valid, or any woman bound thereby. Such would become a rape!"

"Almost I am sorry for Alex," Mary said. "Although I never thought I would say so."

"Be sorry for us all," her sister amended. "For all Scotland is now ruled by this — this devil."

"The more reason to heed my warning," her brother pointed out. "Do not seek conclusions with Robert — any of you."

Jamie shook his head stubbornly. "Nevertheless, we cannot lie down under evil," he said. "You, sir, a churchman, will not deny that? I shall still go after Patrick Ramsay, to Moray. Find him, and wring the truth out of him. About Bickerton and Earl James's murder. I can do no less, now I know where he is gone."

"No, Jamie!" Mary exclaimed. "Do not do it. What value or virtue in it?"

"Neither virtue nor point," Thomas declared. "Since such knowledge can do you no good. Besides, why go to Moray now? Ramsay will have been gone five or six weeks belike. Difficult as travel is in the Highlands, it should not have taken him all such time to reach Bishop Barr at Elgin. He is but a messenger, and the business should not occupy him overlong. The Countess Euphemia lives at Forres — which is not far from Elgin. Ramsay may well already be on his way back. He will, no doubt, return to report to Robert. If see the fellow you must, then await his return."

"That makes sense, Jamie," Isabel agreed. "No need to go travelling the barbarous Highlands. You might well miss him, indeed. We can wait."

"They are right," Mary added earnestly. "It is here, in the South, that all will be decided, not in the North. Bide here with us, Jamie."

He could be an obstinate young man, and he did not commit himself.

Although there appeared to be nothing more to be learned or gained from the Archdeacon Thomas, they stayed for a few days at St. Andrews, where the atmosphere was considerably more cheerful than at Dunfermline. But Isabel was still anxious about her father's health, and Jamie that Ramsay might come back early and he miss him. After an active interlude of hunting, hawking, feasting, music and even play-acting — which gave the young man, at least, an altogether new impression of high ecclesiastical living — they made their return journey westwards, with promises from Thomas Stewart that he would do what he could about the Inchcolm business, and that if any vital word of Ramsay or his mission came to St. Andrews, as distinct from Dunfermline, he would let them know.

With that they had to be content.

XVII

THE AUTUMN AND winter of 1389 was an unsatisfactory period for Jamie Douglas — as well as for sundry others. Having allowed himself to be persuaded not to set off northwards through the Highlands looking for Ramsay, he found himself forced to hang about the vicinity of the Governor's Court, at Dunfermline and elsewhere, indefinitely, to be sure of seeing that elusive young man when he eventually put in an appearance — which in fact he did not do. For an active and not particularly patient character, this endless and more or less idle waiting was a misery — the more so as, the King's health slightly improved, the Lady Gelis removed herself to Dumfries-shire to have her childbirth at Nithsdale, and took Mary with her. Actually the Earl Robert himself did not remain for very long at a time in one place, moving around to Falkland, to Doune, to Stirling and Linlithgow and Edinburgh, although leaving his ailing parent, under heavy guard, at Dunfermline. Since Isabel felt it to be her duty, as well as in her own interest, to remain with the King, with no others of his daughters near, Jamie would have been hard put to it to find excuse to travel round with, or near, the Governor — who so clearly disliked him — had it not been that the new Earl of Douglas came up from his Border fastnesses to be with and support his friend, and Jamie could attach himself not so much to the Earl's company as to his heir's, the Master of Douglas. Archie the Grim was hard hit by the death of his favourite son, Sir Will, and grimmer than ever. He did not particularly love his eldest and legitimate son, but insisted that the Master danced attendance. The latter had his own little coterie of gentlemen and knights, as befitted the heir of Douglas, and in this group Jamie found himself welcome. Drumlanrig, Cavers and other young sprigs of the house of Douglas, were loosely of its number, and gradually more joined it, including Jamie's own brothers Sir James, William and young Johnnie. The Master was a rather gloomy and reserved young man of twenty-seven, but honest enough. He tended to be more preoccupied than usual in that his marriage was imminent and he a less than enthusiastic bridegroom. It was a union planned by his father and the Governor for political and prestige purposes, the bride being the Lady Margaret Stewart, fifteen-year-old eldest daughter of the Earl of Carrick, the Lord David's sister. The marriage would serve to tie the next generation of Douglas to the Stewart cause and at the same time act as a possibly useful lever on the Carrick family. If the Master of Douglas had had other plans, he was not permitted to air them.

Jamie, with the others, was in the little town of Doune, in Menteith, which served the Earl Robert's great main castle — and where the hunting at least was excellent — when the news came that the Lady Gelis had given birth to a daughter, to be called

Egidia. Earl Archie, the grandfather, snorted his disgust and became worse-tempered than ever. Jamie would have sought to go visit mother and child — and Mary — had he not been tied, waiting for Patrick Ramsay to appear.

In late autumn, the fruits of the expedition into England, of the early summer, where displayed, however futile and abortive it all had seemed to most of the participants, in the arrival of a joint embassage of French and English envoys. A decision had been reached at Boulogne, at last, by these two realms, to include Scotland in their mutual treaty of non-aggression; and the ambassadors brought with them a document signed by Kings Richard and Charles agreeing to a three year truce between all concerned, with the recommendation of renewal thereafter if all went well. This was the first major success of Earl Robert's rule, and seemed to justify his peculiar behaviour at Lanercost and the Roman Wall — although few Douglases at least saw it that way. The envoys came to Dunfermline, where the king was still bed-ridden, so that the Governor's Court had to go back there temporarily to greet them. It is to be feared that the Englishmen got but a cool reception, despite their errand, for Robert Stewart was never effusive, and the Douglas faction, being no weathercocks, remained hostile. Archie the Grim went so far as to send the envoys back with a demand to the King of England for the extradition of his subject the Lord Clifford to stand trial in Scotland for the murder of Sir Will Douglas of Nithsdale. The French had a rather kinder welcome and the truce was signed.

As early winter rains and snows and frosts developed, Jamie began to give up hope of Ramsay's return. Travel anywhere in deep winter was difficult enough, with roads turned to quagmires, low ground flooded, rivers too deep to ford and food for man and beast hard to come by; but in the Highlands it was all but impossible, with the passes blocked and the glens closed. If Ramsay had not got through by this time, then he was unlikely to appear before late spring. The same, of course, applied to any idea of Jamie's going looking for him. All development in his quest seemed to be at a standstill meantime.

All was not gloom with Jamie Douglas, of course, as his twentieth birthday approached — not an age for unrelieved depression. For one thing, in early December a preaching friar brought him a letter from the Archdeacon of St. Andrews. In it he announced that, on his instructions, the diocesan chancellor would pay to Sir James Douglas of Aberdour, on return of the enclosed document duly signed and witnessed, the sum of £100 Scots yearly for ten years, in full adjustment and quittance of his claim against the Abbot and Chapter of St. Colm's Inch. A postscript to this added that there was word from Moray that Bishop Barr had issued the desired command to cohabit and sent it to the Earl of Buchan, presently apparently residing in some outlandish mountain hold called Lochindorb Castle in Braemoray, with no reported results to date. Three months were being given to obey. There had been no sign nor word of the man Ramsay, at St. Andrews.

If, in fact, Jamie was more exercised by the postscript than by what went before, this is not to say that he was not grateful and gratified over this financial windfall — although perhaps his first reaction, that Mary would be pleased, was significant. £100 for ten years, £1,000 in all, was far more than he had ever really anticipated, whatever Mary's extravagances, and, added to his own doubled Aberdour revenues, gave him an income of £400 a year, a sum that many a lordling might envy. He had managed well enough on £150; this would be nothing less than riches.

He would have gone, thereafter, to Nithsdale, to pay his respects to mother and child and to convey the news. But with the Douglas-Carrick wedding to be a Yuletide one at Dunfermline Abbey — so that the King's near presence at least would give it added significance — most of the royal family would be assembling, Gelis allegedly intending to make the winter journey in a horse-litter.

He would wait.

It was to be an especial Yule all round, apart from the wedding. It was the first of the new regime; the first of truce with England. The Governor was not the man to court popularity, nor yet to enjoy festivities; but he could recognise the value of public favour for any government, especially that of the lesser nobility and the Church. So this Christmastide he was prepared to spend money fairly lavishly. It would not be his own money, after all.

Isabel disapproved strongly. Her father believed that he was dying and only wanted to be taken home to Dundonald in Ayrshire, to pass away in peace. It was not much to ask, for the King of Scots. This was no time for his family to be celebrating and capering in his house.

Nevertheless, most of the Stewarts came, from one side of Scotland or the other, despite bad weather for travelling — none from the Highlands of course; but then there was only the Wolf and his illegitimate crew, and his sister and nephew of the Isles, who dwelt in those heathenish parts; for Alexander Leslie, Earl of Ross, and his wife, preferred to live in the Lowlands, being no true Highlanders. The Earl John, of course was there, however reluctantly, with the Lady Annabella and their family, the Lord David to be groomsman. The Lord Walter of Brechin came, with his inevitable entourage of giggling young women. The Lady Egidia of Dalkeith brought such of that family as were not already present. The Lady Elizabeth, married to Sir John Hay of Erroll, the High Constable, came with the Lady Jean, widow of the former Great Chamberlain, Sir John Lyon of Glamis, slain in a brawl with the Lady Egidia's son, Sir James Lindsay. The Lady Marjorie attended on this occasion, with her husband the Earl of Moray, however much the latter disapproved of the Governor. And the Lord Murdoch Stewart, Robert's heir, was there, despite his presence underlining the fact that he was not up where he should have been, as new Justiciar of the North, all knowing that he was in fact frightened to venture into his jurisdiction for fear of the uncle whom he was supplanting. Most of the illegitimate offspring were present also, including the Archdeacon Thomas for once, judiciously keeping his distance from the Governor.

The Douglases, naturally, were there in force, to see their young chief wed. Dunfermline had seldom been so full.

Gelis's litter cavalcade, slow-moving necessarily, was one of the last to reach Dunfermline, and after days of hard frost, Jamie, along with most of the other younger folk, was away curling and skating on frozen Loch Leven eight miles to the north, when it did arrive. Indeed, he was back, starting to eat his evening meal in his very humble quarters in the lower part of the town when, of all people to act messenger, the Lord David Stewart burst into the room.

"Your particular friends have come, Jamie," he announced. They were on familiar terms now, the youth seeming to find Jamie's company more to his taste than that of others; indeed they had been skating together most of the day.

"You mean . . .?"

"I mean my beautiful and well-endowed aunts, on whom Jamie Douglas delights to dance attendance! And does not know which he loves best. They came this noontide, it seems, having taken ten days to travel from Nithsdale — God knows how. Although, of course, they have this puling babe with them. And an insolent lad, whom I have already had occasion to put in his place, the late Sir Will's bastard. But . . . man, finish your eating, of a mercy. They will not run away."

But Jamie was on his feet and hastily tidying himself. Nothing would do but that they must hurry off up to the palace, through the nightbound, slippery streets. With the overcrowded state of Dunfermline, there were lights everywhere however, bonfires on eminences, drink flowing and drunken men-at-arms brawling in the wynds, women skirling and coaxing, packmen selling their wares even at this hour, fisherfolk with braziers vending boiled cockles and mussels and oysters for instant eating, preaching and begging friars going about their business, dogs barking, pigs grunting in the gutters and poultry pecking, a lively and inspiriting scene despite the cold.

The palace and abbey were just as full of folk and movement and noise, with even the illustrious of the land having to bed down in ante-rooms, mural-chambers and corridors. Gelis and her party had no option but to share Isabel's apartment in the old wing, and here David brought Jamie. Throwing open the door, he announced him with an elaborate flourish.

"Sir James Douglas of Aberdour, Knight — a man of wealth and substance and the scourge of Holy Church! To pay his too humble duties to beauty, high-born and base-born — having foolishly left his own meal uneaten to do so!"

Frowning blackly, Jamie stood in the doorway. His eyes lighted at once upon Gelis — and remained there. Always she had been lovely. Now she had somehow added an almost ethereal beauty, a fining-down and spiritualising of her features as of her expression, perhaps as the result of childbearing, motherhood and sorrow, which elevated, exalted, her looks to the exquisite, the utterly heart-catching. Certainly they caught at Jamie Douglas's heart. Gone in a moment his former discomfort and slight offence at her pregnant state, his feeling of alienation on account of her so obvious worship of the memory of Will of Nithsdale. He could not take his eyes off her at first, though there were four others in the room.

"Jamie!" she cried. "How good. How kind. We were but talking of you." She rose, near the fireside — although this time she did not hurry to him but waited for him, arms out.

He did the hurrying — although actually he was almost afraid to embrace her, so fine-wrought and fragile-seeming she had become. Not that her person felt fragile in his arms; it was more an aura of delicacy, rarity, which she appeared to have developed. Her kiss, on his lips, was warm but calm, lingering rather than impulsive. Gelis Stewart was a girl no longer, but a full woman.

"Dear leal Jamie," she murmured, stepping back a little to look at him, but still holding his hand. "Darker than ever, I do declare." A brief touch to the hair at his temple. "But, come. Come and see my poppet. She sleeps, after her long journey . . ."

Only then, as he turned, had he eyes for Mary, sitting back with tambour-frame in a corner of the arras-hung room. She was watching him, smiling just slightly, and looking bonny, bonny — but, of course nothing like so beautiful as her half-sister. He raised his free hand to her, wordlessly, as Gelis led him over to the crib.

The baby was pink and plump and fair, with eyes closed, lips slightly open and tiny fists clenched. Jamie, with no great experience of the like, thought it lacking in interest — but did not say so.

"Very good," he pronounced. And, as an afterthought, "And fat."

"Fat! She is not fat. Do you not think that she is beautiful?"

He was not a good liar. "Not, not as beautiful as her mother!" he got out. He pointed to the rolls of fat at the little wrists. "When she has some hair, perhaps . . ."

"All babies are so . . ."

A tinkle of laughter from across the room. "You have much to teach him, Gelis," Mary said. "But . . . he learns quickly!"

"I dispute that last!" David declared.

From the other side of the fireplace, Isabel spoke. "Perhaps he would prefer your other . . . acquisition, Gelis?" she suggested. "More recognisably Douglas."

Where she pointed, a boy stood, quiet, alert, watchful, and slender, dark, almost swarthy. Douglas he was indeed, every inch, and the young image of the late Sir Will. Small wonder that Gelis cherished him.

"Young Will," she announced. "Young Will of Nithsdale. Who grows apace. And will one day grow sufficiently to avenge his father." That was said quietly, without emphasis, as though common-place — and all the more telling for that. The boy did not so much as blink his bright eyes or alter expression — although David made a face.

Jamie stirred uncomfortably. There were too many currents and cross-currents in this room — not all for the best, he felt. Although on vengeance bent himself, he conceived this last to be unhealthy. He went over to the boy and shook his hand. In their lean darkness they displayed a marked similarity.

"Your father was a fine man, young Will," he jerked. "Grow like him if you would please him best. That is enough."

"As one hero of another," David mocked.

"My lord — I am no hero," Jamie said stiffly. "But this lad's father was. If the house of Stewart could produce stock of this sort, but one or two, it would require to fear the future less."

"Bravo! Bravo! Up, the Douglas!" the youth cried, grinning cheerfully. "I love you when you are embattled thus. Eh, Aunts? Are not we Stewarts a poor crew? Not a hero amongst us. So we needs must marry Douglases — and hope."

Into the uncomfortable silence, Isabel spoke. "We none of us heed Davie," she mentioned, in a general way. "Jamie — I have been telling them of your great good fortune, which Thomas has gained for you. We rejoice . . ."

"Though it is but half of what I asked," Mary put in. "Even so, it is excellent, Jamie."

"It is *you* I have to thank," he said. "As I do, Mary. I am truly grateful. £100 a year is a notable sum. Added to the moiety, it is riches. The Archdeacon has been good, kind. He is here for the wedding — I have thanked him . . ."

"Had my esteemed but unfortunate father known of your so great wealth, Jamie, he could have come to you for siller, instead of having to sell his eldest daughter." David observed.

"Sell . . .?"

They all gazed at him.

"Why, yes. Did you not know? My revered and saintly sire is a babe in many things, I fear. Like some others I know. Siller is one of them. Rents, dues, revenues — he lets his tenants and vassals off with them, on any sorrowful tale. In consequence is ever indebted to others, less kind. Certain matters have grown pressing — so my Lord High Steward of Scotland must needs find some hundreds of siller swiftly. His kind brother the Governor found it for him — on condition that he wed his daughter to the heir of Douglas. So, no doubt, the Earl Archie paid for it. Heigho — my valuable sister, at fifteen!"

Struck silent, they digested this.

"I had no notion of such a thing," Isabel said, at length. "It is shameful. So, so lacking in dignity. She will be the first princess of Scotland . . ."

"If her father ever reaches the throne!" Mary put in.

"You think . . . he might not?"

"I think it possible."

"You think father might go the way of Uncle David of Strathearn, Aunt?" young David asked, interestedly.

"I did not say that, Davie. Only that it is possible that he might not reach the throne. Other, other hindrances might come between."

"As such?"

"Your father might be persuaded. To renounce the crown. Or to abdicate when the King dies . . ."

"In favour of Uncle Robert? Then it would be necessary to get rid of *me*, would it not? For I am the next heir, not my uncle. And I would not renounce nor abdicate, I assure you. So I am equally at risk, with my father. Do not think that I have not conceived of it. I keep my eyes and ears wide, whatever my father does."

Jamie looked at the youth, wondering, as so often before. It crossed his mind that here undoubtedly was someone the Earl Robert would have to dispose of eventually if he wanted unchallenged control of Scotland.

It was as though David Stewart read his mind. "So you see, I am in my uncle's road even more than is my father. He considers me child, as yet. But that will change. In another year or two . . ." The boy laughed and shrugged. "In another year or two, my father will either be King, or dead, or else I King. In any case, better able to look after my Uncle Robert! What one Stewart can do, so can another. Let Robert Stewart watch for himself!"

If Jamie, or the Stewart women, had any notion of dismissing that as adolescent bravado or posturing, they had but to remember the rows of dangling bodies at Turnberry Castle, hanged on this boy's orders; or indeed the manner of their initial introduction to him there. David Stewart did not go in for idle posturing.

Smiling at their alarmed expressions, he went on. "As token that two can play this game, I too can take Douglas to be my shield and support. God save Douglas, I say! So I offer myself as groomsman for this wedding. Persuade my lady-mother that Archibald, Master of Douglas is the finest goodson she could find for her firstborn, a true, honest and kindly husband, if something sober. That my uncle would seem to think the same in this, is no matter. Archibald Douglas will be *my* friend, not his. I might even wed a Douglas myself, before too long — the grim and ancient Earl Archie has a belated daughter Marjorie, has he not? I already have made many Douglas friends, and shall make more. Have I not, Jamie? So now you see why I so cherish Sir James Douglas of Aberdour as my dear and close companion. He is as a key to the door of this Douglas strength — as well as being a likeable carl, to be sure." And the insufferable youth patted Jamie's shoulder.

Even as that young man jerked away, however, he knew doubts, misgivings. How much of all this was folly, how much stark truth? This boy could well be King of Scots in a few years' time — if he lived. All that he said, however fleeringly spoken and outrageous, in fact made sound sense. Even the last mocking reference to himself. Put a crown on this beautiful head, and the words became not vapourings but pregnant with meaning, fateful, perhaps prophetic. And that crown was in a highly unstable state, none would deny.

Gelis it was who changed the subject, or at least brought it back to where it had been, young Will Douglas.

"Do not heed Nephew Davie too closely, Will," she advised. "He talks much nonsense. Wiser to heed Sir Jamie, who uses words more carefully! He acts, as one day you must act. Learn from him."

Embarrassed, Jamie looked around him. "I, I fear that I cannot act in anything on an empty stomach!" he said. "I but came to greet you. With your ladyships' permission I go back and finish my meal. Tomorrow there is to be another great bonspiel, skating, curling, jousting on sleds, races, feasting on the ice, at Loch Leven. If I may act escort for any or all . . ."

"It will be *all*, I assure you!" David prophesied. "You will see. Now, I shall come with you, back to your lodging. Perhaps I may win a few more Douglases as friends. Unlike you, I never hazard myself alone with these aunts. I bid you all a good night . . ."

*   *   *

Loch Leven, wide and level under the thrusting Benarty and Lomond Hills, presented a gay and extraordinary scene, basically white with ice and hoar-frost but splashed and dotted with colour as hundreds disported themselves on the ice. Lists, enclosures and even pavilions of a sort had been erected, the servitors and men-at-arms dragged sleds of food and drink and fuel out to the islands, where bonfires blazed and groaning trestles were set. Half-a-dozen curling-matches were in progress, players sweeping busily with birch-brooms to ensure maximum runs for their stones; skating and sledge races were taking place; tumblers, acrobats, wrestlers and even dancers entertained, and groups of instrumentalists dispensed music throughout. There was ample room for all, for the heart-shaped loch was in fact almost four miles long by two wide, with seven islets, two quite large, and the little towns of Kinross and Milnathort huddling on its northern, marshy shore. All save St. Serf's Priory Island belonged, as it happened, to Jamie's father, like so much else in Lowland Scotland, and he it was who was paying for all the festivities, here and elsewhere, as contribution to the Douglas side of the wedding.

Jamie's party did indeed include all the group of the previous evening — save for the baby, left with a nurse; but others also had attached themselves, more to the princesses and the Lord David than to Jamie, Gelis being as a magnet for a large proportion of the well-born males on the loch. The fact that the bride of two days hence was also with them made a deal less stir. She was a quiet modest girl, with the warm beginnings of Stewart good looks — and her brother was unexpectedly kind to her. The bride-groom was nowhere to be seen.

Jamie had bought, begged or borrowed as many sets of bone-made skates as he could find in the little towns, and they all were displaying their differing stages of expertise, those who had been reared on the east side of the country being notably better at it

274

than those from the west, where intense frosts were rare. The Stewarts were mainly from the south-west, and Jamie suitably had elected to teach Gelis the art. Not that he would have had the least chance with her, in view of the many eager and more highborn instructors, had she not made it clear that he was her own choice. The business, of course, involved much clinging and clutching and holding up, which neither appeared to find distasteful. Nevertheless, Gelis did not shout and laugh and skirl as so many young women were doing in like circumstances, but maintained the air of calm dignity that went with her new sort of beauty — however little dignity and learning to skate might seem to match. She was looking utterly lovely in that bright, cold air, cheeks flushed, great eyes glowing, heavy coiled hair golden against the black-and-white hood of her fur cloak. Jamie suffered little of his normal slight impatience.

"You must think me very awkward, clumsy, Jamie?" she panted, not for the first time. "I vow my little Egidia might perform as well at this as do I! Perhaps I am too old to learn this skating?"

"Too old? You are twenty-one years four months. Is that old?"

"So — you know, to the month. Am I to be flattered, or otherwise?"

"I have no concern with flattery," he told her, holding her straight on course. "But I have long grieved that you were sixteen months older than am I. It seemed a sad gap, once."

"But not so sad now, I think?"

"No," he admitted. "Not now."

"I feel a deal older."

"I do, also. But you — you have suffered much. Yet look . . . the fairer."

"Suffered much, yes. And learned much, I hope . . ." She collapsed into his arms again. "Save in this nonsense! How strong you are, Jamie. How secure I feel, in your strong arms."

"They are yours to command, Gelis. Always."

"I wonder!"

"Why say that? What mean you? It is truth."

"Yes, Jamie. Truth in one fashion. I know that you are the lealest of the leal. But . . ."

"But what?"

"These strong arms have held others, have they not? Even more closely perhaps?"

He caught his breath and could not answer her, cursed by his inability to lie convincingly. Was it possible, conceivable, that Mary could have told her?

She searched his face, so near her own. "It is true, then. You see, Jamie? True, the other — only after a fashion." She pushed away. "Now — let me try this again . . ."

"But . . . but . . ." He shook his head, and concentrated on supporting her delectable person. Many watching undoubtedly marvelled that any man, in the circumstances, could manage to look so frowningly displeased — although indeed his dark brows had much to do with it.

Isabel glided close. After years of marriage in the east, she was a good skater. "Spare poor Gelis, Jamie," she called. "She has suffered enough, surely! Come — escort me over to the isle where they are roasting beef. I vow I can smell it, from here. I am hungry." That was slightly imperious.

"Yes," he nodded. "Very well. Perhaps the Lady Gelis is hungry also? Will you come . . .?"

"Not now, no, I thank you. It may be that I can find some other strong arms, meantime. Later, perhaps . . ."

His frown unabated, he skated off with Isabel.

"Gelis wearies easily," her sister mentioned. "In her present condition. I scarce think it wise for her to try to skate, meantime."

"She seems well enough. And nothing loth."

"She is not eight weeks from childbirth. Not truly herself. Do not encourage her towards foolishness, Jamie."

"Yes, Princess."

She looked at him sharply, as they sped together over the ice. "I mean it kindly, Jamie. For you both. Gelis is too recent a widow, and mother, for, for cantrips! And folk will talk."

He seemed to have heard that before, somewhere. He forbore to enlarge on it, however.

They came to the islet, not far from that of the castle, where the food was being dispensed. A dozen fires blazed here, whole sides of oxen roasting on two of them, on spits, wildfowl, capons, venison on others, with boiled lobsters, crabs and shellfish on braziers.

There were wines and spirits and ale, hot if desired. A gipsy with a fiddle and a dancing-bear entertained here.

The Lord Murdoch Stewart sat on a sled, watching the bear with lack-lustre eyes, and toying morosely with a whole roasted mallard. His young gentlemen had drawn some distance back, so that it seemed that he was in one of his moods. He was a strange and difficult man — perhaps not to be wondered at, with the father he had — tall, well-made with reddish hair, and good-looking in a heavy way that could frequently turn to sullenness. In his late twenties and still unmarried, he had been kept too closely under his father's thumb, and while resenting it, lacked the strength to break free.

"I hear that you almost won the sled race, Nephew," Isabel greeted him civilly.

"Almost — but did not!" he returned shortly. "How should I, when others have better horses?"

"You showed the greater skill, then."

He shrugged.

"Cousin Murdoch will remedy his lack of good horseflesh soon enough now," a musical voice declared behind them. "When he can take the best from all the North. A poor Justiciar and Lieutenant who could not!" The Lord David, who must have skated after them, had come up quietly.

Murdoch eyed his young kinsman without delight, and made no comment.

"To be sure, it will be necessary to take over from Uncle Alex first," David went on judiciously. "He, now, will have a fine stable, I warrant. Perhaps he will leave it for you, Cousin. When do you go?"

"When I am ready."

"Ah, yes. Good. Readiness is vital, in dealing with our good uncle. And discretion likewise. But I have little doubt but that you are most suitably discreet, Cousin Murdoch."

Hastily Isabel intervened. "I would think that Murdoch is waiting for tidings from the North. To determine when he should go."

Her older nephew nodded. "That is so."

"And it is scarce the time for journeying, my lord," Jamie put in. "For couriers or for Justiciars." He had no urge to rescue the Governor's sullen son from his gadfly relative, but he hoped that

277

this conversation might be steered to the subject of Ramsay — of which, of course, David knew nothing.

Murdoch nodded again.

"What tidings do you await?" David asked interestedly. "That Uncle Alex has died a death? Or perhaps so dreads your coming that he sends abject terms. For the surrender of his powers and offices?"

Stung, the other raised his head. "The Earl Alexander will have good reason to be abject!" He jerked. "You speak truer than you think, boy."

"Ha — you say so? That will be a new role for the Wolf of Badenoch!"

"A new role, yes. He has never yet been, been . . ." Murdoch swallowed the dread word just in time. He coughed. "Been faced with the full rigours of Church and state," he substituted.

"*Church* and state?" the quick-witted David asked.

"And you await a courier bringing tidings of this?" Isabel inserted.

"We do. He is delayed. Or I could well have been in Elgin by now."

"Delayed? Or lacking the desired tidings?" his cousin wondered, sceptically.

"Delayed. He left Elgin in mid-October. A friar of Bishop Barr's brought the word to the Abbot of Dunfermline. But the Highland passes were closed early, with snow, floods . . ."

"But insufficiently to halt the friar, it seems!"

"He came came round the coasts."

"So you still await this courier and his message before you venture North?" Isabel asked.

"I mislike your word venture, Aunt." That was heavily said.

"Travel, if you will. Journey. And if he comes not?"

"We have sent another. To ascertain conditions."

"Such caution, Cousin, will serve you but oddly in dealing with Uncle Alex, I think!" the youngster observed, pulling a face. "Come, Aunt, Jamie—let us see if the beef here is as tender as is Murdoch Stewart." And he strolled off.

After a moment or two, Jamie followed him, leaving Isabel apologising to one nephew, who scowled, for the behaviour of another who smiled.

"Ox-roasting is but poor sport!" David commented, as the other came up with him. "How think you, Jamie?"

"I think you make enemies needlessly, my lord."

"You do? That one is my enemy whether I make him so or not. His kind, one might bait into indiscretion, I say." He paused. "What is this of the rigours of *Church* and state?"

Jamie shrugged, and moved faster, ahead.

At the true ox-roasting they found Mary and her niece, the bride, nibbling daintily but effectively at steaming ribs of beef, and joined them gladly. But when, presently, the Countess Anabella of Carrick came and carried off her two children to present them to the Primate, Bishop Trail, who would conduct the wedding service two days hence, Jamie was less at ease. He had not been alone with Mary since her arrival from Nithsdale, hardly indeed since the day on Inchcolm, and he was uncomfortably aware that the young woman might well have remarks to make. He chewed the more attentively at his rib.

"I saw you talking with that odious Murdoch," she said, after a space. "You would get little out of that one, I think?"

Much relieved, he answered her, his mouth full of meat. "More than I thought to. We learned that Ramsay left Elgin in October. They still look for him to come. So they wait as impatiently as do I. They have sent another messenger to the Bishop of Moray meantime."

"To learn how Alexander has received the cohabitation command?"

"Yes. That, and to discover if may be what reception would greet the Lord Murdoch should he venture into his new jurisdiction. He mislikes the word venture, which Lady Isabel used — but it is clear that he is afraid to go North until he learns that his uncle is sufficiently cowed. But if what the Archdeacon Thomas said is so, then the Earl Alexander could not yet be cowed. If ever. For he was given three months to comply with the command. Under threat only of fining. The excommunication, which they think alone could cow him, not to be mentioned. Three months are not yet gone."

"So-o-o . . .?"

"I think that the Earl Robert may not have told his son all. That Murdoch believes the excommunication threat to have been made, and does not know of the deceit, the trap."

"It could well be so. Robert would deceive his own self, if he might. Does, perhaps." She paused. "It may be that we all do."

"In what fashion?"

"Why, in our everyday hopes and fears and wishes. *I*, see you, had believed that you had been weaned from your doting on Gelis. But I find that it is not so. You are more besotted than ever, I think! I it is who deceive myself."

He drew a sharp breath. "You have no right to say that," he protested.

"No? Even after, after ..." She shook her head. "No *right*, Jamie, perhaps. But must a woman have a right before she may speak her mind? To one who, who has been close to her?"

It was that word close which sparked off the little blaze — that and his own too lively conscience. Gelis had used the same word, or closely. These arms, she said, had held others even more closely.

"So you must needs tell Gelis of this closeness!" he jerked. "Was that why you did it? There on Inchcolm? To unbesot me of your sister!"

She drew back from him as though struck. "Jamie — how unkind. How cruel!"

'Belike, for the same reason, you gained me those moneys from the Church," he blurted on, his long-repressed doubts and emotional tearings bubbling up unchecked at last. "I did not desire those moneys. I was well enough, lacking them. *You* shall have them — for they are yours. You plotted for them and won them, not I. Take them, then. I will make a charter of gift ..."

"Stop!" she commanded. "Before you say the unforgivable! Before you call me whore, harlot! And keep your moneys. For you will need it all, and more, if Sir James Douglas seeks to wed himself to a princess. Not that Gelis will ever wed *you*, or any. She will use you, yes. Hold you to her side. But not wed. She is wed to the memory of Will of Nithsdale, only. And the person of his son. She will wed no other. I ... I ..." she turned and ran from him then, voice choked in her throat.

Almost he went after her, but did not and stood biting his lip, hating himself.

Isabel found him, presently, staring at his rib of beef unseeing. She linked her arm in his. "Come — take me to see this castle on the other island," she said. "My brother Alex was imprisoned there by Queen Margaret of Logie, when a young man, twenty years ago. Did you know . . .?"

He went with her, wordless.

*   *   *

Two days later, the wedding itself was something of an anti-climax. It was, indeed, a strange admixture of extravagance and parsimony, of splendour and apathy, of the formal and the make-shift. The fact was that, when it came to the bit, neither Earl Robert nor Earl Archibald had been prepared to dip their hands too deeply into their pockets for the business, and the Earl John could not afford to. As a result much was skimped. Where the Lord of Dalkeith had had a hand, and sundry other Douglases, there was amplitude, colour, richness — but this was only on the perimeter, as it were, the inessentials, where they were spending to enhance the credit of their house. The churchmen were, as always, magnificent to look at; and Dunfermline Abbey a brilliant setting. Most of the guests were at their finest. But that said, the proceedings were all but humdrum, the ceremonial cut to a minimum. The Master of Douglas looked well enough and suitably clad, but scarcely interested — indeed much outshone by his lively and youthfully beautiful groomsman in royal cloth-of-gold and scarlet, who for that matter, equally outshone his light and shrinking sisters, all three of them, the bride included. The wedding-feast after the ceremony was lavish enough but lacked sparkle—the Governor's presence something of an inhibiting factor perhaps, and neither the Earl Archie nor his son at their best in such social occasions; while the bride's father contributed nothing to gaiety. Indeed, the Lady Egidia of Dalkeith was heard to exclaim loudly that they required her nephew Alex to liven matters up suitably, by God!

Jamie himself added little enough to the jollity. He stood through the ceremony and sat through the banquet, in lowly position and dark reserve, at odds with himself and all else. He could have placed himself near Mary, but she would have nothing to do with him — and of course in such formalised proceedings the princesses were far out of his reach. Not that Gelis was being very gracious to him either, and he was finding Isabel trying. He cursed himself for what he had said to Mary — but that would not unsay it. Yet, in a way, she had deserved it, undoubtedly; he was tired of being warned and reproved and tugged this way and that. He had never felt less of a knight or hero, less chivalric, less sure of his direction. He was, in fact, not good at waiting, at inactivity and looking on.

After the wedding there were the usual Yuletide festivities. But somehow conditions were not favourable, despite official encouragement, Holy Church's cooperation and the unusual peace with England. For one thing, the weather broke down to continuous rain, chill and windy, and with outdoor occasions excluded, all indoors became so overcrowded as to lose appeal. But there was more to it than that. There was a kind of undefined and unexpressed fear hanging over the land, a fear for the future. The old man slowly dying up in his tower-room scarcely helped.

Folk began to leave for home early. Jamie's twentieth birthday passed almost unobserved.

It was, in fact, the King who achieved for Jamie his immediate desire — to get away from Dunfermline quickly; or, at least, Isabel it was who persuaded her brother to allow her father to go home to Dundonald, his childhood home, as he wished. The monarch was scarcely rational now and seldom spoke lucidly. But when he did it was of his longing for Dundonald, to die there. The Governor at last agreed. He was himself a restless man. He decided to wind up affairs at Dunfermline and take the King home himself, with a large guard, of course. Isabel was not to be parted from her father — and Jamie, as ever, provided her escort.

The parting from Gelis and Mary was a strained and straining business, with the boy Will watching, level-eyed, silent. Neither of the young women had ever looked more fair. Stilted farewells expressed nothing of what might have been said, should have been said. Gelis kissed him goodbye, with a sudden little rush. Mary did not. But as he moved to the door, it was Mary who had the last word.

"Take heed, Jamie, how you go. Always," she said. "Be not . . . so great fool as . . . as sometimes!"

After a moment he nodded his head at that, and left them.

III

XVIII

USED AS HE WAS, by this time, to the rugged and spectacular, in scenery, Jamie Douglas involuntarily reined in his garron as they topped the rise, to stare at what opened before them, beyond the birches. Two massive, hulking mountains reared themselves threateningly a few miles ahead, steep-sided from this angle, harsh, sombre even, with the forenoon April sunlight gleaming on their still snow-clad flanks — where the flanks were not so abrupt or riven by corries and ravines that the snow could not lie. In that vast welter of hills in which they rode, and had ridden for days, these two stood out dramatically, menacingly; and between their mighty buttresses a great abyss yawned, dark, daunting. There appeared to be no other break in the solid phalanx of mountain and ridge in front.

Nodding towards it all, he turned in his saddle to the young Highlander, Gregor MacAlpin, whom he had hired on the advice of the Bishop of Dunkeld, when they entered Atholl, as necessary guide and interpreter.

"Those mountains? That gulf? What are they?" he demanded.

"*An Muc Ath-Fodla* and *An Torc Baidheanach. Druimoch-dair* between," the other said, in his pleasing, lilting voice. "The Sow of Atholl and the Boar of Badenoch. Also the Pass of Drum-ochter."

"Badenoch . . . !" Jamie, despite himself, repeated that ominous name with a hint of dread.

"Badenoch, yes. Och, Atholl ends at the Sow — with the Boar

seeming like to be mounting her!" Gregor smiled briefly at the significance of his little joke. "But it is through this Badenoch that you are after coming to travel, is it not, lord?"

He part-nodded, part-shrugged. "Yes. To be sure. And that pass — must we go through that?"

"There is no other way, at all."

He signed to the other three to ride on.

They were five days north of Dunkeld — and in this land one counted distances by days rather than miles — eleven since they crossed the Highland Line at Aberfoyle in Menteith. It seemed scarcely credible for Border horsemen, but they were averaging no more than a dozen miles in the day. They had left their good horses at Dunkeld, of course, and now rode the stocky, short-legged, broad-hooved Highland garrons, which nothing would make speedy but which were sure-footed and tough enough to cover country which would have foundered any ordinary mount. Jamie had heard plenty about the difficulties and dangers of Highland travel; but he had not fully realised the scale and scope of the problem until he actually experienced it — made worse, to be sure, by his own impatience in starting out too soon, before the worst of the spring snow-melt and flooding was past. With every burn a hazard, every river a rushing torrent, every loch swollen, every glen-floor a bog, every drove-track — for there were no true roads — a succession of peat-broth quagmires, progress was as slow as it was uncomfortable and dangerous. And devious — for circumnavigation was the constant procedure; often half-a-day was spent reaching a spot tantalisingly in view only a mile ahead. The fact that beauty and grandeur were everywhere around quickly lost appeal, in the circumstances — although every now and again sheer and dramatic scenic loveliness did halt the Lowland travellers in their tracks.

Progress had proved to be expensive as well as slow, and Jamie had reason to be glad of his new-found wealth whatever he had said to Mary Stewart. Not that food and forage cost the wayfarer more than in the Lowlands; considerably less in fact, although the choice was severely limited, for human consumption, to oat products, beef, venison, salmon and scraggy poultry, with milk and cheese. The expense arose from a sort of passage-toll. Every area of the long route, however vacant-seeming, was in fact the territory of some clan, or part of a clan, under its chief, chieftain or tacksman; and each of these exacted payment for way-leave or so-called safe-conduct across their domain, however small, barren or empty. They might pay as much as three such tolls in a single day, with fierce-looking if superficially polite clansmen assessing them shrewdly at each stop, deciding on how much to make the charge, on the basis of how much the victim could probably afford to pay — and it was by no means always the greater territories and more powerful chiefs who charged the most. Jamie at least had had the sense to take good advice on this matter before setting out, and had decided to limit his escort to a mere three – for the larger the party the larger the toll, it seemed. It was of little avail to use a numerous and heavily-armed retinue, evidently — short of a small army — for food and forage was just not provided for such, and the Highlanders had innumerable ways of blocking the already difficult passage of those whom they did not like, without actually resorting to arms; although this they could do also, for these chiefs could call up surprising numbers of savage swordsmen from the apparently empty mountains and glens, who were far more at home fighting in bogs and on steep hills than could be the travellers. Three, therefore, was probably sufficient for immediate personal protection from small robbers and the like, whilst being no pro-vocation to the more powerful. That last thought had been very much in Jamie's mind, also, for the final stages of his journey and quest, where any seeming provocation towards a much more dire authority fell to be avoided at all costs.

There was one advantage, however, about this expensive toll-paying process, other than the fact that it was usually linked with providing hospitality — if that was the word — in the form of ele-mentary food and shelter; and that was, since it was compulsory on all travellers, it provided a fairly reliable means of checking who and what had come this way recently. So Jamie, through Gregor MacAlpin the interpreter, could question each wild toll-gatherer anent Patrick Ramsay. There were, in fact, very few Lowland travellers in the Highlands, save for the ubiquitous churchmen, wandering and mendicant friars who moved con-tinually between monasteries, abbeys and dioceses wheresoever situated, and tended to act as couriers, messengers, even packmen for other than religious institutions. Church advice at Cam-buskenneth, Dunblane and Dunkeld had been unanimous that this, by mid-Atholl and Drumochter, was the route almost certain to have been taken by Ramsay or any other wayfarer to and from Elgin. The alternative, by Ericht and the passes of Glen Shee and the Mounth, was longer and higher with many more hazards — whilst the route round the east coast would take a half-month longer. Despite all his questioning, however, Jamie could glean no hint nor trace of anyone approximately resembling Patrick Ramsay. Young, red-haired, broad-built and hot-eyed, he was the sort of Lowlander the clansmen would note and remember. Some indeed said that they could recollect one such travelling northwards in the autumn, alone. It seemed that Ramsay was still in the North.

Now, as they approached the beetling Pass of Drumochter, under the rearing Sow of Atholl, they were as usual accosted by typical tartan-and-calfskin-clad brigands, with ingratiating smiles and bows but armed to the teeth, requesting *màl*, or mail, as they called it, in the name of the mighty and potent chieftain MacConachie of Dalnamine, own cousin to *Donnachaidh Mor* himself, lord of all Atholl. They had to pay not a few contributions to this resounding potentate already, but this was the costliest of all, as final quittance, as it were, for after this they would be into the lands of the barbarous Macphersons, Cattanachs, Shaws and other members of the unspeakable Clan Chattan — where the good God preserve them! Jamie, who had anticipated any threat to come from the Wolf of Badenoch and his minions, was concerned to hear of these new terrors. But MacAlpin indicated that this was likely to be no more than exaggerated clan rivalry and animosity, or else a desire to detain the travellers here for prolonged 'hospitality' — which assessment seemed to be substantiated when the MacConachies switched their pressure to the dangers and appalling horrors of the Pass of Drumochter just ahead, than which there was apparently, nothing to compare and which demanded days of preparatory feeding and toughening for man and beast, here in the clan township of Doire Dhonaich, as well as no doubt expensive escort through eventually. Warnings were also given as to the extortionate habits and sheer wickedness of the thieving monks in front — from which it transpired that the Church, in its charity, has established a hospice of sorts for wayfarers in the very mouth of the Pass, which the MacConachies clearly resented. Pressing on to this, despite almost tearful dissuasion, in a mile or two, at Dalnaspidal, they found a small and modest establishment, not to say primitive, although no doubt a very grateful haven for many a stormbound or weary traveller. It was kept by three Cistercian friars and half-a-dozen very tough lay-brothers. These likewise did their utmost to prevail on Jamie to linger, harping on the dramatic severities of the Pass rather than on the Clan Chattan bandits — though, the visitors suspected, really only desiring more prolonged converse and gossip with folk who spoke other than the local Erse. However, it being no more than noonday, Jamie was determined to press on. When they took their leave, the friars reluctantly admitted that there was, in fact, another similar hospice at the other end of the Pass which they ought to be able to reach before nightfall, if God and the Virgin were kind.

Drumochter, which now engulfed them, was certainly a daunting place, as befitted the main and major access from the Southern Highlands into the wilder upland fastnesses of Badenoch and Braemoray, one of the greatest such gateways in all Scotland. One thousand five hundred feet above the level of the sea, it was a six-miles-long deep defile between close-shouldering high and barren mountains, so steep that for much of the year the sun never reached its rocky and narrow floor. Cataracts poured whitely down its harsh flanks, so that the noise of falling water prevailed, punctuated by the frequent scream of eagle and buzzard circling above, all against a strange rumbling sound like distant thunder, which MacAlpin said was actually the noise of wind amongst the high tops — although there was little wind here in the gut of the Pass. Apparently these mountains, outliers of the mighty Monadh Ruadh to the north, made their own weather, and storms of great fury could rage up there about the peaks and corries, in a totally different climate unsuspected below. Many a hillman, herdsman or hunter had perished for failing to remember that. Sometimes that weather descended into the Pass itself — and then let travellers beware.

As well as these hazards, Drumochter was declared to be the haunt of wolves, wild boars and other terrors; but Jamie, considering its bare and stony sides argued that any such creatures would be highly unlikely to seek out these singularly barren and unproductive hunting-grounds if they had a grain of natural sense.

In fact, although the traversing of that great defile took them the remainder of the day, it was water, bog and fallen rocks which delayed them rather than animate creatures or climatic conditions. Apart from the eagles, buzzards and ravens, and a few deer and white hares, they did not set eyes on anything that moved throughout — save for the everlasting cascading white water which scored the hillsides and made a prolonged marsh of the boulder-strewn floor, eventually to turn into the north-flowing River Truim.

Weary, soaked and splattered with peat-mud to the eyes, they came to Dalwhinnie, where this river, running fast now, began to drop somewhat to a wider though still high and enclosed upland valley. Here was the second hospice, with a scattering of turf cabins and more mail to pay, this time to Macphersons whose patronymic, the Sons of the Parson, possibly only enhanced their cupidity. Fortunately, by Lowland standards, the scale of these tolls was small, a single silver piece obviously representing great wealth to a people whose normal medium of exchange was in kind not coin. The Macphersons proved to be no worse than the Mac-Conachies however, in other respects.

They spent the night at this hospice, and Jamie found great difficulty in keeping awake during the prolonged session of questions, discourse and report which followed the meal and went on by the hour, with Friar John, from Stirling, avid to gain and dispense news and views with one of his own race. But out of all the talk, the travellers did learn something of value other than that no one answering the description of Patrick Ramsay had passed this way. They gained a new insight into the ways and regime of Alexander Stewart, Earl of Buchan, still Justiciar and Lieutenant of the North so far as the local inhabitants were concerned.

Clearly there was a sort of love-hate relationship between the Wolf and the people here. He was a hard, cruel man, yes — but he kept the warring, plundering clans in order. He took his own heavy taxes and dues from all, but let them off others' claims, including the King's. He allowed no robbers, thieves and sorners to operate in all Badenoch, Braemoray and Lochaber — other than his own sons and minions. Above all, he made constant war and frequent descents upon the fat lowlands of the Laigh of Moray and the like, which all Highlanders were prone to do, and did not prevent others from doing likewise. It ill became a churchman to defend such raidings, Friar John admitted, especially as the Prior of Pluscarden and the Bishop of Moray were his superiors in God; but the fact was that all these low-countrymen were rich, and arrogant in their riches, referring to all Highlandmen as caterans and Erse savages and treating them accordingly whenever they might. Clearly the good friar had become somewhat contaminated through his long stay in the mountains.

Jamie was too sleepy to pursue the matter at length, rarified mountain air and Highland travel tending to have that effect; but he did gather that the Wolf had three main strongholds, strategically sited where they could best control his vast domains, or at least the accesses and drove-roads and passes through them — Lochindorb, on the high moors of Braemoray, above the Moray plain, to the north, which was his favourite seat and home; Loch-an-Eilean, a smaller fortress, also on an island in a loch, amidst the great pine-forests of Rothiemurchus, in the centre and heart of the territory; and Ruthven, not so very far from Dalwhinnie, guarding both this route to the south and that which probed right across the Highlands to Lochaber and the West, as well as all the great upper Spey valley. He had lesser holds too, of course, but these three represented the government of one-fifth of Scotland, as far as acreage went. Their captains were all sons of the Wolf, young men as hard and tough as their sire, illegitimate to be sure but none the less authoritative for that. There were five of them, all by Mariota de Athyn, a noted concubine; and though he had innumerable other brats by other women scattered over the face of the land, these were very much the ruling family, with more power, according to the friar, than any prince or earl in the South.

The Wolf, it seemed, was a king in all but name — and a far more potent one than ever his father had been.

Jamie sought his couch heavy-eyed, that night — but with a correspondingly heavy feeling that he ought to be exceedingly thoughtful.

Next morning, as they rode on down Glen Truim, his mind was indeed very busy. It seemed clear that with the Wolf's grip so strong and all-embracing, nothing was likely to be achieved in these territories lacking his permission, since it seemed that he was not to be avoided as Jamie had hoped. On the other hand, if anyone was apt to know the whereabouts of Patrick Ramsay, the Wolf was, undoubtedly. So instead of avoiding him, if possible, as intended, might it not be more profitable actually to seek his presence? He had no reason to think well of the Earl Alexander, but nor had he reason to loathe him as he did his brother. And since the Wolf also loathed his brother, might he not in fact be sympathetic towards this quest? Moreover, he had the where-withal to bargain, had he not? The knowledge of this excommuni-cation trap. For that knowledge the Earl should be prepared to pay. And if it was to help convict his brother Robert of the murder of the Earl of Douglas . . .?

Would such approach and revelation be in some way wrong, a tale-bearing, a breach of faith even? But against whom? Isabel? She did not love Alex — but again she did not hate him as she did Robert. She could not particularly desire his excommunication, her own brother, just to further an evil plot in Robert's game of power? The Archdeacon Thomas, then, who had revealed it? The same applied to him; and though it was partly a churchmen's plot, he had had no hand in concocting it. None would suffer, then, from its revelation save the instigator, Robert Stewart. Which was as it should be. Well, then!

He had got so far in his debate with himself when, as on the previous day, he suddenly drew up his garron, to stare. Not, this time, at ominous, threatening grandeur but at sheer heart-break-ing loveliness. Rounding a corner of the steepening glen of the now rushing, foaming Truim, there far-flung before them opened a tremendous prospect of dizzy immensity, a vast low-lying am-phitheatre, all colour and light, rimmed by range after range of mountains slashed with snow and shadow, purple and mauve and every shade of blue. All the foreground was the rich dark-green-and-copper of Caledonian pine-forest, stippled with the verdant emerald of young birch-buds and just bursting out. It took a moment or two to realise that half the colour of the middle-ground was in fact water faithfully reflecting hills and woods and sky. After the constriction of the Pass and close-shouldering mountain-sides, the vista was breath-taking.

"Badenoch," MacAlpin nodded. "The Drowned Land."

"Drowned . . .? It is beautiful. I had no notion . . ."

"Drowned, yes. That is the great valley of Spey, twenty miles long and a mile broad, lord. In this season of melting snows, the Spey cannot contain it all, and is after spreading over all the valley. Each year it does so, for it carries the waters of all the land.

That is no mighty loch, but flooded meadows. *Bàth-eanach*, the Drowned Land."

"It is beautiful, nevertheless."

It was amazing how abrupt was the transition from bare, bleak and stony heights to green and heavily-forested uplands, grassy slopes and wide vistas. A populous land, too, such as they had not seen since South Atholl, for though villages as such were not in evidence, cabins and little townships were everywhere and blue smoke-columns rose out of all the woodlands, the sweet scent of burning birch-logs on the air.

Jamie now saw that any idea he might have had to avoid the Wolf's whereabouts, at this Ruthven Castle or elsewhere, would have been in vain, without actually taking to the mountain-sides like goats — where they quickly would have been spied anyway. The configuration of the land, the hills, the rivers and the flooding, all conspired to channel the travellers into a very limited choice of route. And where spurs of low hill jutting from either side narrowed the strath to a waterlogged half-mile or so, in the centre, like an island in the floods, rose a steep-sided, flat-topped mound crowned by the towers of a castle. The Wolf certainly knew where to site his strongholds. Nothing could move up or down this upper Strathspey without being observed from this hold.

Seeing it from some miles distance, to the south, Jamie was congratulating himself on having decided to visit it anyway, when his thoughts were rudely interrupted. Out from the cover of pines and junipers flanking the track, near the junction of Truim with Spey, without warning, leaped a rough and ragged crew of Highlanders brandishing swords and dirks, shouting and gesticulating threateningly. Less alarmed than they would have been six days earlier — for this was not an entirely unusual approach for the toll-collectors — the travellers reined in, and sighing, Jamie prepared to dip once again into his pouch. But fairly quickly he recognised that this hold-up differed from the normal pattern. There were considerably more of the clansmen than usual. There were no smiles; indeed they all looked distinctly hostile and prepared to use their weapons.

Jamie raised a hand above his head, and turning, nodded to MacAlpin. That man made his accustomed speech, in Gaelic, explaining that this was Sir James Douglas of Aberdour, a peaceful traveller, and pointing out that they had paid mail back at Dalwhinnie, but if further payment was customary, then let their leading man speak and it would be considered.

There was a pause at this, and many dark eyes turned towards the woodland from which the caterans had emerged. Looking, Jamie perceived a youth sitting a garron there, under an ancient, gnarled pine. He was the youngest of the band undoubtedly, but the only one mounted, though bareback, and clearly the leader.

"I am not a mail-collector!" this youth called, in English, though with a Highland accent — and managed to make it sound as though he had been insulted. He rode forward. "Who are you? Where are you going? And what does any of the name of Douglas do in Badenoch?" That was peremptory. "I considered you all Border thieves?"

Jamie eyed him assessingly. Although dressed in stained and ragged tartans, short kilt and plaid, with the usual calfskin sleeveless jerkin, this one had an air about him. He seemed to be about sixteen years old, with quite good features — had they been recently washed — and a mass of tawny hair to his shoulders, badly in need of a combing. Youthful and ragged as he was, he bore the unmistakable stamp of authority. Also there was something slightly familiar about those features — a Stewart, at a guess.

Jamie took a chance. "I am Sir James Douglas, as you have heard. And we Border thieves at least do not demand payment from lawful travellers crossing our lands! I come to Badenoch seeking my lord Earl of Buchan. With information for his private ear. I request, sir, that you aid me on my way to his house."

The youngster rode close, beardless chin high. "You are bold with your request, Douglas!" he said. "I advise a more respectful tone!"

"Respect from a Douglas requires to be earned. Civility I offer to all." That was evenly said. "I have not won my way here through all your Highlands by bowing in respect before all who challenge me. On the other hand, I have offended none, paid all asked of me . . ."

Quick as a snake might strike, the youth leant over from his garron's broad back and slapped Jamie sharply across the face, first one side then the other, with fierce efficiency. Clearly he had done this many times before.

"*Learn* respect, fellow!" he snapped. "I am Sir Andrew Stewart." Jamie had drawn back in his saddle, cheeks flaming from more than the blows, eyes flashing. His hand fell to the hilt of his sword — but immediately gleaming steel tips of broadswords and dirks thrust forward within inches of him by dismounted caterans on all sides.

"Curse you — you will pay for that!" he panted. "Pay, Stewart! Pay for those felon's strokes. *You* will learn that no man strikes Douglas and does not suffer. Call off your, your animals, boy!"

The other looked as though he was about to repeat the blow, but thought better of it. "We will teach you how to be respectful, in Badenoch!" he said briefly, and rapped out some Gaelic commands to the clansmen.

Swiftly these leapt upon the five horsemen and dragged them down to the ground. There was no point in fighting or struggling. Expertly if ungently their wrists were pinioned behind their backs. Then, surprisingly, they were ordered to mount again, their horses' reins held by caterans. Stewart turned his beast round, and without another word kicked it into a smart trot. Promptly the entire company set off after him at a loping run, the lead horses in the midst.

So they went northwards, at an astonishingly fast pace, through the woodlands of birch and pine and juniper. Jamie had heard of the running gillies of Highland chiefs. Now he knew the reality.

In about three miles they came to the floodlands of the main Spey valley, the great river presumably flowing somewhere through the midst. Keeping up their spanking pace they skirted the eastern edge of the water, scattering large herds of grazing cattle from the open woodland slopes. Another two or three miles of this and ahead, islanded amongst the floods, rose the lofty walls of Ruthven Castle on its mound, a strong and extensive place. Could this arrogant youth be its captain? It seemed scarcely credible. Yet Stewart he seemed to be — although the *Sir* Andrew part Jamie very much doubted.

Almost opposite the castle their leader rode straight into the water, without hesitation or casting about, although at a somewhat odd angle. Splashing out on this course, he abruptly changed direction after about a score of yards, through almost a right-angle, but without pause, the gillies running after heedless of the water up to their bare thighs. Another change of course halfway out made it clear that they were in fact on a zigzag underwater stone causeway.

Still without moderating their speed, the caterans wet and breathing deeply but far from gasping, they breasted the steep slope by a spiral track which wound round the mound, all of it entirely vulnerable to defensive assault from the sheer walls above. The mound itself, which Jamie had taken to be a natural outcrop or moraine, now, from its regular outline and smooth stoneless sides, appeared to be artificial, a work of men's hands. But not the motte-hill of a typical motte-and-bailey castle; by its great size, prehistoric rather, a monument to silent, giant races long gone. A couple of standing-stones on the summit, near the entrance-gateway, further testified to this.

Through that gateway they ran, into a wide courtyard surrounded by low, thatch-roofed lean-to buildings within the high walled perimeter, more like a village than a castle — and a slovenly village at that, with a high central midden of dung in the midst, poultry clucking around, deer- and calf-skins stretched to dry, peat-stacks in corners and half-naked children at play. Here young Stewart barked a few cryptic orders, leapt down from his garron and strode off into the main tower or keep without a backward glance. The prisoners were pulled down from their saddles and hustled away to the keep basement, where MacAlpin and the three Tantallon Douglases were flung into one small vaulted cell and Jamie alone into another, the door slammed on him and the key turned.

He had reached the Wolf of Badenoch's domains, with a vengeance.

*   *   *

Jamie spent two days and nights in that vaulted basement. The fact that he was held alone in it appeared to be his only privilege, for otherwise conditions could scarcely have been less privileged. A heap of old and distinctly smelly skins in a corner of the stone floor for bed, a wooden bucket and the tiny grilled window represented the sole amenities. He could not complain about the food, for it was no worse and no better than they had been able to purchase all the way up through the Highlands, plain but adequate as to quantity, though thrust wordlessly into the cell

twice a day by a grinning gillie who knew no English. This was his sole contact with his fellows, his shoutings and door-bangings going quite unanswered. There were no facilities for washing or shaving, only the sanitary bucket — which was soon far from sanitary.

In those two days and nights, Jamie had opportunity for serious thought. He could not see where he had gone wrong. They could not have avoided this encounter. Their approach had obviously been reported to this Ruthven Castle and they had been deliberately ambushed. He could not admit that he should have reacted differently to that slap on the face, nor said other than he had anent respect. He had told this young insolent the truth. A man, and a Douglas, had to keep his *self*-respect. He had also informed him that he was seeking the presence of the Earl Alexander — presumably his father — with tidings for his private ear. Surely the youth could not ignore that completely, however arrogant? Detaining him like this might please his vanity — but it was inconceivable that he would not send to the Wolf to inform him. In which case it was to be assumed that the Wolf would wish to hear the alleged private information. Even he would not dismiss as of no interest a Douglas come all this way north on a special mission? In which case he could look for developments before very long. The Wolf would either send for him, or send an intermediary to question him, someone less high-handedly autocratic than this deplorable Andrew. And he could then refuse to speak until he saw the Earl himself.

With this line of reasoning Jamie consoled himself during his lonely incarceration.

When, on the forenoon of the third day however, the cell door opened to admit three men, none of them ordinary gillies, it was not quite as he had anticipated. Indeed to call them men was scarcely accurate, for all were younger than himself. There was the insufferable Andrew, a slightly older, taller youth dressed in somewhat tarnished finery of Lowland style, and a heavier, more stolid individual, seemingly older again, in kilt and shirt, though this last was of tattered silk not the usual coarse linen, but none the cleaner for that. It was the middle one who drew the eye. He might have been the Lord David, save that he was fairer, older, taller, a brilliantly handsome, slender and debonair character, all smiles and self-confidence, with long and lustrous well-combed hair, a tiny silky beard and scimitar of moustache. The finery which he wore with such élan did not quite fit him, having clearly been made for a somewhat heavier-built man — the Wolf himself probably by its richness. This character bowed with a flourish to Jamie. The others did not.

"Sir James Douglas, I am told. Of Aberfoyle, is it? I greet you kindly. I hope you find your quarters, er, secure? And have had a sufficiency to eat?" Even the voice was like David's, musical and light, but with the typical Highland lilt and sibilance — and the mockery not amissing either.

"Aberdour, not Aberfoyle. Son to Douglas of Dalkeith — of whom even you may have heard!" Jamie gave back stiffly. "And not used to such accommodation or such treatment, sir."

"To be sure. Sir Andrew, my brother, is plaguey short on accommodation here, unfortunately. And other things, perhaps." That came out with a cheerful laugh. "But sound at heart, see you. I am Alexander Stewart, at your service, Sir James. And this is another of the family our half-brother Rob, of Glentromie. A stalwart — although lacking the accolade as yet."

The third individual glowered like a Highland bull, and said nothing.

"I am relieved to hear that you, at least, are at my service, sir! And appear to have better manners than this brother of yours. I am rejoiced that *I* do not have to claim him brother!" Jamie said. "Perhaps you will bring me out of this stinking hole and convey me to the Earl of Buchan, to whose house I was bound when this savage waylaid, struck and imprisoned me here. I demand release, escort and redress."

"God damn your soul, Douglas . . . !" his captor began, when his brother Alexander gripped his arm. Seemingly the one had some authority over the other, for Andrew stopped speaking, though obviously with a major effort.

"All shall be attended to, I assure you," the other said soothingly. "But I would prefer if you would speak of Sir Andrew more courteously, sir. We do not like the term savage, on Lowland lips!"

"Then, Stewart, school your brother not to act like one! He struck me twice, unprovoked. And one does not strike Douglas without paying for it."

"In your Borderland perhaps not, Sir James. But in Badenoch, Douglas may cut less wide a swathe. Still, if Sir Andrew struck you without due cause, I am sure that he will give you due satisfaction — as one knight to another. And in this regard, Sir James, it would pleasure me if you addressed me as *Sir* Alexander, rather than just Stewart. Since we have been knighted just as truly as yourself — although admittedly not on the field of battle. But at least by a royal prince, not a Border earl! And we are all bastards together, are we not?" That was said with a winning smile.

Jamie considered, and decided that perhaps it was time for some civility, at least towards this less barbarous individual — who presumably was in fact King Robert's grandson. They all were, to be sure. Evidently the Wolf knighted certain of his offspring, but not others — as, of course, he was entitled to do, and they were as true knights as he was.

"You know much of my circumstances, sir," he said, less stiffly. "I am surprised at that, up here . . ."

"We are not wholly ignorant, my friend. Even in Badenoch! Especially where deeds of valour are concerned. But we hear of other matters also. Such as the fact that you, sir, enjoy the intimate favours of more than one of our aunts, our father's royal sisters. A matter we, in our ignorant northern fashion, found strange to account for — and you younger than seemed likely! I . . ."

"How dare you! How dare you speak so!" Jamie burst out. "Of these ladies. The princesses. Your own kin. It is false — false, I say! They are noble and virtuous ladies . . .'

"My, oh my! Such heat, such fervour! Have we been misinformed? It is not like our royal sire to have his notions wrong. Especially of his own sisters . . ."

"Nor has he, I swear!" Sir Andrew declared. "This, this insolent Border adventurer would deceive in this, as in all else."

"Hush, Andrew! We must respect Sir James's knightly word! In especial where ladies are concerned." The sarcasm was only slightly veiled. "Moreover, it may be that it is the same royal ladies who have sent him on this journey to our father? It would ill become us to seem to doubt their goodwill! As their virtue. Or indeed, their messenger's. Not so, Sir James?"

Jamie began to speak, and then perceived the possibility of

benefit in this. "The Ladies Isabel and Gelis *are* concerned in the matter," he agreed. "I am but their servant and courier. I left them at Dunfermline, to journey north."

"And our aunts' message, sir?"

"That is for my lord Earl's ears alone, Sir Alexander."

The brothers exchanged glances.

"*We* shall decide on that," Sir Andrew said. "We have the means to open close lips, believe me! Our father does not suffer impostors and interlopers gladly. You will do better to tell us first."

"No!" the prisoner said baldly.

"I think, Andy, that we should take him to Lochindorb," his brother said. "This is your territory — but in a matter between our sire and his sisters it might be wise. If it is indeed so. The hazard is Sir James's!" He turned to Jamie. "You understand, my friend, that if our potent father deems you a liar, or in deceit, you will be happy indeed, in due course, to hang! I swear that you might be safer, more comfortable, to let us be judge, first!"

Despite himself, Jamie swallowed — for he had no reason to believe that this young man exaggerated or misrepresented. But he shook his head nevertheless. What he wanted, had come all this way for, he would not gain here, he was sure.

"Very well, Sir James — to Lochindorb you shall go. I shall take you there myself — with Sir Andrew's permission. For he is captain of this castle and territory. And I wish you pleasure of the exercise!"

"I thank you. I would wash, cleanse myself. My men the same, no doubt . . ."

*   *   *

They rode away from Ruthven Castle within the hour, Sir Alexander Stewart, with the silent Rob of Glentromie and a troop of mounted caterans. Now Jamie and his men rode unbound, even with their swords and dirks restored to their sides, their new escort adopting a totally different line from that of his brother, and chatting pleasantly as they trotted through the bright noontide. For all that, they were none the less prisoners, and all knew it. They could no more have escaped than taken to the air.

Their route, north by east, took them through a wonderland of scenic beauty and attractiveness. The vista seen from afar was not belied by closer acquaintance. On every hand was colour and light and fairness of form and outline. The hills near at hand were gentle, green, wooded, those behind sculptured in granite, blue shadow and white snow-cornices. The woodland glades on every hand were mainly of graceful silver birch, purple branches and twigs bearing their lightsome pale tracery. The Caledonian pines, growing often out of heather, were ancient giants spaced well apart, massive rounded trees quite unlike the pines of the South, combining strength with grace. In every glade the juniper bushes not only glowed rust-red amongst their rich green but were festooned with myriads of glistening spiders'-webs which the night's heavy dew had decked with tiny diamonds. There was water everywhere, not only the flooded meadows and tributory burns but still, dark pools in hollows and shaws of the wood where water-lilies floated. Through it all the roe-deer flitted like silent, brown shadows, the occasional woodland stag stood at gaze, the capercailzie and blackcock swooped and blundered and all the lesser birds of the forest twittered and sang.

After a few miles, Jamie remarked on it all. "You live in a land of surpassing beauty," he said. "How many perceive it, I wonder?"

"Ha — a lover of more beauty than women's, Sir James! But — do I detect blame here? Accusation? That we barbarians cannot perceive such delight? Pursue only our own uncouthnesses?"

"I meant nothing such. Only that when seen every day, even such beauty might pall. I think you wear thin skins in Badenoch, Sir Alexander."

The other paused, and then laughed. "You are right there, no doubt," he agreed. "Or some of us. The result of being . . . who we are, perhaps, Lords of all here — but despised and hated whenever we set foot out of our own glens and forests."

"Feared, also."

"Feared also, yes — for that is necessary. The Douglases — are they not feared in the South, on the Border? Is not fear necessary? For respect. Even in the so courtly Lowlands? I understand that men respect our Uncle Robert. But do not respect our Uncle John — since none fear him. Although he heirs the throne."

Jamie could not deny it. "If that is so, it is a sorry judgment on us all!"

"True. But . . . we have strayed far from beauty, have we not, Sir James? Myself, I much rejoice in the fairness of this land. On all we see around us. But it is a matter of taste. I doubt if Rob, here, sees it all so lovely?"

That stolid individual, thus brought into the conversation, shrugged. "I see this as difficult and dangerous land. When we most need the meadow pastures, for the beasts after winter, they are flooded. These forests harbour wolves, wild-boar — and worse, broken men. Those mountains breed storms, and little else. We cannot eat beauty, nor yet keep our enemies from hiding in it."

"And there you hear the voice of most sensible men, my friend! We stand rebuked, do we not?"

"No," Jamie said shortly.

Alexander Stewart laughed aloud. "On my soul, I like the rocky style of you, James Douglas!" he exclaimed. "A man who knows his own mind, and speaks it. Let us hope that our lordly father finds a similar liking — for I would not wish to hear that sturdy voice choke on the end of a rope!"

On that ominous note they rode on through beauty.

They presently skirted round the eastern shore of what was more than just flood-water, a large loch, although still only a widening of Spey, Insh by name. This lay at the mouth of the major glen of Feshie, opening from truly mighty mountains, still wholly snow-covered, the Monadh Ruadh, highest range in all Scotland. Here they had to ford the magnificently rushing River Feshie, a hazardous business even for sure-footed garrons, with the tremendous weight of white water to be negotiated in channels cut in solid rock. Thereafter, however, the floodlands ended, the valley sides drew closer, and the track lifted high above the Spey.

It was here that they began to smell burning, not the sweet scent of birch-logs in domestic fires but a more acrid smell, heavy, persistent. The breeze was from the east.

Rob Stewart quested the air. "Inchriach?" he jerked. "Tullochgrue?"

"Further than that," his brother judged. "Thin on the wind.

And nothing to be seen. No smoke-clouds. No blue haze. More like Glen More. Beyond Rothiemurchus. Aye, Glen More."

"Then a big fire. If we smell it here."

"Yes." Both brothers had involuntarily urged their mounts to a faster trot.

"Who? Seath Mor Shaw? The Cattanachs? MacGillivray? Or just a chance fire?"

"Too early in the year for a chance fire. Undergrowth is still damp. Who knows who it is? But discover we shall."

Soon they left the main north-going track to turn away from the river, due eastwards, climbing quickly to a tiny pass between two rounded birch-clad hills of no great height. At the summit of the coll, though none paused in their hurried progress, Jamie at least drew a quick breath.

They were on the lip of a huge basin, many miles across, wholly covered by dark pine forest save for a loch just below them, tree-grown to the very edge, and just the glimpse of another far beyond to the east. All around this wooded depression high hills stood guardian, wholly isolating it from the main Spey valley and all else. On an islet in the middle of the first loch below, a castle rose, much smaller than that at Ruthven, consisting only of two square towers of no great height, linked by curtain-walling, but taking up every inch and angle of the islet nevertheless so that the grey walls seemed to rise straight from the still waters. It was a fair place, as castles went, a jewel in a sylvan setting.

But Jamie's companions were not looking at castle or loch, but beyond, towards the far north-eastern side of the great basin. There great clouds of brown smoke were billowing high, tinged with a murky orange and every few moments slashed with bright red bursts of flame as whole pine-trees went up like torches. It was indeed a big fire, possibly half-a-mile wide and approaching twice that in depth, a terrifying sight even at this distance.

"The Luineag! Geadas!" Rob Stewart exclaimed. "That is not Seath Mor and the Shaws. So near their own places. Damnation — if it is those Cattanachs again . . .!"

Sir Alexander was pointing, stabbing with urgent finger. "See that! And that! The line of that fire. Where it has been lit. How it burns. Whoever raised that blaze knew what he was at! It is controlled. Look — the ravine of the Luineag that side. The line of

Geadas Burn at the other. The flames will not pass these. They are eating back into the east wind. Those two sides narrow in, run almost together at length, to Loch Morlich. Yonder." He stabbed again. "Do you not see? As good as an eel-trap! An ever-narrowing funnel of fire."

Jamie could not tell what he meant, but his half-brother appeared to understand. "Then . . . what? Who?"

"Not the Cattanachs, for sure. How could that serve them? I know but one man who would think of that device! Come, you." Alexander pushed on, at speed.

They pounded down to the loch, and along its shore, threading the trees, until opposite the castle-island. There Sir Alexander drew rein.

"Sir James," he said, "I regret that I must leave you here. Rob also. To discover this of the fire. Here is the castle of Loch-an-Eilean, formerly mine, Rob now its captain. In this Rothiemurchus. You will be comfortably enough bestowed here, for this night. Lochindorb is too far to reach in a day. Some of these gillies will see to you. A boat will come for you . . ."

"Do not be fool enough to attempt an escape!" the brother put in, roughly. "You would not get far — and could have your throats cut before nightfall!"

"Truly if crudely put," Alexander nodded, smiling. "But Sir James is no fool."

"If you doubt my safety, allow that I ride with you," Jamie suggested. "I have languished behind stone walls sufficiently these last days. I would rather ride — and learn how you deal with your forest afire."

The two Stewarts exchanged glances.

"You may learn more than you reckon on!" Alexander said grimly. "But, as you will. No harm in it."

The entire party beat on round the west side of Loch-an-Eilean.

Thereafter, round the loch-foot, they turned to ride east by north through the vast forest, all pine this, with the great trees well scattered and growing out of heather and juniper-clumps, the surface hillfoot country with the high Monadh Ruadh rising steeply, close on the right. Vistas were intermittent and seldom lengthy, save up towards the tall summit ridges. But ever the dark smoke-clouds thickened ahead, and the smell of burning became harder on the nostrils and throat. There were many cabins in the forest, single and in groups, some quite large communities, for foresters, wood-workers, charcoal-burners, herdsmen — for shaggy and semi-wild herds of cattle roamed amongst the glades — and hunters to protect these from wolves and the like. This Rothiemurchus seemed to be something of a world unto itself, with quite a large population living under the canopy of the great pines. Pine-needle-carpeted tracks criss-crossed the vast area everywhere. Clearly it would be an easy place to get lost in.

It was difficult to judge distances in the forest, with its twisting tracks and lack of lengthy prospects; but they seemed to go for some three or four miles before the noise of the fire before them, the crackling roar, became evident above the hollow drumming of their garrons' hooves on the pine-needles, a grim and frightening sound. Presently they could feel the heat of it, on the easterly breeze. They came to a sizeable stream, the Geadas, and moved along its north bank. Ahead now all was darkened by the pall of smoke.

At last they emerged from the trees into the area of devastation, a blackened, smoking desolation stretching widely across their front, patterned still with flame and glowing red, out of which thrust innumerable great skeleton trees not yet wholly consumed and blazing like torches. It made a hellish scene. As Sir Alexander Stewart had predicted, it was half-a-mile wide, and more; also, as suggested, its flanks were controlled, limited, on this south side by the stream they had been following — or by its course, at least, no ravine but a broad belt of bleached stones and pebbles ten times as wide as the Geadas itself, witness to the fury of the floods which could sweep down from the high hills behind laying down this wrack of stones two hundred yards across; the other, northern side apparently would be similarly confined by the still larger River Luineag's course.

Many men, clad in short kilts, some entirely naked, blackened with soot and streaming with sweat, laboured all along this base-line of the fire, wielding besoms of birch-twigs to beat at the creeping flames to prevent them from spreading further westwards. The head of the conflagration was far to the east now, almost a mile probably, although it was hard to judge in the smoke and heat-quivering air. Alexander Stewart shouted brief words, in Gaelic, to the first of the men they came to, who grimaced, shrugged, and pointed away north-eastwards.

They rode on northwards, along the base of the fire-area, without pause, panting and choking with the heat, the garrons rearing and nervous. Small wonder that the beaters looked exhausted. Presently they reached the south bank of the Luineag, a wider stream and, oddly enough, flowing in the other direction, westwards not east. This had no margin of stones, for it flowed out of Loch Morlich ahead, not into it as did the Geadas; but it ran in a wide grassy course nevertheless quite sufficient to prevent the flames from leaping across to the trees on the other side. Along this grassy corridor, coughing and spluttering, they turned eastwards again.

In just under a mile they were gulping deeply, their mounts all but unmanageable, for now they were level with the actual fire-front, an appalling inferno showering out sparks and blazing fragments, exploding in constant bursts and reports, the flames fifty feet high and more, the heat blistering, intolerable even here a hundred and fifty yards from the edge. But it was less dark now, the smoke itself largely left behind, what there was lit up by the red glare. Ahead could be sensed rather than seen, light and space.

At last, streaming-eyed, they were ahead of the fire — and suddenly all was clear, open, bright, the sinking sun gleaming on the wide levels of Loch Morlich, backed by all the soaring magnificence of the Monadh Ruadh mountains and the Glen More hills. But it was not so much that abrupt widening of the background which held the riders' painful and bleary gaze, but the men in the foreground. For, a few hundred yards in front, where the Luineag River emerged from the loch, at the sandy shore itself, many men and horses stood waiting behind a screen of junipers. Two or three boats also lay just a little offshore south of the river-mouth, oars at the ready. Nobody here was sweating, active or seeking to deal with the fire, most obviously. Just waiting.

But even as the riders pounded up, there was a flurry of activity. Out from the small unburned area of forest still left between the fire and the loch-shore, burst two animals, strangely matched, racing most differently, one long-legged the other short, one a great-antlered woodland stag the other a massive-shouldered and tusked wild-boar. Bounding gracefully, head up, and rushing purposefully, head down, these made straight for the sandy shore, the stag quickly gaining on the other. Then the shouts arose, as men out there in the boats yelled, waved arms and plaids and splashed oars. In fresh alarm the stag swerved and turned left, to race instead for the mouth of the Luineag; and after a moment or two the boar did likewise. And hidden behind the barrier of uprooted bushes, the main group of watchers waited, arrows strung, spears at the ready.

There was only a fairly narrow corridor between the row of junipers and the shore, for the fleeting animals to pass before the river-mouth. Arrows sped, and the stag's graceful bounding suddenly changed to a desperate shambling scrabble, before it pitched forward and lay still.

An authoritative shout then rang out above the roar of the flames, and right over the barrier of bushes a single figure vaulted, tall, lithe, in Lowland clothing, spear in hand. Out to meet the rushing boar this individual ran, on a collision course. Only a pace or two from the charging animal he somehow achieved a leap to one side, an approximate halt and a rising on his toes. Down drove the spear into the massive bristling flank, just a hand's breadth behind the heavy shoulder, as the crazed brute went hurtling past with a bare inch or so to spare. Spear standing out from its side the creature careered on almost to the river's edge, dead on its feet, before the heart gave out and it fell, tusks goring the sand. Its slayer turned to face them all, laughing, handsome head thrown back.

"My father loses little of his art with the years — in this as in other matters!" Alexander Stewart the Younger observed. "You are spared the ride to Lochindorb. Though — I shall not announce you yet, Sir James. My lord's sport must not be spoiled, you understand? Achieved at such . . . pains!"

Jamie nodded, silent.

XIX

THE EARL OF BUCHAN and his companions paid no least attention to the newcomers, being much too busy. Clearly these had arrived just in time for the climax of this extraordinary proceeding, with the fire reaching this apex of the long triangle between the rivers, and all trapped within now penned in this diminishing corner — or else burned to death. Creatures had been seeking to escape for some time previously for the ground between Luineag, loch and fire, the killing-ground, was already littered with carcases. Now, the Earl Alexander, leaving his boar, had barely got back to his cover before three grey-brown shadows slipped out from the woodland and ran swiftly, belly-down, directly for the river. These were lean and fast, and one was badly burned as to coat and tail, limping on one foreleg — wolves, yellow eyes glaring, red tongues hanging from parched mouths. Arrows sped at them, and two fell, twitching; but the limping one ran on, although transfixed by a crossbow shaft. A couple of wolf-hounds leapt out from the junipers after it, and managed to pull it down in snarling fury just as it reached the water.

There were already further creatures bolting from the shrinking cover — a mixed bag now, two dainty roebuck leaping high, a stag and three hinds in great-eyed terror, and a female boar. The deer all fell under the hail of arrows. But a young man emulated the Earl — he looked like another Stewart — racing forward with spear to meet the boar. He was less expert at the business than the other however, drove in a slant-wise blow which failed to penetrate the tough hide and glanced off, the spear jerked out of his grip. Whether it was the hooted scorn from behind or on his own initiative, the youth thereupon hurled himself bodily after the animal as it rushed past, falling upon it, arms encircling its hind-quarters. Down they both crashed.

"God-sakes — Walter was ever a headstrong fool!" Sir Alexander exclaimed. "As well it is only a sow, or he would have himself killed!"

But in fact this new brother of his was fortunate, however foolhardy — and determined. For though a female wild-boar could be almost as dangerous as a male, this one was terrified by the noise and the fire, rather than angry, and already scorched by blazing embers. This new attack probably seemed to it just a continuation of the horror in the wood, and instead of rounding on its assailant it merely struggled to regain its feet and continue its flight, squealing loudly the while. The youth hanging on grimly, was dragged along the ground — to the shouted laughter from behind the junipers. Walter Stewart was actually clutching the sow's little tail now, to the further delight of the watchers. But he was by no means put off in his determination by this ridicule. Bumping over stones, roots and pebbles, whilst clinging to the tail with one hand he was reaching with the other for his belt, where hung his dirk. Somehow he managed to unsheath it.

But to use the weapon effectively on the sow, in his present position was well nigh impossible. Desperately he sought to get to his feet. The brute was running too fast, and had enormous strength in those massive forequarters. Young Stewart managed to get approximately to his knees, still being pulled along, and from this most awkward and unsteady of stances began aiming a series of wild stabs at the only part of the creature's anatomy he could reach, its hindquarters and rear orifice — with delighted and distinctly rude advice yelled by the bystanders.

Right to the river the animal ran, the King's grandson still attached and smiting. In the water, however, all was changed, for the pig family are not the best of swimmers and Walter Stewart was. The pressure went off him, likewise the friction on his legs. Now he could use his dirk to better effect and at a better target-area. It was still a messy, protracted, splashing and bloody affair, but the end was no longer in doubt. Presently the poor brute was in its death-throes and being towed back to the bank.

"I warrant you have never seen boar hunted so!" Alexander cried. "But then — nor have I! My brother Walter goes his own way."

The exodus from the burning forest had by no means stopped for this interlude, and most of the hunters were too busy to watch the end of it. Creatures of all kinds were emerging now, mainly deer, but more wolves, singly and in groups, foxes always alone, bewildered-seeming badgers, even a great wild-cat in spitting, tail-lashing fury — which the Earl shouted was his, and slew with a crossbow-bolt, laughingly shouting death to Clan Cattanach. There were hordes of lesser animals also, of course — red squirrels, mountain hares still half-white, stoats, weasels, marten, the ground a moving carpet of voles, mice, shrews and the like. Most of the birds had already flown but some there were still low-fliers like capercailzie, woodcock, blackcock and owls.

Then suddenly Jamie gasped, and pointed. "Look!" he cried. "A man! Dear God — a man! There, behind those alders. Save us — another! Men — in that inferno! Why? Why do they linger? In there. Are they mad? With safety here."

Alexander Stewart did not answer. The figures in the trees disappeared.

"Are they *your* men? Your father's?" Jamie demanded. "What do they there?"

"Wait, you," Rob Stewart advised shortly.

"More! Saints alive — there are more! See yonder. Beyond the fallen tree. The upturned roots. Two more — no, three."

The others were not looking where Jamie Douglas pointed. For, a little further forward, a single man had run out to the very edge of the trees, staring towards them, clad only in a philabeg or short kilt, body blackened and gleaming with sweat. He paused, pant-ing. And even as he did so, an arrow zipped out from the juniper barrier and took him full in the throat. With a bubbling scream, hands up trying to tear the thing out, he fell, spewing blood.

"God in Heaven!" Jamie whispered.

Almost immediately thereafter two more men burst out at the front of the woodland, with a red deer hind alongside, and ran straight to the loch-shore. One was in ragged tartans, the other completely naked, with all hair burned off. They got almost to the water's edge before marksmen in the boats dropped them both. The deer sped on, unchallenged now.

A cheer rang out from the junipers.

Jamie turned to stare at the Stewart brothers. "Murder!" he choked. "Cruel, bloody murder! The most heartless kill-ing . . .!"

"Killing, I agree," Sir Alexander nodded, although with less calm confidence than his usual. "But not murder, no. Justice, shall we say? Execution. These are Cattanachs, a broken clan. Rejected

310

by the chiefs of Clan Chattan. They live by robbery, rapine, slaying. As fierce as yon wild-cat — which is their emblem . . ."

As he spoke another blood-curdling scream rang out, and a
fourth racing refugee dropped, to thrash about in agony.

"Murder, I said!" Jamie repeated, hoarsely. "Savage, merciless
murder. Hunted down like brute-beasts . . .!"

"Justice, fool!" Rob Stewart grated, gripping his arm hard.
"Watch your tongue, Douglas! I warn you! Our father is Justiciar
of the North. These are felons, outlaws. The scourge of the forests.
They can be taken no other way . . ."

"Burned out! Hunted as though for sport! All the fire was for
this? Not the wolves and boars and deer? *This! For men* ! The rest
but by-play waiting? This is your father's justice? Small wonder
that he is named the Wolf of Badenoch!"

"I advise that you hold your tongue, Douglas!" Sir Alexander
said gratingly. "For your own sake. Since *you* are now within that
jurisdiction!"

Small point in reminding that any such jurisdiction was now
withdrawn by Crown edict. These Stewarts would make their own
edicts and laws. Jamie, belatedly sensible, kept his lips tight
closed.

There were fourteen of the so-called Cattanach slain, the last
two with hair and beards aflame, before the fire reached this last
corner of the trap and the sport was over. Gillies gathered up the
game and began to gralloch the deer. But there was no attempt to
collect the human victims, who were left to lie where they had
fallen — on the principle apparently that they were not fit for
Christian burial and that their own kind would no doubt deal with
them in due course.

Jamie found himself curiously dealt with. He was not brought
and presented to the Earl, but indeed kept carefully out of that
man's way, by the young Alexander. He could not believe that
the Wolf had not noticed his presence, even recognised him — for
he had seen him often enough in the past in the Earl of Douglas's
company; but no move nor sign was made towards him. Alexander went and spoke with his father, alone, leaving Rob to guard
the prisoner. When he came back, it was to order a turn-around
and the ride back to Loch-an-Eilean.

It was some little time before Jamie realised that the Wolf's
party was not following them. He mentioned the fact.

"My father has set up a hunting-camp for this night in Glen More," Alexander told him. "There is no accommodation for you there. Moreover it is best, I think, that you do not see my lord in your present state of mind, Sir James. I have no cause to love you, but I conceive you to be honest after your own fashion. I would not wish to see you sealing your own fate by hot words to our sire — who suffers such less than kindly! Some breathing-space is advisable, I say — during which it is my hope that you will learn to mind your words, and take that black Douglas scowl off your face! Tomorrow we shall ride for Lochindorb."

"You are very . . . careful, sir!"

"Perhaps I am the careful one of a scarcely careful family. Though not all would call me that, I think! Eh, Rob?"

That youth smiled, for the first time in Jamie's experience.

*　　*　　*

It seemed that this Lochindorb Castle lay something under a score of miles to the north, well beyond the Spey valley and amongst the high moorlands of Braemoray. Why it should be necessary for Jamie to be taken there for his interview with the Earl was not fully explained; but leaving the churlish Rob behind at Loch-an-Eilean, Alexander took him off next morning, wrapped in plaids against the chill rain-storms. They went through the dripping woodlands, by Inverdruie and Loch Pityoulish, through a small pass close above the Spey and so into another vast forest area, that of Abernethy, separated from Rothiemurchus by outliers of the Glen More hills.

There was no fording Spey, so wide and deep a river; but there was a ferry at a township called Boat of Garten, where quite a fleet of large flat-bottomed scows were maintained by brawny Highlandmen, seemingly in the Stewart pay. Clearly no one would cross Spey from north or south unless with the Wolf's permission. The cattle-droves of the North on their way to the southern markets had to come here — and pay the required mail.

In the distance, eastwards, down the great valley, they could glimpse from sundry eminences another smallish stronghold; Castle Roy, Alexander explained, of which the boar-slaying Sir Walter Stewart, his younger brother, was captain. It seemed that the Earl had knighted all his five sons by the Lady Mariota de

Athyn, to distinguish and raise them above his other innumerable bastards, as the ruling family of Badenoch.

They forded another quite major river, the Dulnain, and soon thereafter began to climb out of the woodlands, and the wide Spey valley itself. Gradually open heather succeeded the pine trees, bare rolling moorlands the glades and glens. In intermittent rain-showers, the change was not for the better.

Nevertheless, Alexander Stewart was friendlier again today, good company indeed. Perhaps it was because he had none of his brothers with him, as witnesses. No direct references were made to the fire or the slaying of the Cattanachs, indeed little to his father at all. But of his mother he spoke warmly, of his brothers amusingly, and of their life here in the North spiritedly. In return he asked a great many, and pointed, shrewd and intelligent questions about conditions and personalities in the South and at Court. Clearly this Wolf's whelp hankered after a wider and fuller life than Badenoch offered him.

As well that their converse was interesting, for the journey was not. Jamie had not realised that there were such endless barren moors in the land, treeless, almost featureless, seemingly extending almost to infinity. In the Douglasdale country of Lanarkshire there were long, dreich moorlands; but nothing to compare with these. It was a high plateau, really, and they often were riding through the skirts of chill clouds, far from flat, dotted with legions of small dark lochans and peat-pools. But the unending brown desolation of the heather, pitted with black and ominous peat-hags, was what predominated. When that heather was in bloom it would be a scarcely believable sea of purple; but meantime it was a lost and dreary wilderness. Great herds of deer were there, as brown as the heather; but apart from these, the whirring grouse and the circling buzzards and eagles, the entire land appeared to be empty.

It was mid-afternoon, and the weather improving, before there was any major change. Summits and ridges with some definition had gradually been taking the place of the everlasting heather billows and troughs. Ahead these now steepened and grew into true hills, not so very high above the surrounding plateau but no doubt of quite substantial height above sea-level. Ascending the long southern flank of one of these, they topped a shoulder and there opened before them, with no prior indication, a wide am-phitheatre, an oval green hollow amongst all the surrounding and prevailing brownness, perhaps three miles long by half that in width, not actually forested but dotted with trees, pine and birch, the first seen for hours. In the centre the hollow cradled a loch of the same general shape, of approximately half its dimensions; and in the loch was an island from which rose a many towered castle. A more unlikely place in which to find a fortress would be hard to imagine.

"Lochindorb?" Jamie exclaimed. "That? There?"

"None other. You are surprised?"

"This your *home*? The Earl your father's seat? Lost in this wilderness?"

"Scarcely lost. But well hidden, is it not? Secure. There is no more secure hold in all Scotland than that, I swear!"

"Secure, perhaps, yes. But to what purpose? Out here? Well hidden from what? Eagles? Deer? Your Cattanachs? Security must serve a purpose, surely? What, here?"

"An excellent purpose, my friend," Stewart asserted. "From that secure hold most of the North is governed. In the wilderness, yes — but none so remote. From Loch-an-Eilean and upper Spey, perhaps. But from what is important here, not so. See those stout towers. Why think you Edward Plantagenet built them here? For the King of England it was who turned this from a mere eagles' nest of the Comyns into a strong fortress, near a century ago. One of the greatest soldiers of Christendom, however much he hated Scotland. Not for any whim or fancy. From this hold two or three hours' riding will put you astride every route into the North, or out of it — by Findhorn and the Streens, the Slochd and Strath Dearn, Strath Nairn and Drommossie, Strath Errick and the Great Glen, Latterach, Glen Lossie and Lower Spey. The Laigh of Moray lies open to the east, Cawdor and Inverness to the north, with the Ness crossings, and all the Mondath Liath passes to the west. He who holds Lochindorb not only sleeps secure in his bed but has all the North by the throat! English Edward knew it, if *you* did not!"

Suitably abashed, Jamie rode on down towards the loch.

Halfway down the slope the horns were ululating from the castle.

"That is to inform all hill-top guards and outposts that it is a friendly party which approaches, that boats will put out from the island — for none are permitted to linger at the shore — and that no aid or reinforcement is required," Alexander explained, with a hint of pride. "We keep but fifty of a garrison — but a thousand can be here within the hour. Your wilderness is less empty than you think perhaps, Sir James!"

"They cannot tell *who* we are, at this range, surely?"

"They have known who we were and where we were since we left Dulnain ford," the other asserted cryptically

As they drew near, Jamie could see that any superficial resemblance to Loch-an-Eilean was confined to both castles being built on islands. This was a major strength by any standards, five times as large as the other perhaps, a great oblong of high curtain-walls with round towers rising at every angle. There were outer defensive walls to form a bailey or basse-cour, all strengthened by earth-works, ditches and portcullis gateways and draw-bridge — although any attack, necessarily by boat or raft, would have to be on a vast scale and long maintained ever to win a toehold on the island, which had been artificially extended and steepened by timber and masonry to provide only one possible landing-place. The castleton for men-at-arms, stables, byres and farmery were all on the mainland.

Used as he was to powerful castles, Jamie was impressed.

Boats were waiting for them, and Jamie and his four attendants were ferried out to the island. A large cheerful woman and a good-looking girl of about fourteen awaited them at the landing-stage. Alexander embraced them both warmly.

"Here is Sir James Douglas of Aberdour come seeking my lord, Mother," he announced. "Come the long road from Fife, on some especial mission. He looks stern, but is less stiff than he seems!" He laughed. "Sir James — the Lady Mariota de Athyn. And our sister Margaret."

The lady beaming on them, Jamie bowed warily. He was after all a prisoner, and this was the most notorious concubine in the land, in a situation with its own delicacy.

The woman at least appeared to feel no need for wariness nor yet delicacy — which indeed was a word scarcely appropriate to her. In her forties, she was generously made, tall, still handsome with much red hair, open, comely features, a wide mouth, a ready smile and great vitality. She was, in fact, of chiefly Celtic blood, being a daughter of Mackay of Strathnaver, in Sutherland, chief of the name, descendant of the noted MacEth line from which also sprang the Earls of Ross. So she was oddly enough distantly connected with the Wolf's true wife Euphemia, Countess of Ross. Her brother Farquhar Mackay of Strathnaver was physician to King Robert. The Celtic MacEth, meaning the Son of Hugh, had like so many another, been 'Normanised' to De Athyn.

"Welcome to my house, Sir James," she said genially, as though this was the most ordinary domestic establishment. "I have heard of the brave Sir James, and Otterburn fight. I rejoice to meet such a hero! In especial one who looks the part!" And she half-curt-seyed to him smiling, like any girl a third of her age. "We live very quiet here, at Lochindorb — I fear you will find us exceeding dull. We cannot offer you the excitements of the Court." She chuckled. "Not that I have ever experienced them! But my house is yours. Use it as your own." She had a deep, throaty voice, highly attractive.

Astonished at such a reception to the Wolf of Badenoch's lair, Jamie swallowed and muttered disconnected inanities — the more so as, turning towards the great portcullis-hung gateway, they were confronted by a long beam, on the left, projecting from the southern corner parapet of the outer bailey walling, a beam from which dangled six men, in varying stages of decomposition.

Alexander noted the visitor's expression, if his mother did not. "Prime malefactors those, Sir James," he sang out. "We have to keep the King's peace, here. Fortunately the wind is very seldom from the south."

The girl Margaret trilled a laugh. "I think Sir James is shocked!" she said.

"We certainly must have them taken down soon," the Lady Mariota nodded.

Within the curtain-walled enclosure, the castle was not unlike Ruthven, save that it was larger and cleaner, a small walled town in miniature. There was almost a street down the centre, with single-storey subsidiary buildings on either side, all of stone here, with no dangerous thatching to burn, and including a quite hand-some chapel, kitchens, brewhouse, laundry and the like, also an armoury. At the upper end of the street were the great and lesser halls and a two-storeyed range of domestic quarters, where Jamie was conducted, his men being bestowed near the kitchens.

There was no sign of the master of the house.

A peculiar interlude followed, almost unreal to Jamie's mind. For two days he was the honoured guest in a hospitable, comfortable and well-found house, treated with courtesy and respect. There was no least hint that he was, in fact, a captive, that his very life might be in danger, that any sort of threat hung over this establishment. Only those dangling bodies in their creaking chains in the outer bailey spoke of any sort of abnormality. He was free to go where he would to see what he would — and if he did not say all he would, that was of his own choice. Of course, he was unable to leave the island without requesting the services of boatmen; and once over there, it had been made entirely obvious that he would be under observation all the time and could go no further in any direction than his hosts desired. He went hunting and hawking with Alexander and the girl Margaret, although it was now May, and the breeding-season limited sport. He fished in the loch and chased mountain-hares with greyhounds. He attended chapel — for there was a resident chaplain. He talked much with the Lady Mariota — and came to the opinion that in many ways she was a woman to be admired. More than once he was on the point of touching on the subject that had brought him here, and the matter of the Bishop of Moray's injunction. But each time he drew back, in embarrassment, believing that it might be the end of the good companionship—moreover, for best effect, it would be put directly to the Earl, when he elected to return.

That happened on the evening of the third day. Just as dusk was falling, there was a blowing of horns from hilltop outposts, answered loudly from the fortress, and presently a large cavalcade of horsemen, laden pack-horses and running gillies appeared over the skyline to the south. An air of anticipation came over the castle, Jamie's contribution less than joyous.

He kept discreetly out of the way while the Earl was being welcomed home with three of his sons, Duncan, Walter and James. When, later, Jamie was summoned to the lesser hall for the evening meal, the Wolf greeted him with superficial civility, although with the arched eyebrow and fleering smile which was more or less habitual.

"Ha—the Douglas knight-errant!" he exclaimed. "One of the paladins of Otterburn come to my poor table in the wilderness. I regret that I was not here in person to receive you, Sir James. But my lady and young Alexander would serve you well enough? Perhaps better than might I!"

Uncertain what that last might mean, the other bowed. "I have been most kindly used, my lord — since I reached Lochindorb," he said, with emphasis on that last word. Two could barb their remarks at the end.

"Say you so? Journeying in these parts can have its hazards, young man. We all suffer them on occasion. Even I, the Justiciar! However, you have reached my house safely — for which you may think to thank your Saint Bride. Your Douglas saint, yes? Was she not burned to death, poor woman? Or do I mistake?"

Jamie moistened his lips, recognising the warning. He inclined his head.

"My lord — how gloomy an invitation to your table! You will quite put our gallant guest off his meat," the Lady Mariota said cheerfully. "You will all be hungry, I swear. Sir James—sit you beside me, and tell me more of Sir Will of Nithsdale's son and the Lady Gelis. I have not understood this . . ."

That meal was a very different one from the others Jamie had had at Lochindorb. There was a tension in the air, a lack of ease — although to be sure, neither the Earl nor his lady appeared to be aware of it. Alexander and his sister certainly were restrained, almost anxious — whatever the attitude of their brothers. Jamie came to the conclusion that this aura of wariness, discretion, was endemic when the Wolf was present, an inevitable reaction to his dominant, predatory and unpredictable character. If he did not frighten Mariota de Athyn, she was alone in that. The three sons who had arrived with him, aged about fifteen, fourteen and twelve, Sir Walter, the middle one, a twin brother of Margaret's, had the air of savage cubs ready to snarl and bite — but not in their father's presence. Alexander appeared to be the only one with a mannerly veneer. Jamie's efforts to respond frankly and cordially to the Lady Mariota's amiable conversation were less than successful.

His relief when the Earl abruptly rose from the table was short-lived. For when the older man strode off, it was to pause at the door.

"Young man," he called back. "If, as you say, you have a privy message for me, I will hear it now. Come."

"Allow that he finishes his meat, Alex," the lady protested — but Jamie got to his feet, bowed, and followed the Wolf out. This thing had been put off for sufficiently long.

In a small first-floor chamber of the domestic range, the Earl shut the door on them and turned on his visitor.

"Well?" he demanded — and there was no attempt now to disguise hostility and impatience, as they stood facing each other. "Who sent you? And why?"

Jamie endeavoured — more successfully than he knew — not to show his trepidation. "My mission in the North, my lord, is two-fold," he said. "Firstly to find a man whom I believe may give *me* information as to the murder of my lord the Earl of Douglas. Secondly to bring to *you* information which you may find to your advantage. I come from Dunfermline and your royal sisters, the Ladies Isabel and Gelis."

"My sisters never sought to advantage me ere this, Douglas!" the other barked. "Why should they do so now? Why should they think that they *could*? And send such a stripling as yourself. To me!"

"As to that, my lord, I cannot answer you. But I was coming anyway. On my own quest. To try find this man I spoke of . . ."

"Well, well — out with it, boy! What is this information to advantage me?"

"It concerns the matter, the delicate matter, of, of your marriage, my lord. And the Bishop of Moray's injunction . . ."

"Christ God! You, *you* dare come here to talk of that! You, sprig of Douglas, to me — Buchan!"

"Only as a messenger, sir. If the message I bring is to your advantage, does my lowly estate concern you?"

"Boy — do not use that tone of voice with me! 'Fore God — I have hanged better men than you for a deal less than that!"

"No doubt, my lord. But you will not hang me, I think, until you have heard my message! When you may have cause to thank me, instead."

"That we shall see. But I warn you — speak with care. For I am not gentle with those who offend — and I like not your tone of voice."

"I little require your warning, my lord. Since I have seen your way with those who you esteem offensive — in Rothiemurchus fire! So I speak with due care. If I may?"

"Speak, then."

319

"The injunction I spoke of. From the Bishop of Moray. That you should forthwith forsake the Lady Mariota to cohabit with your true wife, the Countess of Ross, under penalty of £200 . . ."

"Damnation — how know *you* this?"

"You think that it comes from Bishop Barr, my lord. But in fact it is your own brother, the Governor's doing. In conjunction with the Primate, Bishop of St. Andrews. And it was your *half-* brother, the Archdeacon Thomas, who learned of it at St. Andrews and informed your sisters. I was there."

"Go on."

"You have not obeyed the injunction, my lord — as they conceived that you would not. It is a trap. For though they declare the penalty to be but £200 payment if you do not, the truth is far otherwise. You were given three months to comply — which is now overpast. Then the true penalty is excommunication — the greater, not the lesser. Excommunication by Holy Church!"

If Jamie had hoped for astonishment, dismay, even fury, he was disappointed. The other merely nodded, hot eyes narrowed.

"And they think that clerks' rigmarole and ranting will terrify me, Alexander of Buchan! My brother Robert at least should know me better."

It was Jamie who was astonished. "You, you knew?" he said.

"Aye, I knew. I am none so ill-informed, in my wilderness. Your precious information is a mite stale, boy!"

"But, but . . ."

The Wolf snapped his fingers. "That for your excommunication!" he added.

Floundering, the younger man sought to recover his lost confidence. "My lord — have you considered well? What excommunication can mean? Not just prelates' pronouncements and anathemas. But the loss of all rights, in law. The excommunicate becomes as dead before the law. They will declare your earldom, titles and lands forfeit. All rights and privileges as the King's son likewise. All offices taken from you. And you unable to contest it, in law . . ."

"*I* make the laws in Badenoch, boy!"

"Perhaps, my lord. But in the realm at large? In the South? There the Governor controls all. It would serve you ill to become an outlaw there, with no rights . . ."

"When I go south, my young friend, I will take my rights with me, never fear! A thousand broadswords will speak louder than any bishops' anathemas!"

"Yet your brother, the Earl Robert, does not think so. Or he would not be going to this trouble. And he is not a man to misjudge in such things."

"Then I must teach brother Robert that he can misjudge indeed! Teach him, and his bishops, a lesson they will not forget. I will teach him who rules in the North — and what will be the fate of his wretched son Murdoch should he show nose north of Atholl! I have already made plans to do the like. It may be that, if I do not hang you first, you may have the pleasure of witnessing that showing and teaching, Douglas!"

"Why should you hang me, sir?" Despite himself, Jamie's voice quivered a little. "I have done you no hurt. I came to *serve* you, with this information — not knowing that you already had it. Wherein do I offend?"

"You came from my brother's Court — and I trust none who do so. I mislike the liberties you take with my sisters, Douglas — even though they may encourage you. And you called my son Andrew savage, did you not?"

Jamie cleared his throat. "He struck me. Twice. Imprisoned me without cause. You knighted your sons, my lord. You know that one knight does not strike another. As to your royal sisters, I have taken no single liberty. They have been kind to me — but only as to a servant they favour. And I am not of the Governor's Court, misliking it — as it mislikes me!"

The Wolf was eyeing him assessingly. "You talk overmuch for a stripling," he said softly. "Even for a Douglas! I may have to still that tongue, I think. As I stilled the other from the same airt."

"I, I cannot stop you, my lord — since I am in your power. But ... I am your guest, am I not?"

"Not mine, boy — not mine! *I* did not bring you here. You are my captive — which is something different."

"But why should you conceive me your enemy? When I came to serve you. And when our true enemy is the same, my lord. The Governor. He it is who seeks to trap you and bring you down. And he it is who, I believe, caused the murder of the Earl James of

Douglas, at Otterburn. Why I came seeking Patrick Ramsay, his minion . . ."

"Patrick Ramsay, you say? You came seeking Ramsay?"

"Yes. He is the man who can tell me whether the Governor paid Bickerton to slay the Earl James . . ."

The Wolf hooted a laugh. "Ramsay will tell you nothing! Come, boy — over here." He strode to the window, and threw open the lower timber-shutter. "See you, yonder. The second from this end. Or it may be the third — I mind not. There is your Patrick Ramsay." He was pointing at the row of hanging corpses.

Jamie stared. "You mean . . .? Ramsay — he is dead? You hanged him? Hanged Ramsay."

"To be sure. Few more deserved it. I hanged him in November. Or it may have been earlier."

Jamie let out his breath in a long sigh. Here, then, was the end of his quest — and nothing decided. Ramsay silenced, like Bickerton, for ever. This hazardous journey into the North for nothing. All but wasted time and effort. He would never now uncover Robert Stewart's guilt.

"Why did you hang him?" he asked, flatly.

"For the best of reasons. He it was who carried the insolent Bishop's letter to me. As to this of my wife. I made him talk. We have means here to open the tightest lips! From him I learned of this excommunication. Before he died."

"Need you have killed him?"

"Why not? He was a rogue, employed by rogues. Working against me. All such that I lay hands on die. I warn you! Besides, it was necessary, having spoken, that his lips be closed."

"He said nothing of the Earl James? Of his murder? Of Bickerton?"

"I did not ask him, boy. I know naught of that. Nor greatly care."

"Yet could you prove that the Governor had my master slain, my lord, you would have forged a strong weapon against him. The Douglas power. Even the new Earl Archibald could not save him from the Douglas wrath!"

The other stared at him for long moments. "And this was what you sought?" he demanded. "To prove this — to seek to bring down my brother?"

322

"Yes."

"And my sisters? They are in this with you?"

"Yes."

"I see. Aye — well, then, I may come to think a little less ill of you, Douglas! Who knows? Though do not rely on it, my friend! I will think on what you have said. Have you more to tell me?"

Jamie shook his head. "Nothing that I would think would interest you. But . . . may I go now, my lord? Leave your house? Return to the South? For what I came to do is done. Or no longer able to be done. My purpose here . . ."

"That you will not, sirrah. You will bide here, during my pleasure. Go when I say you may go, not before — *if* I say it!"

"Then I am your prisoner still? Why?"

"Was it not guest you said, earlier? Guest will sound better meantime. My lady's guest — not mine!" The Earl laughed, and waved towards the door.

More depressed than he had been for long, even in the Ruthven vault, Jamie followed him out.

XX

IT was nearly a month later, strange and difficult weeks, before there was any major development, any sign of the reason for Jamie's detention at Lochindorb. During that period he was well-treated by the Lady Mariota, her daughter and Alexander, ignored or mocked by Duncan and Walter, and tolerated by the youngest son, James. Fortunately or otherwise, the Wolf himself, with one or more of his sons, was from home for most of the time, on and off: when present at the castle he varied his reactions towards the reluctant visitor through careless bonhomie and utter disregard, to scornful railing and sheer abuse. In the period Jamie saw three men hanged, others lashed with whips, and one old woman, allegedly a witch, thrown into the loch to drown. All in the name of the King's justice. Otherwise he hunted, hawked, coursed, fished, fed well, listened to Alexander on the lute or singing — and he was a notable performer — and talked much with the lady of the house.

Then, one evening in early June the Earl, who had been away overnight, this time with all his sons, came riding back in especially boisterous state, seeming to be in a strange combination of satisfaction and frustration. All who had been with him were noisier than usual, save Alexander, who was indeed more silent, preoccupied. Clearly something significant had happened, but what was not vouchsafed to the captive; and when a few leading questions elicited no explanations, his pride forbade him pressing the matter. Alexander was undoubtedly unhappy, however, his brothers distinctly elevated, and their father varying between extreme irritability and loud cheer. The Lady Mariota remained her friendly, genial self, but there was no question that she was concerned about something and that there was tension in the air.

It was a few nights afterwards that Alexander came to the prisoner's little chamber, with the rest of the house retired to bed. "Your waiting is over, Sir James," he announced, though somewhat grimly. "We ride tomorrow — and you with us. You have been chafing, I know, in this idleness. Well, at least there will be an end to that."

At the distinctly ominous tone of voice, Jamie reserved expressions of rapture. "You ride where? To do what? And in what way am I concerned? I gather that it is not that I am to be released?"

"Scarcely that. Since you have been kept here for a purpose. No — my father has been waiting. Waiting for too long for his patience — or yours, perhaps. Now there is to be an end to waiting. But whether you will enjoy the doing, instead of the waiting, remains to be seen."

"I have been waiting for my release, Sir Alexander, for some reason for my confinement here. Any reason may be easier to accept than none. But ... what have *you*, and your father, been waiting for?"

"In the main, for the old King, my grandfather, to die. He is gone now, at last. We had word from the South some days ago. Now it is confirmed. So there is no longer need to wait."

324

"The King dead? Poor old man — but he is better away. He had no pleasure in his life, for long."

"As to that I know not. I never saw him. But he has died at Dundonald, his own house. At a great age, seventy-four years, no less."

"God rest his soul," Jamie said. "The Lady Isabel will mourn him, at least. It, it will mean great changes."

"Changes, yes. And so we act quickly, here in the North."

"Act quickly?"

The other nodded, but did not amplify.

"What does the Governor now? Do you know?"

"He continues to govern. But not us! As my father will demonstrate."

"But the Crown? What of the Crown? The Earl John is heir. But . . . ?"

"The Earl John is now King. By the Grace of God and his brother Robert! Though not King John. John is considered an unlucky name for a king — too many Johns have come to grief. So he is to be crowned King Robert the Third. An apt enough style, since the true Robert Stewart will rule him and through him!"

"So! I, many, feared that the Earl Robert might seize the Crown for himself."

"As did we all. That is why my father waited. Much depended on it. But he, Uncle Robert, has chosen to remain Governor . . ."

"Governor, *still*? But—will his brother the new King, permit that? An old bed-ridden man might appoint a Governor; but the Earl John is none so old."

"Nevertheless, the word is that he has reappointed his brother as Governor to rule in his stead — or Robert has appointed himself and the King has acceded. He is weak, gentle, as we all know. He will be just as wax in Robert's hands, even more so than the old man, who had some strength once. In this way Robert will have all the power — but when aught goes wrong, the King it is who will bear the blame!"

"Yes, I see it. Though, John is weak and gentle, yes — but he has a son who is neither. And the Lord David, your cousin, is now heir to the throne. Young as he is, I swear there will be trouble."

"The more trouble for Robert Stewart the better! *We* plan to make some, forthwith!"

325

"What trouble will you make which can hurt the Governor, far in the South?"

"That is for my father to show you, not me. We have already made a start — but only a start." He shrugged and sighed in one, but left it at that. When Jamie pressed for details, the other shook his head and made for the door. "I came but to prepare you, Sir James," he said. "To be ready to ride tomorrow. For the rest — you will find out. A good night."

Next day, then, a major cavalcade rode out northwards from the castleton of Lochindorb. Always the Earl went heavily escorted and well armed; but on this occasion the company not only bristled with arms but went dressed in their finest, a colourful admixture of Highland and Lowland, tartans, Celtic jewellery, velvet doublets, chain-mail shirts, calf-skins and breast-plates, the Wolf himself splendid in gold-inlaid half-armour. Sir Andrew from Ruthven and Rob Stewart from Loch-an-Eilean arrived to join them, with another half-brother named Thomas, captain of some castle called Drumin. All five of the Lady Mariota's sons were present, however many other of her lord's bastards were included in the noisy, laughing retinue — and certainly there were not a few who might have claimed Stewart features. They rode, or ran, under many banners and pennons, a gallant-seeming concourse.

Parties began to join them almost at once, from every valley and township — and there were more of these latter than was apparent. The Dorback Burn, quite a major stream, flowed out of the north end of the loch, and down this they proceeded in the brilliant early summer sunshine. Soon, on the slightly lower levels of the vast Moor of Dava they had collected contingents large and small, doubling their strength to fully five hundred, all wild-looking, bare-shanked Highlandmen under their chieftains and tacksmen. Only a small proportion were mounted, the rest no less mobile for being afoot. They went at a tireless lope which easily matched the garrons' trot.

Presently they left the Dorback and the well-trodden drove-road to turn away eastwards and climb up and up over the shoulder of a long low double-summit hill and across a bleak upland watershed of mosses, peat-hags, pools and tall old heather, with the prominent landmark of the pointed Knock of Braemoray rising blue out of the prevailing browness some miles to the north-west. It was the sort of terrain no Lowland force would dream of traversing; but these Highland caterans took it literally in their stride, caring nothing for the quaking bogs and the splattering peat-broth, leaping the tussocks, skirting the emerald-green treacheries, splashing through the burns and shallows, and making rather better time indeed than did the garrons.

Jamie rode between Alexander and the boy James, a little way behind the Wolf and his chieftains. He had been so far vouchsafed no hint as to their mission and objective, his enquiries eliciting only that they were making for Dallas, on the River Lossie, only some half-dozen miles from the sea at Findhorn Bay.

Dallas, when reached in its own hidden valley amongst the lower cattle-dotted foothills, proved to be a quite large community, and now something in the nature of an armed camp. The Wolf had already proved Alexander's assertion that he could summon up a thousand men within an hour or two; now fully another thousand was awaiting him here. It was a notably secure place, at a joining of waters amongst low green hills, for a secret mustering of an army. But why should the King's Lieutenant and Justiciar of the North require such secret army?

It was mid-afternoon when they arrived at Dallas, having covered fifteen difficult miles. They appeared to be halting here for some time, with fires lit by the riverside, cattle being roasted whole, liquor available in abundance and a general air of good cheer. The Wolf seemed to be in the best of spirits now — but evidently was not in the least interested in his prisoner, who was left to languish alone, although strictly guarded. More clansmen kept coming in as the day wore on.

Jamie was dozing, sitting with his back against a tree, seemingly the only non-cheerful individual of that great company, when Alexander brought him a smoking rib of beef, for his evening meal, with a beaker of ale, and sat to partake with him.

"What does your father want with me?" he demanded, sourly. "Has he any reason? Any reason, at all? For bringing me today? Or for holding me captive these months? I do not believe that he has — only that I am in his power and he enjoys showing that power. A despot. He oppresses for the sake of oppression . . ."

"Have a care of your words, Sir James!"

"Care? I am past caring. I can see nothing in which I may be of use to him. Is there to be no end to this . . .?"

"You have a use, yes. My father does nothing without due purpose." The other spoke thoughtfully. "I am not sure, but I believe that it is partly because of your friendship — if that is the word — with his sisters, my aunts. The princesses. He conceives you to have a possible value there. In his continuing battle with his brother Robert, he might well find his sisters' support useful. He believes you to be very close to aunts Isabel and Gelis, and thinks that they might be prepared to do much to gain your release. I heard him say as much to my mother."

"But surely he cannot keep me endlessly a captive in case such opportunity arises?"

"Not endlessly, no. Matters come to a head, now. It is a trial of strength, between these two brothers of the King. And you are caught up in it. We all are. But *you*, to be sure, entangled yourself! You came here, to Badenoch, for that purpose."

"I cannot see that it is necessary to hold me prisoner . . ."

"Do not think that I have not sought to convince him of that. But you have given him much offence, with your too outspoken tongue. I have warned you, many times. He has told me that you are fortunate — and that is true, I assure you. He could as easily have killed you, for crossing him, struck you down with his sword, or had you hanged. As he has done so many. That he has not done so is because he thinks to find you useful. As a witness. And possibly out of some respect for your courage — for he much admires courage. But he has no patience with foolhardiness."

Jamie shook his head. "This possible usefulness I cannot see. Even if he does believe that my safety may carry some weight with the princesses, why bring me on this expedition? What is the object? You said something of witness? Of what am I to be a witness?"

"Let us say of what can happen to those who oppose the Earl of Buchan and Lieutenant of the North. For he still is that, whatever the Earl Robert may say."

"And what parliament may say?"

"Parliament, indeed! What power has your parliament here? My father rules the North, and will continue to rule it. If he must needs take stern measures in that rule, he is not the first to do so. This land needs a strong hand. No dispensing of edicts and decrees will rule the North — only the clenched fist. And not only the North, in the end, but the entire kingdom. The Governor recognises that, and uses deceit, plot, murder, to enforce his clenched fist. That is not my father's way. He is a more honest man, whatever else. He uses his power openly, before all men. He stabs in the front, not the back!"

"And for whom am I to witness his stabbings?"

Alexander drew a quick breath, but controlled his voice. "For Robert himself, I would think. And your Douglas earl. The King also, it may be. Certainly the princesses. All those who have influence in the South. A Douglas witness will be believed. See you – my father does not confide in me, in any of us. But I would say that he reasons thus. The new King is an even weaker monarch than his father. He will not *rule*, only reign. So others must rule for him. He, my father, hates and despises his brother Robert, and would displace him, as Governor of the whole realm, if he could. There is only a year or two between them in age, both strong men. You do not love the Earl Robert. Which would you prefer as Governor?"

"God save me — I do not know!"

"Aye. So there you have it. Even the man of convictions, Sir James Douglas, does not know! My father, then, will seek displace Robert. But if he cannot, he will at least seek to maintain his rule of the North. He will not be turned aside by excommunications and threats. Hence his present harsh measures. Edward of England burned Berwick-on-Tweed and slew 17,000. As warning, to save him burning all Scotland . . ."

"Harsh measure? What mean you by that? Is that what we are at, here? Imposing harsh measures?"

The other shrugged and rose to his feet. "We shall see. As I say, I am not in my father's full confidence." He was moving away when he paused. "I would sleep now, if you can. I understand that we ride three hours before sunrise."

"Three hours before sunrise? Why that, in God's name?"

He was not vouchsafed an answer.

Sunrise was in fact timed for five thirty a.m., and in the small hours of the morning the Wolf's augmented force, now perhaps 3,000 strong, left the Dallas area to proceed down the valley of the Lossie, a lengthy column. Scouts rode ahead and to the flank, along the wooded slope of the Hill of the Wangie.

Through the sleeping and quite heavily wooded foothill country they rode and marched, by the side of a now quite large river, by Kellas and Buinach to where the Latterach joined Lossie, and on by Manbeen, with the land ever sinking before them and the hills lessening and drawing back. It was not so dark, of a northern Scotland June, that much of the landscape was not fairly evident, and it was clear that they were coming down into more settled lowland country — although of course Jamie Douglas had scant idea as to where they were. They halted for a while, after perhaps ten miles, at a ford and milling community called Pittendreich, apparently waiting for a flanking company to arrive, which had for some reason been sent round by an alternative and more northerly route.

"Where are we?" Jamie demanded of Alexander, who alone of the leadership ever troubled to come to his side. "We near the coastal plain, that is clear."

"We are at the mouth of the Vale of St. Andrew. Wherein lies Pluscarden, up yonder. It is a populous vale, and a small force has been sent round that way, to ensure that all is well, there."

"All well! For whom — at this hour of the morning?" Jamie frowned. "Pluscarden, you say? There is a famous monastery there, is there not?"

"There *was*. A great Priory. But it underwent a ... chastening!" On that cryptic remark, Alexander moved off.

When the newcomers arrived, and the Wolf seemed to be satisfied that his rear was secure, they proceeded for another mile or so, and it was noticeable how a quiet had descended upon the entire force now, a sort of furtiveness. When, presently, they emerged from woodland, on a well-defined drove-road, to the Lossie again, which it seemed they must now ford, it lacked less than an hour to sunrise. And Jamie was surprised to see before them, in the strengthening light to the east, the towers and pinnacles of a town black against the yellow. Soon he recognised that it was more than a town; the soaring spires and steeples of a mighty cathedral dominated a host of lesser columns and turrets. That could only be the celebrated Lantern of the North, Elgin Cathedral, seat of the Bishopric of Moray and capital city of the greatest province north of Tay.

Here, having crossed the river, the force divided, swiftly, silently now, into four sections, the Earl retaining perhaps one-third of the whole with himself, the other three being placed each under a son — but not Alexander, who was ordered to stay near his

father, and Jamie kept with him. The others had apparently received their orders already, and melted away with their ragged
but well-armed companies, in various directions.

The Wolf's thousand proceeded south-about around the city's
perimeter at a distance of about a mile, by Hardhillock and Dun-
kinty. Although the sun had still not actually risen, it was now
possible to see most of the city in outline, a dark shadow on its
gentle ridge, the towering cathedral at its far, east, end. There was
a castle at Elgin too, and a royal one, to the west — actually
official seat and court-house of the Lieutenant and Justiciar, Alexander pointed out; but compared with the famous Lantern of
the North it was but a poor place, crowning the low Lady
Hill — and clearing the Justicar was not making for it now. There
were many other steeples and spires, including the tall square
tower of a large church midway between castle and cathedral,
indicating numerous fine buildings, rather after the style of St.
Andrews it seemed to Jamie.

The eastern approaches to the city were through a succession of
low sandy banks grown with birch scrub, providing good cover, if
that was required, for even a large body of men. Amongst the last
of these the Wolf drew up his contingent, facing west now, whilst
he and his lieutenants moved quietly forward to an isolated mound
beside a deep, glooming pool in a hollow, unusual in being some
little way from the river and apparently unconnected therewith.
This pool was evidently well known to all, an adjunct of judiciary
known as the Ordeal Pot, for the drowning of witches. On the
knoll, where a few trees hid them, they waited, Jamie now
brought up with the leaders. The air of hushed secrecy and
damped-down elation and anticipation was very evident.

Low-voiced, Alexander described at least the physical situation to the prisoner — who certainly did not pretend lack of
interest. Just ahead, they could see the quite large buildings,
outside the walls of the city, of what he identified as the
Lazarite leper hospital. This was one of the largest such places in
Scotland, and the brothers of the knightly Order of St. Lazarus of
Jerusalem who manned it, were noted for their dedication. Just
beyond this, in the high perimeter walling, was the gate known as
Pann's Port, where the lepers each morning got their daily
bread — hence the name — issued to them from the Bishop's
bakery within the city; the lepers were not allowed, of course, to

enter this, or any other town, as unclean. At sunrise this charitable distribution was made.

It was at this stage that Jamie realised that he was not the only unwilling spectator of this curious enterprise. A tall white-robed friar was now also included in the leadership group, although manifestly holding back from the others. A powerfully-built man of notably proud carriage for a monk, he had been brought to the Pittendreich rendezvous by the company which had there joined them from the Vale of St. Andrew, and so was presumably one of the clerics of the Priory of Pluscarden which Alexander had described as having undergone a chastening. Although there was no communication between the prisoners, it seemed as though he was being held as some sort of hostage.

Alexander was further quietly describing the scene, as they waited. The walls in which this Pann's Port opened were actually those of the cathedral precinct, or chanonry; for the great church had its own walled city-within-a-city, wherein rose innumerable religious edifices and establishments, monasteries, nunneries, friaries, hospices, chapels, shrines and the manses of the cathedral clergy. The secular city had its own walls and gates, of course; but at this eastern section of the perimeter the chanonry wall was the outer one, and this Pann's Port opened directly into the cathedral-yard.

Jamie began to understand, and stared from speaker to leper-hospital to walled gateway, with dawning apprehension, almost horror.

Alexander's voice tailed away as his father came strolling up to them, at length apparently prepared to recognise the existence of his captives.

"So, Douglas," he said genially, holding out a leathern bottle. "A mouthful of wine, for your sustenance, as we await our churchly friends. Come, drink with me — to your further education!"

Jamie bowed stiffly from the saddle of his garron, warily—but did not refuse the proffered refreshment, whatever was meant by this of education.

"Alex has looked after you well enough, I hope?" The Earl seemed to be in expansive mood. "Perhaps you have found it all dull, lacking incident? But we will put that right, never fear. Show you incident in plenty. For you to relate hereafter to your so

332

notable friends in the South. In but a short while now, to be sure. That is, if our churchmen are not over-lazy — like so many of their kind. Eh, Master Sub-Prior?"

The tall Valliscaulian Order friar inclined his tonsured proud head briefly, silently.

"The Church, *Holy* Church, has its uses for once, this day," the Wolf went on. "Prior Moray will no doubt guide us in the matter, where necessary. Keep us right. As is suitable. After all, he has learned our methods. And if he is sufficiently helpful — who knows? He may greatly benefit, rise much higher on the road to Heaven than mere Sub-Prior of Pluscarden — especially as Pluscarden no longer needs a sub-prior, or a prior either! With the good offices of the Lieutenant and Justiciar of the North, he might even aspire to a bishop's mitre! And, by God, the See of Moray is going to require a new Bishop after this day!" And he barked a laugh.

Neither captive said a word.

"So, Sir James," the Earl went on, conversationally, "we have both spiritual and military advice here, eh? You are a soldier of a sort, are you not? Experienced in war and siegery? Although I do not think that you won into any of the cities you assailed, yon time in England! But perhaps you know the business, in theory? How would you advise that we gain entry to this walled city of Elgin, wherein lies my castle and courthouse — aye, and my lady-wife, mark you, my *wife*! Yet whose gates remain ever shut against me, the King's Lieutenant, on the orders of Bishop Barr, the Excommunicator! Your good counsel, sir — since it lacks yet a few minutes to sun-up."

Jamie moistened his lips. "Do I understand, my lord, that you mean to *attack* this city?"

"Attack? I mean to *enter* it, sir, one way or another. And thereafter remonstrate with Master Barr. He claims that it is *his* city, the Bishop's city. I say, as in duty bound, that it is the King's city. We must come to a conclusion on this matter, if there is to be any rule in the North."

"And you require 3,000 men, my lord, to speak with the Bishop?"

"Why, we must needs find a way in, somehow. Many gates to ask at. By stealth — or as we did at Pluscarden last month. Eh, Master Moray? So, Sir James — what is your advice?"

"I scarce think you need any from me, my lord. Clearly you plan a surprise assault at sunrise. On an unsuspecting city, on citizens of your own brother the King. My fellow-subjects, and yours. Who have done no hurt to any." Jamie drew a deep breath. "I would counsel restraint, since you ask me."

"A-a-ah!" That was very quiet. "So you offer me advice on policy. Not tactics, boy? Ah, well, I must be grateful! Meantime, we shall just have to use our own poor wits, lacking your experienced military guidance. This city is guarded. But at sunrise its night guards may be weary and heedless, their duty over. And the day guards may still be part-asleep. There are six gates in all, four in the town-wall, two into this precinct. We seek admittance at them all! But here at Pann's Port, Douglas, we shall seek with especial humility. The lepers from yonder Lazar-house each morning come out to get their bread — provided by Master Barr's bakers. They are not permitted to enter this godly city — but the Pann's Port is opened to let them draw their loaves. So, this fine morning, we shall join the unclean — and in our modesty win more than bread! Will it serve, think you?"

The younger man swallowed. "Only you, my lord, would have thought of that. To use the Bishop's charity to destroy him ... !"

Jamie Douglas got no further. A mighty backhanded swipe struck him full on the throat, snapping back his head and toppling him from his saddle. He crashed to the ground, and lay still.

*   *   *

When he came to himself again, he was sitting up, against Alexander Stewart's knee, held by the other's arm. His head throbbed, his vision swam and his throat ached so that it was an agony even to swallow. The friar, Moray, stood nearby, watching. The Earl had gone back to his chiefs. He must have been unconscious, but only for a very short while, presumably.

"You are a fool!" Alexander said, when he saw that the other was conscious again. "Will you never learn, Douglas?" He bit his lip. "I am sorry — but the blame was your own. My father will not be spoken to so. You should know it."

Jamie sought to speak, found it too much of an effort, and forbore.

"Are you hurt, man? Sorely?"

334

"I think not. My throat . . ."

"Why cannot you hold your tongue? As must others. He might have taken his sword to you, instead of his fist. Why?"

There was no answer to that.

The first dazzling golden level rays of the sun were just surmounting the dark band at the seaward horizon as Jamie struggled to his feet, dizzily. With the sudden increase of brightness the scale and detail of the city ahead became more evident, a riot of towers and gables, spires and turrets, domes and battlements. Something of the power and wealth of the Bishop of Moray — and of the reasons for the Wolf's envy and malice — became apparent. But it was the cathedral itself which inevitably drew the eye, quite the most splendid Jamie had ever seen, more noble than St. Andrews or Durham, its two great square towers to the west balanced by a lofty turreted gable to the east, and in the centre another and still mightier tower with soaring spire, the whole edifice three-hundred feet in length, its buttresses, clerestoreys, blindstoreys, arches and triple-tiered windows a challenging symphony in golden-brown stone. The Lantern of the North was well-named.

As the golden dazzle from the east lit up the magnificent building, a deep, sonorous but tuneful, joyful pealing of bells rang out from the cathedral towers to meet the new day, a rich and commanding paean of praise and thankfulness which throbbed and swelled and maintained — and which, even when joined and supported by what seemed to be scores of lesser bells from the other religious houses of Elgin, still clearly sounded through, behind and above all, so that the rest appeared to be no more than a background harmony to a major theme.

Soon after the bells began to ring people started to emerge from the leper hospital, people who limped and scurried and hobbled and crawled, a few at first, then a stream, a crowd, and all making for the Pann's Port gate.

Rob Stewart was already hurrying back to the main body of the Wolf's thousand behind.

Quickly thereafter, in ones and twos, Highlandmen came unobtrusively from this side and that to mingle with the waiting throng before the gate, seeking to appear not too strong and lusty for the pathetic company they kept, wrapped in their plaids, stooping, stumbling. Then the gates were unbarred and opened, from within, and the crowd surged forward. Trestles laden with steaming loaves were pushed and carried through the gateway by black-robed Lazarite brothers, some actually set up within the entrance itself.

The Earl of Buchan hooted. "They could scarce be kinder!" he declared. "No need for our would-be lepers. They could not close those gates in time, now. Come, friends — to our sport! Master Prior — come break your fast!"

The leadership, mounted and otherwise, trotted down to the Pann's Port unhurrying. In through the pitiful crowd of lepers they rode and pushed, knocking the unfortunates over like nine-pins, the white-robed friar striding amidst all in frowning sternness. Leaning from his saddle, the Wolf snatched up a warm loaf of bread from a trestle-table and tossed it to him, and another for Jamie.

"Of Bishop Barr's bounty!" he called, grabbing a third for himself. "He bakes good bread," he added, as he bit into it appreciatively. "I might put him into my kitchen at Lochindorb instead of hanging him!"

The Sub-Prior stared ahead of him, expressionless.

Everywhere now the caterans were snatching up the lepers' bread, knocking over the tables — and any of the black-robed, green-crossed brothers who got in their way or made protest.

The Earl rode on into the cathedral precincts, his fierce horsemen behind. It was as simple as that. They were in Elgin, and had not even had to draw a sword, as yet.

Before the great fluted and shafted western door of the cathedral, twenty-four feet high, the Wolf reined up, just as the bell-ringing died away. "You all know your tasks," he said to his lieutenants. "*I* will attend to Barr and to his property! They will be singing the Angelus in yonder, now. But not the Bishop, I warrant! He will still be in his bed, with a whore on either side, like as not. Wattie — have your men guard all these cathedral doors. Do not enter yet — but none to leave. They will have heard nothing, because of the bells' din. Alex — bring Douglas and the Prior with me. Mackintosh — the Dean's manse is yonder, behind that wall. See to it. Next is the Chanter's, I think, MacPherson." He pointed again. "That one is the Chancellor's, Mac-Gillivray. Aye, and the Sub-Dean's. God in Heaven — they serve themselves well! Off with you. And remember — tinder and fuel to be sent back. Thatch, straw, plenishings, timbering. Plenty of citizenry to carry it! Aye, and find that Archdeacon Spynie for me — he who brought the Lady Euphemia here from his Forres. I want him, alive — and my wife!" He rode on.

Jamie looked at Alexander Stewart. "This is beyond belief!" he said. The other did not answer but gestured him onwards.

A short distance west of the cathedral rose a tall, slender building, in dressed stone, of three storeys and an attic, within its own little courtyard and walled garden, the Bishop's town-lodging. It was more of a little castle than the senior clergy manses round about, defensible — but within the walled precinct and city its defences were left latent, its courtyard gate wide, its door shut but not locked and barred. This last the Wolf discovered when he rode up. It was a massive door and he made no attempt to kick it open but ordered a gillie to try it. When it opened, he laughed, and shouted, "Barr! Barr, I say! Knave! Clerk! Rouse yourself, excommunicator! Come down and break your fast with me. I have some bread here — lepers' bread. Come share it with Alexander Stewart!"

There was silence in the house.

"Come, man! Slug-abed! Come and tell me whether I should hang you or drown you or burn you! Your St. Lawrence toasted on a grid-iron, did he not? Will you follow the good Lawrence? Or prefer that I slit your throat for the rogue you are? Come — aye, and bring my wife with you!"

When still there was no least response, he hurled his loaf at the statue of a saint in a niche of the vaulted vestibule, sending it crashing to the floor and shattering. "Ho — servants! Scullions! Rascals! To me — to me, I say!"

A scared face peered round from the turnpike stairfoot. "Lord — he is not here! From home," the apparition wailed. "My Lord Bishop is not here."

"God's Death! Where is he?"

"He is gone to Spynie, sir. He is at Spynie."

"God damn and shrivel his soul! The foul fiend roast him! He came back from Spynie three days agone. I had sure word."

"Yes, sir — yes. But he left again. Yesterday's noon. He entertains company at Spynie . . ."

"Christ in Heaven!" The Wolf's fury all but choked him. He made an awesome sight, purple in the face, gasping for breath like a landed fish, his clenched fists raised above his head. Spynie Castle, the Bishop of Moray's episcopal palace, lay some three miles to the north, a powerful stronghold set most securely in the saltmarsh of the Lossie estuary.

Storming out, the Earl spurred back to the cathedral, speaking to none. At the great western entrance, where the boy Sir Walter stood on guard with a score or so of caterans, he pushed past all, gesturing peremptorily for the door to be opened, and rode inside. Behind him surged his party — but none of these had quite sufficient of their lord's spirit to ride horses into God's house.

Within, the scene and aura, the tenor and tempo, was so utterly different as to be scarcely believable, acceptable. The building itself was so vast and lofty and glorious as to completely dwarf all men, even mounted men, and their puny doings, the orderly forest of tall pillars, the multi-storeyed arches criss-crossing, the soaring vaulting and groined ribbing so high above as to be but dimly seen in the mellow light of the rank upon rank of stained-glass windows and the blue haze of generations of incense. The prolonged narrowing vista of aisles and transepts, side-chapels and galleries, was all but overpowering — and uniquely so, for this was the only cathedral north of France to boast double aisles in the nave. The wall-paintings and hangings and memorials were so rich and varied and colourful as to take away the breath at first glance, the gold-coated screens of the choir a glowing joy. In all this sublime splendour the presence of men was scarcely to be noticed; but their music and praise was. Far ahead, up in the choir, sweet chanting rose high and clear, the pure notes of boys' treble voices lifting through the undertones of tenor and bass, as those cathedral bells had risen through the cacophony of the rest. There was no congregation; only the lesser cathedral clergy and choristers at early morning worship, up there below the high altar.

The Earl of Buchan was not impressed; or if he was he betrayed no sign of it. Without pause he drove his garron up the great central aisle. Presently the hollow clatter of its hooves penetrated to the singers' ears, and gradually the chanting died away as men and boys turned to stare appalled. Behind the Wolf, but at some distance, came his distinctly doubtful and overawed minions.

Past the golden screens and up the steps into the choir or chancel he went. Opposite the stalls where the gaping, white-surpliced choristers waited, he reined over to where a massive multi-armed candlestick stood, and, lashing out with his foot, kicked it over, to crash on the tiled flooring, as introduction. He jabbed a finger towards the officiating priest and his assistants up before a secondary altar.

"Begone!" He barked the single word, and gestured away.

Terrified, the clergy hurried off, only one remembering to bow briefly towards the Presence-light above the high altar. The choristers were commencing to depart likewise when the Wolf turned in his saddle to his followers.

"These," he said pointing at the singers, men and boys. "Use them. All woodwork to be stripped. All timbering. All vestments and hangings. All that will burn. In heaps. Where it will best serve. In especial at the stair-foots, in the galleries, under the roof-trusses. Find where the lamp-oil is stored. And candles. More fuel will be coming from the town — thatch, straw, wood — much more. See to it. And quickly. Andrew, Wattie — all vessels of gold and silver, crosses, gewgaws and the like, to be collected."

Thus commanded, like a horde of destructive ants, the caterans swarmed off over the magnificent edifice, smashing, breaking, wrecking, dragging and heaping. Instead of sweet music and chanting was shouting, laughter, cursing, banging, splitting and clanging. The Earl sat his horse in the midst throughout, stationary but overseeing all.

"May we go outside?" Jamie said, voice cracking. "If we ... stay here, I swear ... I will assail him! With my bare hands ...!"

"If you will." Alexander sounded little loth.

In silence they hurried out, through the spoliation. The smell of burning met them before they ever emerged through the western portal, carried on the westerly breeze. Outside, great gouts and billows of smoke and flame were already surging up from various parts of the town, with near at hand the clergy manses beginning to blaze.

"They should not have excommunicated him!" Alexander Stewart said heavily.

"Can you do nothing? *Nothing?*"

"What can I do? What can anyone do? You have seen him. He is not as other men. You know that. He is a law unto himself. He *is* the law, in all the North!"

Jamie shook his head, beyond words.

339

Presently the first of the columns of fuel-bearers began to arrive at the cathedral, frightened citizens, men, women and children, driven by dirk-brandishing caterans, burdened with their own or their neighbours' furnishings and roofing. They made a sorry sight.

To burn a lofty, stone-built cathedral was, of course, a very difficult and major task. The Earl had anticipated this, and went about the business with a carefully thought-out and grim efficiency which gave the lie to any suggestion of mere savage wrath. He permitted no firing until a vast quantity of tinder was accumulated, and disposed at heedfully selected points where it would achieve most damage. With much of the city alight, a terrifying sight, the cathedral itself was darkened, all but hidden, huge as it was, in the roaring, swelling smoke-clouds pouring down on the wind, creating their own hot wind. Before all was ready for the torches, conditions within were menacing enough. The final touch was somehow the more odious, the wholesale smashing of the richly lovely stained-glass windows the better to create ample through-draughts to fan the flames. Only then were the fires lit.

Even so, it took a while for the blaze to get a grip. But when it did, the effect was tremendous. The many narrow turnpike stairs which led up to the clerestory galleries in especial acted like great chimneys, with the flames roaring up in daunting fashion. The galleries and the nave roofing took fire first, therefore, with added frightening effect for those still working dragging fuel below, showers of sparks and flaming fragments raining down. With the choking smoke, conditions inside became quite horrifying. But still the Earl remained there, dismounted now since he could no longer control his maddened horse, directing, superintending.

The tall person of the Sub-Prior of Pluscarden materialised out of the smoke before Alexander Stewart and Jamie, just outside the western doorway, his eyes running, as were all others.

"Where is he? Where is the Earl?" he demanded. "In the name of God, tell me! This is . . . beyond all. Even Pluscarden and Forres . . ."

"My father is within, Sir Prior," Alexander said, shaking his head. "But it will serve you nothing to see him, speak with him."

"It must. It *shall.* God in Heaven above — the mighty Trinity

340

to which this church is dedicated — should strike him down! The King's brother . . . !"

An explosion of flame and smoke above them burst out a window too high for the wreckers to have reached, showering all below in broken and molten glass. Starting back, seeking to protect themselves, they scattered.

"Perhaps God will!" Jamie panted, to the cleric. "Since the Earl is still in there."

Without a word the other pushed past the cowering guards and plunged within.

"The fool!" Alexander jerked, when he realised what had happened. "He can do nothing. None can do anything now. Even my father himself." He shook his fair head. "This is madness. He should be out — my father. He could die. This smoke could overcome him . . ."

"And just retribution! I pray that he does die."

The other only frowned. "He is my father. And my brothers are in there still, also . . ."

"Only because their own savage lust for destruction keeps them there."

"I am going in. I must! Wait you here . . ." Alexander Stewart, in turn, hurried back into that inferno.

Jamie waited, a prey to conflicting emotions. Should he also go in? What good could he do? Alexander was the only one he would lift a finger to aid. And the Prior, of course. On the other hand, for the first time in long weeks he was in a position to try to escape. None stood close guard on him. If he could make a dash through the smoke and into the city? Better still, out through Pann's Port and into the open country. Lie low somewhere, then make his way south. He had no arms, no money, only the clothes he stood up in. But he could steal a garron . . .

He gnawed his lip. Alexander Stewart would suffer for it, if he did. Could he help that? He had given no sort of parole. He had been maltreated, threatened, wrongly imprisoned. He owed nothing to any of this wretched family. He peered around him in the lurid flame-fingered gloom. Caterans were milling about everywhere — but most might not know who he was. Or conceive him any responsibility of theirs. The smoke could be his opportunity.

He edged a little way further out from the doorway, peering.

Then, just as he was preparing to stroll away, a hand fell on his shoulder and jerked him round. Two Highlandmen stood just behind, dirks held at the ready, threatening. They said nothing, but there was no mistaking their warning. He had been in error in thinking that he was no longer closely guarded.

Shrugging, he moved back to his former position.

In a short while the Sub-Prior Moray came stumbling out of the cathedral, coughing, clutching a burned hand, his white robe blackened by embers. Gulping the slightly better air, he stood beside Jamie.

"The man is Satan incarnate!" he panted. "Filled with the spirit of hell. Sheerest hatred. Possessed. Nothing avails with him."

"Nothing. Save a sword keener and stronger than his own!"

"Who is there to raise that sword? You are also held captive? I saw you struck down. You at least are no friend of his."

"No friend," Jamie agreed. "I am James Douglas of Aberdour. His prisoner."

"Douglas? You are far from your own country, sir."

"Aye — too far. Would God I were home again. Out of this devil's clutch."

"He is a destroyer. And must himself be destroyed. If we would save Holy Church in the North."

"Less easily done than said."

"I will do what I can, God willing. A month past he burned down my priory of Pluscarden. After burning the whole town of Forres . . ."

"Forres? He burned Forres? And Pluscarden. That is what he was doing! They did not tell me. But why? Why Forres?"

"Because his true wife dwelt there. The Countess Euphemia, whom he has long deserted. Over whom he was excommunicated." The Prior was having to shout, above the roar of the flames and the cries of men. "Holy Church cared for her. Archdeacon William de Spynie, in particular. He is Rector of Forres as well as Archdeacon of Moray. He escaped this evil prince, and brought the Countess to Pluscarden. Then on here to Elgin, to the Bishop. So now he comes destroying here. Beelzebub, the prince of devils. Flinging down God's houses. Defiling His altars. Abusing His servants. Stealing His treasure. I shall make him pay, by all the saints of glory! I shall go South forthwith. To the Primate. To the Governor. To the King himself."

"What can they do. Even the King?"

"They can, and must, do something. I have powerful friends, kin. I am of the great house of de Moravia. If it is the last thing I do, I shall see that he suffers for this. I will go to the Vatican, even!"

"The Vatican can do no more than your Bishop of Moray, I fear — excommunicate. That is the direst sanction — and he scorns it. But, sir — if you do win to the South, will you inform the Lady Isabel Stewart, who was Countess of Douglas, of my state? Or the Lady Gelis . . ."

"But these are princesses. Sisters of this royal monster!"

"I rejoice to call them friends, nevertheless. I am the Lady Isabel's knight and servant. If you cannot win to them, see Mistress Mary Stewart, their half-sister. Tell her. Indeed, best tell her first. Say that I am the Wolf's prisoner. But will return as soon as I may, God willing. And tell her . . ." He paused, and shook his sore head. "Aye — tell her that, sir."

"I will do so. If I can. If either of us escape with our lives from this monster, this fiend in human form."

"You are not a prisoner as I am, are you? Brought here but for this day? You they will not hold, I think. Why not try to slip away now, sir? I tried — but me they know for long, and restrained me. You, a churchman, might move around. Slip away in the smoke, if you may. You can serve no good purpose here."

Looking around him in the thick gloom, Sub-Prior Moray nodded. "I can attempt it. God keep and preserve you then, my son," he murmured. And head down, clutching his burned hand, he paced slowly off and was quickly lost to sight. None appeared to see it as their duty to follow him.

Presently Alexander emerged again, with his father and brothers, all staggering, blinded with tears, lungs bursting, faces red. Sack-loads of valuables were dragged out after them, some of the bags on fire. The Earl coughing terribly, hair and beard singed gasped in debate whether to ride on the three miles north to Spynie and launch immediate assault on the Bishop's palace, whilst his sons pointed out that Barr would have had ample warning. Moreover his hold, protected by the saltmarsh, was impregnable, save by surprise.

The Earl allowed himself to be convinced. In fact, he was exhausted with the heat, the smoke and lack of any sleep the night before, a man in his fifties, for all his physical strength and energy.

Gazing blearily, for once like his late father, on all blazing Elgin, he nodded. He handed his horn to someone with more available wind than he had left, to blow the Retiral.

Only a small number heard that summons, of course. Leaving most of his force, now largely dispersed, drunken and ungovernable, to wreak their wills on what was left of the capital of Moray, the Wolf trotted off south-westwards, with his long train of booty.

At the crest of the ridge of Hardhillock he looked back. Out of the holocaust of the city the cathedral now towered like a mighty furnace, spouting flame.

"We have lit the Lantern of the North!" he exclaimed huskily. "Douglas — you perceive? You have seen how Alexander Stewart deals with those who misuse him. Remember it. Remember all of it. So that, one day, you can tell those who ought to know. For their own good. If God and I spare you!" Without waiting for answer, he rode on.

XXI

DESPITE THE WOLF'S repeated mentions of his role as witness, he seemed to be in no hurry to despatch Jamie upon this duty. He was taken back to Lochindorb from Elgin — which at least was better than Loch-an-Eilean or Ruthven — and thereafter the Earl more or less ignored him. He could scarcely be said to forget him, for the reluctant visitor was permitted to revert to the status of restricted house guest, and therefore could not be entirely overlooked by the master of the house. Fortunately or otherwise, the Wolf was much away from home in the weeks that followed, apparently holding justiciary courts here and there, at Inverness, Nairn, Rothes and as far away as Lochaber — of which he was also lord — however extraordinary a proceeding this might seem for the man who had just deliberately burned two towns, a cathedral and a monastery. What sort of justice he meted out must be debatable — although Alexander defensively declared that his father made an excellent, shrewd and fair judge. He took different sons with him on these journeys, so that Jamie suffered a variety of jailers, not all so accommodating as Sir Alexander. However, the Lady Mariota was consistently kind and indeed seemed to enjoy the captive's company; as, to a lesser extent did the girl Margaret.

Jamie was intrigued by Mariota de Athyn. A woman of character, intelligence and considerable charm, and gently bred, she nevertheless appeared to be quite content with her life and situation. Stranger still, she clearly was very fond of her savage paramour. To be sure he was apt to behave comparatively well when in her company, so that she undoubtedly saw the best of him. But how she could condone his behaviour elsewhere was beyond Jamie Douglas's understanding. Despite his own evident attraction for the other sex, he still had a lot to learn about women. They never actually discussed the Earl's outrages together, of course; although they came near to it time and again, the woman always skilfully turned the conversation. But they discussed much else, and Jamie had constantly to remind himself that he was talking with a notorious courtesan and not a perfectly normal and admirable wife and mother.

Had it not been for the sense of freedom restricted, plus the uncertainly as to the future, Lochindorb Castle would have been none too bad a place in which to pass a Highland summer. The immediate surroundings were scenically attractive, activities for an energetic young man numerous and unfailing — although he was never permitted to indulge in them unescorted — and the provender excellent. When Alexander was at home, he had no complaints as to the company. But with anyone as unpredictable and unrestrained as the Wolf as arbiter of his fortunes, none of all this permitted easement of mind.

As to repercussions from Elgin and Forres burnings, strangely enough, they heard nothing at all. No word came from the outside world, and the matter was seldom referred to at Lochindorb — although Jamie did gather that, as well as what he had seen to be burned at Elgin, the Maison Dieu Hospice, the Greyfriars and Blackfriars monasteries the main parish or Muckle Kirk and no fewer than eighteen clergy manses had been destroyed. But as far as reactions and retributions were concerned, it might all never have been.

The captive, of course, made constant demands to be allowed to leave for the South. But none could give him that permission, save the Wolf; and he would not until he was ready, he said. And Jamie was past the stage of protesting more than automatically, formally. Having learned all too clearly of what the man was capable, in one of his rages, and perceiving at long last that argument, like protest, was profitless in the circumstances, he held his peace.

In a period of some seven weeks, one quite welcome and enlightening interlude did occur. For reasons undisclosed but probably because he desired to have Alexander with him and none of the other sons happened to be at Lochindorb that week, the Earl elected to take Jamie with him also on one of his judicial excursions. This trip, far up the valley of the Findhorn, according to Alexander, was in a somewhat different category from the usual, where courts were held in towns and castles and populous areas. This one involved the settlement of a dispute between two Clan Chattan chiefs, the Mackintosh himself, Captain of Clan Chattan, and MacGillivray. Apparently it was the sort of problem which would formerly have been decided by simple recourse to armed conflict — in which case the Mackintosh would presumably have won, for he was much the more powerful, and as head of the Chattan confederation could have called on other members for support. But, surprisingly enough, under the Wolf's regime as Justiciar, such age-old customs were frowned upon and the matter fell to be settled by due process of law — the King's Justiciar's law. Hence this journey.

A party of about two-score, they rode off northwards across the bleak Braemoray moors in the last week of July, in no hurry, enjoying a fine summer's day in what were presently pleasing surroundings when they came down into the fairly narrow and picturesque Findhorn valley at Ardclach. Jamie was surprised indeed at the general holiday atmosphere, something he had by no means associated with the Earl. In fact it was almost like a royal progress, on a small scale, with Buchan greeted at every small community with smiles, respect, acclaim even, himself genial, friendly and consistently good company. Gone was the savage tyrant; instead a father-figure, authoritative but benevolent and accessible, prepared to talk and listen to the humblest of the cateran families and clansmen, the herders, peat-cutters, woodmen and the like. That they responded, indeed came to welcome him, showed that this was no unusual manifestation, no mere demonstration for the occasion. It occurred to Jamie, belatedly, that these Highlanders must in fact approve of their fierce overlord or they would scarcely turn out at such short notice and in such large numbers to fight for him.

They crossed the lofty area known as The Streens, wild and supporting no townships or settlements but at this season pastured by great herds of cattle, up from the lower lands for the summer grazings. Parties of young people tended the herds in some fashion, living an idyllic and carefree existence up there on the roof of the land, untrammelled by their elders' presence, domestic drudgery or indeed much in the way of moral codes. The life of the shielings, as it was called, given passable weather, was obviously a pleasant one, a kind of prolonged annual holiday. Yet, according to Alexander, it was about just such shieling controversy that the present errand was concerned.

The Streens crossed, they came down into the wider strath of Moy, The Mackintosh country, wooded and more like Strathspey, and here they found the Captain of Clan Chattan himself waiting, with a large company of his clansmen, Lachlan, 9th chief and Baron of Moy, an elderly but still powerful man of huge stooping frame, hooded eyes and beaked nose. But he greeted the Earl warmly and they seemed to be on excellent terms.

The augmented company, now with pipers to cheer them on their way, proceeded on up the Findhorn, whose valley now assumed the character of a normal Highland glen, the hills rising ever higher as they pushed deeper into what were now the mountain masses of the Monadh Liath. This Strathdearn as it was called was a fairly populous valley, with strips of oats on every level haugh and terrace, cot-houses dotted the length, even a little church at Dalarossie, low-browed and thatch-roofed like the cabins. Everywhere the Earl and Mackintosh were hailed and welcomed, clearly popular, in a way no great lord would be greeted by common folk in the South.

Where the side-glen of Kyllachy came in from the north-west, another company awaited them, Farquhar MacGillivray, 5th of the name, with a selection of his chieftains and tacksmen, from

Strathnairn to the north. He was a youngish man, thick, stocky, rather like a bull, with a sort of brooding stillness to him which might well explode into sudden and drastic action. He was stiff with The Mackintosh but gruffly amiable towards the Earl, who handled him jovially. The two sets of clansmen eyed each other like wary dogs.

A mile or two further up the main valley another glen came in, Mazeron by name. This was their destination. For the tacksman of Glen Mazeron, one Conal Dubh MacGillivray, was the transgressor and cause of the present trouble. He was accused of stealing cattle up on the shieling pastures between this Strathdearn and Strathnairn, one of the most heinous crimes in the Highland calendar, which struck at the very roots of a pastoral way of life based on common grazings. It appeared that he had been caught actually with the stolen beasts, red-handed, so that there was no doubt as to guilt. What was being contested, and what had brought the King's Justiciar all this way, was who should try him and what the sentence should be. The MacGillivray chief, *Mhic Gillebráth Mor*, claimed that as the offender was a tacksman of his, the duty and privilege fell to him; whereas the Mackintosh held that, since the beasts had been stolen from the Kyllachy shielings, Mackintosh land, the jurisdiction was his. The aggrieved owners certainly could not rely on adequate penalty being meted out by any MacGillivray trial, or even be sure of getting their cattle back. So the chiefs brought in the Justiciar. It was interesting that the Wolf agreed to come.

It was early evening before they reached Glen Mazeron, over thirty miles, and much too late, all agreed, for any serious debate or trial. Strangely enough the atmosphere at the township was anything but gloomy and foreboding, almost the same holiday spirit prevailing as elsewhere, even the offender himself playing host with a fair degree of aplomb. He was a swarthy eager little man of early middle years, voluble, lively and far from crushed by the enormity of his sin. He was not locked up. There was no place here to incarcerate him and nowhere to which he could effectively flee anyway. In the Highland polity a man stayed within his own clan, right or wrong. But he was the tacksman here, superior tenant, and recognised his duties towards the distinguished visitors.

The two chiefs had come well provided, and the encampment

348

suffered no lack of cold meats — more beef carried, undoubtedly, than could have been produced from the stolen cattle which brought them here — venison, oatcakes and *uisage-beatha*, the fiery spirit of the North. A lively evening developed, with singing, tale-telling, piping and dancing. Even the cattle-stealer contributed notably on his fiddle, for he was a renowned performer, and was roundly applauded. The Wolf himself was not above singing powerfully, dancing, and finally impersonating a pompous cleric at his devotions — which went down well. He insisted that Jamie, after Alexander had borrowed the tacksman's fiddle and played with expertise and feeling, should render an offering, so he sang a haunting Border ballad of lost love and hopeless sacrifice — which, of course, being in English, was understood by few, but with most of his hearers three-parts drunk anyway, this mattered little.

Presently all who were sober enough to do so wrapped themselves in their plaids and slept under the stars, around the aromatic birch-log fires.

In the morning a brisk purpose prevailed, although many of the company seemed to breakfast on whisky. They all moved to a nearby knoll, whereon the Earl and the two chiefs seated themselves. The clansfolk, reinforced now by what must have been a large proportion of the local population, gathered round in a wide circle, in the best of spirits. When Conal Dubh MacGillivray was escorted to the judgment seat he had to pass through the crowd, to cheerful raillery. It was noted that he brought his fiddle.

The proceedings were, of course, conducted wholly in the native Gaelic, and had to be translated for Jamie by Alexander Stewart. After a brief introductory speech by the Earl, here known as *Alastair Mor Mac-an-Righ*, Big Alexander Son of the King, genial, even humorous, the MacGillivray chief launched into a prolonged and vehement declaration that it was elementary and age-old custom that a *ceann cinnidh* or clan chief was responsible for the administration of justice within his own clan and its territories, save insofar as this did not conflict with the jurisdiction of the *Ard Righ*, the High King. If a chief was held responsible for the actions of his clansmen by the Crown, it followed that he must be able to discipline, try and punish offenders. Conal Dubh was undoubtedly his clansman, tacksman of this clan territory of Glen Mazeron. There was no possible cause for dispute. He, *Mhic Gil-*

lebráth Mor, had in fact sat in judgment, and adjudged Conal Dubh as guilty of the crime of cattle-stealing from open shieling grazings, and passed sentence. This sentence was that the said Conal should have his right hand struck off from his right arm; that he should thereafter be banished from the clan and its territories for five years and five days; and that restitution should be made from his goods to the owners of the said cattle. Confident of the correctness and fairness of this judgment, he, *Mhic Gillebráth Mor*, submitted the case to the superior jurisdiction of the High King's Justiciar.

Nodding, the Wolf turned to The Mackintosh.

That fierce old man, who introduced himself as *Mac an Toishich Mor*, Captain of Clan Chattan, Senseschal of Badenoch and Baron of Moy, poured scorn upon MacGillivray's pronouncements, on various counts. While there was no question that the wretched and infamous Conal Dubh was a clansman of MacGillivray, yet *Mhic Gillebráth Mor* was himself a clansman of *himself, Mac an Toishich Mor*, since MacGillivray was only a sub-clan of the great and mighty Clan Chattan federation of which he, *Mac an Toishich Mor* was Captain and chief. The greater included the lesser before the law. Secondly, the cattle had been stolen from Glen Kyllachy shielings, which were and always had been Mackintosh territory, the aggrieved owners Mackintosh clansmen, entitled to look to their chief for justice on his and their territory. Thirdly, he was Baron of Moy, which rank and status conferred upon him a superior jurisdiction to that of *Mhic Gillebráth Mor*, including the right of pit and gallows over the entire barony lands of Strathdearn, to which Glen Mazeron indubitably belonged. *Mhic Gillebráth Mor* held no such baronial status. And, since this was undoubtedly a hanging matter, the power of pit and gallows was involved. He therefore claimed the right to try and sentence the said Conal, as inadequately tried and sentenced by *Mhic Gillebráth Mor*.

The Earl, who of course knew all this anyway, thanked both contestants for their clear and concise statements of the position. He pretended to ponder for a little, and then put forward his own observations, in entirely moderate fashion. Both sides appeared to have much to be said for them, he held. Much seemed to depend on the definition of the terms sub-clan and federation. It seemed to him that a clan was a clan, or else it was not. A federation was an association or alliance, in which the members, in this case the constituent clans, were partners. This, to his mind, did not lessen the status of the members, which remained clans, with all their privileges and responsibilities. There might be greater and lesser clans within the federation, but they were all *clans*. A captain was necessary in such a confederation, but for leadership in war rather than before the law. MacGillivray was undoubtedly a clan, and had been one from early times. Therefore, it seemed that *Mhic Gillebráth Mor* had uncontestable right to try and sentence his clansmen.

While The Mackintosh frowned darkly, MacGillivray's bull-like features broke into a grin.

Nevertheless, the Earl went on, judicially, there was much in what *Mac an Toishich* had put forward, not so much as Captain of Clan Chattan as Baron of Moy. The barony *was* a superior jurisdiction, just as the Crown was superior to both. In this regard, the right of pit and gallows was important. Had *Mhic Gillebráth Mor* sentenced the offender, Conal, to death, there might have been no dispute — save perhaps that the Crown might possibly have contested the sentence as infringing on its prerogative. But he had not done so, imposing a lesser penalty. So the Baron of Moy might well claim that the sentence was inadequate, as he did, and since he held the right of pit and gallows, it might be that there should be a re-trial with a view to revising the sentence. Was not cattle-stealing normally considered to be a hanging matter, on open grazings?

The Mackintosh forcefully declared that of course it was so. All knew that. It was merely that this Conal Dubh was a tacksman, not just an ordinary clansman, and a distant cousin of *Mhic Gillebráth Mor* — who was therefore shielding his kinsman. MacGillivray hotly asserted the contrary saying that it was within his right to impose what sentence he thought fit. But that if hanging it was to be, then *he* would impose that sentence and do the hanging, not Mackintosh.

The two chiefs were now glaring at each other angrily, and clansmen on either side beginning to growl ominously and finger their dirks.

Smiling benevolently, easily, the Earl raised his hand. It would be a pity he asserted, if his good and true friends were to come to blows over such a small matter as who should conduct a hanging!

If they were both now agreed that hanging was the most suitable penalty, he would be glad to resolve the difficulty for them by himself, as Justiciar, carrying out the sentence. Would this be agreeable? As between friends? He could insist, of course, since they had both appealed to him for a final decision.

Both protagonists, after a doubtful moment or too, looked relieved, and nodded their agreement.

The Wolf beamed on all. A most happy outcome, he declared. All should be satisfied, and the Clan Chattan federation preserved from schism. There was only the one point remaining outstanding. Had the guilty party Conal Dubh MacGillivray any relevant observations to make? And he turned to the offender.

That man, who had listened to the debate with the greatest of interest now bobbed his head eagerly and launched into a monologue which Jamie would have assumed to be a plea for mercy but which did not seem to be in the right tone for that. Alexander explained that the little man was in fact expressing his favour for the amended sentence. He had never relished the notion of his right hand being cut off — for it would mean that he could never play his fiddle again; which was his greatest joy. He would far rather be comfortably dead, especially if he was to be banished from Strathdearn which had been his home always, the valley he loved and about which he had composed more than one fiddle tune. There was only the one thing that he would ask, of the lord's mercy and goodness. Might he be disposed of some other way than by hanging? He had always disliked the idea of hanging on a rope, an awkward, uncertain and undignified end for any man — he had seen a few hangings.

The Earl nodded kindly. He would prefer not to die by hanging, himself, he admitted. Cold steel was much to be preferred. Might he make a suggestion? As a younger man he had been rather good at beheading people with a sword. On a chivalric expedition to France he had had the privilege of winning a tourney where the prize was the opportunity to execute six malefactors. He had whipped off the heads of four of them with single strokes. Only with his arm flagging a little had he required two strokes each for the final pair. Would Conal Dubh like to essay that?

Conal Dubh would be delighted, it seemed. He was at his lordship's disposal, there and then. There was only one small matter first. He would very much like to play them all a piece on his fiddle before he went. If he might, he would give them his own favourite composition, *In Praise of Strathdearn*. It was not very long and would not delay their lordships unduly.

This request was graciously granted, to general applause. The little tacksman took up his instrument, briefly tuned the strings, and plunged into a lively, spirited and tuneful air, linked by a simple but effective refrain, which soon had all feet tapping while the Wolf beat time with his dirk. Imperceptibly, however, the lilt changed to a sweet and lingering melody, wistful, poignant. He ended on a high note, pure, quivering, which brought lumps to many a throat.

Beaming round, Conal Dubh bowed to the Earl and the chiefs. Holding up his fiddle, he said something which Alexander failed to finish translating. He was asking the Wolf if he might present the instrument to one whose fiddling he had admired the previous evening? In the fiddle he was leaving behind the best of him, he said, and wished the creature to be in good hands. He would break it over his knee if he was not permitted to present it . . .

Alexander Stewart's interpretation faded away as the little man turned to him and held out the instrument. With the Earl nodding agreement, the young man stepped forward to accept the gift, his face a study. Haltingly he promised to look after the fiddle well and truly.

The Wolf sent a gillie for his great two-handed sword, and came down from the mound. The tacksman turned to face him and spread his hands eloquently, ready.

"He says that, since there is no priest present, he trusts the good God to receive a sinner's soul unshriven," Alexander reported unsteadily.

"Must this be . . .?"

"I fear so. Cattle-stealing is a more grievous crime here than is murder."

The sword handed over to the Earl, he tried a few swishes with it, in the air to flex his muscles, the condemned man watching, critically concerned. Then the latter asked whether he should kneel down on the grass, thrust his head forward or how otherwise dispose himself? He was told that the other usually did his decapitating standing up, and that since he was only a small man there should be no difficulty.

353

Conal Dubh bowed again, half-smiling — and on impulse the Wolf outthrust his hand to shake that of his victim. Then, stepping back, with great swiftness and a remarkable explosion of strength, he swung the five-feet-long blade up, back and forward again without pause, his eyes and those of the tacksman remaining locked until the very moment of impact.

With a notably final snapping sound, the grinning dark head flew right off, to land on the grass feet away and roll over and over, still smiling. The headless trunk, however, spouting blood like a fountain, stood its ground for a few timeless moments before taking three or four uncoordinated steps, sideways and backwards oddly enough, then, as the knees gave way, pitching forward.

A great sigh arose from the company. A woman began to wail, some way off, presumably the wife.

The Justiciar of the North, *de facto* if not *de jure*, had dispensed justice, maintained the royal authority, prevented a clan squabble from escalating into wholesale bloodshed, and kept the favour and support of two useful lieutenants.

The air of holiday had reasserted itself well before the Earl's party left Glen Mazeron to ride down Findhorn again, with Jamie Douglas meditating on Badenoch and the Wolf. He was beginning to suspect that judgment, like justice, was less straightforward north of the Highland Line than he had supposed.

XXII

THE WOLF AND his household knew of the impending visitation, of course, an hour and more before it arrived, knew even that a woman was involved. But identities they could not know, for this company was large enough to escape the escorting attentions of Sir Andrew Stewart of Ruthven, unlike lesser predators. When, eventually, in the late afternoon of the last day of July, the cavalcade did appear in sight of Lochindorb

Castle, over the final shoulder of Carn nan Clach Garbha, it was to reveal something that the busy scouts had omitted to mention — that it now rode under two banners, one that of Stewart, the other no less than the Lion Rampant standard of Scotland.

That set tongues urgently to wag in the island stronghold.

The Earl, presently, sent his son Alexander in a small boat to meet the newcomers at the opposite shore, to enquire their business and to question the presence of some fifty armed men in his territories, uninvited and unheralded, Stewart banner or none.

Sir Alexander was rowed back notably quickly, alone and in some agitation. He had just a little difficulty in enunciating his message to his father. "It is the new High Steward," he declared. "David, Earl of Carrick and Prince of Scotland. He, he requires your presence before him. He said . . . forthwith!"

"God's eyes—*requires!*" The Earl all but choked. "Requires, he says? Me! That insolent brat, my nephew Davie!"

"He says that he comes directly from the King, his father, my lord. And sounds . . . confident."

"Let him, the pup! Now — what has he come here for, young David Stewart? This is passing strange. And the woman? The woman — what of her? Who is she?"

"He did not say, my lord. She did not speak. Save that she is mighty good to look at, I learned naught of her. He was short in speech. Most masterful."

"So-o-o! We will change that! But . . . good-looking, eh? He is on the young side to be trailing a doxie around with him — although perhaps I did at his age! She would not be one of the princesses, my sisters?"

"I know not, sir. I have never seen them."

"They have come a long way. Why? Why, I wonder?" The Wolf turned to look speculatively at Jamie, when there sounded a loud and continuous blowing of horns, peremptory, imperious, from the shore. "Curse the malapert!" he barked. "This one needs a lesson — and will get it."

"Perhaps you should go, Alex," the Lady Mariota suggested mildly. She did not often do the like. "This is the heir to the throne. It will serve you nothing to give unnecessary offence. Your brother is not young, nor strong. This David could be king sooner than you think. Better not to have him as enemy."

"Let him learn discretion, if he is to be king! Aye, and manners too. In the North, *I* rule. He will discover it — as others have done!" He swung round. "How say you, Douglas? You have learned who is master here. You will know this stripling, I swear?"

"I know him, yes, my lord. And would counsel you — beware!"

"Save us — you would? Then you are a bigger fool than I thought you! When Alexander Stewart begins to heed striplings and shavelings, it will be time to bury him!"

"This stripling, sir, is . . . unusual! And does not resemble his royal father."

The Wolf began to speak, then stopped, staring. There was some commotion over there, which resolved itself into men-at-arms, dismounted, pulling heather-thatch off the roofs of two or three of the castleton cot-houses. Even as they watched, the heaped roofing began to smoke, burst into flames.

"As I said, the Lord David is an unusual youth . . ." Jamie commented — but the Earl was already striding down to the island landing-stage. When Alexander hurried after his father, Jamie went also.

The Wolf did not speak once during the row over to the mainland, and no others sought to intrude on his thoughts. Anyway, by halfway across Jamie's interest was elsewhere. Against the background of blazing thatch and smoke columns, a small group of riders still sat their horses, apart from the busy men-at-arms a little, waiting. The slender figure of the Lord David, now Earl of Carrick, was easily picked out. And beside him sat a rather less slender but still trim figure, even better-known to Jamie Douglas — unmistakably Mary Stewart, and the only woman there. His heart gave sufficient leap within him almost to make him splutter a sort of cough.

After that recognition, for a little while, he was less than sure of the exact sequence of events, his mind and emotions in a whirl. He was vaguely aware of the boat grounding, of leaping out after the others, of David's ringing call — which should of course have been directed towards his uncle but was in fact addressed to him — of shouts and hot words and tension. What he was entirely aware of was Mary's lovely face, flushed, eyes sparkling, lips parted, gazing at him — and him only. That made up for a lot of captivity.

He pulled himself together. The Wolf and his nephew were confronting each other, a sufficiently dramatic situation in all conscience. The barely fourteen-year-old High Steward, with the musical, high-pitched and mocking voice, had assumed the initiative.

". . . and having come so far, looked for a kinder welcome than this, my lord," he was saying. "To be kept waiting, like packmen at a gate. After insolent attentions by sundry creatures of yours since we entered this Badenoch."

"How dare you! How dare you fire those my cot-houses!" the Wolf thundered.

"I dare more than that, in this kingdom," the boy answered easily. "A deal more, Uncle, as you shall discover. I am here representing its liege lord, by his express command. Let none forget it."

"Damn you, boy — keep that sort of talk for those it may impress! Here *I* command — in the King's name. And by my own right hand!"

"Then command to better effect, sir. To receive me, and your sister here, better than this."

"How am I to know who may come chapping at my door, unannounced . . .?"

"You did not know that we came, then?" That was quick. "Your bastard at, at — I misremember the barbarous name — declared that none approached your robber's hold unknown and unannounced. An idle boast, it seems?"

The Wolf, frowning, drew a great breath. And Mary Stewart took the opportunity to put in a word.

"My lord Alexander," she said. "Greetings. It is no little time since we saw each other. But you may recollect my identity, nevertheless! I hope that I see you well?"

Her half-brother ignored that, entirely. "You will discover no idle boasting at Lochindorb, Nephew, I promise you," he said. "Indeed you will discover much that you ought to have been taught before this! Including regret for allowing your ruffians to damage my property." And he gestured to the burning thatch.

"Ha!" The boy tinkled a laugh. "I thought that such would commend itself to you, Uncle. Are you not an expert with torch

357

and tinder? We hear of whole towns and even cathedrals set alight. Is it only *Alexander* Stewart who may burn houses? Besides, was it not effective? To bring you, belatedly, to your duty."

It appeared that the youth had actually achieved the well-nigh impossible. The Earl of Buchan was rendered speechless.

Pressing his advantage, David spoke more formally — yet the subtle mockery was unmistakable still. "That duty, my lord, is to hear and receive the King's command. I am sent to summon you, as His Grace's brother and an earl of this realm, to attend the royal coronation at Scone on the 14th day of August next. God save the King's Grace!"

The Wolf moistened his lips. "What folly is this?" he demanded.

"Folly? You name the King's coronation folly, my lord? Before witnesses? The crowning of the Lord's Anointed! Is that not as good as high treason?"

"The folly is in sending such as you all this way to tell me. As good as a play-acting. Why?"

"You are entitled to be summoned, my lord. Would a lesser messenger have better pleased you? Or should it have been a greater? Is the heir to the throne insufficient to invite the Earl of Buchan? Must the King himself come to Badenoch and humbly seek your lordship's attendance?"

"Think you I care who acts messenger? I would no more attend this coronation flummery than seek to fly in the air!"

"So — that is the answer I am to take back to my father? In response to his royal command."

"Take what answer you like, boy. I care not. But not to Johnnie, or whatever he now styles himself. He is but a puppet. Take it to him who sent you, to my brother Robert, the Governor."

"The Earl Robert did not send me. Indeed he knew naught of my coming. We are scarce the best of friends. I came from the King alone."

"Think you that should comfort me? If I appeared at Scone, it would be to deliver myself into Robert's hands. He would have me taken and bound within the hour."

"So that is it, Uncle? You are afraid! The Earl of Buchan and Wolf of Badenoch is afraid to venture out of his lair! For fear his sins may catch him up? I will tell my father that."

358

"Fool! If it is fear to beware of treachery, then I am afraid, yes. I know my brothers. Even if the King were honest in this, he could not save me from Robert. So — would you have me take an army down to Scone? Perhaps I should!"

"Take whom you will, my lord. I but bring the royal summons. But I have another royal command, see you. You are holding here, without right or cause, a leal subject of the King, who has served him well. Sir James Douglas, a friend of the princesses. And of my own. It is my father's express command that he be released forthwith. To return with us."

The Wolf turned, to stare at Jamie with that blank yet calculating look of his, which could be frightening. "The wind blows that way, does it?" he said. "Now, how did that tale arise? So far away?"

"We had it on excellent authority," David said briefly. "I rejoice to see him here, and in seeming good health. Despite ... blows!"

"And why not? He has been my guest, my welcome guest, these two months and more. Although he came unbidden. He has fared well, dining at my table. My son here, Alexander, has looked after him like any brother. Is it not so, Douglas?"

Jamie hesitated. "I have no complaints as to Sir Alexander's treatment of me," he said.

"I think not!" That was grim, warning. "Held without right or cause, heh? So much for your excellent authority."

"Then, my lord, he *can* come back with us, without hindrance?" Mary put in.

"To be sure. If he so wishes." Narrow-eyed now, the Earl looked at his captive.

"I do so wish, my lord," Jamie contented himself with saying. He was only too well aware that this was a very much more delicate game than probably either of his friends realised. He knew a great deal better than they did of what the Wolf was capable, and how utterly devastating one of his rages could be. The fact that David had fifty men-at-arms immediately available might look decisive, for the moment; but that was not likely to affect his uncle's reactions in any major way. Nor was the nephew's now lofty status. Alexander was looking exceedingly anxious, on edge — and Jamie had found that was the best guide to watch.

359

The older man suddenly seemed to have had sufficient of this verbal exchange. "Enough!" he jerked, in a different voice. 'Come, you. Over to the castle. We have stood here over-long. Nephew, and you Mary, come in this small boat. Leave your men and horses. I will send over a barge for such as you would have with you there."

"No, Uncle."

"Eh? What mean you — no?"

"I mean that we bide here. With my men. Who knows, if we went out to your island yonder, some h'm, some storm might blow up! And we could not win back. We will bide here, very well. Send us victual . . ."

"But — God's eyes! You cannot roost out here. All night. Lacking all comfort."

"We have journeyed over two hundred miles of mountains, Uncle, lacking better comfort. And will do so again. We return to the South tomorrow. In the morning."

"Tomorrow? What nonsense is this? Not yet dismounted and talking of riding again. Come — over to the castle and rest you."

"I say no. Here we stay."

"Mary — you at least will have a grown woman's wits. Come."

"I have, my lord—and elect to stay likewise."

"Save us all! The bairns' folly of it. What of your two hundred miles of mountains, to journey back? Unrested."

"The reason for our swift return, Uncle," David said. "We have little time. The coronation is in but fourteen days. And it seems that it is necessary that I be present! Whether you are or not. We must start back in the morning."

Tight-lipped, the Wolf considered them. Then he shrugged. "As you will. I shall send over some meats. Alex — come. And you, Douglas."

"Sir James stays here, with us," David said, "since he rides with us, in the morning."

"Curse you — he is my, my . . ."

"Your captive, Uncle? Hostage?"

The Wolf glared around him, at the watchful ring of men-at-arms. Many of his own people stood behind them, the occupants of the castleton; but mostly they were women and children.

Almost all the men were away at the bog-hay harvest in the floors of the side-glens, so vital for winter forage. A supreme realist, he recognised realities now. Without another word he swung about and strode back to his boat.

Alexander waited a little, then shook his head unhappily at Jamie, and hurried after his father.

The boat was barely launched on its return journey before Mary had slipped from her saddle and run to fling herself impulsively into the young man's arms.

"Oh, Jamie, Jamie, Jamie!" she cried. "I feared ... that I would never ... see you again! Jamie, my dear — my very dear!"

He could not answer anything, just then. Not that he tried so very hard. Her lips were very close to his own, lips he had thought of, dreamed of, at some length in recent weeks. He conceived of better use for them than chatter. There had been a sufficiency of talk, anyway. He closed them with his own, onlookers or none.

David Stewart, however effective and mature-seeming, did lack certain of the attributes of the grown man, prominent amongst them an inability to take this sort of situation seriously. He did not give them long, therefore, before dismounting, to come and clap Jamie on the shoulder in cheerful reproof.

"Come, Sir Jamie man — have you no better greeting for your future king than slobbering over his auntie!" he exclaimed. "Here's gratitude, by the Mass! And me coming all this road just to rescue you! Shame on you!"

"Aye, my lord — to be sure." Jamie released Mary — who still kept hold of his hand, however. "I am sorry. I crave pardon. Forget myself. In my, my ..."

"Yes, yes — we all know your weaknesses, friend! It is our royal pleasure to forgive you, this once. At least, it seems that you are little the worse for all your troubles."

"I am entirely well, yes. Is it true, what you said? That you came all this way for *my* sake?"

"Of course we did," Mary assured. "This of the coronation was but an excuse. To gain the King's permission. And this escort. We never believed that my curious brother would come to Scone ..."

"She would have come for you if she had had to walk all the way!" David interrupted. "As, perhaps, might I! But this way we

361

journeyed secure, in a troop of the royal guard. At the Treasurer's cost!" He chuckled. "Which guard I had better see to . . ."

While the boy and an officer ordered the men-at-arms to prepare camp, Mary sought reassurances that Jamie was as well as he looked, had not suffered hurt at the Wolf's hands. "That friar, Alexander Moray, told us that he had seen you knocked off your horse. By that brutish brother of mine. When you tried to stop him burning the cathedral. We have been direly anxious, Jamie."

"No need," he told her. "He is a hard and savage man; and I have seen some ill things. But he has his own honesties — if that is the word. Once he decided not to hang me, he has treated me fairly, by his lights, preserving me as some kind of witness. Little as any witness would seem to his credit! I was to testify to his power and ruthlessness, as warning to others. In the South. That none would dare oppose him. He has held me prisoner but has done me no hurt."

"Thank the good God for that. When we heard of the burnings and slayings . . ."

"And yet, you, a woman, came all this way! Into like peril. I can scarce credit it, Mary — even yet. Through all these wild and dangerous Highlands. You, a king's daughter . . ."

"I am no shrinking flower, Jamie. Nor have I to play at being a princess! Neither Isabel nor Gelis could come. It would scarce have been suitable. But Isabel is in Galloway and Gelis has the child to see to. So I went to David. Now that his father is King, and he the High Steward, he can do much. Too much, perhaps, for one so young. Though Robert hates him, and seeks to clip his wings. He leapt at this venture. For he admires you greatly . . ."

The young prince came back. "Will that uncle of mine truly send us food and drink, Jamie?" he asked. "If not, we must see what these caterans' cabins can provide."

"He will, I think — if only to save *them*. He looks after his people well — and will guess that you would do that. But do not think, my lord, that he will forgive you for this. Or allow you to outwit him. He is a dangerous man to cross. And no fool."

"So we understood — and so we planned it. We were not going to be lured out to his island, and held. We were not to be parted from our men. We were not going to stay sufficiently long for him to be able to gather together a force to overwhelm us. If he had not brought you across with him, it would have been more difficult. We would have had to bargain for you."

"With what?"

"With another dear cousin of my own!" He grinned. "A surly oaf, calling himself Sir Duncan Stewart, who thought to interfere with our free passage, some leagues back. We taught him otherwise and took him into our custody to teach him manners, bringing him with us in case of use! He is in a herd's cabin in a valley a mile or so back under guard. If his sire had refused to yield you up, I would have offered this oaf in exchange — if you will forgive the insult, my friend? Hanged him, if need be. Now it may not be necessary."

Jamie swallowed. "Praise be you did not do that!" he said. "For assuredly I would have hanged likewise, and promptly. And you never won South again. You do not know the man, I tell you. Even now, I fear that he will seek to counter you. He will not like being outreached. And by one so young, and on his own doorstep. He will do *something* to stop you."

"What can he do? He can have no force, large enough to stop us, on that island, to bring over against us. If he sends out messengers, we shall see them and stop them. I have men on watch. Any boat leaving the castle will be seen . . ."

"Under cover of darkness?"

"It is never so very dark of a night, we have discovered. But such darkness as there is will serve us as well as Uncle Wolf! We shall not wait until morning, but slip away during the night. We have all we came for — you! We shall be many miles away from this Lochindorb by daylight."

"He would follow."

"Let him. I still have his bastard as hostage."

Jamie was doubtful still. Presently his doubts were justified. A barge was rowed across from the castle, laden with cold meats, oatmeal, ale and whisky in generous measure. With it came Alexander, again with the invitation for the visitors to come over to the island, to meet its chatelaine at least, whose provender was thus provided. When this was politely refused, Alexander sent back the unloaded barge but remained behind himself, with half-a-dozen tough and well-armed Highlanders as a sort of bodyguard, explaining that in this case his father had told him to stay and offer such aid as he might to their comfort, all night if he must.

363

This of course, upset the plans for stealing away unobserved. Jamie, who had scarcely believed that the project could be successful anyway and was likely to have unpleasant consequences, was almost relieved; especially as Alexander was his usual civil self again and seemingly in excellent spirits. His doubts gathered again however when, almost casually, the other announced that he had decided to come with them, to the South. It was a notable opportunity. Always he had wanted to visit the Lowlands, to attend the King's Court, to see the life led there. He loved this mountain land — but a man should know more than that, especially a Stewart. So he intended to travel with them, if they would take him. He would represent his father at the coronation — for nothing was more sure than that the Earl would not go.

Jamie stared. "But . . . but . . . do you realise what you say?" he demanded. "If you come south with us, alone, without your father, for how long do you think you will remain a free man? The Earl Robert would sieze you, almost certainly."

"If I was in this young prince's protection? He is High Steward and heir to the throne. Surely his name and state would protect me?"

"You do not know the Governor. He is as hard a man as your father, however cold. I say that you dare not risk it, man."

"And you would care, so much? You so long *our* prisoner!"

"*You* have always treated me well. And your lady-mother." That was gruff. "What does your father say?"

"He calls me a fool," the other admitted. "But will not gainsay me if I am resolved. As I am. He too says I will be taken and held — for he despises your young Earl David, as I do not. But he declares that *he* would get me out of such imprisonment quickly enough! He will have his own methods, see you. Moreover, I think he sees some advantages in having me in the South for a space, speaking directly with the King, my uncle, and with others. It would also ensure that he was not accused of deliberately disobeying the royal command to attend the coronation — which might be used against him. If he sends me as deputy. The fact that he has not forbidden me to go means something of the sort, I am sure."

The news of this change of stance on the part of the Wolf put the visitors in something of a quandary — as was no doubt anticipated. David suspected a trap, and said so; but Alexander assured that it was not so. That young man was so obviously pleased with the prospect that it seemed highly unlikely that his part was not genuine. As to his father's, they reserved judgment. It would, of course, enable the party to take their leave of Badenoch without further difficulty.

Although still wary, the sudden improvement in the situation brought about a general relaxation. The food and drink was distributed and appreciated. Mary was found quarters, of a sort, in one of the cot-houses; but the rest of the company remained encamped in a fairly tight group. There was now no point in planning to leave before sun-up, but an early start would still be advisable, for time was indeed short.

When he decently could, Jamie steered Mary off a little way along the lochside — although there might in fact be some small doubt as to who actually initiated the move. Alexander and David were discussing routes for the southward journey. In the gloaming light, the young woman may have found a variety of obstacles, roots and the like to trip over, and took Jamie's arm. They went unspeaking for a while.

He made three false starts, and then in sheer disgust with himself burst out, "A mercy, Mary — here have I been thinking of you, dreaming of you, longing to talk with you, all these weary months, and now, now I cannot think what to say or how to say it! I am the greatest fool . . . !"

"You are doing fairly well, I think, so far," she said.

"No. How can I say what I want to say? To thank you . . ."

"If that is what is troubling you, Jamie, say no more. Am I to be thanked for doing what I wished and sought and planned to do?"

"You are, yes — if that is so. For wishing it. To come all this way. Yourself. Not just to send another. For me. Endangering yourself."

"I could not allow David to come alone. He is able, yes, and keen. But young, headstrong. And I it was who sought *his* aid. I could not leave you in the Wolf's hands. Has he really treated you none so ill?"

"Yes and no. He has held me captive, threatened me with hanging — as he hanged Ramsay of Waughton, the man I came seeking — mocked and made fool of me. Yet, save when he felled me at Elgin, he has not mistreated me. For much, I have to thank

365

his son, this Alexander, much the best of his brood. And his — I was going to say his wife, for wife is what she is to him in all but marriage — his concubine, the Lady Mariota. She is kind, warm-hearted, keeps a good house. She has treated me as guest . . ."

"Then I need scarce have come?"

"No, no — save us, no! I have been waiting, hoping. Not knowing when he would let me go — if ever he would. I hoped and prayed that Prior Moray would not forget, would deliver my message. I told him that *you* would be best. To tell. But never intended that you should come, in person . . ."

"Did you hope for Gelis?"

"No. I never thought of any woman coming."

"At least you conceived me to be the one to send to. I must console myself with that!"

"I believed you to have the soundest wits of, of my friends."

"I thank you, kind sir! Further consolation. Although I much mislike clever women! It was not as such that I hoped to commend myself!"

"I am sorry. I was never very good at saying the right word. I . . . I did not dream of you as a clever woman, Mary."

"No? This is better." She pointed to a bleached tree-trunk cast up on the shore by a flood. "Come, let us sit on this and you can tell me how you dreamed of Mary Stewart."

"That I would not dare!" he asserted, as he sat down.

"So bad as that, was it?" She smiled. "You but make me the more eager to hear. Was it worse than on Saint Colm's Inch?"

He swallowed. "To be honest — yes!" he said.

The young woman laughed aloud. "My dear honest Jamie! I love you for your honesty — as perhaps you love me for what you call my wits! So I am a fallen woman, am I — or as good as one? Does not Holy Writ declare that for a man even to desire a woman in his heart is as good — or as bad — as to have bedded her? Alas for my poor virtue!"

He shook his head. "Mary — I wish that you would not mock at me so. Laugh at my, my feelings for you . . ."

Sensing actual distress, she quickly changed, "I am sorry, Jamie — we Stewarts have the tongues of scorpions. Our men flay with their swords; we women do it with our lips! Forgive me. But . . . these feelings for me, that I laugh at? What are they? Will you not tell me?"

Thus abruptly brought to direct decision, as it were, he drew a long breath and stared straight ahead, across the darkling waters, to the Wolf's castle.

"I think I need you," he said. Which was not really what he intended to say, out of his sudden acceptance of commitment.

She waited for more; but when it did not seem to be forthcoming, she spoke. "Need? What does that mean? There are many needs."

He nodded. "Many. I need you in many ways. I have had long to think on this. As a prisoner, in cells, on journeyings, in the heather. I need your *wits*, yes — but also your courage, your steadfastness, your resolve, your swift strength. Aye, and your disregard for all obstacles . . ."

"You have me sounding like a good mare for breeding, with your catalogue!" she observed. This time there was no laughter in her voice.

But he was not to be put off his recital, now he had screwed himself up to it. "No. But I lack much that you have, could give me. I am dull, slow-spoken, stiff of manner. Lacking your laughter, even . . ."

"Certainly you might laugh more," she agreed.

He had not finished yet. "These things you have. As well, you are very lovely. Of face as of person. These I need too, I have found. Your . . . your body."

"Ah! So we do come to that!"

"Yes, I fear so. These months I have learned about myself. Found myself longing for you, Mary, these qualities, yes — but also your person. All of you, lass. I have near cried out for you . . .!"

"Me? Not Gelis? Or just a woman, perhaps? A ready woman?"

"You. You only. I know now. Gelis was . . . otherwise. I did not know myself, then. My need is for you . . ."

"*Need*, again!" she interrupted him. "What is this, Jamie? A declaration of dire need, necessity? A proposal to cohabit? Or could it even be marriage, as last resort!"

"Of course it is marriage, Mary. Think you I am like the Wolf, a lecher . . .?"

"Both our fathers were lechers, were they not — since we are bastards," she exclaimed. "It would be none so strange. But . . .

dear God — here is Jamie Douglas proposing matrimony to Mary Stewart at last, at very long last! And she talks of parents and bastardy! And he of qualities and excellences and bodies — but never a word of love nor yet fond affection!"

"But — but Mary! Of course I love you. Love you most dearly. With all my heart. You must *know* that. It is to be understood. I would not be talking this way otherwise . . ."

"Then *say* so, of a mercy! Do something. Why sit we here, debating . . .?"

They stared at each other, then, on their tree-trunk. And simultaneously both burst into laughter, a strange, rueful, frustrated but releasing laughter, which had tears somewhere behind it on the girl's part and helpless apology on the man's, yet was basically joyful, joyful.

Leaning over, he fondled her in his arms, still laughing. Kissing and being kissed, he declared incoherently, most interruptedly and with monotonous repetition — although entirely convincingly — that he loved her, loved her more than anything else in this world or the next, loved her wholly, entirely, exclusively, and would she be his wife? Would she? Would she? Her answer was implicit rather than explicit, but entirely positive, not in any doubt — even though they both appeared to require repetition, even continuous confirmation of the entire situation, however gasping and breathless a process, Mary's splendid bosom partly responsible for this last, being considerably compressed on the one hand and obtrusively impact-making on the other.

They were still in this state when David and Alexander Stewart came up to interrupt. The latter would have held back, considerately; but there was nothing like that about the High Steward.

"Come, come, you two!" the former reproved. "You have been at this sufficiently long, surely? Besides, it is no way to behave, in decent company! In fullest view of the camp! We have been observing you this considerable while, and wagering on how long you could maintain it . . .!"

"Not so," Alexander asserted hurriedly. "My lord jests."

Jamie glared at them both, with comprehensive hostility.

"For the aunt of the heir to the throne, it will not do," the boy went on. "Even the illegitimate aunt! The royal house must ever present an example. And in front of this son of the Earl of

368

Buchan! What if his sire was to perceive you from yonder castle? Corrupting all . . . !"

"I'll thank you to speak more respectfully of the lady who is to be my wife," Jamie began stiffly — but was interrupted by Mary's peal of laughter, in which the Earl David promptly joined. When Alexander commenced to chuckle also, Jamie had no option but to relax to a somewhat shamefaced grin. He rose to his feet — and was surprised to find the High Steward throwing his arms around him in an impulsive embrace.

"Bless you, Jamie! God be praised!" he cried. "So you have come to it, at last. I will be groomsman at your wedding! Here is the best news we have heard for long. Mind — what sort of a wife she will make I know not. But she is the right shape for child-bearing and like frolics . . ."

"Nephew — hold your tongue!" Mary commanded. "And wait until you are asked to attend the wedding before you offer your services . . ."

David stopped more of that by going to kiss his aunt heartily, while Alexander came to grip Jamie's hand with obvious pleasure.

After that they had to drink more of the ale and whisky the Wolf had sent over than was really good for them, in celebration. Even the men-at-arms got extra, until all was finished.

When at length, the night well advanced and all sleepy with the drink and the camp-fire heat and smoke on top of a long day, the trio escorted Mary to her cot-house quarters, it was David who completed an elaborate goodnight slapping Jamie on the shoulder and pushing him towards the cabin door also.

"With your troth pledged before all, you will be thinking to share this night's accommodation, I swear!" he asserted.

Jamie looked at the young woman — who paused but did not speak. He sighed a great sigh. "No," he said. "Not so. We will do this thing decently, properly. Mary . . . Mary deserves no less."

She turned to consider that, and him, for a long moment, then nodded. "No doubt I will thank you, Jamie — one day," she said. "Good night." And she hurried within.

"M'mmm," her nephew said. "And you may make a kirk or a mill out of that, Jamie Douglas!"

"A kirk, surely!" Alexander adjudged, but soberly.

Together they went back to the camp-fire.

In the morning, and earlier than might have been expected, the Earl came over, with the Lady Mariota and their daughter, to suggest again that the visitors delayed their departure; also to urge Alexander to change his mind about this journey to the South. But since it was altogether out-of-character for the Wolf to urge and suggest anything, rather than to command and since Mariota had brought a bundle of Alexander's best clothing and gear for her son to take with him, it looked as though they were reconciled to his going — which was as good as saying that his father wished him to go.

All was now approximate amity, with good wishes for the travellers, and even congratulations forthcoming to Jamie on his betrothal. Also regrets, from the ladies at least, that they were going to lose their visitor. That young man was perhaps suspicious of mind, but he remained cautious, feeling that there was probably something more behind all this than met the eye or ear.

As they were preparing to move off, and Alexander had embraced his mother and sister warmly, the Wolf raised his voice to rather more like his normal tone and manner.

"Nephew — and you, Douglas," he said, "remember that I am placing my son in your care. He is going with you, amongst men of ill will, against my advice. I have told him that if he does this, if he makes his own bed, he must needs lie in it! Nevertheless, I shall expect you both to ensure his good treatment. As part price of my releasing you, thus. Mind it."

David shrugged. "We shall try, to be sure," he said. "But as you well know, Uncle, none can ensure anything in this realm as it is governed today. Sir James discovered that, when he came here to your Badenoch, did he not? Sir Alexander may be more fortunate, but we cannot swear to it."

"No? The King's only son cannot warrant protection for one in his care? I think you can. I shall require it of you, have no doubts. Unless Alex prefers to think again? More wisely?"

"No, my lord," his son said firmly. "I wish to go. Moreover, I think that I perhaps can look after myself."

"We shall see. Although, to be sure, I think even Robert Stewart, or any other, will consider twice before interfering with a son of mine! For I promise you, if I hear aught of hurt to Alex, I will not sit idly in Badenoch wringing my hands! Let all know that." The Wolf stared round at them all. Then he jabbed a finger at Jamie. "Douglas—you will not fail to remember what you have learned here. What you have been shown." That was no question, but a statement. "You will tell those who ought to know. You have seen what sort of hand rules the North. Let none mistake or forget it. I let you go, now — and might not have done. See that you are duly . . . grateful!"

Jamie inclined his head, wordless. He moved forward to salute the Lady Mariota and her daughter, more hurriedly than he would have intended. Then he leapt on to his garron's broad back.

The Wolf had the last word, hand and voice raised. "Make no mistake, all of you," he called. "It might have been otherwise, here — much otherwise. The decision was mine. Go in peace."

* * *

The journey south was a deal less trying and prolonged, for Jamie at least, than it had been northwards. A good summer had dried up the land, and the innumerable rivers and lochs and the unending marshes and peat-bogs were less of a barrier. Also, of course, having *Alastair Mor Mac-an-Righ*'s eldest son with them, as well as the force of men-at-arms, greatly facilitated progress, the endless haggling about mail and passage miraculously evaporating, smiles and bows ushering them from one clan territory to another, food and forage provided at much more modest rates throughout; so that frequently Jamie and his three Tantallon Douglases, with MacAlpin the interpreter — all of whom the Wolf had returned to him the morning they left Lochindorb — exchanged rueful glances. For all that, he would have been well content had their progress been less expeditious, since it developed into something of an idyll for him, traversing a most lovely country day after day with Mary ever at his side. Even though they could seldom be completely alone for any length of time, they did manage to lag behind quite frequently, wander apart of an evening, make small unaccompanied ventures. On occasions when there was no separate sleeping accommodation for the young woman, Jamie had the joy of lying side by side with her, on sweet-smelling bog-hay or straw. It was all one of the happiest episodes of his life, young and cheerful company, long carefree days in the saddle, learning sides of Mary's character which he had not known — and rejoicing in all he learned.

This carefree aspect of the journey was something new for

371

Jamie Douglas. Since Otterburn he had never been carefree. He had been plunged from youth into manhood too swiftly, had saddled himself with responsibilities in the Lady Isabel's service, taken his knightly status perhaps too seriously; above all been oppressed by the horror of the Earl of Douglas's murder and his own vow of vengeance. Now, the failure of his quest here in the North, far from depressing him actually lightened his mind. The deaths of both Ramsay and Bickerton somehow seemed to clear the account. And it was evident now that if the Earl Robert was indeed guilty, it would never be confirmed, much less established before all men. Jamie had, at last, come to accept that he, a very minor figure on the realm's stage, could never hope to bring the Governor to book — and that acceptance was like a weight off his shoulders. Admittedly this journey was only a sort of timeless interlude, a very temporary hiatus; but he knew an abiding sense of relief, of freedom from onus and obligation, nevertheless. For that, of course, Mary Stewart was to be thanked in large measure.

Only one incident marred the pleasant tenor of their progress, and that at the very beginning. When they released young Sir Duncan Stewart from his incarceration, under guard, in a rude shieling cabin in Glen Tarrock, a bare hour after leaving Lochindorb, he had not taken the situation well, being surly and resentful to a degree, despite his brother Alex's soothings and explanations. He had ridden off eastwards, not to Lochindorb, without farewell. But later in the day, in the Forest of Abernethy, they saw him again, with the other brother Andrew and a small group of mounted caterans. They sat their garrons high on a hillock above the track, to watch the south-bound party go by. They did not come down or seek to waylay them. But as the travellers passed below, the two brothers raised clenched fists high, shook them, and cursed with a ferocious violence and intensity. Even David was taken aback, and Alexander remained silent for a long time thereafter. But there was no pursuit nor further demonstration.

They won out of the true Highlands at Dunkeld, collected Jamie's Lowland horses and said goodbye to Gregor MacAlpin. Then on to Stirling, where the King was said to be in residence prior to moving to Scone in a few days' time. They saw many fine and colourful cavalcades already on their way to the coronation. The heir to the throne was just in time.

XXIII

THE CORONATION OF Robert the Third was a strange affair from the start. The new King himself would probably have been glad enough to dispense with the entire occasion; certainly to have had it on a very abbreviated and modest scale, a mere gesture. But this did not suit his brother the Governor. Just why the Earl Robert was so determined that it all should be a great and memorable proceeding was not entirely clear, for he was not a man who cared much for display and was no waster of money. Yet that August of 1390 nothing was spared, all was conducted with much formality and dignity, and everyone who mattered in Scotland was expected to be present. It might indeed have been the Earl's own crowning. Perhaps he felt that it established his own position as king-maker more clearly. Perhaps it served his purpose to summon all the realm together under his eye — for although a summons to parliament might be ignored or rejected, to refuse to attend a coronation could be construed as treasonable. Possibly he felt that the Stewart hold on the throne was still too new and less than secure — this was only the second of the line, after all — to risk dispensing with any of the traditional formalities. Whatever his reasons, the Governor arranged all, decided all.

The Abbey of Scone, considering its importance as the principal shrine of Scotland, was surprisingly modest compared with such as Dunfermline, Melrose, Cambuskenneth and the like. It had belonged, of course, to the ancient Celtic Church polity, ever much less spectacular in its display than the Romish; and Scone had been the capital of Pictavia, the Pictish kingdom, retained as such by Kenneth MacAlpin when he united Picts and Scots. Here was installed the semi-legendary talisman of the Scots monarchy, the Stone of Destiny; and here all Kings of Scots had been crowned from time immemorial. But its modest size meant that there was but little accommodation for such great state occasions, and with the King's and the Governor's personal households occupying the abbot's and monastic quarters, there was no room for others. Large numbers of the commonality, servitors, scullions and the like were installed in tents and pavilions in the haughland of the Tay nearby; but for the quality this would not do. Fortunately Saint John's town of Perth was only three miles to the south, and there the great majority of the nobility, gentry and dignified clergy found lodging, riding to and fro each day, the burghers of Perth charging exorbitant sums for the use of very inferior houses for the few days of the event.

Although the Lady Gelis had not yet arrived from Nithsdale, so that Mary had to wait for her, Jamie found his father installed in a wing of the large Blackfriars monastery of the Dominicans, on the north side of Perth, with the Lady Isabel and her husband, Sir John Edmonstone, allotted a room therein. His father greeted him rather after the style of the returned prodigal — for Jamie's journey into the North had been taken contrary to Dalkeith's advice — rejoicing at his safe return. He had been uncertain as to how his sire would react to the news of his betrothal, for he was not yet of full age by a few months, and fathers could be awkward about such matters. Mary, a more or less penniless bastard, was not provided with the tocher or dowry normally so important. But the old lord took it very well, making no objection and declaring that although Jamie was young he had shown himself to have a mind of his own; and having gone his own way for these past two years, he was entitled to choose his own bride — especially one who had shown her acumen by improving his financial position notably, as she had done over the Inchcolm affair. That would serve in lieu of dowry. And the link with the royal family was in the Douglas tradition and might well prove useful. Moreover, it was probably time that Jamie married, if he intended to remain in the Lady Isabel's service; it would look better thus. That was as far as the careful Lord of Dalkeith committed himself, in words, on what he fairly evidently considered was his son's unsuitable entanglement with the former Countess of Douglas. Clearly this betrothal was something of a relief.

This first duty over, Jamie went in search of the said Lady Isabel, and in some little trepidation.

374

He found her, with the Lady Egidia, strolling in the orchard of the monastery, which lay just within the city wall, overlooking the open parkland of the town common called the North Inch — and did not know whether to be glad or sorry that she was not alone. At sight of him she came quickly over to embrace him, with undisguised delight — to his rather more than usual embarrassment.

"Jamie, my dear! My very dear!" she exclaimed. "How good, how good! Praise God that you are safely back. Oh, Jamie — I have been so worried. In those terrible Highlands. And in that ogre's hands! How you must have suffered . . ."

"I did not suffer at all," he jerked. "I . . . I am very well."

From the background her aunt hooted. "He does not look to me like a great sufferer! Never seen him look better — if you would stand back somewhat, girl, so that I *may* see him!"

Isabel ignored that, still clutching him. "We heard grievous tidings of you. At the sack of Elgin. Made prisoner. Struck down by that monster. You should never have gone, Jamie — I told you it was too dangerous."

He shook his head. "Not so. But it is all past. I suffered no hurt. Learned much. And now — now I am betrothed to be wed." That came out in a rush.

She drew back now indeed, staring at him. She parted her lips but did not speak.

"Ha!" the Lady Egidia said. "Are you now? To that minx Mary, for a wager!"

"Mary, yes." It was at Isabel that he looked, half-defiantly, half-pleadingly.

"You will *wed*?" she said, almost in a whisper. "Wed . . . Mary?"

"Yes. I love her. She is . . . good."

"High time, too," his father's wife put in briskly. "Time you were wed, young man. You are too fond of women — without being able to take care of yourself! And women too fond of you! That Mary has a good head on her shoulders. She will keep you right. This is best. Is it not, Isabel?" That was almost a command.

The younger woman touched her hair, her cheek. "No doubt," she murmured.

"She came. To gain my release. A long way. With much courage. She loves me well, she says. And, and she is a bastard, as am I!"

375

"So! My own leal knight no longer!"

"But yes. To be sure, I am. Why not? I made my knightly vow to serve you. I will not cease to do so because I am wed. I am ever yours to command."

"Unless your Mary says otherwise!"

He shook his head. "Why should she do that? She is your sister. She loves you also. She has always known me to be in your service."

"Yes. No doubt. Yes — forgive me, Jamie. If it is your wish, if you are happy . . ."

"Then I may continue to serve you?"

"If you so will."

"I will, yes." He paused. "But — I fear that I achieved little in that service, in the North. I failed. Failed to find what I sought. The Wolf, the Earl of Buchan, had hanged Patrick Ramsay. As bearer of the excommunication letter. So I learned nothing. Nothing which would establish the Lord Robert's guilt. With Ramsay dead, I fear we shall never establish it."

"For which you should praise God, I say!" Egidia Stewart asserted. "A less profitable employ I never heard tell of! I swear your life is the safer lacking that information, Jamie. Yours also, it may be, Niece. Dangerous knowledge."

Isabel spoke levelly. "I will discover that knowledge if it is in my power to do so, nevertheless. And charge Robert with it, before all. If it is my last act!"

"Then do not also sign this lad's death-warrant in doing it, girl! Enough is enough. Three young men have died. Is that not sufficient, Isabel?"

When the other did not answer, Jamie spoke. "I do not think that it will be possible to learn more now. None can keep a closer mouth than the Governor. If he ordered Bickerton to do the deed, he will never tell. Bickerton will not tell! And Ramsay, who could have told who paid him to silence Bickerton, will not tell either. Who else would know? None, I doubt. So I fear our quest is ended, Lady Isabel."

She turned and hurried away from them, back into the monastery buildings, without word or backward glance.

"Let her be, boy," Lady Egidia told him, as he made to follow her. "She will be herself again presently. You dealt her two strokes there. Give her time."

The Lady Gelis arrived that night, in the Earl of Douglas's train, from the South-West. Since the death of Sir Will of Nithsdale, Archie the Grim had taken more interest in his royal daughter-in-law than when her husband had lived — although it was probably more on account of the boy Will, in whom he seemed to find something like a reincarnation of his favourite son. The lad was with the party also, and dressed like a prince by his grandsire.

After his interview with Isabel, Jamie was a little anxious as to how Gelis would react to his news. He need not have worried. Once again he did not see her alone, for she had the boy Will with her — indeed she seemed to keep him at her side always. She was looking as beautiful as ever, almost more so, with her features more chiselled, her eyes seeming larger. But there was something strange about those eyes, a fey look which he had not seen before, a sort of preoccupation as though she was concerned with something which she alone could see — and which was certainly not himself. She greeted him warmly enough, but fairly quickly seemed to grow almost abstracted. The impression grew on him that it was not lack of affection but rather lack of interest which was the trouble. Her mind was not on what he had to say. It turned out that she knew of his betrothal, for she had already seen Mary; but it did not appear to make much impact upon her. She made conventional remarks of congratulation and goodwill, but there was little conviction therein. As assuredly, however, she was not in any way resentful or hurt. On the subject of Patrick Ramsay she listened attentively enough, but made little or no comment, expressing no emotion either way. He noticed that, all the time he was talking to her, her eyes kept turning back to the boy Will, as though that was where her true concern lay. As for himself, Jamie discovered no regrets, no hankering for what might have been, no trace of what he now could look upon as a former infatuation with the princess. If she had changed, so presumably had he. He still could admire her, have an affection for her; but the ache and the desire had gone — to be replaced, indeed, by a disquiet for her, an anxiety. There was something far from right about her. If it was still preoccupation with her murdered husband and vengeance therefore, it had taken an even more unhealthy turn than had her sister's. There seemed to be a strange balance in the Stewart nature, which if upset could grievously swing to direst

377

extremes. Mary, thank God, appeared to have escaped this flaw—
unless an occasionally flying tongue might be an aspect of it!

The following two days were busy ones, with preparations for
the coronation interrupted, strangely enough, by a state funeral.
This was the Governor's idea, and many were the questions and
discussions as to why he ordained it, the significance of the
thing — for Robert Stewart seldom did anything without due calculation. It was the old King's burial. Robert the Second had died
on May 13th; but his body, embalmed, had been kept unburied
until now. He was to be interred at Scone Abbey on August 12th,
and the new monarch crowned there the next day. The Governor
said this was to emphasise the continuity of the royal line and
kingship, that Robert II was theoretically king until he was interred; and Robert III was not really king until he was crowned the
next day. But most men saw it as one more device for ensuring
Robert's own supreme power in the new reign. He was still con-
stitutionally Robert II's Governor and Regent, so long as his
father remained unburied. There was to be no possibly dangerous
hiatus between that event and the next day's when the new monarch would confirm him in the rule.

The funeral, in the end, was in fact a somewhat hurried and
makeshift affair, grief and regard for the old man having tended
to cool, and the morrow's more dramatic and vital celebrations
overweighing all — indeed the elaborate decoration and fes-
tooning of the Abbey and its surroundings was more apt for a
wedding than a funeral. Isabel Stewart was possibly the only one
to shed tears.

That evening, however, tongues were more busy than ever in
speculation and debate, with even more significant tidings. All in
Perth and Scone were agog with two further items of news. One,
that the Queen's personal coronation was to be postponed until
the day after her husband's; and two, that the Governor himself
intended to place the crown on his brother's head. The King had
apparently agreed to both these departures.

After the evening meal, the group at the Lord of Dalkeith's
lodging were discussing the implications, with a variety of reactions. The general opinion was that both were deliberately in-
sulting to the monarch — and the first, of course, still more so to
his wife; but that the second might be the more significant.

The women were indignant about the slight to Queen Annabella, whom they had all come to admire, and some to love, during the Turnberry affair. Even Egidia forgot to be cynical and voiced her disgust at her brothers, both brothers, one for being so hard and the other so weak. Isabel declared that it was Robert's bitter way of paying back Annabella for his rebuff at Turnberry, and that they all ought to unite again to demand a reversal. Gelis said nothing, but Mary pointed out that they had not much time to do anything such. Robert had heedfully delayed the announcement until the last moment no doubt for that very reason. The ceremony would be beginning in not much more than fifteen hours.

"Too short a time to achieve anything to any purpose," Dalkeith agreed, shaking his grey head. "It is a sorry business — but not really important. The Queen remains the Queen whether her coronation is one day or the next. Nothing alters that. As an example of Robert's spleen it is vexatious, but only that. What is more important is this of the actual placing of the crown on his brother's brow. This, I fear, is symbolic of much greater danger."

"Why?" his wife demanded.

"Do you not see? He, Robert, is demonstrating to all that he, and he alone, is making his brother the King. The Crown is *his* gift. Not only does it make his position as Governor more secure, but it could be used to imply that what he could do he could also undo! The king-maker might unmake. Or, even put him in a position hereafter to refuse to crown the boy David. He must have good reason for this move — he always has. I do not like it."

"He is Earl of Fife," Sir John Edmonstone pointed out.

"Only by a trick, a device. The right to place the Crown on the King's head is hereditary in the MacDuff family — not necessarily in the earldom of Fife. Up till this, the head of the MacDuff line has been Earl of Fife — but today is not. When old Earl Duncan died, eleventh of his line, he left only a daughter, Isabella, to succeed to his earldom. She wed, as her second husband, the Lord Walter, the King's eldest son. They had no bairns — she was forty-six years old when they married, to be sure — no more than a ploy to get the premier earldom in the land for the Stewarts. When Walter died young, and the Countess wed yet again, an Englishman, by an intrigue she and he were prevailed upon to settle the earldom on Walter Stewart's brother, Robert, in exchange for lands elsewhere. The true heir of the MacDuffs was otherwise. The senior of them, the Lord of Abernethy, by tradition should have the privilege of crowning the monarch at his coronation — not the holder of the Fife earldom."

"Are no MacDuffs here to uphold their claim?" Jamie asked. "This Lord of Abernethy — where is he? I know nothing of him."

"He is a quiet man, retiring, older than am I. He will never oppose the Earl Robert, I fear."

"Can we do nothing, then?" Isabel demanded.

"What is possible? At this stage. He lives far away in the sheriffdom of Banff. If he has not come South . . ."

It was at this juncture that there was an interruption. An esquire came hastening from Scone, from the Earl David, seeking Jamie Douglas, to announce that the Governor's men had arrested Sir Alexander Stewart. Sir James was to come, at once.

"You heard?" Jamie cried, to his father. "He has taken Alexander! Despite all. Despite the Earl David's protection. Despite the King's own kindness towards him. We believed that he was safe, since he had fair audience of the King. The Earl Robert has held his hand these three days. Now . . . ! What can we do?"

Dalkeith eyed him unhappily. "I do not know," he admitted. "He *is* the Governor. Where the affairs of the realm are concerned only the King can gainsay him. And if the King will not . . ."

"He relied on us to preserve him. His father put him in our care . . ."

"His precious father is scarce in a position to demand care from *you*, boy — or any other who has suffered his attentions! I wonder greatly why he allowed this young man to come. He needed not to be a seer to foretell this . . ."

But Jamie had gone, with the esquire, to ride hard for Scone.

He found David Stewart in the Abbot's quarters of the monastic wing, displaying rather more agitation than he had ever seen in that self-possessed youth — but it was the agitation of anger rather than dread or uncertainty.

"You have heard?" the prince exclaimed. "The insult of it! He has taken him in despite of me. And of my father. Fall foul him — he scorns us both! This is not to be borne, I say!"

It occurred to Jamie that David was more concerned for his

own pride than for Alexander's safety. "What has he done with him? Alexander? Where is he, my lord? Is he in any danger of hurt?"

"God knows! He was here, talking with one of my sisters, when my uncle's creatures came for him. This afternoon. I was in Perth, so knew naught of it till I returned. They rode off with him — that is all I am told."

"And your father? What does the King say?"

"My royal sire wrings his hands and moans! Prays, belike! But will *do* nothing. He says he will talk with Robert anon — but, God be good, that signifies nothing! Oh, to have a *man* for a father!"

Jamie sighed. "What can we do, then? If the King will do nothing. When a guest, his own nephew, is taken from his own house . . ."

"Do! We will go speak with my accursed uncle here and now! I but waited for you. He is here in the monastery, with that oaf Murdoch. And your precious Earl Archie . . ."

"Me? *I* cannot go denounce the Governor to his face! A mercy — not me, my lord. I am only a small man, a mere knight . . ."

"You are the Wolf of Badenoch's witness, you told me? You can tell Robert Stewart matters no one else can. Come, you."

"But . . . this is folly . . ."

"Do you not desire to aid your friend? Never fear, I will say most of what has to be said. You will know when to support me." Without further instructions, David hurried off.

Across a pleasant courtyard and into the cloisters the young prince strode, with a very reluctant Jamie behind. Guards stood at the door of the refectory — but none dared to halt the heir to the throne. Pushing through the crowded eating-hall, full of the Governor's minions who eyed the pair askance but did not seek to question them — some even bowing uncertainly — David made for a far door protected by two more guards. When one of these began to interpose himself and ask, respectfully enough, his lordship's business with the Governor, he was actually dug in the stomach by a sharp elbow.

"Out of my way, fool!" the boy snapped. "Do you dare oppose *me*, Carrick?"

Hastily the other guard opened the door, and they marched in. David slammed it shut behind them.

Four men lolled at ease behind a table, with wine-flagons and platters — at least, three lolled, for Robert Stewart never did such a thing but sat stiffly upright. The others were the Earl of Douglas, the Lord Murdoch Stewart and Bishop Peebles of Dunkeld, the Chancellor. The last got heavily to his feet, while the rest stared.

"What is this, this intrusion . . .?" the Governor was saying, frowning, when he was interrupted, and vehemently, as his nephew shot out an accusing hand and pointing finger.

"My lord of Douglas — do you not stand when the High Steward of Scotland enters the chamber?" he demanded. "On your feet, sir. As for you, Cousin Murdoch, I swear you have not the breeding to know how to behave. Learn, then!"

Astounded, that awkward young man rose, looking alarmedly at his father, whilst the Earl Archie, muttering, raised posterior a few inches from his bench before sinking back again, craggy brows down-drawn.

"Nephew — how dare you burst into my chamber, with your infantile arrogance!" the Governor jerked, remaining seated. "I will have a word with your father on this, believe me!"

"I dare a deal more than that, sir," the boy gave back, strongly. "And refer to me more respectfully in the presence of these . . . persons! I am here because a friend and kinsman has been shamefully, unlawfully and indeed treasonably taken out of my father's house by your ruffians, whilst under the King's and my own protection. I require Sir Alexander Stewart returned to that house forthwith, sir, and due apology made to him, and to me!"

His uncle considered him expressionlessly. "Have you overlooked the fact, boy, that *I* rule this kingdom, as its lawful Governor? And do not require to answer to you, or any, for my actions."

"You were Governor for my late grandsire, now buried, sir. My father, after tomorrow's coronation, *might* continue you in office, in some fashion — or might not. *I* certainly would not. But meantime you only *act* Governor. Whereas I am High Steward and Prince of Scotland, next in rank to the King. Do not forget it." He turned. "Chancellor Bishop — you are aware of the truth of this, if my uncle has forgotten. Am I right?"

The heavy old cleric cleared his throat unhappily. "I . . . ah . . . my good young lord. That is so, in a manner of speaking. But . . ."

"Manner of speaking, sirrah? Is it true or is it false?"

"Er, true, my lord. But . . ."

"But nothing! Uncle — you will return Sir Alexander Stewart to my father's lodging here, immediately."

"I shall do no such thing, boy."

"Not if the King commands it?"

"Has the King commanded it?"

"*I* command it. And His Grace will, if I ask him, confirm. He is much disturbed by your action."

"I shall see His Grace then, in due course, and inform him of the matter. And of your insolence. Now leave us, Nephew — we have important matters in hand."

"You have important matters to *explain*, sir! And I will have that explanation, now! Where is my cousin Alexander? Where, and why, have you taken him?"

"I need not answer your ill-mannered questions, Nephew — even as *acting* Governor! But for your information, your Uncle Alexander's bastard is by now halfway to my house of Falkland, in Fife. For his own security. His father is an outlaw and excommunicate, and has grievously injured many. Not only in Elgin and Forres. His son could be endangered. I will see that he is preserved, secure."

"Do you expect any to believe that? Only you would dare assail him, when in the King's care and protection. I say that you have taken him for your own ill purposes. Out of hatred for his father. And, no doubt, because you think to use him to force his father to your will. In which case, I say, you have made your greatest mistake, Uncle. And are like to pay dearly for it. Indeed, I believe that you may have fallen into a cunning trap."

The Governor looked coldly unimpressed. But the Earl Archie spoke.

"Trap, my lord? What mean you — a cunning trap?"

"I mean that my Uncle Alex is fully as clever as is my Uncle Robert, my lord! He as good as *sent* Sir Alexander south with us. He would never have permitted him to come had he not wished it. And he warned his son, before all, that you might act to his hurt. Demanded *my* protection for him. Why send him then, think you? The Wolf knows well what he is at. I say that he *wanted* you to move against his son. So that he might have excuse to move against you! And now you have given him it, my lord acting Governor."

Robert Stewart moistened thin lips. "My shameless brother can do nothing against me, from his barbarous mountains. He may burn and slay in the North — and we shall halt that in due course. But he is powerless here in the South."

"You believe so?" The boy smiled. "*He* does not believe so — and Uncle Alex is a man of action, remember. Unlike some others! He has, h'm, designs on this southern part of my father's realm, I am told." He turned. "Has he not, Sir James? You were held by him for months, in his house of Lochindorb. To be his witness — chosen to give his warnings. Were you not?"

Jamie drew a deep breath. "Yes, my lords. He told me so. Said that I should make it known to you all, to all who have the rule in the South."

The Governor sniffed, not even looking at the speaker. He sipped from his wine goblet.

The Earl Archie sat forward, however. "What did he say, Jamie?"

"He said that he would come South, one day. And when he did he would claim his rights. Rights the excommunication had sought to take from him. He, he knew of the excommunication device, my lords, and what was behind it, before ever I reached Badenoch."

"Ha! He did? And you say he spoke of coming South?"

"Yes. He promised to do so. And said that he would bring his rights with him. That was the way he said it. And that a thousand broadswords would speak louder than any bishops' anathemas."

"Wind!" the Governor said. "Bluster. Vain pretence — such as is Alex's custom."

"Sir James has it otherwise," David put in. "Was Elgin, Forres, Pluscarden wind and bluster?"

"Aye, my lord — these things were done by way of warning and example," Jamie went on, looking from one to the other. "I was taken to see, as witness. And told to tell you. How, he, my lord of Buchan, acts. And will act. To other than Elgin and Forres. If he has to come South. He meant it — that I swear. And it was ... terrible."

384

For a moment or two there was silence in that chamber.

"You see?" the prince resumed. "The Wolf is sufficiently wolfish! He refused to come to my father's coronation — but he sent his son. Why? Now you have taken his son. May not this be the excuse he looked for? Now he can come, to rescue his son. You said a thousand broadswords, Jamie? But he has more than that, I think?"

"He had over 3,000 at Elgin, my lord. Sir Alexander told me he could raise 10,000 and more in a week."

"Wild savages — Highlandmen!" the Earl Robert snapped, scornfully. "Mere threats, bairn's boastings. What could such do against our knightly array and armoured chivalry? Burning cathedrals and defenceless towns is one thing, assailing a steel-clad host another. Alex is not fool enough to risk that. You will not frighten grown men with such tales, boy."

"Then you refuse to heed? You, in whose hands the safety of my father's realm is supposed to lie?"

"I refuse to heed the tales and threats of fools and bairns. Now — leave us, if you please, to our important business. Tomorrow's observances occupy my time sufficiently."

David Stewart moved forward, to lean over the table towards his uncle. "There are more sorts of fools than bairnly ones!" he said. "I declare that my father is ill-served — and shall not cease to tell him so. And when *my* time comes, my lord of Fife and Menteith — watch you, I say! Watch you!" He swung about and strode for the door, Jamie hastily following. But before opening it he paused. "You may resume your seats, my lord Bishop and Cousin Murdoch," he said, and so left them.

It was a fair exit — but they had failed in their task and no flourish would disguise it. The boy mouthed blasphemies all the way back to his room.

Coronation day, August 14th, dawned bright if breezy — and with much of the ceremonial taking place outdoors, the weather was important. The exodus from Perth started early, and even by sun-up the roads were packed with folk making for Scone, from all over the Lowlands, in holiday mood and in their best clothing. Even the mounted nobility and gentry, ploughing their impatient way through the unending crush, could not spoil the popular good humour.

Isabel not requiring his services today, and Mary in attendance

385

on Gelis, Jamie attached himself to his father's party — otherwise, undoubtedly he would not have gained admission to the Abbey-church, which was not nearly large enough to contain all who wished and considered themselves entitled to occupy it. Even so, although his father had a prominent place amongst the lords of parliament, he and his brothers were installed in only a fairly lowly position at the back of the south aisle, where sundry pillars tended to interfere with the view. But it had its advantages for young people who might seek to lark about somewhat during the long period of waiting, and moreover provided a visual alleyway to the seats reserved for the princesses and their ladies at the front of the opposite aisle. Jamie at least could see and make signs to Mary.

The Scottish coronation was a mixture of religious service and secular ceremonial, its procedures laid down and ordered over the centuries, with little scope for innovation. Only in minor details could there be variations — as, for instance, in this of the Queen's share in the programme being put off till the next day. Annabella walked to the church from the Abbot's house, in a small procession of her own, to take her seat in a chair-of-state in front of the princesses. Her eventual arrival signalled the start of the ceremony proper.

Sweet chanting introduced a choir of singing boys, and, flanked by acolytes swinging censers, the Lord Abbot of Scone led in the prelates, the bishops and mitred abbots and priors, in their gorgeous copes, dalmatics and canonicals. These paced up to the chancel, which was hung for the occasion with magnificent tapestries, and seated themselves in the stalls on either side. Then, to the sound of fifes and tap of drums came the lords of parliament, in their robes, two by two, Dalkeith among them with half-a-dozen other Douglases, Lindsay of Crawford, Montgomerie of Eaglesham, Maxwell, Seton and others to the number of some two score. These did not sit but went to stand just above the chancel steps facing the altar but leaving a passage in their midst.

Clash of cymbals heralded the earls, led by Dunbar, and all present save only Buchan, resplendent in scarlet and gold — Carrick and Fife having different roles to play. The earls went to sit on chairs in front of the prelates on the north side of the chancel.

There followed a flourish of trumpets, high and clear, to announce the royal approach. Lyon King of Arms brought in the great officers of state, the High Steward, a slight but brilliant figure in cloth-of-gold, the Chancellor, Chamberlain, Treasurer, Standard-Bearer and Keepers of the Great and Privy Seals, who brought the symbols of their offices to lay on a green-velvet-covered table before the altar. As these took up position in front of the prelates on the south side, the Primate, Bishop Trail of St. Andrews, led in the limping monarch, flanked on one side by the Constable, Sir Thomas Hay, bearing aloft the sword-of-state, on the other by the Marischal, Sir William Keith, bearing the sceptre. Behind, looking inscrutable, walked the Earl of Fife and Menteith, bearing the Crown of Scotland on a crimson cushion, his son Murdoch at his heels.

The King, of sadly noble appearance, wore the white velvet of purity and truth under a prince's robe of crimson, his hair and beard already almost as white as his doublet — scarcely credible as brother to the Wolf. A throne without canopy was set on a small dais behind the green-covered table; but the monarch was led by the Bishop to a lesser chair at the side. The sword, the sceptre and the crown were placed on the table. All was ready.

The Abbot of Scone, a dignified and venerable figure, moved up to the high altar, with his assistants, and commenced the coronation mass. This said, the celebrant and monarch alone partook of the elements. The Abbot then turned to bow to the Primate, who moved over to the royal chair and raised the King to his feet. Standing thus together, he administered the Oath, in which the monarch swore in a husky voice to be a father to his people, to keep the peace in his realm so far as God allowed, to forbid and put down all evil, crime and felony in all degrees, and to show mercy and righteousness in all judgments — in the name of God Almighty, merciful and compassionate. By the time he came to an end, the royal voice was the merest whisper.

The Bishop was then given a vial of consecrated oil from off the high altar, by the Abbot, and with this he anointed the King's head and brow in the name of the Father, the Son and the Holy Ghost.

A great shout arose within the crowded church; and led by the choristers, the company burst into the singing of the Twenty-third Psalm. But when the fourth verse was reached, all fell silent for a high, clear solo voice which sang heart-breakingly the significant lines:

Yea, though I walk through the valley of the shadow of death,
  I will fear no evil;
For Thou art with me; Thy rod and Thy staff they comfort me.
Thou preparest a table before me in the presence of mine
  enemies;
Thou anointest my head with oil; my cup runneth over.

When there was silence again, Bishop Trail led the monarch down from the dais, which he negotiated only with difficulty, and a little way towards the ranked lords and people.

"I present to you the Lord's Anointed, your liege-lord and undoubted King!" he intoned impressively.

The building all but shook to the eruption of bellowed chanting. "God save the King! God save the King!" The monarch blinked, shaking his head.

Now the Lord Chamberlain came forward to divest the King of his prince's crimson and put on him instead the robe of royal purple. He was led to the throne, not to his former chair, and seated. The Constable came over with the sword-of-state, the monarch rising to have it girded on by a shoulder-belt — for it was five feet tall and two-handed. Sitting again and finding the sword awkward to dispose at his side, he was brought the sceptre by the Marischal, easier to hold, in the left hand.

Another flourish of trumpets, loud in the enclosed space of the church, heralded the actual crowning. The Earl Robert came up with the crown on its cushion, still with Murdoch behind. Many present beside the Douglases undoubtedly resented the Governor's appropriation to himself of this especial honour. The emphasis was obvious. He handed the cushion to his son, took the handsome, indeed magnificent crown from it, lavishly made by Robert the Bruce out of the spoils of Bannockburn, and placed it on his brother's brow with the minimum of ceremony. Stepping back, he inclined his head slightly, rather than bowed.

The trumpets sounded a prolonged fanfare.

The crowned and anointed King sat, one hand high on the hilt of the great sword, the rod of the psalm, the other holding the sceptre, or staff, while the coronation anthem surged out from hundreds of throats. Although some of the throats were a trifle choked for singing, just then, some from emotion at the age-old and significant thing that was done, representing their pride of nationhood; some at the essential mockery of all so solemnly represented; some at the personal tragedy of the gentle, kindly, ineffectual man whose twisted fate it was to sit there.

Just before the singing ended, there was an unrehearsed incident. Out from the line of officers of state the dazzling, slender figure of the High Steward stepped, to sink before the throne on one knee, head bowed to his father, hands out. Relinquishing his awkward grip of the sword-hilt, the King extended his own hand, trembling, towards his son, who reaching up, took it between his palms, in the traditional gesture of fealty. Kneeling there, he repeated the fealty oath, his young voice firm, unhurried, whilst the Earl Robert frowned blackly but could not interfere, and from the nave a great sob came from Queen Annabella, hastily suppressed.

Rising to his feet, relinquishing the royal hand, David Stewart bowed low to his father, turned to stare blankly at his uncle, and then returned easily to his place. Jamie Douglas, for one, could scarce forbear to cheer. The great sigh that went up from the congregation was eloquent.

But now it was the Governor's turn. Striding forward, he raised his brother from the throne in brusque fashion, and with two flicks of his forefinger summoned the Constable and Marischal to come and take the sword and the sceptre. A further beckon brought Sir Alexander Scrymgeour, Constable of Dundee and Standard-Bearer of Scotland, to lift the Lion Rampant standard from off the table and hold it aloft above the royal brothers. Then, without further ado, and gripping the King's arm, he set off at a pace on the fast side for a man with a limp. He led the monarch, who still wore the crown, down through the ranks of the bowing lords, out of the chancel and into the nave, making for the great west doorway. He did not pause or even glance at the Queen as he passed her chair, although his brother attempted a shambling bow.

Out of the church they passed, and hurriedly the officers of state, the earls and prelates and lords, sought to form up in their due order and follow on, the Constable and Marischal to get into their flanking positions and the Standard-Bearer to come close behind with the banner.

The church stood on a kind of terrace above the level haugh-lands of the Tay, with the monastic buildings to east and west. But to the north, a little way back, was a slightly higher ridge, grass-grown, and all about this a vast crowd was congregated. In their thousands the people of Scotland waited to hail their new-crowned sovereign on the famed Moot-hill of Scone. Un-fortunately, the renowned Stone of Destiny, on which the new King should have seated himself, was not available. When Edward of England had come storming for it in 1296, it had been hidden away, and the invader palmed off with a lump of Scone sandstone roughly quarried, instead of the ornate and highly carved talisman long known as the Marble Chair. The true Stone had been produced for Bruce's hurried coronation; but on the hero-king's death-bed, he had entrusted it to his loyal supporter, Angus Og, Lord of the Isles, well knowing the dangers to it im-plicit in his infant son David's succession and the unending Eng-lish threats. Angus Og had taken it to the Hebrides, and there it still was, succeeding Lords of the Isles refusing to yield it up until their claims to the earldom of Ross, and otherwise, were met — the present Donald being no exception. So there was no Stone today. But the Moot-hill presentation could still be made, the motions gone through.

As the now distinctly straggling procession began to climb the hill, another royal brother arrived from Perth. Walter, Lord of Brechin, had somehow managed to miss the church ceremony but was in good time for the feasting. His two elder brothers ignored him entirely.

To the ringing cheers of the populace the principals reached the top of the Moot-hill, the King distinctly breathless. There, turning to face the crowd, the Earl stooped to pick up a fistful of the sacred earth, already loosened for the purpose, and thrust it into his brother's hand.

"I, Robert of Fife and Menteith, give you the land of Scot-land!" he said, level-voiced. "I will aid you to hold it secure." And his hand clenched over the other's. With the other hand he gestured towards the assembly, and raised his voice — a thing he seldom permitted himself. "On this Moot-hill of

Scone," he called, "I, Robert, give you your crowned King."

The cheers rang out, unperceptive of the double meaning, and continued. The monarch inclined his head; but it was more an act of infinite regret, almost of apology, rather than a bow of acknowledgment. His son came and stood beside him, at the other side from his uncle.

Presently the Lyon King had his trumpeter blow a flourish for silence, and, as successor to the ancient Celtic sennachies, commenced to intone from a lengthy parchment roll.

"Hear me, all men high and low — behold the High King of Scots, *Ard Righ Albannach*, Robert, son of Robert, son of Marjorie, daughter of Robert, son of Robert, son of Robert . . ." On and on he went, tracing the royal descent back through the Bruce generations to David, Earl of Huntingdon, brother of William the Lion and Malcolm the Fourth and so by Malcolm Canmore through seven more generations to Kenneth MacAlpine who united Picts and Scots, and on through the misty Celtic names to Fergus MacErc of the semi-sacral Fir-Bolg who followed the missionaries from Ireland, but who claimed descent from the pagan Eochaid, the Horseman of the Heavens, god-spirit of the early Celts. It took a considerable time to rehearse, but the huge crowd listened intently throughout. The Scots had ever been a race of genealogists.

Now servitors came carrying the throne from the church, on which the King seated himself thankfully. He was barely thereon when his brother Walter, the second Walter of the family, came to drop unsteadily on one knee and take his hands between his own in token of fealty, muttering something approximating to the oath — for he was three parts drunk as usual — seeking the prominence of being first to do so. Thereafter, in more dignified fashion and due order of precedence, starting with the earls, all the great ones of the land — save the ecclesiastics — formed up to do likewise, a lengthy process; and not only the great ones, for every holder of a barony was expected to make fealty, although not all on coronation-day, and even Jamie in due course came forward to swear loyalty for the barony of Aberdour. He was moved with real compassion as he took those soft hands within his own, wishing that he could say something of what was in his heart instead of the oft-repeated and all but meaningless formula. And he was much aware of the stern features of the Earl Robert regarding him unfavourably from behind the throne on one side, and those of David Stewart half-smiling at the other.

At last it was all over, and Lyon could announce that the King graciously invited all and sundry, high and low, to come feast with him in the Abbey-park below, to celebrate together this great day. Long live the King's Grace!

Later, Jamie sat with Mary, and other dependants of the lofty, at a modest but well-placed trestle-table not far from the royal and Douglas ones. Well-fed, they discussed the day's events. All around them was repletion, satiety, even excess, gluttony and drunkenness, folk great and small, young and old, gorged with meats and wine and ale and now being entertained by a variety of musicians, jugglers, tumblers, bear-dancers and the like. Only at the royal table itself was there little aspect of ease, relaxation and content. The King sat exhausted but still tense, only toying with his food, the Queen on his right seeking to sustain, encourage and comfort him, David on his left making no major attempt to disguise his boredom but amusing himself by intermittently baiting his cousin Murdoch who sat next to him. The Governor was on the Queen's right, but sat at a distinct remove, expressionless, staring straight ahead of him, Isabel on his right finding no more to say to him than to her other brother Walter who sprawled asleep over the board. Gelis and the other princesses present sat at the far side of Murdoch. However good-looking, none would have called the royal family a happy or congenial company.

"By all the saints, when may we slip away?" Jamie murmured. not for the first time. "Must we sit here all day? I planned to take you to Shortwood Shaw and Kinclaven, where Wallace fought the English — fair woodland and river. It is but eight miles . . ."

"I cannot leave until Gelis does — as you know well. And she may not until the King does, as you also know. What has happened to my staunch and patient Jamie?"

"You have! I am weary of being patient, of putting up with other folk, of *sharing* you! I want you to myself, Mary — do you not understand? We are never alone . . ."

"I understand only too well, foolish one," she said. "Since my need is as great as is yours — immodest as it may be to admit it! Perhaps you should not have chosen a princess's maid-in-waiting for your betrothed? But — wait you lad. Rein in! I shall make it up to you, I promise!" And she gripped him beneath the table.

"That makes it but the worse, woman! If I could catch young David's eye. He looks sufficiently wearied of it all, himself. He might induce his father to make a move . . ."

"His unhappy Grace, my brother, would welcome a move, I swear. But until his master, there, gives the word . . .!"

"How can a man be so, so helpless? So lacking in all spirit? *He* is the master now, King of Scots. He can command, and none gainsay him. Why submit to the Governor so?"

"Well may you ask. John was born tired, I think. And being the weary one of a forceful family must have been a sore business, wearing him down. Alex and Robert ever dominated him harshly. Being lamed was the final blow. The habit of deferring to others will not change now, at his age, I think. Being king will mean nothing to him, save irksome duty and more pain. All he seeks is peace, quiet and his books."

"Yet he could make a good king. He is kind, honest, just . . ."

"No, Jamie — these are not the qualities demanded of a king, today. Or ever, I believe. If the king has them, so much the better. But what he *requires* is rather strength, vigour, ruthlessness, an ability to be harsh and to frighten men. Some might love John, but none could ever fear him. And the ruler needs to be feared." She pointed at the Earl Robert. "Yonder is the man who *should* have been king. And does he not know it! He has all those qualities I named, and none love him. But all fear him. I mislike the man with all my heart – but my head tells me that he might have made a good king for Scotland. As even might Alex. Both have been denied what could so easily have been their birthright. And have fought against that denial differently. But they are strong, determined men, and could have given this land the strong rule it has lacked since the Bruce died. Robert may do so still, as Governor. John never would, or could."

"You talk like my father."

"I am glad if I do — a mere woman! For your father has one of the wisest heads in Scotland, Jamie. If you were to choose to follow *him*, instead of dancing attendance on Isabel, you could rise high in this realm, Sir James Douglas!"

He looked at her thoughtfully. "Do you want me to rise high, Mary?"

"No-o-o. I think not. But I am a Stewart also, see you, and the lust for power is in us. So beware! I would sooner have you always the true and modest Jamie I know and find to my taste! But you may have little choice, lad. Do you not see it?" She pointed again, on either side of the King, to Robert and David Stewart. "Those two will, and must, come to blows, one day. Over the rule of this kingdom. The Governor and the heir to the throne. Nothing could be surer. In not many years from now, I vow, there will not be room for both of them in Scotland. For Davie has the qualities a king needs also. And Robert, I swear, will never yield the power to him, gracefully. Many will have to choose whom they will support. And Davie calls *you* his friend. He will demand not a little of his friends, that one. I think that you will need all your father's wisdom one day, Jamie."

"I would not wish to be caught up in any struggle for power."

"Perhaps not. But you have to choose sides. And if you choose for the boy you have come to like, as against the man you have come to hate, you will not keep out of it."

"You are warning me? *Against* David and *for* the Governor?"

"Lord, no! Since I mislike Robert as much as you do, even though he is my own kin. I but remind you that it may not be so easy to remain aloof when battle is joined. For Jamie Douglas in especial."

They sat in silence for a space, watching yet scarcely watching a juggler.

"What will he do now? With Alexander?" Jamie demanded. "Your precious Governor!"

"Who knows? But he will not heed *us*, in the matter, that is certain. There is nothing you can do, Jamie."

"I have tried the Earl Archibald. He is the only man the Governor heeds. But he will not act. He says it is for the best. That the Wolf and all his brats deserve nothing better, but worse indeed. My father besought him also, but could do no better. My hope is that David may later prevail on the King to assert his authority and order a release. He says that the Queen will keep reminding his father on this. Will you speak with her also?"

"To be sure. But, I grieve for Annabella. Her lot is the sorriest of all. For John can blame none but himself; or, at least, his nature. But the Queen, although quiet, calm, is a woman of spirit. It must greatly try her to see her husband so used. And herself slighted."

"Tomorrow she will do better. At her own coronation."

"We must seek to see that she does. For that is not Robert's intention, I swear. The service here is to be direly short, and held early in the day. Moreover, Gelis says that he is contriving a great tourney, race-meeting and wapinschaw, on the Inch at Perth, for all day long. As a celebration, he says — but it will mean that a great many will not come to Scone. He will ensure, I vow, that few indeed do come . . ."

"This is shame! A sorry, contemptible stroke. Does David know of it?"

"I do not know. We must ensure that *many* learn of it."

"And yet you say that Earl Robert might have made a good king!"

"If his ambition and yearning for the crown had not been soured and twisted thus, I think he might have been, yes. For he is able, competent, shrewd, forceful. He is a man thwarted, seeing others doing ill what he could do well. He has become a man eaten up with resentment."

"And all Scotland must pay . . .!"

XXIV

JAMIE DOUGLAS, MAKING plans now, with Mary, for their wedding in October, spent the next few weeks on the move between the houses of Edmonstone, Dalkeith and Aberdour — where they were going to set up home and where much refurbishing was necessary after years of neglect, before any self-respecting man could bring a bride to it. Mary's position, in this interim period, was difficult. Gelis had retired again to Nithsdale in Dumfries-shire, with her step-son, the remote situation of which seemed to suit her present withdrawn mood — but was highly inconvenient for Mary. Besides which, the coronation over, she seemed neither to require nor desire her half-sister's attendance. So Mary, who would have relinquished her position as maid-in-waiting anyway, on marriage, did so in advance. But being illegitimate and having no property of her own, this left her more or less homeless. And though, as a royal bastard she could have always found some sort of lodging and employment about the Court, this did not suit her independent frame of mind, especially as the Court was now really the Governor's, the King himself retiring to the seclusion of Turnberry on every possible occasion. The young Earl David had been allotted a suite of rooms for himself in Stirling Castle, in recognition of his advancement as heir to the throne and High Steward, although he used them but seldom. The boy was glad to bestow one of these chambers on his favourite aunt, so that she might have somewhere that she might call her own meantime, and keep her belongings; but that great hilltop fortress was hardly a suitable residence for a single young woman, when the Court was not present, and she was no more often there than was David. Moreover, she felt slightly less then welcome at Edmonstone, for though the Lady Isabel had fully recovered her equanimity and treated Jamie almost as before, there was still a reserve between the half-sisters, and Mary's aforementioned independence of spirit made her avoid Isabel's house. Happily she was always welcome at Dalkeith, where the old lord, and Lady Egidia also, had come to approve of her. Since it would not do that she should openly cohabit with Jamie before the marriage ceremony, when he went to Aberdour he found quarters with her half-brother the Archdeacon Thomas — or at least provided by him, at a nunnery at Dysart, reasonably convenient. It was all in rather irritating contrast, nevertheless, to their fine free ride south from Badenoch; but they put up with it in moderate patience since it would soon be over — and, to be sure, they contrived to be alone together with fair frequency.

They were, in fact, busily planning and arranging their house at Aberdour one day in late September when a messenger from Dalkeith summoned Jamie urgently to his father's bedside. The old lord was ill and desired to assemble his family around him. Much concerned, for neither his sire nor the Lady Egidia were of the alarmist type, Jamie, and Mary with him, set off for Queen Margaret's Ferry without delay.

They reached Dalkeith Castle to find a large family concourse, in considerable gloom, for the lord thereof was well loved. He had suffered some sort of heart attack four days before, and though he had shown some small improvement since, he seemed to be convinced that he would not recover. Presently Jamie was summoned to the bed-chamber, alone.

His father did not look so very different from when last seen, hale and well, but his eyes somehow appeared to have grown larger. His voice also was less strong, and breathless.

"Jamie, lad," he said, mustering a faint smile. "You gladden my old eyes. You are the eldest of my brood. And though born out-of-wedlock, you have ever been close to my heart. For I loved your mother dearly. She was not such as I might wed — a small farmer's daughter. But we were close, close." His voice sank to a whisper. "Closer than ever were my two wives!"

Embarrassed, Jamie gripped the older man's arm. "God rest her soul," he said. "I never knew her."

"To your loss, boy — to your loss. The plague took her, young." He sighed. "If only I might have wed Meg . . ." A pause. "But *you* are more fortunate, Jamie. You can wed the lass of your own choice, as not all can. Your Mary — she will serve you very well. A young woman with a head on her — as well as the parts young men show more interest in! You have chosen well, in the end."

"I thank you, sir. But . . . you must not tire yourself. The Lady Egidia said I was not to stay long, to tire you . . ."

"Heed her not, lad — heed *me*! I have two matters to speak of. And I may not be spared for another chance. I have made up my will and settlement of my affairs. I have left you certain tokens. When I pass on. The lands of Stoneypath and Baldwinsgill, in Lammermuir, with the castle of Stoneypath. And Roberton, in Teviotdale. The tower there is long broken by English raiding. But the barony itself is well enough. These are larger, richer lands than your Aberdour . . ."

"But, my lord — there is no need! I thank you — but I have sufficient. I do not seek wide lands . . ."

"Wheesht, lad. You will have bairns soon enough, you and yon lassie. They will need to be provided for. Forby, Jamie, I leave you to look to and provide for young Johnnie. Your brother, your *full*

397

brother. He has not your wits nor steadfastness. Belike he will grow in sense. But I durst not leave him lands yet. He would but squander them. So see you to him, out of yours. For the rest . . ." He paused, panting. "For the rest, I would have you to have my second gold girdle — you'll mind it. And my suit of tilting-armour. It will fit you well enough. Inlaid with gold. And two silver plates, with my arms. To remember me by . . ."

"My lord, my lord — do not speak so! Do not talk as though you were, were dying. You are not, I swear. And I do not require such tokens to remember you by. You have always been a true and kind father to me, a bastard though I am . . ."

"I have tried to be, lad. I . . . I . . ." A fit of breathlessness shook him. Jamie straightened up.

"I will go now, sir. You have spoken more than enough."

"No, no. Bide you, boy — a little longer. I told you. I had two matters to speak of. Hear me. You know that the lassie Borthwick died a while back? Her your brother James was betrothed to. Janet, Sir William's daughter. Aye, poor lass. But I have arranged another match for James. With the new King's second daughter, the Lady Elizabeth. Aye, a more suitable match. For my heir."

"But . . . but, sir, she is but fourteen. A child, yet . . ."

"Old enough to be wed. Her sister wed but a year older. To Archie's son."

"And James? What says he to this?"

"It is not what James says, boy — it is what *I* say. Forby, James knows his part and place. He is heir to Dalkeith and Morton. Unlike you, he may not wed just whom he fancies. James will be the second man of the Douglas power. One of the richest lords in the land. So he weds the King's daughter, a princess — where you wed a King's bastard! There is the difference. Aye, the difference."

Jamie said nothing.

"They are to wed on St. Martin's Mass. Here in my church of St. Nicholas, Dalkeith. My wish . . . that you are wed together, you and James. A double wedding, Jamie . . ."

"But we are to wed the month before. In October, not November."

"A month's wait will not hurt you, boy. And it will serve you well. A great occasion. Although I will not be there to see it, I think. The King, the Governor, Archie, all the highest in the land. To see you wed."

"I care naught for that. Nor does Mary, I swear. We would be wed quietly . . ."

"No doubt, my son — no doubt. But I choose to make the decision mine, not yours. You are not yet of full age. The cost of all will be mine. You are a Douglas, and will accept the responsibility of that." His father's eyes glowed almost eerily, even though his voice was little more than a dry whisper. "It will be a great day for Douglas, for Dalkeith. I am near my end, but this I can do. The Stewarts, and therefore the Crown, will be bound closer than ever to Douglas. Do you not see it, lad?" In his eagerness, the old lord half-raised himself from the pillow, but fell back, unable to sustain the effort. His gasping, rustling voice however, went on. "My wife, the Lady Egidia, the King's aunt. James's bride, the King's daughter. Your bride, the King's half-sister. All wed to Douglas. Archie's son wed to the King's eldest daughter — just as his bastard Will wed Gelis, the King's sister. His second son is to wed the Governor's second daughter. Young George of Angus is to wed the Lady Mary, the King's youngest. You see? The Douglas design!"

Jamie swallowed. "I see . . . something. Something I had no thought to have part in! Mary and I are not for this design, my lord. Marrying for design, for power. And I would scarce have thought that Douglas was so admiring of the Stewarts to wish to be allied only to them! I have heard you name them upstarts, sir, have I not? Compared with our own more ancient power."

"Fool! Do you not see?" The mottled hand, surprisingly strong, gripped his own. "The Stewarts themselves are naught to care for. It is the Crown! The day will come when most Stewart lines end in a Douglas! And there are none so many lawfully-born males in line for the throne. Young David. The Governor. The Governor's two sons. Walter of Brechin. That is all. And none save the Governor married. Bastards innumerable, but these cannot succeed. You see? Douglas meantime will surround and support the throne. One day, Douglas may mount it!"

The younger man shook his head. "So this is what the Earl Archibald and you plan. With other's lives! I . . . I mislike it, my lord. And cannot see why Mary and I, illegitimates both, have to contribute to it. Why involve us?"

"You add weight, boy. To this wedding ceremony. A double wedding is the more notable. And you are something of a hero, Jamie. Since Otterburn. And now your Badenoch venture. Aye, and your Mary riding North to rescue you. She is bonny, well liked. Folk speak of you both. You will add weight."

"I mislike it . . ."

His father spoke sharply, seeming to forget, for the moment, that he was reputedly on his death-bed. "It is my will. You will obey. Remember it." Then he sighed, and wearily waved a hand. "Pleasure an old done man, Jamie. It is not much to ask. Go now, lad. I will see Mary later. Not now — for I am tired . . ."

Distinctly upset, Jamie went to tell the young woman. Surprisingly, Mary was less perturbed than was he. If it would please his father, she said, it would not greatly hurt them. They would survive the added three weeks. This design for linking Douglas and Stewart so closely was scarcely new, after all. And anyway, no concern of theirs. She could see nothing sinister about it, as Jamie seemed to do. Nor, clearly, could the King and the Governor think so, since they must agree to all these marriages. Indeed, she would not be at all surprised if it was not so much a Douglas design as a Stewart one. For the Earl Robert was ten times more of a plotter and planner that ever could be the Earl Archibald and the Lord of Dalkeith; and if he allowed these marriages, then he had his reasons. Let their wedding be held at St. Martin's Mass, and before all the Court — it would but serve to demonstrate how well and truly wed they were. And Isabel and Gelis would have to be present to acclaim them! She laughed cheerfully. Besides, these great new lands willed to Jamie, in Lammermuir and the Borderland, were well worth three weeks of waiting.

Jamie Douglas, it is to be feared, was due to learn what it meant to have a wife with a clear and practical head on her bonny shoulders.

The next day, delayed by events, the Earl of Douglas arrived, in his usual striding stir scarcely suitable for invalid visiting. Indeed, when Jamie escorted him upstairs to his father's bedchamber, he was in grave doubts as to the wisdom of admitting him — not of course that he could have kept Archie the Grim out had he decided that was best. Stamping in, panting from the climb, the Earl wasted no breath on sick-bed sympathies.

"Sakes, man James — you lying there yet!" he cried. "Here's a poor state of affairs! This winna do, James. With a wedding, two weddings, to get by with. Aye, and worse than weddings, a sight worse!"

"Archie ...!" the sufferer faltered. "I'm sick, direly sick. I doubt I am not long for this life. Aye — maybe the next will be better, kinder ..."

"Faugh, man — the next life'll need to look to itself! This one needs looking to with a deal more haste and swink. Precious soul of God — I'm like to be needing five hundred men from you any day now, weddings or none!"

"Eh? Eh?" Dalkeith stared. "Men ...? What's this? What's this, of a mercy?"

"Trouble, James — trouble. Alex Stewart — a curse on him! He's on the move — or his heathenish bastard sons are! They've come spreenging out of their Hielant hills, with thousands of their bare-shanked caterans. Over the Mounth passes into the lowlands of Angus, Strathmore and Gowrie. Fire and sword and dirk ..."

"God a mercy!"

"The Wolf has struck, my lord?" Jamie demanded, at his back, forgetful of his place. "In force? Invaded the South?"

"Struck, yes — a plague on him! No warning or declaration. He's loosed his barbarian horde on to honest men's lands, slaying, burning, ravaging. It is no cattle-reiving, this, but bloody war."

"Not war, Archie — never war!" Dalkeith quavered. "They'll be making a bit stramash, a gesture, just ...?"

"If this is a gesture, man, it's a sore one. They've already defeated the force sent against them — God knows how! At a bit called Briarachan or something such — Glen Briarachan, north of Glasclune on the edge of Strathmore. We'll need to do something about it, James. I doubt I'll have to muster Douglas."

"But ... but ..." The invalid spread his hands, helplessly.

"This is the Wolf's answer," Jamie said. "To his son's arrest and imprisonment. I ... I ..." He could hardly say I told you so to the Earl of Douglas. "I feared something of the sort. He warned me. Who commands this Highland host, my lord?"

"Some brigand sons called Duncan and Andrew Stewart, they say. A pair of savages, by God! But they must be stark fighters — for they've routed the Sheriff of Angus, slain him indeed — Sir Walter Ogilvy of Auchterhouse, a fair enough soldier. And Lindsay of Glenesk and a wheen more. A bad business."

"There has been a battle?"

"You could name it that. When the word of this inroad came in, I wasna there. I was in the Borders and knew naught of it. Robert, the Governor, sent his good-brother, Sir David Lindsay of Glenesk to deal with it, with the Sheriff — since it was his own country. They mustered a force from the knights and lairds of Angus and Strathmore, a fair force by all accounts — but these caterans defeated them. A slaughter, no less. Hundreds slain, including the Sheriff and his brother, Guthrie of that Ilk, the Lairds of Ochterlony, Cairncross — och, many more. David Lindsay himself sore wounded, like Sir Patrick Gray and other knights . . ."

"Armoured chivalry defeated by the scum of Hieland bogs!" Dalkeith exclaimed, in agitation.

"It seems so. They should never have fought them in these upland glens — damned folly! But, even so . . ." Douglas shrugged. "When Robert heard of it, he sent for me. All Angus and Gowrie and the Stormonth, even Fife itself and Strathern, lies open to these barbarians. He'd have me raise the power of Douglas. But that will take time. God knows what they may be at before I could hold them."

"There's others besides Douglas, Archie," the sick man protested. "Nearer to the bit. Mar, Crawford, Drummond, Hay, Lyon . . ."

"Aye — no doubt. And they'll no' be standing idle. But none can field an *army* as can we, James." That was said not in any pride and eagerness but almost wearily. Archie the Grim had reached sixty-six years.

Jamie spoke, greatly daring. "You do not *wish* to raise Douglas, my lord? To engage in war. For an ill cause, if ever there was one — the, the Governor's folly!"

"Of course I do not, boy — do you take me for a sword-brandishing fool! Fighting the English is one thing; fighting our own countrymen, even these bare-shanked Hielantmen, and on our own land, another. But we canna let them over-run and destroy the realm."

"I do not think that they will aim to. They will not keep up any sustained campaign, I reckon. How would that serve the Wolf?"

"The foul fiend knows! What does he want? Is he coming South to try to release that precious son of his?"

"More than that, I think." Jamie frowned in concentration. "I

402

believe that he expected this. Sent Sir Alexander with us knowing that his brother might well lay hands on him. And so give him good and extra cause to make this invasion. I believe he would have invaded anyway — but that shameful arrest, when under the King's and prince's protection, aided him. I know what he wants — he made it very clear. He wants to ensure the continuation of his rule in the North, as Lieutenant and Justiciar. And he wants the excommunication lifted. To this end, and for vengeance on Bishop Barr, he burned Elgin and the rest. As example. For the same reason he sent this host South—and can send many more . . ."

"Well, man — well? What of it? How will this save us from outright war? And me from raising Douglas?"

"It may not be too late to save both, my lord. And to spare much bloodshed. The Governor's policy towards his brother has failed. The excommunication plot, his substitution of his son Murdoch as Lieutenant, and how this of Sir Alexander. He has *provoked* this invasion. But surely it is not too late to change his policy, perceiving his mistake?"

"Robert Stewart does not easily change his mind. And he is a proud man. Besides, it is too late by the Mass !"

"Perhaps not. If the Wolf gets what he really wants? And to give him it will cost the Governor little, save in his pride. If he released Sir Alexander, said he would press the Primate to withdraw the excommunication, and offered to restore the Justiciarship, in return for his brother calling back his forces to Badenoch?"

"He would never do that. Give way on all these — to a lawless brigand and his unholy tribe !"

"Why not, sir? What would it cost him, in truth — compared with civil war? Alexander held in a Falkland cell serves him nothing. The excommunication would be lifted by the *Church*, not seemingly by the Governor. And the Wolf *is* still Justiciar, and accepted as such by all in the North — the Lord Murdoch's appointment never taken up. He would rejoice to be relieved of it, I vow! Three scrapes of the Earl Robert's pen, and the danger would be lifted."

The Earl Archie tugged his beard. "Would it be sufficient? And would Buchan credit it? Believe it would all be done? He trusts none, that one."

"I think he trusts *me* — however humble an instrument! Else why make me his witness? Why release me to come South again? If I sent him a message, assuring him that Alexander was released, and would not be taken again — on *your* surety, my lord! — I think that he would agree."

"Robert would never lout so low to his younger brother, boy. He could not do it. To restore the Justiciarship would be as good as eating dust before all the kingdom. And parliament, mind, confirmed that dismissal . . ."

The invalid took a hand. Dalkeith was sitting up now, indeed, and looking a deal less near death's door than when his friend had entered, despite the alarming news. "It might be done judiciously, discreetly, Archie," he declared. "Made to sound better — so that Robert Stewart might swallow it. A contrivance. He need not actually restore his brother — since it was only in name that he was ousted. If Robert was to announce that his son Murdoch wished to resign his appointment — which all know he has never desired — this would serve. No other being appointed. Would it not?"

"That is right," Jamie agreed eagerly, "no need for more."

"And this of the excommunication," his father went on, life in his voice again. "Since the lifting of it would in fact be Holy Church's doing, not Robert's — if Alex could be persuaded to express some form of regret for what he has done. Not so much in the matter of his wife perhaps but in this burning of the cathedral and towns. Then the Governor's name need scarce come into it."

"Express regret — Alex!" the Earl exclaimed. "As well expect the Devil to! Or Robert!"

"A form of words could be devised — only words, man. To cover the matter. I could contrive such, I believe. Something Alex Stewart could say, or sign, which would save the faces of the churchmen. Make some small payment, perhaps. A token, just . . ."

It was Jamie's turn to look doubtful, even though he rejoiced at his father involving himself, rousing from his despond, displaying the shrewd and experienced statecraft again for which he was renowned. "It would be difficult," he said. "With the Wolf holding all the cards. He is not a man to be cozened by skilful words. Any more than he is to express regrets . . ."

"But neither is he a fool, Jamie. He must know that Holy Church would have to have *something* before the Primate could lift the anathema. To preserve the bishops' credit. He cannot expect to be freed of excommunication without at least a gesture that they could call repentance. Even Alex Stewart! I say that he will recognise that."

"This *I* say, my lord — that he will never apologise to any bishop, to his brother. The Governor, that is. To the King himself it might be different. That might serve. But to none other, I'd swear."

"Aye — that might be contrived, likewise. John — King Robert — will do anything to save his realm from war, I think. How say you, Archie? Could you convince Robert? He needs must listen to you, after all — for he requires you. And he must see that only something such as this can save him, in this pass."

"I can try," the Earl agreed. "Aye, devil burn all stiff-necked Stewarts — I can try! James — can you write a letter? For Robert to send to Alex. You are good at words. And I will tell him to sign it — or whistle for Douglas support! And you, boy — write one to Buchan himself, as you said. To go with it. And by the fastest courier we can send to Badenoch."

"And Sir Alexander? You will get him out of Falkland Castle, my lord?"

"To be sure, to be sure. God help me, I'll get him moved out of there and back to the King's keeping — damn him for a plaguey pest! Aye, and meantime I'll have to set up some sort of a defence to keep his ruffianly brothers from splurging further South into decent country. While we treat with their father. A curse on them all, I say . . . !"

"Better that than flinging all Douglas into war, Archie — all the realm. Jamie — fetch me paper, quill and ink, lad . . ."

XXV

THE ATMOSPHERE IN the church of the Dominican or
Blackfriars monastery at Perth was tense. It was already
well past noon, and the small but illustrious company
waited uneasy, on edge, offended in some cases. It was unthinkable that the King himself should be seen to wait for anybody, even his own brother, and he remained hidden in the
chapter-house, young David shuttling to and fro cheerfully
enough, probably the only non-tense member of the congregation.
Bishop Trail of St. Andrews, the Primate, and Bishop Peebles of
Dunkeld, Chancellor, looked distinctly nervous in their stalls up
near the altar, Archdeacon Thomas Stewart demonstrating
greater ease by strolling constantly from one to the other with a
sort of alert reassurance. The Earl of Douglas, representing the
Governor, also paced about, huffing and snorting. The Ladies
Isabel, Elizabeth and Jean Stewart sat silent, no longer even whis-
pering, with Mary in attendance behind — the other royal sisters
unable to be present for one reason or another, Marjory because
her husband, the Earl of Moray, had just died as a result of a
tournament wound in England, Katherine being at the bedside of
her wounded spouse, Sir David Lindsay of Glenesk, Gelis preoccupied in Nithsdale, and Margaret, as ever, lost in Donald's
barbarous Isles. Walter of Brechin should have been there, but
was not. The remainder of the congregation, apart from the prior
of the monastery and one or two priests and monks, consisted of
Jamie and Sir Alexander Stewart, released for the occasion, standing beside Mary and behind the princesses.

Jamie himself was agitated, undeniably. Although both Mary
and Alexander kept reassuring him that no real responsibility
rested with him, he could not but feel that it must, to some extent.
The details and timing of this encounter had been no concern of
his, admittedly, but the general situation was — or at least he had
been the vital link and largely the instigator. People kept looking
at him. Alexander revealed little concern, but there was a stillness

about him unusual in that lively character. He looked pale from his confinement.

David came back, a gay figure in peacock clothing. "Look not so fearful," he called out, grinning, to Jamie but loud enough for all in the church to hear. "We are entirely comfortable here, are we not? And Holy Writ enjoins us to pray as well as watch, I seem to recollect. I perceive little praying in progress — but perhaps my lords Bishop are doing so silently, for us all!" He laughed, uninhibitedly. "My royal father, at least, is an example to all. He is lost, through there, in a dusty manuscript, sacred I have no doubt. And Her Grace contemplates, as is her wont — eternity perhaps."

Archie the Grim emitted a choking sound. Otherwise the heir to the throne's observations were received in silence.

Jamie whispered to Alexander. "We should have posted a lookout, up on the monastery bell-tower. To tell us if he approaches. From the north. We still could do so."

"What benefit in that? If he comes, he comes. If not, no watchman will bring him. He may already be in the city. But never fear, my friend — if he said that he would come, come he will. Sooner or later."

"Thank God that it is the King, in there, not the Governor! He would have been long gone ere this, and all lost."

"Perhaps. But my father knows his brothers."

The Lady Isabel turned in her seat. "Jamie — you are sure it was noon?" she murmured. "Not mid-day — which might mean a less certain hour. Or noon*tide*, perhaps?"

"I did not make the arrangement, Princess," he said. "The Governor planned it all. Used his own messengers . . ."

"My esteemed Uncle Robert said *noon*," David declared. "And we all know what weight he puts on truth and accuracy. In small matters!"

More than one throat gulped at that.

The Archdeacon Thomas, after conferring with the bishops, came down to the lower chancel area to speak with his royal relatives.

A noise, a disturbance, from outside, galvanised the company — clattering hooves, shouting and the clank of mail. And since the church opened off the cloisters, deep within the monastery complex, this was unlooked for, to say the least.

407

Jamie had a vivid mental vision of the Wolf riding his horse right into the cathedral of Elgin, and something quailed within him.

Then the west door of the nave was flung open in unceremonious style, and a knight in full armour, helmeted, came clanking in bearing aloft a large banner displaying the arms of Buchan, three golden sheaves on blue. Behind him paced a gaudily-tabarded herald in the Stewart colours, and thereafter two trumpeters. These blew a resounding fanfare which set the hammer-beam roofing ringing. The herald then raised his powerful voice.

"The mighty prince Alexander, Earl of Buchan, Lord of Badenoch, Lochaber and Kinneddar, Lieutenant and Justiciar of the North, *Alastair Mor Mac-an-Righ*!" he announced.

Shaken, all stared.

There was a distinct pause before the Wolf walked in. He had elected to dress simply, if rather oddly for the occasion, wholly in gleaming chain-mail, girded with a golden earl's belt. A great two-handed sword hung from a shoulder-belt, also of gold, and over the other shoulder was draped a voluminous tartan plaid. His head was bare, his shoulder-length silver-gold mane gleaming to match the chain-mail. He was chatting easily with his two sons, Sir Duncan and Sir Andrew, leaders of the current invasion, these dressed as though straight from the field of battle. Behind came a colourful throng of Highland chieftains in an eye-catching display of varied tartans, eagles' feathers and Celtic jewellery, all armed to the teeth. The excommunicate of Holy Church had arrived to offer penance, oblation and satisfaction.

Brushing past his banner-bearer, herald and trumpeters, the Wolf walked up the nave some way, and paused to stare round the church. His eye lighted on his son. "Ha, Alex!" he called, but did not move forward or discontinue his survey. He greeted none other. "Where is my brother the King?" he rapped out. "Douglas — where is he?" It was not at the Earl thereof that he looked, but at Jamie.

David Stewart stepped out. "Greetings, Uncle," he called pleasantly. "What delayed you?"

He was ignored. "Sir James Douglas — I said, where is the King? Whom you engaged would meet with me here."

"My lord, he is here, I assure you . . ."

"Earl of Buchan, His Grace is occupied, in the chapter-house," the nephew announced, now fully as stiffly as his uncle. "I shall enquire whether he is ready to receive you!"

The Wolf started forward angrily, but restrained himself with an effort. He did not know this church and where might be the chapter-house. Undoubtedly it would look highly undignified to go trying at various doors. He stood still, frowning. The boy by no means hurried off.

Archdeacon Thomas cleared his throat, in the hush. "My lord — the Primate and my lord Bishop of Dunkeld have been awaiting you . . ."

His half-brother eyed him remotely, up and down, and then looked away, unspeaking.

The Earl of Douglas hurrumphed strongly. "We have been here a long while waiting, Buchan," he jerked. "I have more to do with my time."

"Then go do it, man. Your presence is not required."

Hotly the Douglas snarled something incoherent; but he had no answer to that.

No one else ventured a remark.

Presently, preceded by his son, the King came limping through a sidedoor near the chancel-steps, Queen Annabella on his arm — or more accurately, he on Annabella's arm, since she it was who did the supporting. He looked around him, moistening his lips, a stooping, nervous figure, as all rose and bowed, managed both to shake and nod his head at the same time in acknowledgment, and without further ceremony hobbled over to the high-chair provided, and sank down, opposite the bishops. The Queen remained standing at his back, to one side, the young prince at the other. An entrance more different from his brother's would be hard to conceive.

He cleared his throat. "Aye, Alex," he said thickly. "You've come, then."

"We have both come," the Wolf returned shortly. "I hope to some purpose."

"Oh aye, to be sure — to be sure. But . . . this is all none of my doing, Alex. Much here."

"Meaning, Sire?"

"I mean that it is Robert's contrive. All of it. I would not have had yon excommunication . . . if I had been asked. Nor this end to

409

it. It was ill done. But, Alex—you shouldna have burned Elgin. You should not. The cathedral. Yon was a sin, a great sin. I wouldna like to have that on my conscience, Alex. No, no . . ." The hesitant voice trailed away. Only one or two there knew how much resolution it had taken to enunciate those words.

The Wolf knew, and his pale eyes narrowed. "There are sins and sins, Brother," he said, levelly for him. "You at least will never have *that* sort on your conscience! And Robert's conscience died at birth!" He took a deep breath. "Shall we say, Sir, that, like yon fire, I, I got something out-of-hand! To my. . . regret." That last was like a trap shutting. Undoubtedly it represented fully as great an effort as had the King's statement.

There was silence then, as people eyed each other, wondering.

When it was clear that the supreme sacrifice had been made and that they would not get more, the monarch cleared his throat again. "Aye, well," he said. "So be it. God forgive us our sins—and *I* have ower many! But see you, Alex—the Bishop here, my lord of St. Andrews, has this matter in hand. This of excommunication — the lifting. There is some form of words for it. My lord Bishop . . .?" Thankfully the King pushed, almost physically, all over to the Primate.

"My lord of Buchan," Trail began, in sepulchral tones, rising to his feet, "where grievous sin has been committed, in especial sin against the Holy Ghost, Christ's Holy Church has power to pronounce solemn excommunication, the supreme anathema, banishment of the creature from before the face of the Creator."

"Who said so, man? Christ?" the Wolf interrupted.

The Primate coughed. "Holy Church says so, my lord. The successors of Saint Peter . . ."

"Not even Saint Peter himself? Only his successors! But which one, Clerk? He in this Avignon? Or he in Rome? There is a difference, is there not?"

"My lord — this is a solemn matter . . ."

"God's truth, man — do I not know it! My eternal soul, no less — as you would have me to believe! Have done with your preachings, Sir Priest — if you would have me to bide in this kirk much longer!"

The Primate twisted his hands together and looked unhappily from the King to his fellow-bishop. "I protest!" he exclaimed. "I do most solemnly protest!"

"So do I, sirrah — so do I! So there are two of us! Now — get on with it a God's name! Or I leave, you hear — leave!"

"Alex," the King quavered, "the Bishop is your friend. Here to do you a good service . . ."

"Then let him perform it, and be done. I did not come here to be preached at."

Drawing a quivering breath, Trail tried again. "My lord of Buchan — before excommunication may be lifted, repentance is necessary. Repentance in sackcloth and ashes . . ."

The guffaw which interrupted that was sufficiently eloquent.

"Do, do you so repent, my lord?"

"How think you, Clerk?"

The Bishop drew a hand over his lips. "You have *come* here. Presumably for that purpose. You have said that you, h'm, you regret . . ."

"So I seem to recollect."

"M'mm. God's judgment against impenitent sinners is terrible, my lord. I, ah . . . the regret you speak of, to my mind referred to the wicked burning of Elgin Cathedral. But . . . but that is not what the excommunication was pronounced for. Indeed it pre-dated it. The excommunication was on account of the failure of your marriage to your lawful wife, the Countess Euphemia, and, and . . ."

"And that, Christ God, I *do* regret!" the other shouted. "More than anything else on this earth — a curse on it!"

"Ah. I . . . m'mmm . . ."

The Bishop of Dunkeld plucked at the enriched loose sleeve of the Primate's magnificent cope, and muttered a few words.

"I, ah, can take it then, that your lordship repents sufficiently on both scores," he said. "Which is . . . satisfactory." He coughed. "There is but the matter of the robe, now. This of sackcloth and ashes." Hurriedly he stooped, to pick up a coarse grey gown which lay on the floor beside his stall. "To, to ease and expedite the matter, my lord, we have here a garment, a vestment. Made of sackcloth. It, it is already sprinkled with ash. If you would . . . if your lordship might . . . the required formality . . ."

The Wolf barked a great laugh, and slapped his mailed thigh. "Mary Mother of God!" he cried. "Here's the best jest I've heard these long years! Holy Church comes prepared for all! Sackcloth — with the ash provided. And no doubt dust, likewise? Lord,

I make profound reverence!" And he bowed low, with a flourish. "It would take a clerk to think of that." He turned. "Duncan, lad — go fetch me this notable provision, without which naught can be done. I would inspect this wonder, this miraculous mummock! Fetch it."

The youth left his side to stride forward, up to the chancel where, smirking and without ceremony he grabbed the grey robe and returned with it to his father. The Earl held it up, to examine it with assumed interest, this way and that, and turned to display it to the chiefs behind him, laughing. Mystified, not understanding anything that had been said, they laughed dutifully, in turn. Draping the thing casually over his right arm, amongst the folds of his plaid, he looked at the Bishop again.

"I swear you could have done better than this!" he commented. "More ash. But proceed, Sir Priest. What now? What further mummery have you in store?"

The Primate began to speak, thought better of it, and stooped for a hurried word with Bishop Peebles. Shrugging as he straightened up, he adjusted his cope. "It is intended that the garment should be *worn*," he muttered. "But perhaps this will serve, so." He shook his head, sighing, and moving over to before the high altar, turned to face them all, raising a beringed hand.

"Dearly beloved in the Lord," he announced, in a sort of weary monotone. "With God's mighty assistance I do hereby ordain and declare, before all here present as witness, that the awful and condign sentence of excommunication, duly pronounced upon our erring brother in Christ, Alexander, in person before us, be lifted, removed, effaced and nullified; the said Alexander by God's grace, being duly penitent and seeking the forgiveness of the Lord Jesus Christ and of His Holy Church. In the name of the Father, the Son and the Holy Ghost. Amen." He paused. "I also . . ."

"I agree," the Wolf announced loudly, briskly. "That's over, then. And not before time!"

The Primate blinked, mouth open to continue. Clearly he had by no means finished his rite. "But . . . there is more, my lord," he said.

"More? What need we with more? You have said the word. Before witnesses. The thing is done. Why waste more time on more words? *You* may, if so you wish. For myself, I am off. This has taken overlong, as it is. And my good caterans up in Strathmore may be growing restless. Heigho — I'll have them turned and marching back to Badenoch by nightfall — for I have matters to attend to with all the rule and governance of the North on my unworthy shoulders — not so?" He chuckled. "See you, my lord Bishop— I will keep this notable garment of yours, as memento! I will put it on the man Barr when next I see him. With some additional ash of my own! Alex — come you home with us, lad."

"My lord, my lord — there is more yet, I say . . ."

"I told you — enough is sufficient. Sire — I bid you a good day. All of you."

The Primate hurried down to the royal chair and spoke urgently to the monarch, the Bishop of Dunkeld also coming over, anxiously.

"Alex," the King called, as his brother turned away. "There's the matter of the compensation, mind. Restitution. For the damage. Making good, man. Was that not agreed? Their lordships are exercised on that score, see you."

"Indeed? Filthy lucre! Sordid gain, to be chaffered over in this house of prayer — making it but a den of thieves! My lords, my lords — here's a fall from all the sanctity! But, as you will. Two thousand merks."

There was a tingling silence, with even the bishops exchanging astonished glances. Undoubtedly not only had they expected to have to fight for their money, but this was far in excess of what they might have hoped for.

When no verbal response was forthcoming, the Earl swung on one of his lieutenants, who bore a satchel in place of a claymore. From this he took two leather bags, obviously very heavy. The Wolf tossed these in the direction of the chancel, scornfully, where they fell to the floor with a clinking sound.

"Gold!" he jerked. "Two thousand — with thirty pieces of siller, in addition. As seems suitable for the occasion, my friends! Will that serve you?"

The Primate seemed to have difficulty in swallowing. "My lord," he got out, "this is, this is . . . munificent! A, a signal contribution. It will not pay, of course, for all the damage done to the Cathedral of Elgin. The Bishop of Moray will require a deal more. But . . ."

"A pox — it has naught to do with Elgin!" the other snapped. "And not one plack will I give to the man Barr. That gold you may use as you wish — save that none goes to Barr. Perhaps you will purchase a better sackcloth gown, in the place of this! Aye — and let it buy for me and mine some place of sepulture before an altar. A fair place of sanctity, for when I am gone. As befits so repentant a prodigal! You will see to this, my lords spiritual?"

"In, in Elgin Cathedral . . .?"

"Not so. Never in Barr's rickle o' stanes! Besides, yon will not be rebuilt in a lifetime! No—in some other kirk as yet unburned!" He grinned. "It might keep such a one safe, to be sure!"

Bishop Peebles spoke up. "My lord of Buchan — you may have sepulture under the shadow of my altar at Dunkeld. If so you desire."

"Ha — that you may win a moiety of the gold, Sir Chancellor! So be it — as you will. I will hold you to that. Dunkeld, eh? It will serve as well as any other." He shrugged, and looked round. "Alex—I said, come you."

Sir Alexander pressed Jamie's arm. "Another day, friend," he murmured. "We shall celebrate this! And—my thanks, my true thanks." With a bow towards the King and a smile at Mary, he went to his father.

As the young man moved across the flagged aisle, Mary gripped Jamie's arm. Turning to her, he discovered, alarmed, that she was repressing laughter only with a major effort, her eyes dancing, her features working.

"He is going!" she whispered. "Jamie — he is going *now*, I do believe! No more — that is it all. Saints of mercy — it is beyond belief! If only Robert could have been here, to see and hear!"

"Hush! He is here," he told her, frowning. "David has just told me. Watching unseen through yon lepers' squint."

"Lord — you say so?" She all but choked. "That makes it perfect. I shall never forget this day, so long as I live!"

"It is all mockery, Mary, almost a blasphemy. From start to finish. On both sides. The bishops merely out-mocked . . ."

"Sssh!"

"Brother—God save you," the Wolf was now calling, his hand on Alexander's shoulder. "God save the King — especially from Robert Stewart!" He bowed elaborately, and turned. "Nephew — I wish you well, but tremble for you! Sisters — my salutations." He looked at the Earl of Douglas slightingly, but said nothing to him. To Jamie he nodded. "Watch you the company you keep, young man. You might do better in Badenoch!" He signed to his trumpeters, and to their somewhat ragged flourish, without even a glance towards the clerics, he laughed and swinging around, pushed his way through his colourful entourage, marching out, the penitent at large.

"Aye, well," the King said, and with a sigh heaved himself to his feet. "That was Alex, aye." And on the Queen's arm, he limped slowly whence he had come.

David, joy writ large on his beautiful face, skipped gleefully down towards his friends.

The clergy clustered together for a few urgent moments, seeking to school their features, and then paced out with great dignity. From the small congregation the buzz of talk and exclamation arose and maintained.

Scotland, it seemed, could breathe again. The terrible Earl of Buchan had been brought to heel, had confessed, repented and made restitution, and in the infinite mercy of Holy Church, was restored to the communion of saints. The Governor of the realm was the Governor still, and had disposed of armed invasion and the threat of disaster to his rule. Even John, the King, had been forced for once to play monarch, in some degree, and to demonstrate that he could do what his Governor could not.

Jamie Douglas drew a long quivering breath, and turned to his bride-to-be. "That is it, then," he said. "What now?"

"Now—us!" she declared strongly. "For in three days' time we shall be man and wife. I charge you, sir — forget all else . . . !"

HISTORICAL NOVELS FROM CORONET

NIGEL TRANTER

☐	16213 9	Montrose: The Young Montrose	50p
☐	21237 3	The Wallace	£1.25
☐	18767 0	Gold For Prince Charlie	40p
☐	18768 9	The Clansman	40p
☐	18769 7	MacGregor's Gathering	40p

JOHN CREASEY

☐	20801 5	The Masters of Bow Street	£1.25

MARTHA ROFHEART

☐	20799 X	Burning Sappho	£1.00

RICHARD SUMNER

☐	20003 0	Mistress of the Streets	60p

All these books are available at your local bookshop or newsagent, or can be ordered direct from the publisher. Just tick the titles you want and fill in the form below.

Prices and availability subject to change without notice.

CORONET BOOKS, P.O. Box 11, Falmouth, Cornwall.

Please send cheque or postal order, and allow the following for postage and packing:

U.K.—One book 22p plus 10p per copy for each additional book ordered, up to a maximum of 82p.

B.F.P.O. and EIRE—22p for the first book plus 10p per copy for the next 6 books, thereafter 4p per book.

OTHER OVERSEAS CUSTOMERS—30p for the first book and 10p per copy for each additional book.

Name ....

Address ....

....